MW01598103

The Great Accident

Ben Ames Williams

Alpha Editions

This edition published in 2022

ISBN : 9789356232594

Design and Setting By
Alpha Editions
www.alphaedis.com
Email - info@alphaedis.com

Contents

BOOK I

THE GREAT ACCIDENT

CHAPTER I

HARDISTON

THERE are two kinds of people: small-town folks, and others. The others are inclined to think of the people of the small towns as men and women of narrow horizons and narrow interests and a vast ignorance of such important things as cocktails. But, as a matter of fact, the people who dwell in the little mid-western cities and towns are your real cosmopolites. They know their own country, east, west, north and south, at firsthand. The reason for this is simple. When a city dweller goes to the country, he is careful to remain a city dweller; but when a small-town man goes to the city, he becomes a city man for as long as he is within the city's gates. Your Bostonian knows Boston, has a smattering of New York, and a talking acquaintance with London. Your New Yorker knows New York—perhaps; and he desires to know nothing else. But the men and women of Hardiston, for example, know New York, and they know Boston—and they prefer Hardiston with a steadfast and unshakable preference.

This little town of Hardiston—it is really no town at all, since the last census showed it with a population above the five thousand mark, and so entitled it to be called a city—stands on a plateau above Salt Creek, and it is overlooked by a circle of hills, and at three corners of the town the gaunt, black iron furnaces stand sentry at the gates. The hills, of clay and iron ore and conglomerate rock, are pink with apple blossoms in the spring; and in the fall the hardwood growth which clothes them where the orchards have not yet spread presents a dazzle of reds and yellows that blind the eye with their splendor. It is a rich and fertile country, with well-watered bottom lands; and Hardiston town and Hardiston county have a past, a present and a future.

The past goes back to the Indians and beyond. Salt Creek won its name by no mere chance. There have always been traces of salt in its water; and in the ancient days, the Indians used to come to a riffle below where Hardiston now stands and boil the water for this salt. There was a big encampment here; and the tribes came from all over Ohio, and from Kentucky, and farther, too, to boil salt and take it home with them. They brought Daniel Boone here once; and you may still see, to the north of Hardiston, a crumbling precipice of sand conglomerate over which Boone is said to have jumped in making his escape. Also, at the foot of that sandy bluff, you may dig in an ash bed twenty feet deep, and find the skeletons of Indian braves, buried there beneath the campfires, with perhaps an arrow head of flint between their ribs.

When the whites came in, they took up the making of salt where the Indians left off. The state recognized the industry, and chartered it. But at last cheaper salt came in, and the salt boilers found themselves with their occupation gone. So, seeking about them for work for their hands to do, they discovered black coal in the hills, and rusty brown ore; and they digged the coal and the ore and made iron. It was good iron; none better in the world; and it commanded the highest prices in any market.

The county was all undershot with coal; the hills were crowned with iron. Twenty years ago, every valley in the county had its gaunt tipple and its pile of crumbling slack; and every road was dotted with the creaking, rusty wagons that hauled the ores to the furnaces in Hardiston. To-day, much of the coal is gone; and the ore has vanished. But the furnaces fetch ore from Superior, and smelt it into heavy pigs of iron; and their roar is eternal about the comfortable little town.

A stranger, coming to Hardiston, is inclined to think the place is dead; but the town has a deceptive vitality. It is true the brick yard is gone, and the occasional imported industry usually dies after a brief and uneventful life. It is true the big hotel that was, ten years ago, the finest in a dozen counties, goes now from bankruptcy to bankruptcy without a struggle. And Morgan & Robinson's dry-goods store has shrunk from three floors to one; and the interurban traction that used to run half-hourly between Hardiston and the B. & O. main line has given place to a dirty, jerky train that makes two trips a day. The car tracks along Broadway and Main have been ripped up, and the fine brick paving on these streets bids fair to endure forever, for lack of traffic that would give it wholesome wear and tear.

But the town is not dead; it is only sleeping. You may see signs of the awakening in the apple blossoms on the hills. These Hardiston hills produce apples of a surprising excellence, and some day the Hardiston apple will be as famous as the Hardiston iron was in the past. But for the present the town sleeps, a gorged slumber. For Hardiston is rich. There are three banks, and each has more than a million in deposits. Hardiston folk have made money; they have built themselves homes, they have bought themselves automobiles, they have sent their boys and girls to college, and now—save for an occasional trip into the outer world, there is little more for them to do. But the money is there; it feeds the prosperity of three or four moving-picture houses, half a dozen soda fountains, and two sporadic theaters; it fattens the purses of a street carnival or so every year, and it delights the heart of every circus that comes to Hardiston County.

It is a friendly town, a gay little town. People make their own good times, and many of them. And the stranger is always made welcome within their gates. Every one is quite honestly fond of Hardiston and proud of it.

When you go there, the Chamber of Commerce does not buttonhole you and demand a factory. That is not Hardiston's way; and besides, there is no Chamber of Commerce. No, when you go there, Hardiston does not ask you to do something for Hardiston; Hardiston tries to do something for you. For instance, it invites you out to the house for supper. And you go, and are glad you went.

Perhaps it is because of this taste for friendliness that Hardiston loves politics so ardently. Politics, after all, corrupt it as you will, is the art of making and keeping friends. Hardiston County, and the Congressional district of which it is the heart, form one of the prime political battle grounds of the state. Summer and winter, year in, year out, politics in Hardiston goes on. The county officials in the Court House, when their work is out of the way, tilt back their chairs about the most capacious cuspidor and talk politics; the men of the town gather at the Smoke House, or on the hotel corner, and talk politics; the farmers, driving to town, stop every man they meet upon the road and canvass the political situation. Even the women, at their bridge clubs and their sewing circles and their reading clubs—Hardiston is full of clubs—talk politics over their cards or their sewing, or after the paper on Browning has been read.

Hardiston politics is very like politics everywhere; it has not much to do with platforms and principles, and it has a great deal to do with men. In a political way, Congressman Amos Caretall was the biggest man in Hardiston County. And so the home-coming of Congressman Caretall, on the eve of the mayoralty election, was a matter that furnished talk for all the town.

CHAPTER II

AMOS CARETALL

PETER GERGUE is a public figure in Hardiston. Every one knows him, and—what is more to the point—he knows every one. Not only in Hardiston town, but in Hardiston County is Gergue known. He is an attorney, a notary, a justice of the peace. But his business under these heads is very small. It has always been small; and he has never made any great effort to increase it.

He is a man of medium height, thin and rusty to the eye, with a drooping black mustache and black hair that is too long, always too long, even when he has just emerged from the barber's chair. This long, black hair is Gergue's sole affectation. It is his custom, when the barber has finished his ministrations, to rumple the hair on the back of his head and rub it with his fingers until it is matted and tangled in a fashion to defy the comb. He is conscious of doing this, and has been known to explain the action. And his explanation is always the same.

"When I was a boy," he says, "I used to comb the top of my head and slick it down, but I never got at the back much. So I got used to having it tangled; and now I don't feel right if it's smooth."

So he keeps it religiously tangled; and at moments of deep thought, his fingers stray into this maze as though searching for his medulla oblongata in the hope of finding some idea there.

Gergue's office is above that of the Building and Loan Company, on Main Street, opposite the Court House. There are spider webs in the corners and on the windows; there is dust on everything. The floor of soft wood has been worn till every knot stands up like a wart, and every nail protrudes its shining head. Against one wall, there is a wardrobe of walnut, higher than a man. Within this piece some law books are piled, and a few rusty garments hang. In the summer, moths nest here; in the winter they hibernate in their nests. The garments have not been disturbed for years, and now their fabric looks more like mosquito netting than honest broadcloth and serge.

Gergue has an old kitchen table, covered with oilcloth, near the windows that overlook the street. There is an iron inkwell on this table, a pen, and a miscellaneous litter of papers, while at one side of the table, on the window sill, stands his notary's seal and a disused letter press. The oilcloth top of the table has worn through in many places, and the soft wood beneath is polished to a not unlovely luster by constant usage.

Toward train time of the day Congressman Caretall was to come home, Gergue was in this office of his. James T. Hollow was with him, sitting stiffly in a chair that was too narrow for his pudgy bulk. James T. Hollow was a candidate for Mayor. Amos Caretall was supporting him. And Gergue, as Caretall's first lieutenant, had asked Hollow to go with him to the train to meet the Congressman. Hollow had obeyed the summons, and now waited Gergue's pleasure. He was smiling with a determined, though tremulous, amiability.

"I've always aimed to do what was right," he explained hurriedly. They had been discussing the chance of his election.

Gergue nodded his head. "That's what you always do," he agreed. "Trouble is, Chase has aimed to do what wa'n't right, and looks like he'd get away with it."

The other flushed painfully, and his mouth opened as though he would like to speak, but it was some time before he managed to ask: "Is that—the reason Congressman Caretall is coming home?"

The Court House clock, across the street, struck four. The train was due at four-twenty-two. Gergue rose slowly. "Well, now, let's go down and ask him," he invited.

Hollow assented weakly. "Yes, I guess that's the right thing to do."

Gergue looked at him with faint impatience. "Why do you guess it's the right thing to do?" he inquired.

The other hesitated, lifted his hands, spread them helplessly. "Well—isn't it?" he asked.

"Oh, dear!" said Gergue sweetly. "Well—come on."

Hollow was a man with very short legs. This gave him an unfortunate, pattering appearance when he walked with a taller man; and as he and Gergue turned down Main Street toward the station, this fact was commented upon. Some of the comments were direct, some subtle. For example, one of a group of four men at the hotel corner, when the two approached, looked all about him and whistled shrilly.

"Hey, doggie! Hey, doggie! Heel!" he called.

James T. Hollow was not without perception. He blushed painfully. But Gergue took no notice of the jest, for as they approached the group, one of the men detached himself and came to meet them.

This was Winthrop Chase—Winthrop Chase, Senior—the candidate opposing Hollow for the mayoralty. Hardiston felt that it was gracious of

Chase to offer himself for the office, for he was a man of affairs, chief owner of the biggest furnace, a coal operator of importance in other fields, and not unknown in state political circles. He was an erect man, so erect that he leaned backward, and with a peculiarly healthy look about him. He had a strong jaw and a small, governed mouth. His manner was courtly and gracious. Some considered it condescending.

"Good morning, Gergue," he said now. "Good morning, Mr. Hollow."

"Howdo," Gergue returned. Hollow was more loquacious. "How do you do, Mr. Chase."

"The Congressman comes back to-day?" Chase asked.

"Yep," said Gergue.

"We ought to have a reception for him at the station. He has made a name for himself at this session."

"Always had a name," Gergue commented, and spat carelessly, so close to Winthrop Chase, Senior's polished shoes that the great man moved uneasily to one side.

"I suppose he is coming to take a hand in the mayoralty campaign," said Chase urbanely. He could afford to be urbane.

"He didn't say," Gergue declared.

"I'm sorry we're on opposite sides of the fence in this squabble. Tell him he and I must work together hereafter."

"You tell him."

Chase laughed. "I believe he will see it—without being told," he said loudly, and the three men at his back smiled. "He will, no doubt, find some change in Hardiston affairs."

"He will if there is any."

"Perhaps even in the district. Though of course he does not have to seek reëlection this fall."

"No."

"Still—"

Gergue interrupted maliciously: "By th' way, how's Wint?"

The question had a curious effect upon Chase. It surprised him, it seemed to embarrass him, and it certainly angered him. He opened his mouth to speak. "He—"

But before he could go on, Gergue interposed: "I hear Columbus would've gone dry in spite of itself, if they hadn't sent him home from State when they did." And he departed with the honors of war, leaving Chase to sputter angrily into the sympathetic ears of his companions. When he and Hollow were half a block away, Gergue permitted himself to smile. Then he frowned and looked at Hollow. "Why don't you talk up to him, Jim?" he asked disgustedly.

"I—always try to do what is right, Peter. I'd like to, I really would."

"Would you, now?" Gergue echoed mockingly.

"Yes, I really would," insisted James T. Hollow.

"Well, all right then," said Gergue affably. "Le's go along."

They went along, down shaded lower Main Street, and took at length the left-hand turn that led toward the station. Gergue walked in silence, and Hollow, after a few futile efforts at conversation, gave it up and pattered at the taller man's side without speaking. Gergue seemed to be thinking, thinking hard.

A branch line connects Hardiston with the main line of the B. & O. to Washington. Two trains a day traverse this branch in each direction. One of these trains is called the Mail; the other the Accommodation; but the source of these titles is not apparent, for both trains carry mail, and both are most accommodating. Perhaps the Accommodation is more so than the Mail, for at times it has a freight car attached between tender and baggage car, and this is an indignity which the Mail never suffers.

The station at Hardiston is a three-room structure of imitation hollow tiles. That is to say, it is built of wood sheathed with tin which is stamped in the likeness of tiles. These tin walls have an uncanny faculty for keeping the rooms inside the station at fever heat, summer and winter.

One of these rooms is the Men's Waiting Room; another is for feminine patrons of the road; and between the two is the ticket office and dispatcher's room, with telegraph instruments clattering on a table in the bay window at the front.

The station agent is a busy man, with three or four hard-worked assistants; for all the supplies for one of the big furnaces come in over this branch, and the furnace's product goes out by the same route. The furnace itself towers above the very station, great ore piles spraddling over acres of ground waiting for the traveling crane that scoops them and carries the ore to the fires.

On the other side of the station, across the street, there are two buildings with ornate fronts—and locked doors. They proclaim themselves as buildings with a past—a bibulous past. County local option was their ruin, county local option locked their doors and stripped their shelves and spread dust upon their bars. They are ugly things, eyesores, specters of shame. Whatever may be said for the wares they dispense, there is nothing more hideous than a saloon.

Gergue and Hollow crossed the street at a diagonal, past these locked saloons, to the station platform. They found on the platform a familiar throng. Hardiston was the county seat, and served as market place for the southern half of the county. Many people came and went daily on the dirty, rattling, uncomfortable trains; and this, the afternoon train, always picked up a score or so of passengers southward bound.

In addition to these travelers, there were folk at the station to meet every incoming passenger; for Hardiston still meets people at the train. Guests, home-comers, even the commercial travelers find a welcome waiting. Every one in the neighborhood stops at the station at train time to pick up matters for gossip.

Gergue made it his custom to meet a train whenever no more important matter occupied his time; for by so doing he saw many men of the county whom he would not otherwise have seen, and renewed acquaintances that would otherwise have languished. He was, as it were, a professional meeter of trains, like the editors of the three weekly papers, and the bus men from the hotels. He left Hollow at one end of the platform, while he traversed its length, exchanging a word with every one, observing, inquiring, cultivating.

On this business, he was fifty yards away from Hollow when the Caretall touring car whirled down the street and stopped beside the platform. Hollow took off his hat in greeting, and the four young people in the car acknowledged the salutation carelessly.

Agnes Caretall was driving, with Jack Routt beside her in the front seat, and Wint Chase and Joan Arnold in the tonneau. They remained in the car, the two in front turning half around in their seats to talk with those behind. Agnes Caretall did most of the talking. She was a gay little thing, with fair hair and laughing eyes and flying tongue. Joan Arnold was darker, brown hair, eyes almost black. She was quiet, with a poise in sharp contrast to Agnes' vivacity. Routt and Wint Chase were just average young men, pleasant enough in appearance. Routt was dark; Wint had a fair skin, his father's strong jaw, eyes that inclined at times to sulky anger, and a head of crisp hair that was brown, with golden flashes when the sun touched it. There was a healthy color in his cheeks, but his eyes were reddened, and there were faint pouches beneath them. While they waited for the train, he rolled a cigarette, fizzling his first attempt because his hands were faintly tremulous. Routt laughed at him for this.

"You're shaky, Wint," he jested. "Better take a tailor-made one."

And he offered the other his cigarette case; but Wint shook his head stubbornly, tried again, and this time succeeded in rolling a passable cigarette, which he lighted eagerly.

Peter Gergue, coming back along the platform, saw the four in the car and came toward them. He caught Joan Arnold's eyes and took off his hat, and she smiled a greeting; and he came and stood beside the car, exchanging sallies awkwardly with Agnes Caretall and with Routt.

When the attention of these two was concentrated, for a moment, upon each other, he asked Joan: "Is anything wrong, Miss Arnold? You look worried. You hadn't ought to look worried, ever."

She laughed. "Why, no, of course not. I—must have been thinking. I didn't know."

"Thinking about what?"

"I don't remember."

Wint had climbed out of the car and was talking to some one on the platform a dozen feet away. Gergue looked toward him, then back to Joan. But he said no more.

"Isn't the train late?" Agnes asked, forsaking Routt abruptly.

Gergue nodded. "Ten minutes. Dan says they got a hot box, or something, up above the Crossroads."

Agnes pouted. "They're always late."

"They're whistling now," Gergue assured her, and a moment later every one heard the distant blast. "At the crossing beyond the cemetery," Gergue supplemented. "Be here right away." And he turned back to the crowd.

A moment later, they heard the whistle again, this time where the B. & O. and D. T. & I. crossed; and after a further interval, the train came in sight, rounding the last curve into the station. Agnes jumped out of the car, touching Routt's extended hand when he sought to assist her; and then the engine roared and racketed past, vomiting sparks and cinders over them all.

The rear end of the last car was opposite the automobile when the train stopped; and Agnes and Gergue pushed that way; for Amos Caretall always got off at the rear end of a train. "If you do that you can't get run over—

unless she backs," he was accustomed to explain. The two reached the steps just as the Congressman emerged from the car, and Agnes flew up to meet him so that her arms were around his neck when he stepped down to the platform. He was a stocky man of middle height with sandy hair, shrewd, squinting eyes, and a habit of holding his head on one side as though he suffered from that malady called stiff neck.

He hugged Agnes close, affectionately, for an instant, then held her away from him with both hands and surveyed her. "You sure look good, Agnes," he told her, and hugged her again.

She slipped her hand through his arm. "We came down to get you," she explained. "Come along—quick. These cinders are awful."

He laughed. "In a minute. Hello, Peter. Hello, Jim." He shook hands with Gergue and with Hollow. "Looking for somebody, Peter?"

"Just come down to see you come in."

"Well—" The Congressman grinned amiably. "I'm in."

"We wish to welcome you home, Congressman," said James T. Hollow.

"Thanks, Jim."

The three men were silent for a moment. The situation had its interesting side. When Gergue and Hollow had been alone together, Gergue was the dominant figure of the two. Gergue seemed then like a superman, calm, assured, at ease; and Hollow, beside Gergue, had been almost pathetically docile.

Now, however, in the presence of the Congressman, Gergue seemed to shrink to Hollow's stature. He and Hollow were both mere creatures, Hollow if anything the stronger of the two. And Amos Caretall towered head and shoulders above them both.

It was the Congressman who broke the silence. "All right," he said. "Drop in any time—both of you." And with his grip in one hand and Agnes on the other arm, he crossed the platform to the car.

Routt and Joan and Wint were there. He greeted them with comfortable affection, and surveyed them with keen and appraising eyes. "Climb in," he invited. "Glad to see everybody."

Agnes and Routt took the front seat again, and Joan sat between Wint and the Congressman behind. Just before the car started, Amos Caretall leaned across to ask Wint:

"Well, young man—how's your father?"

Wint's eyes burned sulkily. "About as usual," he said.

The engine roared, they turned up the street; and the Congressman turned to wave his hand to Gergue and Hollow on the platform.

CHAPTER III

WINT CHASE

AMOS CARETALL'S home was not a pretentious affair. He lived in a house that had not been built as other houses are; it had, like Topsy, "just growed." It began as a one-story, four-room brick structure, and spread in wings and "ells" and upper stories until now it numbered ten rooms and was a thing fearful and wonderful to behold. In these ten rooms, Agnes and her father and old Maria Hale, the darky who cooked for them and looked after them, rattled around in a somewhat lonely fashion. For Mrs. Caretall was ten years dead, and the two Caretall boys had gone away to college and afterward had builded homes of their own in other regions.

Amos Caretall was not rich; but he was well off. He had made his money in coal, and when the visible supply of coal began to peter out, he had looked into politics, gone to the state legislature for two terms, and then to Congress. In Congress he had done well. The Hardiston district forgot, where he was concerned, the old rule that a Congressman shall have but two terms. They sent him back again and again. He was now in his fifth term, and his power at home and abroad was growing.

His most valuable quality was imagination. He was not an able man; he knew little about political economy, national finance, sociology, the science of government. He knew little and cared less. For by virtue of a keen imagination, he was able to construct in his own mind hypothetical situations, and then hire experts to meet them for him. Peter Gergue was one of these experts. Gergue's field was human nature and Hardiston County. He knew every one in the county, and he had an uncanny faculty for predicting how a man would react to given circumstances. This faculty extended to men in the mass, and enabled him to predict the political effect of a given course of action with surprising accuracy. Amos Caretall had learned to take Gergue's advice blindly. His home-coming at this time, for example, was in response to Gergue's message of a week previous. That message had been brief.

"If Chase is elected Mayor, he'll beat you for the House next year," Gergue had written.

Caretall wired: "I'm coming home." And he came.

But there was no trace of concern in his amiable countenance as they rode to his home now. He joked Joan Arnold into gayety, laughed Wint Chase out of his sulkiness, and pinched his daughter's cheek until she threatened to ditch the car if he kept it up. Thus, when they stopped before the house, every one was in good humor.

They stopped, and Wint Chase was the first to alight. A muffled bark greeted him from the house, and he laughed and ran up the walk and opened the door. A wiry, tan-colored dog rushed out and engulfed him; Muldoon, an Irish terrier of parts, who had been left behind because he would neither ride in an automobile nor calmly suffer his master to do so. Muldoon was one creature whom Wint unreservedly loved; and Muldoon returned the affection. Master and dog, the first transports over, came down the walk again as the others climbed from the car.

Amos Caretall was urging them all to come in. Jack Routt said he would; but Joan shook her head. "I can't," she laughed. "I promised mother to bring home some bread."

"I'll take it out in the car," Agnes pleaded. "Please...."

Joan stuck to her guns. Agnes pouted. Wint did not commit himself; he seemed to take it for granted that he would go with Joan. She turned to him. "You stay, Wint!"

The old sulky light flamed in his eyes again. "No—I'm going with you."

They left the others, amid a little flurry of farewells from Agnes, and turned uptown. Muldoon circled them madly, running at top speed in a desperate effort to work off the spirits generated during his confinement. Joan laughed at the dog, whistled him to her, stooped to tug at his ears affectionately. "You're full of it, aren't you, Muldoon?"

He whined aloud in his desperate desire to answer her, then darted away again. She straightened and they went on, the girl still smiling. Wint looked at her once, and then again, and then he, too, smiled—at her and at the dog.

"He's a clown," he said.

She nodded. "He's a fine dog, Wint."

"He's a dog of sense. He thinks well of you." He laughed. "I'll give him to you some day."

She looked up at him seriously, understanding in her eyes. "I hope so, Wint," she said.

There was something besides understanding in her eyes, something faintly accusing; and he flushed and said hotly: "Don't look at me like that. Please. I'm—I mean to—make it come true."

"I hope so, Wint," she said again.

They spoke no more for a time. Presently she stopped at the bakery and they went in together. The sweet odor of hot bread and sugar and spice clouded about them as he opened the door A round little woman greeted them.

"Is your cream bread all gone, Mrs. Mueller?" Joan asked.

"No. Not yet. How many loaves?"

"Two, please."

The little woman brought two loaves, still soft from the great ovens and still warm, and wrapped them gently, careful not to bruise them. She handed the package to Joan. Wint tried to take it, but Joan shook her head, laughing at him. "Last time you mashed them flat," she said; "I'll carry them."

"I'll be careful," he promised, and took the package from her with calm mastery, a mastery to which she yielded with a faint tremor of happiness. They continued more swiftly on their way.

Presently she asked: "How does the work go?"

He shook his head. "Badly. I've no—knack for it. And father and I weren't meant to pull in double harness."

"You must learn to, Wint. Give him a chance."

He nodded. "But we—grate on each other. He fires up at the least mistake."

"You've been hard on his patience."

He stiffened faintly. "Possibly."

She laid her hand on his arm. "Now don't sulk, Wint. Please."

"I'm not sulking."

"You're too quick on the trigger. You get angry at the least thing." She laughed softly, in a way that robbed her words of sting. "Wint, you're as proud as a peacock, and as stubborn as a mule. As soon as any one criticizes you for doing a thing—you go right off and do it again. That's no way to do, Wint."

He made no comment, and when she looked at him, she saw that his face was set and hard, and she laid a hand on his arm. "Wint—don't you think I'm a—good friend of yours?"

"If you're not more than that, Joan—I'm through." His eyes searched hers; she met his bravely.

"I am—more than that, Wint. So you must let me tell you things frankly. Wint, you must learn to see that when people criticize you, or advise you, it's more often than not because they really wish you well. Most people wish other people well, Wint."

"That has not been my experience."

She shook his arm, laughing. "Wint! Don't be silly! You talk like a disappointed man—when you ought to talk like a fine, strong, hopeful one."

He laid his hand on hers, where it rested in the crook of his arm. "You're a big-heart, Joan. You like every one, and trust them and every one is good to you. You—can't get my viewpoint."

"I can too, Wint. For you haven't any viewpoint. You're just the plaything of a little devil of perversity that makes you do things you know you—oughtn't to do—just to prove that you can."

They came, abruptly, to her gate. She paused to say good-by. His eyes were angry; but he said quietly: "May I come to-night?"

She shook her head. "Not every night, Wint. To-morrow?"

"Please?"

"I—no, Wint."

He straightened stiffly. "Very well. Good night." He lifted his hat and stalked away.

Joan looked after him for a moment, her eyes disturbed, unhappy; then she smiled a tender little smile, as a mother smiles at a wayward boy, and turned into the house.

At the corner, Wint looked back. She was gone. He went on toward his own home, Muldoon at his heels, in a hot surge of rebellion. Halfway home, he asked himself what it was that made him rebellious, angry; and when he could find no reasonable answer to this question, he became more angry than ever. He was angry at himself; but he convinced himself that he was angry at others....

Winthrop Chase, Senior, had built a home for himself a dozen years before, in the first rush of great wealth from the furnace. It was a monumental house, of red, pressed brick, with a slate roof and a fence of iron pickets around the yard. It had been, when he built it, the finest house in town. Now, however, its supremacy was challenged by a dozen others, and the elder Chase had half decided to tear it down and build another that would defy competition. Mrs. Chase opposed this, gently and half-heartedly. She thought they were very comfortable.

But it was a losing fight, and she knew it. Her husband was accustomed to have his way. He would have it in the end.

Wint pushed open the iron gate—it dragged on its hinges so that it had worn a deep groove in the stone paving that led to the porch—and closed it behind him, and went up to the door. He opened it and went in; and in the dim light of the hall he encountered a girl. For an instant, he failed to recognize her; then:

"Why, hello—Hetty," he said.

"Hello, Wint."

"What are you doing here?" He dropped his hat on the hall bench.

"I've come to work for your mother." She hesitated. "Supper's ready. They're sitting down."

"Oh!" He looked at Hetty again. They had been schoolmates. Her seat had been just in front of his one year. He remembered, with sudden vividness, the day he stuck chewing gum in her hair. Her hair was red; a pleasant, dark red; and it was very luxuriant. "Oh—all right," he said, and went into the dining room. His father and mother were at the table. "I see you've got a girl, mother," he said.

"Yes—I've got Hetty Morfee." Mrs. Chase sighed. "I've had the most awful time, Wint. I do hope she stays. Girls are terrible hard to get, in this town. They—"

Mrs. Chase was loquacious. Her speeches were never finished. She was always interrupted in mid-career. Otherwise, she would have talked on endlessly.

"That steak looks as though she could cook," said Wint. "Give me some."

CHAPTER IV

JACK ROUTT

ONE of Mrs. Chase's difficulties with hired girls was that Winthrop Chase, Senior, liked style with his meals.

Mr. Chase was no provincial. He had traveled; he had lived at good hotels; he knew New York, Columbus, Cleveland, Cincinnati. He had been a guest at fine homes. He knew what was what.

"It adds tone to a repast," he would tell his wife, over and over. "It adds tone to a repast. A neatly dressed maidservant, in apron and cap, handing your dishes around. I tell you, Margaret, it gives that—that—that style...."

"I know it, Winthrop," Mrs. Chase always agreed. "I'd like to have it so, as much as you would. Land knows I've tried. I've trained, and I've trained; but you can't expect a girl to do everything for two dollars a week, or even three. Why, Mrs. Hullis had—"

"Well, pay more, then. Pay more. Five, or ten dollars. I make money enough. I surely make money enough, Margaret, to have comfort and—and style in my own home."

"You can't get a girl in Hardiston that's worth more than three dollars," Mrs. Chase insisted. "They come and they go, and they're always getting married, and—"

Mr. Chase always carved the meats at his own table. He took pride in his carving. When Wint appeared now, he looked up with a hostile eye, at the same time lifting the carving knife and fork. "You're late, young man."

"Am I?" said Wint stiffly.

"The dinner hour in this house is five-thirty. If you wish to have your meals here, you would do well to observe that fact and regulate your movements in accordance."

"Oh, give the boy his supper," Mrs. Chase urged. "You get me all mixed up, calling supper dinner and dinner lunch that way, Winthrop. Wint, don't you mind what your father says. He—"

"Margaret," said Mr. Chase sternly, "I wish you would—"

"I went to the station to meet Caretall," said Wint slowly. "Sorry to be late. But—"

"Caretall?" his father echoed sharply. "You—"

"Now, Wint—don't aggravate your father," Mrs. Chase urged. "You will drive me to—"

"Hetty, pass my son's plate," directed the elder Chase, discovering the girl in the doorway. "Your place is in the kitchen while the meals are being served, not in the hall."

"All right," said Hetty cheerfully, and she took Wint's plate and went around the table to his father's side. Thus relieved of the elder Chase's scrutiny, she winked lightly at Wint and smiled. He made no response. A moment later, she set his plate before him, and departed toward the kitchen.

Mrs. Chase began at once to talk. Her eating did not seem to interfere with the gently querulous stream of her conversation. She spoke of many things. Housekeeping cares, the perplexities and annoyances of the day, the acquisition of Hetty, her hope that Hetty would prove a good girl, a good cook, a good housemaid. "She's not going to go home at night, either," she explained. "When girls go home at night, they're never here in time to get breakfast. When I have a girl, I want her in the house, so's I can see she gets up. She—"

The elder Chase interrupted obliviously. He had been studying his son. "Wint, have you been drinking to-day?" he demanded.

Wint looked up quickly, a retort on his lips. But he checked it, and instead said quietly:

"No."

"Oh, Wint," Mrs. Chase exclaimed, "you ain't going to do any more of that, are you, son? You—"

"I'm keeping my eye on you, young man," interrupted her husband. "You left the office early to-day. Who gave you permission?"

"The work was done."

"The work is never done."

"You left before I did."

The elder Chase's eyes flashed. "My movements have nothing to do with it. Your place is at the office till four-thirty every day. Don't imagine, because you're my son, you'll receive any favoritism."

"It seems to work the other way," said Wint.

"It does work the other way. You're on trial, guilty till proved innocent, worthless till proved otherwise. Some fathers.... A boy expelled from college for drunkenness.... You're lucky that I am so lenient with you, young man."

"Am I?"

"Now, Wint," his mother interjected. "Don't you aggravate your father. Goodness knows it's hard enough to get along with him—"

"Margaret!"

"Well, I mean, you oughtn't to—"

Wint rose abruptly. "Nagging never did any good," he said. "I mean to—do my part." He flamed suddenly. "But—for Heaven's sake—don't talk me to death."

He went out, up to his room. He was trembling with humiliated resentment. In his room he stood for a moment before the mirror, looking at his image in the glass, frowning sullenly. "Talk! Talk! Talk!" he exclaimed hotly. "Always talk!" He went into the bathroom, splashed cold water into his face, went out again and down the stairs. He took his hat. His mother called, from the dining room:

"Wint—there's ice cream! Don't you—"

"No—thanks," he said. "I'm going uptown."

He closed the door upon their protests, and went down to the street and turned toward the town.

His way led past Joan's house. He paused at her gate for a moment, hesitant, frowning, miserable, lonely. Then he went on.

Almost every one goes uptown in Hardiston at night. The seven-fifteen train, bringing mail, is one excuse. The moving pictures are an allurement. The streets are better filled in early evening than at any other time of the day. Wint began presently to meet acquaintances. At the hotel, he encountered Jack Routt. Routt greeted him eagerly.

"Wint! Hello there! Care for a game of billiards?"

"I'd just as soon."

"Come along, then."

They went through the hotel office, down three steps, and into the pool room. There were three tables, two for pool and one for billiards. A game of Kelly pool was in progress at one table, but the billiard table was free. They chalked their cues.

"Half a dollar?" Routt challenged.

Wint nodded. "All right."

Routt won the draw and shot first. The game went jerkily forward. Neither was an expert player. A run of ten was an event. Wint played silently, his thoughts elsewhere. Routt was cheerful, loquacious, friendly. Wint envied him faintly. Every one liked Jack, respected him....

Routt won the game with a run of four, and laid his cue on the table. "I'll be back in a minute, Wint," he said. "You don't mind waiting?"

"I'll go with you," Wint countered.

Routt shook his head. "Now, Wint—no, I won't let you. You know—play it safe, man. You can't afford to monkey with this."

"Don't be a fool, Jack."

"Oh, Wint, I mean it. Leave it alone. That's the only safe way—for you."

Wint's eyes flamed suddenly. "Aren't you coming?" he asked, and started for the door.

Routt followed, still protesting. "Wint—don't be a darned fool."

"Don't be a preacher, Jack."

"Please, Wint—leave it alone. Come on back. I won't go either."

Wint said nothing, but he went steadily ahead; and Routt yielded. They left the hotel, went half a block, entered an alley, climbed a stair....

County option had closed the saloons; but Hardiston was still far from being a dry town. When they returned to the pool room half an hour later, Wint's cheeks were unnaturally flushed, and he laughed more easily than before.

CHAPTER V

COUNCIL OF WAR

AMOS CARETALL and his daughter had supper—dinner was at midday in the Caretall household—alone together. Old Maria Hale cooked the supper, and Agnes brought it to the table. It was a good supper. Fried chicken, for example; and mashed potatoes as creamy as—cream. And afterwards, apple tapioca pudding of a peculiar excellence. All garnished with little, round biscuits, each no more than a crisp mouthful. The Congressman smacked his lips over it with frank appreciation. "Maria," he told the old colored woman, "you could make your fortune in Washington."

Maria cackled delightedly. She was a shriveled little old crone, bent, wrinkled, and suspected of being as bald as an egg. No one ever saw her without a kerchief bound tightly around her head. She had looked a hundred years old for twenty years, and declared she was more than that. "I mus' be a hundred an' twenty, at the mos'," she used to say, when questioned. Now she cackled with delight at the Congressman's praise of her cookery.

"I don't know 'bout Wash'n't'n," she declared. "But I ain' makin' no great pile in Hardiston, Miste' Caretall."

He laughed, head tilted back, mouth full of biscuit. "You old fraud, you could buy and sell Chase himself, twice over. You haven't spent a cent for a hundred years, Maria."

She giggled like a girl, and went out to the kitchen, wagging her head from side to side and mumbling to herself. Agnes looked after her, and when the door was closed said, with a toss of her head: "She's getting awfully cranky, Dad."

Amos chuckled. "Always was, Agnes. Just the same when I was your age. But she can make mighty un-cranky biscuits."

"She gets cross as a bear if I don't help her with the dishes."

Amos looked at his daughter with a dry smile. "Then if I was you, Agnes, I'd help her."

She started to reply, but thought better of it. A little restraint fell upon them, and this continued until Amos leaned back with a sigh of contentment and pulled a pipe from his coat pocket. It was a horny old pipe, black, odorous, rank as a skunk cabbage. Agnes hated it; but Amos stuck to it, year in, year out. When it caked so full that a pencil would not go down into its cavity, Amos always whittled out the cake, burned the pipe with alcohol, and started over again. The brier had been in regular and constant use for half a dozen years—and it was still, as Agnes used to say, "going strong."

Amos cuddled this pipe lovingly in the palm of his hand. He polished the black bowl in his palm, and then by rubbing it across his cheek and against the side of his nose. Agnes fidgeted, and Amos watched her with a twinkle in his eye until she rose suddenly and cried:

"Dad—that's horrid!"

He chuckled. "What was it you said about dishes?" he asked.

She went sulkily toward the kitchen.

Amos watched her with a certain amount of speculation in his eyes. Amos was always speculating, speculating about people, and about things. He stared at the door that closed behind her for a long minute before the clock on the mantel struck seven and broke the charm. Then he got up stiffly, favoring his big body, and went into the sitting room. Only half a dozen houses in Hardiston had living rooms in those days. Rooms with no other appointed use were, respectively, sitting rooms and parlors. The library and the living room were arriving together.

Amos went into the sitting room and pulled a creaky rockingchair up before the coal fire. His feet were in carpet slippers, and he kicked off the slippers and thrust his feet toward the blaze. He wore knitted wool socks, gray, with white heels and toes. Maria Hale had knitted Amos' socks for ten years. He wriggled his toes comfortably, then searched from one pocket a black plug of tobacco, from another a crooked-blade pruning knife. He sliced three or four slices from the plug with grave care, restored plug and knife to his pockets, rolled the slices to a crumbling pile in his palm, and filled his pipe. When it was lighted—he "primed" it by cramming into the top of the pipe some half-burned tobacco from a previous smoking—he leaned back luxuriously in the chair, closed his eyes, puffed hard and thought gently.

He was still in this position when the telephone rang; and he rose, grumblingly, to answer it. Winthrop Chase, Senior, was at the other end of the wire; and when he discovered this, Amos winked gravely at the fire and his voice descended half an octave.

"Good evening, Congressman," said Chase.

"Evening, Mr. Chase," said Amos.

"Gergue told me you were coming home."

"I guess he was right."

"He thought you would want to see me."

Amos' eyes widened. "Did he say so?"

Chase laughed. "Well—you understand—Gergue has his methods."

Amos nodded soberly. "Yes, yes. Well—you can come to-night if you want."

"Er—what—"

"I said you could come to-night. I'll be home all evenin'."

Winthrop Chase, Senior, hesitated. He hesitated for so long that Amos asked blandly: "Er—anything else?"

"No, no-o," Chase decided then. "No—I'll come."

"That's good," said Amos; and hung up, and came back to his chair with a pleasant smile upon his countenance.

Almost immediately, some one knocked on the door. From the sitting room, the door was open into the hall, so that Amos heard the knock easily. There was a bell, and most people rang the bell; but Peter Gergue always knocked, so Amos called out confidently:

"Come in, Pete."

Listening, he heard the front door open. Then it closed, and Gergue came slowly along the hall and into the room. Amos looked up and nodded.

"Evening, Peter. Glad t'see you. Take a chair. Any chair."

Peter put his hat on the table and dragged a morris chair before the fire. He sat down, still without speaking, and extended his feet toward the fire in imitation of Amos. Amos' hands were clasped across his middle, and Gergue clasped his hands there too. Thus they remained for a little time silent.

But such a position put Gergue under too great a handicap. He had to get his fingers into his hair; and so presently he unclasped his hands and began to rummage through the tangle at the nape of his neck for his medulla, as though hunting for something. Apparently, he found it; for after a moment he said slowly:

"Well, Amos, we're licked."

Amos turned his head and studied Gergue. "Do tell!" he exclaimed at last.

Gergue nodded. "Hollow ain't got any more chance of being Mayor than—than young Wint Chase has."

This seemed to startle Amos. He opened his mouth to speak, hesitated, closed it again, then asked: "Young Wint! What makes you say that?"

"We-ell—no more chance than I got, then," Gergue amended.

The Congressman seemed satisfied with the amendment. He wagged his head as though deploring the situation, then asked: "Why? What's Jim done?"

Gergue looked at Amos reproachfully. "We-ell, you know Jim."

"Always does the right thing, don't he?"

"They ain't no votes in that."

The two considered this truism for a time in thoughtful silence. In this interval, Gergue produced and filled and lighted a pipe in a manner painfully like that of Amos. Every detail—pipe, plug, knife, priming—was the same. Amos watched him with interest, and when Gergue had finished with the rites, Amos asked:

"How big a margin has Chase got?"

Gergue opened his hands as though baring every secret.

"Well," he said, "Jim'll get two votes. Yours and mine. He won't vote for himself. Says it ain't right. So I don't know where we can count on anything else." He hesitated, then: "You know, this Chase has got a holt on Hardiston."

"How?"

"Every way. Four-five hundred men working for him, one way or another. The drys are all with him. The money is all with him. And the Democrats are all with him."

Amos pondered. "I hadn't no notion Chase was such a popular man," he said.

Gergue shook his head. "He ain't. They'd all like to see him licked, just to see his swelling go down some. But—a man can't vote for Hollow."

Amos puffed hard. "You know, Peter, I've a mind to vote for Chase myself."

Gergue was startled; but after a minute he grinned. "Whatever you say goes for me, Amos."

"Chase is a good man, a big man, a public-spirited man. You know, Peter, if he was elected Mayor, things being as they is, he'd stand right in line for Congress next fall. I don't know as I'd even run against him, Pete."

Gergue leaned forward and clapped his knee and chuckled. Something pleased him. Amos watched him with an expression of comical bewilderment, until Gergue caught his eye and sobered abruptly. Then Amos asked, most casually:

"How's young Wint, Peter?"

Gergue looked sharply at the Congressman. "The boy? We-ell—he's over twenty-one."

"Er—is he?"

Amos squinted at the ceiling. "Seems to me he is. He was three years ahead of Agnes in school and high school, and she is twenty now. He must be twenty-two or three."

Peter considered this, but made no comment. After a moment Amos asked again: "So—how is he, Peter?"

Gergue rummaged through his back hair. "We-ell—they kicked him out of State for over-study of booze."

Amos nodded. "I know. But—how is he?"

"Still at it."

"Still at—the booze?"

"He drinks when he has a mind to; and he's got a large and active mind."

"What does his father think of it?"

"Various sentiments."

"Wint is looking badly."

Gergue nodded. "I come along the street this morning," he said. "He was standing in front of the Post Office. His back was to me; and when I says, 'Hello' to him, he jumped a foot. Nerves on edge."

"That's natural."

Peter shook his head. "Not natural; booze."

"Oh," said Amos; and: "But he'll straighten up. He'll come out all right."

Peter shook his head. "I've seen 'em go that way. By and by his face will begin to look old, just over night. And then his clothes will get shabby, and b'fore anybody knows different, he'll be hanging around the hotel corner of nights with a cigarette in his mouth." He hesitated. "He's set in his way, Amos. Nothing but an accident'll change him."

Amos looked across at Peter curiously. "Accident?"

"Yeah."

Gergue volunteered no explanation; but after a little time Amos said slowly: "Well, Peter—some accidents ain't so accidental as others. Pete, you just make a study of Wint Chase for me."

Gergue looked curious, and he threaded his hair for his medulla oblongata, but he asked no questions. Before a direct instruction or command from Amos, Peter was always silently obedient. He looked at Amos, and then he turned back at the fire; and for a long time the two men sat thus, staring into the coals above the smoking bowls of their pipes.

It is one of the merits of cut-plug for smoking that a well-filled pipe gives a long smoke. Amos Caretall's pipe lasted three quarters of an hour before the last embers were drowned in the moisture at the bottom of the bowl. He knocked out the loose ashes into his palm, leaving the half-burned cake in the bottom of the pipe to serve as priming for a later smoke, and then stuffed the pipe affectionately away into his pocket.

Peter was still puffing at his, and Amos watched him for a little, and then he chuckled softly to himself. Gergue looked across at him in faint surprise. Amos chuckled harder, began to laugh, laughed aloud—and instantly was as sober as a judge.

"Peter," he said slowly, "what you reckon Winthrop Chase, Senior, would up and do if he was licked for Mayor?"

Gergue considered for a moment, then seriously judged: "He'd up and lay him an egg."

Amos nodded. "And eggs will be worth fifty cents a dozen, right here in Hardiston, inside a month. It might pay to have him lay one, Pete."

"You'll need a political Lay-or-Bust for that, Amos."

"I've got one, Peter."

Gergue stared slowly at Amos, his eyes ponderously inquisitive. At length he asked: "What brand?"

Amos leaned toward him quickly. "Almost any good man could beat Chase, couldn't he, Pete?"

"He might have—starting at the first go off. He couldn't now."

"Chase ain't rightly popular."

"No—he puts on too many airs."

"Hardiston'd like to see a joke on him—now wouldn't it?"

"Sure. A man always can laugh at a joke on the other fellow. Special if it's on old Chase."

"Pete—I kind of like Congress."

Gergue nodded. "Don't blame you a speck."

"I want to keep a-going back there."

"Fair enough."

"But you say, yourself, that Chase don't agree with me on that."

"He says so too."

Amos tapped Gergue's knee. "Pete, wouldn't a good, smashing joke on Chase put him out of the running for a spell?"

Gergue considered. "I'll say this, Amos," he announced at length. "A joke on a man is all right, if it don't go too far. If you go too far, you'll make 'em sorry for Chase, and then there'll be no stopping 'em. Politics sure does love a martyr. But—short o' that—a joke's good medicine."

Caretall sat up quickly. "That's fine," he said soberly. "That's fine," he repeated. And he fell silent, and after a little said, half aloud and for the third time, "Peter, that's fine."

Peter's pipe smoked out, and he, too, emptied the ashes and preserved the last charred bits of tobacco as Amos had done. Then he rose, reached slowly for his hat. "I'll go along, Amos," he announced.

The Congressman lumbered up out of his chair, his broad countenance beaming. "Fair enough, Peter. But, Pete—I want to ask you something."

Gergue shifted his hat to his left hand; his right went to the back of his neck. "What is it?"

"Take a man like young Wint, Peter. Suppose he was give a job—sudden—that was right up to him. Responsibility, power, something to do that had to be done. Nobody to boss him but himself. Him and his heart. What would that do to a man like Wint, Pete?"

Gergue scratched his head—hard. He thought—hard. Amos said softly: "Don't hurry, Pete. Think it over." Gergue nodded; and presently he said:

"Man just like Wint—that's what you mean?"

"Say—Wint himself."

"It'd depend on the man."

"Say it's Wint."

"Depend on whether he had any backbone—any stuff in him."

"Has Wint got it?"

Gergue shook his head. "Ain't sure."

"Say he has."

"Then—this job you mentioned would straighten him out—likely."

"Say he hadn't."

"'Twouldn't hurt him none."

Amos nodded. "That's what I thought, Pete." He laid his hand on the other's shoulder and propelled him gently toward the door. There he paused, added: "You do what I asked, will you, Pete? Make a study of Wint."

"All right."

"And—Pete."

Gergue turned.

"Tell V. R. Kite I wish he'd come and see me."

Peter's eyes lighted slowly—and after a moment, he grinned. "All right, Amos," he said quietly, and went down the walk to the gate.

CHAPTER VI

WINTHROP CHASE, SENIOR

WINTHROP CHASE, SENIOR, took himself seriously.

When he walked the streets of Hardiston, bowing most affably, smiling most genially, he was inwardly conscious of the gaze of all who passed that way. He felt their eyes upon him; and this gave him a sense of responsibility, a sense of duty. His duty, as he saw it, was to set an example to the town; an example of erectness and respectability and high ideals. And it must be said for Chase that he did his utmost along these lines.

He was not an educated man. He had been born in Hardiston, and had attended the Hardiston schools; but in those days the Hardiston schools were not remarkable. Chase could read, he could write, and he could arrange and classify more figures in his head than most men could manage on paper. But beyond that, he did not go. There was a native honesty in the man; and this led him to recognize his own shortcomings. For example, when he was called upon to address his fellow citizens, he always summoned a collaborator and arranged his speech in advance. He made no secret of this. In the same way, the printed word was a continual surprise and delight to him; every book he opened was a succession of amazing revelations. And this characteristic gave him a profound admiration for such folk as the editors of the Hardiston papers. As business men, he had for them only a benignant contempt; as politicians, they were pawns and nothing more; but for their ability to say what they wished with pen and paper, Chase accorded them all honors.

The elder Chase's sense of responsibility to the town had made him an unsympathetic father to Wint. He expected Wint, too, to live up to the position in which he found himself. It was not hypocrisy that made him gloss over private errors and denounce more public aberrations; it was a feeling that Wint owed a good example to the town. Thus he had never objected to Wint's drinking at home—the Chases always had liquor in the house—but when Wint was expelled from the state university for drinking, his father was furious; and when Wint once or twice was brought home from town in an uncertain state of mind and body, his father raged.

The elder Chase made many errors, most of them wellintentioned, and he accomplished much good, most of it by accident. He was a curious compound of harmless faults and dangerous virtues. And no one regretted his mistakes more than Chase himself.

Five minutes after telephoning Amos Caretall, Winthrop Chase saw that was a strategic mistake, and began regretting it. Until Amos's home-coming the mayoralty campaign had been going smoothly and satisfactorily. Hollow was not a dangerous opponent, and Chase seemed reasonably sure of election by default.

Nevertheless, the coming of Amos had disturbed him. Amos was rightly feared by his political enemies. He had the habit of success; and no matter how secure Chase might feel, the thought of Amos made him secretly tremble.

He was not a man to avoid conflict; therefore he had sought to confront the enemy forthwith, and had telephoned Amos with that end in view. He wished to bolster his own courage by seeing Amos cower; and Amos had disappointed him. Instead of cowering, Amos had told him carelessly that if he, Chase, wished to do so, he might call on Amos that night. And Chase had promised to come.

Now he was torn with regrets. He was sorry he had telephoned; and he was sorry he had promised to come. At first he thought he would stay at home, let Amos wait in vain; and he tried to bolster this decision with arguments. But they were unconvincing. Sure as he was of the election, Amos made him nervous; and eventually, with a desperate feeling that he must know the worst, and quickly, he set out for the Caretall home.

Agnes came to admit him when he rang the bell. He liked the girl. She was pretty and gay, and she was always flutteringly deferential in his presence. She opened the door, and saw him, and cried delightedly:

"Why, Mr. Chase! Come in!"

He obeyed, drawing off his gloves. He was one of the four men in Hardiston who wore kid gloves. "Good evening, Agnes," he said, in his tone of condescending graciousness. "Is your father at home?"

"Oh, yes—he's in by the fire."

Amos called from the sitting room: "Toasting my toes, Winthrop. Come in."

"Let me take your coat," Agnes was begging; and he allowed her to help him off with the garment, and then handed her his hat and gloves and watched her bestow them on the rack. She was graceful in everything she did, and she looked up at him in a humble little fashion, as though to solicit his approval. He gave it.

"Thank you, Agnes," he said gravely.

"Now!" she said, and turned toward the sitting-room door. In the doorway she paused. "Dad, here's Mr. Chase."

"Come in, Chase," Amos called again. "Take a chair. Any chair. Turning cold, ain't it?"

Amos did not get up; but Chase went toward him and held out his hand so that the Congressman was forced to rise. He was in the act of filling his pipe again, knife in one hand, slices of tobacco in the other; and he had trouble clearing one hand for the greeting, but he managed. "Now sit down, Chase," he urged again, when the handshake was over. "Glad you came in. Is it turning cold or ain't it?"

"Yes," said Chase seriously. "Yes, there's a touch of cold in the air."

"Sky looked that way to me this afternoon. Early, too."

"I think it will pass, though," Chase declared. "We'll have some Indian summer yet."

"Had some snow, haven't you?"

"Two or three inches, early this month. But it melted in an hour when the sun touched it."

Amos nodded slowly. He was lighting his pipe. Agnes had come in with the visitor, but after a moment took herself upstairs and the two men were left alone. This made Chase uncomfortable. Even Agnes would have been a support in this encounter. He looked sidewise at Amos, but Amos was studying the fire; and after a minute the Congressman got up and poked out the ashes and put on half a bucket of fresh coal. Then he jabbed the coals again, and so resumed his seat.

"Ain't been over to Washington lately, Chase," he said presently.

Chase aroused himself. "No. No. Been very busy, Amos. Affairs here, you know...."

"I know, I know. Now, me—Washington is my business. But you have to stick to your coal and your iron." He paused. "I sh'd think you'd get tired of it, Chase."

"How are things in the Capitol?" Chase asked importantly. Amos looked at him sidewise.

"Why—I ain't noticed anything wrong."

"Who will the Republicans nominate?"

Amos chuckled. "Gawd, Chase, I wish I knew."

"They'll need a strong man, Amos. The country's swinging again."

The Congressman looked at Chase, and he grinned. "Chase," he said, "you're a funny Democrat."

"Why? I—"

"I guess you're one of these waiting Democrats—eh?"

Chase looked confused. "I.... What's that?"

"Figuring there's bound to be a swing some day—and when it comes, you'll be there and waiting," Amos nodded. "You're right, too. Bound to be a swing some day."

"I'm a Democrat from conviction, Amos. The Democratic party...."

"Fiddlesticks! Tariff has made you—iron and steel. Fiddlesticks!"

Chase fidgeted; Amos fell silent, and for a time neither man spoke. Once Amos reached into a table drawer and produced a cigar and offered it to the other. Chase lighted it. When it was half smoked, Amos asked carelessly:

"Well, Chase, what was it you wanted to see me about?"

Chase put himself on the defensive. "I—why you asked me to come. I supposed...."

Amos grinned. "Have it so, Chase. Have it so." He puffed hard at his pipe, looked at the other. "Well—does it look like the swing was coming in Hardiston?"

Chase stiffened self-consciously. "The town has demanded that I run for Mayor—and—I consented."

"That was a public-spirited thing to do, Chase. With all your business to hinder you—take your time...."

"I was glad to do it. A man owes it.... If there is a demand for him, he must respond."

"Sure! Sure thing! And you've responded noble, Chase."

"I've made a straightforward campaign."

"First-class campaign. You figure you've got a chance?"

Chase's confidence returned. "I'm going to win, Amos. Nothing can stop me. I'll be the next Mayor of Hardiston—sure."

Amos looked thoughtful. "I ain't in touch—myself." He puffed at his pipe. "Gergue says you'll win—barring an accident."

"There will be no accident."

"Eh?"

"I intend to see to it that there is no accident."

Amos nodded. "Well," he commented, "that's your privilege."

Chase leaned forward. "Congressman," he said seriously, "it's a bad plan to stay away from home so long. You get out of touch with affairs here. You ought to—you need some ally here to watch over your interests."

Amos looked up quickly. "Now, I never thought of that," he declared.

Chase clapped his hand on his knee. "It's right. You can't tell what the people are thinking unless you live among them—as I do, sir."

Amos considered this statement, and then he remarked: "Take this wet and dry business, for instance. Now, me—I'm so far away I don't rightly know what the folks here are thinking. But you—" He hesitated. "How does it strike you, Chase?"

"It's the big issue here."

"How? County's dry."

"But the town isn't. The law is not enforced here."

"Why not?"

Chase laughed shortly. "The present Mayor—"

Amos interrupted. "I'm a wet man, Chase. You know that. I guess you are, too, ain't you?"

Chase shook his head sternly. "No, indeed. Prohibition is the greatest good for the greatest number. I want to see it sweep the country—state-wide—nation-wide."

Amos looked startled. "I'm surprised."

"There's no question about it, Congressman. Prohibition is coming. And I'm for it."

"You have—you ain't a dry man, are you?"

"I believe in moderation."

"Now that's funny, too," Amos commented, his head on one side in the familiar posture that suggested he was suffering from stiff neck.

"Funny? Why?"

"You and me. Me—I'm a wet man; I believe in license. But I'm a teetotaller. You're a dry man—but you like moderation. I'm for a wet state and a dry cellar—and you're for a dry state and a wet cellar. Ain't that always the way?"

Chase flushed stiffly. "Many great men have held public views differing from their private practice."

"Who, f'r instance?"

"Why—many of them."

Amos nodded. "Well, you've studied the thing. Maybe you're right."

"I am right."

The Congressman looked at the other with a cold, quizzical light in his eyes. "How 'bout Wint? He hold your views?"

Chase turned red as fire. "He has nothing to do with this."

"I heard he was a wet man, personally. But I wondered if he was dry like you in theory."

The other said stiffly: "My son has disgraced me. I have been very angry with him. But it may have been as much my fault as his. I have tried to be patient. He understands, now, that if he continues—if he does not mend his ways—I—" He stopped uncertainly.

"Reck'n you'd disown him."

An unexpected and very human weakness showed in the countenance of the elder Chase. His features worked; he said huskily, "Well—the boy—he's my only child, Amos."

Amos had never liked Winthrop Chase till that moment. He was surprised at the burst of sympathy that moved him. He nodded. "You're right, Chase. And—Wint's a good boy, I figure."

His tone encouraged the other. Chase leaned toward the Congressman. "Amos," he said, "there's a new day coming in Ohio politics."

Amos looked puzzled. "To-morrow's always likely to be a new day."

"Things are changing, Amos."

"How?"

"Men are dissatisfied with the present—administration of affairs."

"Men are always dissatisfied."

"They're looking around for a new—hired man—Amos."

Amos chuckled; then he said slowly: "Well—there's lots of folks looking for the job."

Chase hesitated, considering his next word; and in the end he cast diplomacy to the winds and came out flatly: "Amos—it's a good time to look around for friends. To make new alliances."

Amos looked at the other thoughtfully. "Meaning—just what?"

Chase said simply: "You and I ought to get together, Amos."

"We're—here together."

"I mean—a permanent alliance—offensive and defensive. For mutual good."

Amos' pipe had smoked itself to the end. He emptied it with his accustomed care before answering. Then he said slowly: "Specify, Chase. Specify."

Chase proceeded to specify. "I'm going to be the next Mayor of Hardiston, Amos."

"Barring that accident."

Chase brushed that suggestion aside. "My victory—in a strong Republican town—will make me an important figure in the district."

"Meaning—my district."

"Meaning the Congressional district."

Amos looked at the other. "You figuring to run against me next year."

Chase shook his head. "I don't want to. There's no sense in our cutting each other's throats."

"That's against the law, anyhow."

Chase leaned forward more earnestly. "Amos—here's my proposition. We ought to get together. I'm willing. I've got Hardiston. Sentiment in the district is swinging. I can make a good fight against you next year—I think I can win. But I don't want to fight you. So—Let's get together. Party politics are out of date. We're the two biggest men in the county, Amos. You step aside and let me go to Congress—I can beat any one else easily. And I'll back you for—the Senate, Amos."

For a moment Amos remained very quietly in his chair; then he coughed, such a loud, harsh cough that Chase jumped. And then he said slowly: "Chase—you startled me."

Chase said condescendingly, grandly: "No reason for that, Amos."

"But my land, man—the Senate! Me in the Senate!"

"Why not? Worse men than you are there."

"Chase—you're the man for the Senate—not me."

Chase bridled like a girl. "No, no, Amos. You've the experience, the wide view—"

Amos seemed to recall something. "That's so, Chase. And you—you ain't Mayor yet. Something might happen."

"It won't."

Amos rose. "Chase," he said, "I've got to know you better to-night than in twenty years."

Chase grasped the Congressman's hand firmly. This was a habit of his, this firm clasp. "It's high time, then, Amos."

"Yes, yes," Amos considered. "Tell you what, Chase," he said at last, "I'll think it over."

"It's the thing to do, Amos."

"I'll think it over, Chase," the Congressman repeated. He was ushering the other toward the door, helping him into his coat, opening the door. "Wait till after election, Chase," he said then deferentially. "If you're elected Mayor of Hardiston—I don't see but what we'll have to team up together."

Chase grasped the Congressman's hand again. "That's a bargain, Amos."

"A bargain," Amos echoed. Then: "Good night, Chase."

The door closed; and Amos, after a minute, began to chuckle slowly under his breath.

CHAPTER VII

V. R. KITE

VICTOR RUTHERFORD KITE was a man about half the size of his name. Specifically, he was five feet and two inches tall with his shoes on and his pompadour ruffed up. A saving sense of the fitness of things had led him to abandon the long roll of names bestowed upon him by his parents in favor of the shorter and more fitting initials. As V. R. Kite, he had lived in Hardiston for twenty odd years; and most Hardiston people had forgotten what his given names actually were.

He was about sixty years old; and he looked it. His eyes were small, and they were washy blue. The eyelids fell about them in thousands of tiny folds and wrinkles, so that the eyes themselves were almost hidden. His eyebrows and his hair and his hints of side whiskers were gray. These side whiskers were really not whiskers at all; they were merely a faint downward growth of the hair before his ears; and they lay on his dry cheeks like the stroke of a brush. His skin was parched dry; it was so dry that it had a powdery look. He walked with a dignified little swing of his short legs, and held his head poised upon his thin neck in a self-contained way that indefinably suggested a turkey.

This man was a member of the session of his church; he was the proprietor and manager of a store that would have been a five-and-ten cent emporium in a larger town than Hardiston; and he was the acknowledged leader of the "wet" forces in Hardiston. He himself had come to the town in the beginning to run a saloon; but after a few years, he submerged his own personality in this venture and opened the little store, leaving a lieutenant to manage the saloon which he still owned. Thereafter, he acquired other establishments of a like nature, until he attained the dignity of a vested interest. When county option came, he suffered in proportion.

But though town and county voted "dry," there were any number of Hardiston folk who still liked a drink now and then; and the city—for the town of Hardiston was legally a city—took judicial cognizance of the will of its citizens to this extent: the prohibition law was not strictly enforced. The official interpretation of it was: "It's against the law to sell liquor if you get caught."

V. R. Kite thought this was reasonable enough, and took care not to get caught.

On the evening of Amos Caretall's home-coming, Kite was not in his store, so Peter Gergue had some difficulty in locating him. As a last resort, he tried the little man's home, and was frankly surprised to find Kite there.

He delivered Amos's message, and Kite, who was at times a fiery little man, and a sulker between whiles, agreed in a surly fashion that he would go and see Amos that night. Gergue was satisfied.

Kite's house was near that of Amos; but he did not set forth at once. When he did, it was just in time to encounter Winthrop Chase, Senior, at Amos's gate. Kite bridled and slid past Chase as warily as a cat. The two men did not speak. If they had spoken, they would have fought; for each of them felt that he had borne the last bearable insult from the other. They passed, and Kite hurried up to Amos's door while Winthrop Chase, looking back, watched with a calmly complacent smile. He felt that he and Amos had come to an understanding; and he rejoiced at the thought that this understanding meant the downfall of Kite as a political power in Hardiston.

Kite knocked at the door while Amos was still chuckling in the hall; and Amos let him in. Kite, once the door was open, slid inside, shoved the door shut behind him, and exclaimed in a low, furious voice: "That Chase met me outside. He was here. Don't deny it, Amos! Did you aim for me to meet him here?"

Amos chuckled and patted Kite's shoulder. "Now, now, Kite," he said soothingly. "You didn't run onto him here. You didn't have to talk to him. So what you mad about?"

"I hate the sight of the man. He makes me sick."

"Come in and set down," said Amos, still chuckling.

They went into the sitting-room, Kite still grumbling at the nearness of his escape. When they were once settled, Amos broke in on this monologue without hesitation: "Chase says he's going to be the next Mayor—whe'er or no," he remarked.

Kite's dry little countenance twisted with pain. Amos saw, and asked sympathetically: "That gripe ye, does it?"

"I'll never live in the town with him Mayor," Kite exploded. "I won't live here. I'll sell out and move away. I'll shoot myself! Or him! I'll...."

He petered out, and Amos grinned. "I gather you and Chase don't jibe. What's he ever done to you?"

"Grinned at me. He's always grinning at me like a—like a—like...."

Amos smoothed the grin from his own countenance with a great hand, and tilted his head on one side. "You and him disagree some on the liquor issue, I take it."

"We disagree on every issue. He's...."

"Hardiston's a little bit wet, ain't it?"

"Of course! And no one objects! But this Chase wants to get in and make it dry. He's a...."

"This county option law's popular, though."

"Popular—with fools and hypocrites like Chase."

"Chase'll make a good Mayor," Amos suggested. "He's a fine, public-spirited man. Always sacrificing himself for the town—sacrificing his own interests—an' all that. So he says, anyhow. Said so to me, to-night."

Kite waved his clenched fists above his head. He fought for words. Amos seemed not to notice this.

"He's a good man, a churchly man," he mused.

Kite exploded. "Damn hypocrite!"

Amos looked across at the other in surprise. "Hypocrite? How's that?"

Kite became fluent. "Take the liquor question. He preaches dry—talks dry—and drinks like a fish. And his son is a common toper."

Amos shook his head. "We-ell, a man's private life ain't nothing to do with his political principles. Lots of cases like that. If a man thinks right, and performs his office, I reckon that's all you can ask. Out of office hours—he's allowed to do what he wants."

"He'll ruin Hardiston," Kite declared. "Ruin it." He whirled toward the other. "Your fault, too, Amos. If you'd put up a man against him, instead of a fish like Jim Hollow...."

"I figured Jim would do. He always tried to do the right thing," Amos protested; and Kite dismissed the protest with a grunt.

"The town don't want Chase," he declared vehemently, "but they can't take Hollow."

"We-ell," said Amos thoughtfully, "what's going to be done about it?"

Kite threw up his hands. "Nothing. Too late. But I...."

The Congressman interrupted drawlingly: "Now if it was young Wint that was going to be Mayor—you wouldn't have to worry."

Kite laughed shortly. "I guess not. But—he's not."

"He wouldn't be likely to make the town so awful dry."

"Not unless he drank it dry."

"We-ell, he couldn't do that."

Kite grinned. "I'd chance it."

They were silent for a moment; then Amos said slowly: "Funny—what a difference one letter makes. 'Jr.' instead of 'Sr.' Eh?"

Kite nodded slowly; and Amos was silent again, and so for a time the two men sat, thinking. Kite stared at the fire, his face working. Amos watched the fire, but most of all he watched Kite. He studied the little man, his head tilted on one side, his eyes narrowed. And Kite remained oblivious of this scrutiny. In the end, Amos spoke:

"Kite—how many votes you figure will be cast at this election?"

Kite looked up, considered. "A thousand or twelve hundred, I suppose."

Amos bestirred his great bulk and drew from a pocket a handful of letters. He chose one, replaced the others. From another pocket he routed a stubby pencil, moistened the lead, and set down Kite's figures on the envelope. "I think that's too many," he commented.

"Maybe," Kite agreed. "What does it matter?"

"How many wet votes can you swing against Chase as it stands?"

Kite frowned. "I can't do much with Hollow to work with. Maybe four hundred."

"Suppose you had a good man to work with?"

"He ought to get close to five hundred out of twelve."

"Everybody so much in love with Chase as that?"

Kite shook his head. "They don't like him. Nobody does. He thinks he owns the town."

"Does he own it?"

"A good part. Three or four hundred votes, anyhow."

Amos tapped his envelope with his pencil, figuring thoughtfully. "I was thinking some of playing a little joke on Chase," he said at last. "Think they'd enjoy a joke on him?"

Kite looked across at the Congressman with hope in his eye for the first time that evening. "Any joke on Chase will find lots to laugh at it," he declared.

Amos nodded. "That's what Gergue said."

"He's right." Kite's face fell. "But shucks! What chance is there?"

"There's a chance," said Amos.

"What is it?"

"Listen, Kite," said the Congressman soberly. "Listen and I'll tell you."

He began to speak; he talked for a long time, and as he explained, Kite's countenance passed from doubt to hope and then to exultant confidence.

CHAPTER VIII

THE RALLY

THE home-coming of Congressman Caretall created a momentary stir in Hardiston; but that was all. Every one knew he had come home to take a hand in the mayoralty election; but every one also knew that the elder Chase was going to be elected Mayor in spite of all Caretall could do, and so the first stir of interest soon lagged. There was no sport to be had in an election that was a foregone conclusion.

Caretall did not seem to be worrying about the situation. He walked uptown every morning, waited at the Post Office while the morning mail was distributed, talked with the men that gathered there, went to the barber shop for his shave, to the Smoke House for his plug of black tobacco, to the hotel, or to the *Journal* office, or some other rallying spot for men otherwise unattached.

Now and then he was seen to drop in at Peter Gergue's office; but the best proof that he was doing nothing to change the election lay in the fact that Gergue was idle. That lank gentleman seldom emerged from his office, and when he did so, the fact that his mind was free of care was attested by the circumstance that he left his back hair severely alone. Gergue was a Caretall barometer; and all the signs pointed to "fair, followed by a probable depression!"

A lull settled over Hardiston. Chase carried on his campaign regularly but without heat. He talked with individuals on street corners and with groups wherever he found them; he spoke most graciously to all who met him on the street; and as the last week before election dawned, he announced two meetings, to which all voters were invited. They would be held in the Rink; otherwise the Crescent Opera House—and at these meetings, numerous speakers would expound the justice of the Chase cause. Chase himself, of course, would be the principal speaker.

The first of these meetings was held on Tuesday night, a week before the election; the second was set for the following Saturday. On Tuesday afternoon, Amos Caretall and Chase came face to face in the Post Office; and half a dozen people saw them greet each other pleasantly and without heat. Chase spoke as though he could afford to be generous, Amos like a man willing to accept generosity.

"I hope you'll come to my meeting to-night, Amos," Chase invited with grave condescension; and he laughed and added: "You might learn something that would be of value—about municipal affairs—"

"I was figuring on coming," said Amos, surprisingly enough. It was surprising even to Chase; but he hid this feeling.

"Fine, fine!" he declared. "Amos, I'm glad to hear it. Partisanship has no place in city affairs."

"That's right," Amos agreed.

Chase laughed. "If you don't look out, I'll call on you to speak to-night," he threatened.

Amos grinned at that. "I reckon I wouldn't be scared," he declared. "I've spoke before."

They parted with no further word save laughing jests; but when Chase turned toward his office, his eyes were thoughtful, and Amos watched his departing figure with a faint smile. While Chase was still in sight, Gergue came along; and he spoke to Amos in his habitual low drawl, and received a word from Amos in reply.

Gergue nodded. "The bee'll keep a buzzing till he does it," he promised; and Amos chuckled. He chuckled all that day; but his countenance was sober enough when he presented himself at the entrance to the Rink that night. He was alone; and he walked boldly down the aisle, responding to greetings on every hand, and took a conspicuous seat near the front.

The curtain had been raised; and the stage was set with a stock scene representing a farmyard, or something of the kind. There was an impracticable well at the right, in the rear; and at the left, the kitchen door of the farmhouse stood open beneath an arborway of cardboard grapevines. In the center of the stage, a table had been set; upon it a white pitcher of water and a glass; and in the semicircle about the table, half a dozen chairs. The stage setting was not strikingly appropriate, but no one save Amos gave it so much as a chuckle.

When he had studied the stage, Amos turned to look about at the audience. The Rink was half filled; but half of the people in it were either women or boys too young to vote. The women in Hardiston were all immensely interested in politics; and as for the boys—well, a boy loves a meeting.

While Amos was still studying the audience, Ed Skinner, editor of the weekly *Sun*, appeared on the stage, walked to the table, rapped on it with a wooden mallet which had obviously been designed for the uses of carpentry, and called the house to order. Amos settled in his seat and the meeting began.

There were four speakers. Skinner talked first; he was followed by Davy Morgan, a foreman in Chase's furnace; and he in turn gave way to Will

Murchie, from up the creek, who had been elected Attorney General the year before, and so won the honor of breaking the air-tight Republican grip on state offices. The testimony of these men was unanimously to the effect that Winthrop Chase, Senior, had the makings of the best Mayor any city in the state ever saw.

After which, Chase himself appeared, to prove the case indisputably.

Chase read his speech. He always read his speeches. Murchie had written this one for him; and it was well done, flowery, measured, resounding. It was real oratory, even as Chase rendered it. And Amos, in a front seat, was the loudest of all the audience in his applause. He was so loud that at times he interrupted the speaker; but Chase forgave him, beaming on Amos over the footlights.

Abruptly, Chase finished his speech. He finished it and folded it and put it in his pocket; and every one applauded, either from appreciation or relief. They applauded until they saw—by the fact that Chase still held the stage without starting to withdraw—that he had something further to say. Then they fell sulkily silent.

"My friends," said Chase then, beaming on them. "My friends—I thank you. I thank you all; and particularly I wish to thank Congressman Caretall, down in front here, who has been loud in his applause.

"That's a good sign. I'm glad he appreciates the fact that it is no use to fight longer. He told me this morning that he was coming here to-night; and in effect he dared me to invite him to speak to you to-night.

"My friends, I have nothing to hide. He cannot frighten me. Congressman Caretall—you have the floor!"

The listeners had been apathetic, bored; but they were so no longer. More of them rose, some climbed on seats and craned their necks the better to see the discomfiture of the Congressman. They yelled at him: "Speech! Sp-e-e-ech!" They jeered at him, confident he would accept their jeers in silence; and so they were the more delighted when he rose lumberingly in his place.

Every one yelled at everybody else to sit down and be quiet. Chase invited Amos up on the stage. Amos shook his head. "I can talk from here," he roared, "if these gentlemen will be seated so I can look at them." He spread his hands like one invoking a blessing. "Sit down! Sit down!"

They sat, rustling in their seats, grinning, whispering, gazing; and Amos waited benevolently, head on one side, until they were quiet. Then he spoke.

"My frien-n-d-s!" he drawled. "I am honored. It is an honor to any man to be asked to address a Hardiston audience. And especially on such an occasion—and in such a cause.

"My friends, the name of Chase is an old one in Hardiston. A Chase was one of the first to settle at the salt licks here; a Chase fought the Indians during those first hot years; a Chase dug salt wells when the riffles no longer proved profitable. And when the salt industry died, a Chase was the first to dig coal in this county, and a Chase was the first to establish an iron-smelting furnace here in Hardiston.

"The Chases have deserved well of Hardiston. They have been honored in the past; they will be honored in the future. But they should also be honored in the present.

"My friends, I came here to cast my vote in the city election. I came home in some doubt as to how I should cast that vote. But I am in doubt no longer, my friends.

"I shall go to the polls next Tuesday, and I shall ask for a ballot, and I shall go into a booth; and there, my friends, I shall cast my vote for Mayor.

"And the man I vote for, my friends, I tell you frankly; the man I vote for will be—a Chase!"

The storm broke; and Amos bowed to it and sat down. But that would not do. Chase climbed down from the stage to shake him by the hand and thank him; and others crowded around to do the same thing; and still others came crowding to storm at him for a traitor. And to them all Amos presented a smiling and agreeable countenance.

But this small tumult ended, as such things will. The crowd dispersed; the Rink emptied; and in the end, Chase and Amos walked up the street as far as the hotel together, separating there to go to their respective homes.

Next morning, Hardiston buzzed with the news. Strangely enough, Amos did not show himself in town. He hid at home, said his enemies—those who had been his friends. He hid at home to escape the storm. That was what they said; but it was observed, in the course of the day, that those who went to Amos's home to accuse him, came away apparently reconciled to the Congressman's course of action. They made no more complaint.

One of these was Jack Routt. Routt was an attorney, picking up the beginnings of a practice. He had ambitions. Other men had been prosecuting attorney, and there was no reason why a man named Routt should not hold that office. To this end, he had hitched his wagon to Amos's star; and he was one of the Congressman's first lieutenants.

Routt had not attended the meeting at the Rink. He and Wint Chase spent the evening together. But when he heard what had happened, he uttered one red-hot ejaculation, then clamped tight his lips and marched off to find Amos and demand an explanation.

He got it. It silenced him. It was observed that he came away from the Caretall home with a puzzled frown twisting his brow above the smile on his lips. But he spoke not, neither could word be enticed from him. Instead, he seemed to put politics off his shoulders, and attached himself, like a guardian angel, to Wint.

That was Wednesday. Wednesday evening, Wint and Routt and Agnes Caretall spent at Joan Arnold's home, playing cards. Thursday, the four were again together, but this time at the Caretall home. Friday evening, Routt and Wint played pool at the hotel. Saturday evening they went together to the Chase rally at the Rink. It was a jubilant gathering; the speakers were exultant; and the elder Chase, again the speaker of the evening, was calm and paternally promising.

Sunday, the four went picnicking in Agnes Caretall's car. And it was not until Monday evening that Wint broke away from Routt's chaperonage. He spent that evening—it was the eve of election day—with Joan.

They were very happy together.

CHAPTER IX

HETTY MORFEE

IN the meanwhile, a single incident. An incident concerning itself with Hetty Morfee, Mrs. Chase's newly acquired handmaiden.

Hetty was a girl Wint's own age. She had been born in Hardiston, had lived in Hardiston all her life. She and Wint had gone to school together; they had played together; they had been friends all their lives.

Such things happen in a small town. Wint was the son of Hardiston's big man; Hetty was the daughter of a man whom nobody remembered. He had come to town, married Hetty's mother, and gone away. Thereafter, Hetty had been born.

Hetty's mother was the fifth daughter of a coal miner. She was an honest woman, a woman of sense and sensibility; and Hetty received from her a worthy heritage. But most of Hetty was not mother but father; and all Hardiston knew about Hetty's father was that he had come and had gone. It was assumed, fairly enough, that he had a roving, rascally, and irresponsible disposition. Hetty, it had been predicted, would not turn out well.

This prediction had not wholly justified itself. Hetty, in the first place, was unnaturally acute of mind. In school, she had mastered the lessons given her with careless ease. The effect was to give her an unwholesome amount of leisure. She occupied this leisure in bedeviling her teachers and inciting to riot the hardier spirits in the school—among whom number Wint.

She was, in those days, a wiry little thing, as hard as nails, as active as a boy, and fully as daring. She had whipped one or two boys in fair, stand-up fight, for Hetty had a temper that went with her hair. Her hair, as has been said, was a pleasant and interesting red.

As a child, she had been freckled. When she approached womanhood, these freckles disappeared and left her with a skin creamy and delicious. Her eyes were large, and warm, and merry. They were probably brown; it was hard to be sure. All in all, she was—give her a chance—a beauty.

Some men of science assert that all healthy children start life with an equal heritage. They attribute to environment the developing differences between men and between women. Hetty might have served them as an illuminating example. In school, she had mastered her lessons quickly, had led her classes as of right; while her schoolmates—including Wint, who was not good at books—lagged woefully behind.

This ascendancy persisted through the first half dozen years of schooling; and then it began, gradually, to disappear. In high school, it was not so marked; and at graduation, she and Wint—for example—were fairly on a par.

Then Wint went to college while Hetty went to work. She worked first in a store and lost that place for swearing at her employer. Then she took up housework, and so gravitated to the Chase household. There Wint encountered her; and within a day or so he discovered that the years since high school had borne him far ahead of Hetty. She now was beginning to recede; her wave had reached its height and was subsiding. He still bore on.

These things may be observed more intimately in a small town; for there, social differences do not so strictly herd the sheep apart from the goats. Thus, while Hetty was his mother's handmaid, neither Wint nor any one else outspokenly considered her his inferior. She called him Wint, he called her Hetty, and his mother likewise.

Wint found her presence vaguely disturbing. That first night at supper, she had winked at him behind his father's back. The wink somewhat chilled him. It savored of hardness—And there were other incidents. Wint perceived that Hetty was no longer a schoolgirl; she was, vaguely, sophisticated. Her old recklessness and daring remained; but they were inspired now not by ebullient spirits but by indifference, by bravado.

He remembered ugly rumors....

Wint and Hetty had been, to some extent, comrades in their school days. Once or twice he had defended her against aggression; once he had fought a boy who had told tales on her to the teacher. Hetty had never thanked him; she had even scolded and abused him for this knight-errantry, declaring her ability to take care of herself. Nevertheless, there was gratitude in her. She brought him apples, hiding them secretly in his desk.

On the Friday evening before election, as has been said, Wint and Jack Routt played pool together at the hotel. Afterwards, in spite of Routt's protests, they went together to the stairway in the alley; and when eventually Wint reached home, he was unsteady on his feet.

His father and mother were abed. The door was never locked, so that he entered the hall without difficulty; but the only light was an electric bulb in the rear of the hall, near the kitchen door, and when he went back to extinguish this, he tripped over a rug and barely saved a fall.

While he was still tottering, the kitchen door opened and Hetty looked out at him. She had on her hat, so that he saw she, too, had just come in. He smiled at her amiably, holding on to the wall for support; and she laughed softly and came and caught his arm.

"Oh, you Wint!" she chided.

He tried to be dignified. "Wha's matter?" he asked. "I'm all right."

She winked. "But if father could only see you now!"

He became amiable again. "Thass all right," he declared, "I'm going to bed. He's sleeping th' sleep of th' just. Thass dad. Sleep of the just!"

"Sure," she agreed. "But you know what he'd do to you."

A door opened, in the hall above. A step sounded. Hetty, quick as light, led Wint under the stair where he was invisible from above, and signed him to be quiet. The elder Chase called down the stairs: "Who's that?"

"Me, Mr. Chase," said Hetty. "I tripped. I'm sorry if I woke you up."

She heard Chase say something under his breath; but when he answered, his tone was affable. "All right. Time you were abed, Hetty."

"Uh-huh! I went to see my mother."

"That's all right. Good night!"

"Good night!"

They heard him go back to his room, heard the door close behind him. Hetty crossed to Wint. She was trembling a little, and she spoke very gently. "Come up the back stairs, Wint. He won't hear you. I'll help you...."

Wint took her arm. "You're a good girl, Hetty," he told her.

"You come along."

They went through the kitchen to the back stairs, and up, Hetty steadying him and encouraging him in a whisper. Wint's room was at the back of the house, on the second floor; his father's at the front. Hetty's was on the third floor. She helped him to the door of his room, and in, and turned on the light. He sat down and grinned amiably at her. She started to go, hesitated, came back and knelt before him. While he watched, not fully understanding, she loosened his shoes. Then she rose.

"Now you go to bed, Wint—and be quiet," she warned him in a whisper. "Good night!"

He waved his hand. "Thass all right now. G'night!"

She closed the door behind her and went swiftly along the hall to the stair that led upward to her room. But there, with her foot on the lower step, her hand on the rail, she paused.

She paused, and looked back at Wint's door, and pressed one hand against her mouth, thinking. And slowly her eyes misted with a wistful light. She turned a little, as though to go back....

Then, eyes still misty, she went up the stairs to her own room; and in her own room, with no one to see, Hetty lay down on her face on the bed and cried.

CHAPTER X

THE ELECTION

THE people of Hardiston are early risers, and their hours of labor are long and strenuous. The coal miners—what few still find tasks to do in the ravaged hills—are up and about before day in the fall and winter months; the furnace workmen change shifts at unearthly hours; and the glass factory and the pipe works both begin their day when most folks are still abed.

To accommodate these early risers, the polls at Hardiston open at six. They stay open until four or five or six in the afternoon. The hour is left somewhat to the discretion of the election officials. If a heavy vote is cast early, so that an extra hour would mean only half a dozen votes added to the totals, they close the polls and begin their counting in time to get home to supper.

But if there is prospect of a close contest, the polls remain open till the last voter has been given his opportunity.

On this election day, the polls opened at six; and the election officials, particularly those representing the supporters of the elder Chase, went about their duties with a careless confidence. In the second precinct, the polling place was an unoccupied store on the second floor of a two-story building at the corner of Pearl Street and Broadway. The lower floor of this building was occupied by a dealer in monuments; and throughout the day the chink and tap of his chisel and maul never ceased their song. These sounds came up in a muffled fashion through the floor of the room where the votes were being cast.

The early voting here was light. Jim Thomas and Ed Howe were the principal election officers; and they sat with their chairs tilted back and their feet on the railing around a red-hot little iron stove while the trickle of voters came and went. Jim Thomas chewed tobacco, and Ed smoked. He smoked a pipe; and he whittled his tobacco from a black plug, thus identifying himself with the Caretall factions. Aside from the stove and their two chairs, the room contained only the voting paraphernalia. Three booths against the wall, with cloth curtains to divide them; two flat tables, each containing a list of the registered voters; and the ballot box itself, on the floor near the door where each voter deposited his ballot as he departed.

At seven o'clock—the little stove, by this time, had raised the temperature of the room to a stifling mark—Jim Thomas spat in a box of sawdust and grinned at Ed Howe. "Slow, Ed," he said.

Ed puffed hard. He had a weakness of one eye, a weakness which allowed the lid to droop so that he seemed to be perpetually winking. He turned this winking eye to Jim. "Yeah," he said.

"I guess Caretall is due to get his."

"You reckon?" Ed inquired listlessly.

"I reckon."

Ed grunted and smoked harder than ever.

At half past seven, the elder Chase himself dropped in. "Good morning, boys," he called from the door. "Splendid day, now isn't it?"

"Fine," said Jim Thomas.

Chase produced cigars; he dispensed them graciously. Only Ed Howe refused the proffered smoke.

"Oh, come, Ed," Chase insisted. "Don't be afraid of hurting my feelings."

"Never smoke 'em," said Ed shortly.

"Want to vote once or twice?" Jim Thomas asked, grinning.

Chase chuckled. "I've cast my vote. Second ballot in my precinct, Jim."

"Better chuck in a few more," Jim advised. "Hollow's running strong." He said this seriously, but every one knew it was a joke. Even Ed Howe grinned.

Chase presently departed, still amiable and gracious. His visit had stimulated the imagination of Jim Thomas; and after a little while he rose and took his hat and went down to a group of men in the street outside. Ed looked out of the window curiously. He saw Jim go among the group, hat in hand, obviously taking up a collection. The man seemed to take the matter as a joke. But Jim was grave.

He came back up presently, hat in hand, and approached Ed. "Give up, Ed," he invited. "A penny, a nickel, any little thing."

Ed looked in the hat. He saw a button, a burnt match, a pebble, and a slice of tobacco. He grunted and puffed at his pipe. "Set down, Jim," he invited. "Heat's touched your head."

Jim explained, in a hurt tone: "No, Ed, not a bit. Only—some of the boys thought we'd take up a collection and send downstairs for a tombstone for Hollow."

Ed swung his head slowly and looked at Jim; and a slow grin broke across his countenance. "I declare," he commented, "you're a real joker, Jim." Then he laughed a cackling laugh, wagged his head, and fell into silence again.

The second precinct was the most important in Hardiston. Its voters numbered half as many again as its next rival. And so the candidates gave it more than its share of attention that day. Chase came early and often. Each time he disseminated cigars and amiability. This was his day of glory; and he ate it with a relish, visibly smacking his lips.

Caretall and Gergue came together about eight o'clock in the morning. Amos had very little to say. He glanced at the voting lists, nodded to Ed Howe, called a greeting to Jim Thomas and departed. Peter Gergue remained for a time, scratching the back of his head and talking with those who came to vote.

Amos came back at noon, and as it happened, he met V. R. Kite at the voting place. Kite voted in this precinct, and he had just deposited his ballot when Amos arrived. The two men greeted each other amiably. Amos said: "Morning, Mr. Kite."

"Good morning, Congressman."

"Just voting?"

"Yes. Overslept."

Amos winked. "I trust you voted right, V. R."

Kite nodded briskly. "Right as rain, Congressman. You too?"

"Sure."

Jim Thomas listened with frank interest. Now he found an opening for his joke. "You'd better drop in a few votes here, Congressman. Chase is running strong."

Amos looked at him with interest. "You don't say, Jim?"

"Yes, I do."

"Well—how do you know, Jim?"

Thomas became faintly confused. "Oh, I can tell."

"You ain't been looking at the ballots, have you, Jim?"

Jim blustered. "Look-a-here—who you accusing?"

"You ain't? Then you must be one of these mediums that can read a folded paper."

"Oh, sugar! You go...."

Amos grinned. "Matter of fact, Jim, I wish I knowed you was right. I'm frank to say, Jim, that I got a bet on a horse named Chase to win." Jim gasped, and Amos nodded soberly. "Yes, sir, Jim. You just hear me."

Jim took a plug of tobacco from his pocket and tore at it with his teeth and stuffed it away again. The operation restored his composure. "Well, Congressman, you'd ought not to bet—and you a lawmaker."

"It ain't rightly a bet, Jim," said Amos. "It's a sure thing." He turned toward the door. "Good aft'noon, Jim."

The voting, beginning slow, had picked up during the noon hour. A steady stream of men came in throughout that period and when this stream subsided, four-fifths of the registered voters had cast their ballots. Ed Howe suggested: "Might as well close up shop at four, hadn't we, Jim?"

"Sure," said Jim. "They ain't no real contest to-day anyway."

"I reckon that's right," Ed agreed.

This was a quarter before two o'clock in the afternoon. At two o'clock, Caretall and Chase came face to face at the door of the voting room. They came in arm in arm; and Chase asked graciously: "Well, boys, how are things going?"

Jim Thomas reported briskly, "Fine, Mr. Chase. Most of the votes in. Ed and me's figuring to close at four."

Chase nodded. "I guess that's safe. Don't you think so, Amos?"

"Whatever you say, Chase," Amos agreed. "Looks to me like the fight's all over."

It was observed at that time, however, that Congressman Caretall was strangely buoyant for a beaten man.

Chase and Caretall separated at the door, and Jim Thomas called to Ed Howe: "I'm going uptown and get me some dinner. I ain't ate yet."

"Go along," Ed agreed.

Jim went along, overtaking the elder Chase, and they walked together along Pearl Street and up Main to the restaurant. Chase was quietly contented and exceedingly courteous and gracious to those whom they encountered; and for the first half of the journey, Jim basked in the great man's smile.

It was at the corner of Main Street that the first fly dropped into Jim's ointment. As they turned the corner, they encountered three men. One was V. R. Kite; another was old Thompson, crippled with rheumatism but fat with wealth, and a lifelong enemy of Chase; and the third was Thompson's son, the shoe man.

Chase said: "Good afternoon, gentlemen," to these men. Kite responded: "Afternoon!" Old Thompson grunted; and young Thompson said: "How do you do, Mr. Chase?" with entirely too much sweet deference in his tones. They passed the group, but when they had gone twenty yards, something prompted Jim Thomas to look around, and he detected the elder Thompson in the act of smiting his knee in a paroxysm of silent and malignant mirth.

Right then, Jim Thomas smelled a rat. He looked up at Chase, but Chase was blind and deaf. Jim started to speak, then thought better of it; and at the next corner, he left his chieftain and turned aside to the restaurant.

It seemed to him that Sam O'Brien, the fat proprietor of the place, grinned at him when he entered. He ordered a veal sandwich, and when it was ready for him, he doused it with mustard and ate it with sips of cold water between each mouthful. It was delicious, but his stomach was uneasy under it.

Sam was frankly grinning at him; and so Jim asked at length, in some desperation: "What's the joke, Sam?"

Sam shook his head. "How's the election going, Jim?"

"All Chase."

Sam threw back his head. He was a fat man, and the mirth billowed out of him. He rocked, he slapped his knee. "All Chase!" he gasped. "All Chase! Oh, Jim! Oh, Jimmy man! All Chase!" He wiped tears from his eyes. "Jim, you'll kill me!"

Jim snorted. He was thoroughly disturbed. Sam was a man whose finger touched the public pulse. Obviously, he knew something. Jim leaned across the counter. "What's the joke, Sam? Come on—let me laugh, too."

Sam waved his fat hands at his customer. "You go away, Jim. You go 'way. You'll kill me."

His chortles pursued Jim to the street. There Thomas paused, irresolute. What was he going to do? Warn Chase? Warn Chase's cohorts? But what should he warn them about? He remembered suddenly that his place was beside the ballot box, and he turned and fairly ran down the street to the voting rooms. And it seemed to him that, as he sped, mirth pursued him.

But he found everything as he left it. Ed Howe still sat by the stove, still smoked. He looked up as Jim entered, and shifted his pipe in his mouth.

"Why, Jim!" he exclaimed in pretended dismay. "You're all het up! You're all of a stew! Jim—have you gone and seen a ghost?"

Jim Thomas glared at him. He had gone away from this place confident and calm; he returned in a turmoil of fear; and the worst of this fear was that he did not know what it was he feared. He glared at Howe.

"What you been up to whilst I was gone, Ed Howe?" he demanded.

Ed looked at him in surprise. "We-ell—I've smoked two pipes."

Jim strode to the ballot box, shook it, stared into its slot as though to read its secret.

Ned Bentley came in. He wished to cast his vote, and proceeded to do so. As he was about to go, he paused for a moment on the threshold.

"Has anybody here seen Wint?" he asked.

It was the stressing of his words that startled Jim. This stress, the emphasis of the verb, suggested that they had been discussing Wint, or that Wint must be in all their thoughts. And Jim had not thought of Wint Chase for days.

"Why should we have seen Wint?" he demanded, and looked at Ed Howe. Ed was grinning.

Of a sudden, light burst on Jim Thomas. It was not all the truth that he guessed. But it was enough of it to make his head swim. Without a word, he leaped for the street and ran across to the hotel—where there was a telephone.

Ed Howe watched him go—and grinned. "I declare—Jim acts right crazy," he drawled.

Jim came back presently, a grim set about his jaw. He had no word for any of them. But he went to the voting list and copied the names of those citizens who had not yet voted, and went to the telephone again. When he returned this time, it was five minutes to four o'clock.

Ed lounged up from his chair. "Well—we've 'greed to close the polls now. Go to counting...." He started for the door, as though to bolt it.

Jim Thomas sprang in front of him. Jim was mad. "Git back there, Ed Howe."

Ed looked puzzled. "Why—what—"

"Yo're tricky; but you ain't won yet. Set down. Legal hour for closing is six. We'll have some law here."

"But we 'greed on four...."

"Shut up!"

Ed lounged back in his chair. "Well—in that case—I got time for another smoke." He filled his pipe and began it.

There followed a hectic two hours. Hardiston had never seen anything like it, anything even approaching it.

Every automobile that could be mustered by the Chase forces was mustered. Every livery stable in town hitched up its most ramshackle team. Even the funeral hacks were pressed into service. Fenney's motor truck brought two loads of men from the glass factory. Even Bob Dyer's old tandem bicycle came into use.

And when the elder Chase met Congressman Caretall in front of the Post Office at half past five, he refused to speak to him.

It was open war, with no quarter asked or given. The joke was out, and the Congressman's men were enjoying it in anticipation. They exulted openly; they gathered at the polling places to watch the voters whom the Chase workers dragged thither. They cheered these workers on, praised them, encouraged them, made bets on their success.

It was a hectic two hours, and it lived long in Hardiston annals. But it had to end.

When the town clock struck six, the polls closed. And at every precinct in town, the strain relaxed and took, forthwith, the form of hunger. Unanimously, the election officials sat down with the unopened ballot boxes on a table, in plain view of the world, and sent out for supper.

Around the ballot boxes, they ate their sandwiches. Jim Thomas ate in grim silence, iron-jawed and moody. Ed Howe had recovered his spirits. He was urbane, gracious. He even gave a fair imitation of the manner of the elder Chase, at which all but Jim Thomas managed to smile.

In the morning, Jim had been jubilant and Ed had been moody and still; but now the rôles were reversed. It was remarked afterward that no one had guessed Ed Howe had it in him; and his imitation of the elder Chase distributing cigars was destined to make him famous.

But this had to end, too. There came a time when the ballot boxes had to be opened. The tally sheets were prepared, pencils were sharpened, the boxes were unlocked; and at a quarter past eight o'clock, Jim Thomas lifted the first ballot from the box and unfolded it.

He looked at it; and a red flood poured over his face, and his jaw stiffened. But it was his duty to call the vote, and he called it:

"For Mayor—Chase!"

He was still staring at the ballot, and it did not need Ed Howe's mild question to confirm his guess at Congressman Caretall's coup.

What Ed asked was simply: "Which Chase, Jim?"

CHAPTER XI

THE NOTIFICATION

WHERE was Wint? Others beside Bentley were asking that question, as the afternoon of election wore along. Where was Wint?

No one had seen him. Every one was asking the question. No one was answering. But the inquirers, casting back and forth along the trail, at length hit upon one fact. Wint, for days past, had been consistently in the company of Jack Routt.

Where, then, was Routt?

On the morning after Amos Caretall's announcement at the Rink that he would vote for a Chase for Mayor, Jack Routt had gone to the Congressman with questions on his lips. He had come away with instructions, instructions to keep much in Wint's company and to keep the young man out of harm's way till election day.

He had done this zealously. Until Monday evening, he and Wint were almost constantly together. That evening, Wint went to Joan's house, and bluntly rebuffed Jack's offer to accompany him. But when Wint came out—and he came out in a sulky and defiant manner—Jack was waiting for him at the gate.

Jack did not appear to be waiting. He seemed to be merely passing, on his way downtown; and Wint hailed him.

"Hello—you!"

"Hello, Wint! Just going home?"

"Home? It's early yet. Going uptown?"

"Yes." Routt hesitated, as though confused. "I—we—I'm going up to get a prescription filled."

Wint laughed. "For snake bite?"

"Oh, no. A real prescription."

"You don't say!"

Jack protested. "Sure. So—good night."

Wint thrust his arm through the other's. "What do you want to get rid of me for? I'll walk up with you."

Jack balked. "Oh, now, Wint—you—your father will be down on you. You ought to cut it out, Wint. There's nothing in it for you. You never know when to stop!"

Wint stiffened sulkily, but his voice was gentle. "That's tough! Too bad about me! And it's a shame what dad will do to me, now isn't it?" He took a step forward. "Coming, Jack?"

So they departed together.

At daylight, the elder Chase, arising early to go to the polls, met Routt. Jack was homeward bound; and he was a weary young man. Wint was not with him. They exchanged greetings, but no more.

Routt did not again appear in public until something after noon, election day. When he came downtown then, he was as spruce as ever, his eyes clear, and his cheeks pink with health. He showed no signs of the— fatigue that the elder Chase had remarked in him.

Forthwith, men began to ask him: "Where is Wint?"

The first man that put the question was Peter Gergue. This was a big day for Peter. He had been busy, whispering and advising and suggesting and laughing a little behind the back of the elder Chase. He had been too busy getting out the votes and directing the voters to think much about Wint until Jack appeared; but the sight of Jack reminded him of Wint; and so he asked:

"Where is Wint, anyway?"

Jack looked to right and left. "I don't know," he said.

Gergue drawled: "It's your job to know."

"I know it is. But—he got away from me."

"Got away from you?"

"Yes. Last night. I couldn't stop him."

Gergue frowned and ran his fingers through his back hair.

"It was your job to stop him."

Jack threw out his hands. "You never saw him when he's going good."

Peter nodded and spat. "No," he said slowly. "No—that's right. Where d'you say you left him?"

Routt shook his head. "I wish I knew. He dodged me...."

Gergue shook his head. "Go along. Don't let 'em see you talking—too much."

As the afternoon passed and especially after that final two hours of scurry and effort began, the inquiries for Wint increased in volume. But at six o'clock Wint was still listed as missing, and he was still missing at eight, and he was still missing when the count of the ballots was completed.

But fifteen minutes later, Skinny Marsh, a man without visible means of support, met V. R. Kite on the street and drew him into the dark mouth of an alleyway.

"Kite," he said huskily, "I got something to tell you."

"What is it?" V. R. asked crisply.

"You know where Wint is?"

"No. Do you?"

"Yes."

Kite was interested enough now. "Where?"

Marsh told him; and ten seconds later, Kite was walking briskly up the street, gathering his clans.

In the valley on the northeast side of Hardiston, there is a network of railway tracks, the freight and coal yards of the D. T. & I. Acres of ground are covered with slack, deposited through many years, and sprinkled over with the cinders from a thousand puffing engines.

This is low land. At one spot, a stagnant pool forms every year, and furnishes some ragged skating for the children of the locality. The ice factory is on a hill above this pool. At the other end of the yards, there is a gaunt and ruined brick structure that was once a nail mill; and this mill gives its name to the section.

Across the tracks, there are half a dozen streets, lined for the most part with well-kept little cottages of workingmen. But in one street there is a larger structure that was once a hotel.

This hotel is called the Weaver House. It fronts on the street, is flanked on one side by a railway track, and is backed by the creek whose muddy waters lap its sills at flood time. This was, in its days of glory, a railroad hotel, catering to the train crews in the days before the roads frowned on drink among the men. When the road threatened to discharge any man seen in the place, its business languished. But prohibition brought the Weaver House a measure of prosperity. There was strategic merit in its situation. A rear room overhung the creek; and a section of the floor of this room was so arranged that when a bolt was pulled the floor would swing downward and drop whatever it bore into the concealing waters.

This was a simple and effective way of destroying evidence; and the owner of the place made good use of it.

The office of this hostelry was a square room at one corner in front. At eleven o'clock on the night of election day, there were five creatures in this room.

Four were human; one was a dog.

The office was lighted by a single oil lamp. The chimney of this lamp had once been badly smoked, and subsequently cleaned by a masculine hand. It was, to put it gently, dingy. Also, its wick needed trimming. As a result of these defects, the light it gave was not blinding.

This lamp stood on a square table in one corner of the room. A wall bench ran along two sides of the table. At the corner, a checkerboard was set on the table, and over this board two old men leaned. They were engrossed in their game. Both were gray, both were unclean, both were ragged. Both were bearded, and the beards of both were stained, below the mouth, with tobacco. Nevertheless, they played keenly, and at the conclusion of each game broke into bitter, cackling arguments. These arguments lasted only so long as it took them to rearrange the men, when the one whose turn it was made the first move, and silence instantly descended on them again.

These gusts of debate which broke from the old men now and then were the only sounds in the room.

Beside one of the men, and leaning forward over the table in a strained and awkward position, was the boy. He may have been fourteen years old. But it was strange and pitiful to see in his face, in his eyes, an air of age and grim experience almost equaling that of his two old companions. This boy was dressed in clothes too small for him, so that his wrists stuck out from his sleeves, his neck reared itself bare and gaunt above his coat collar, and his pale ankles and shins were exposed above the shoes he wore.

This boy was reading. He was reading a copy of the bulletin of the Ohio Brewers' Association. He was spelling it out word by word, with the closest attention. When the old men burst into argument, the boy shook his head a little as though annoyed by their outcries. But for the rest, he read steadily, passing his fingers along the lines as he read.

The dog slept on the floor at his feet. The dog was just a dog.

The other person in the room was the manager of the Weaver House. The manager was a woman. The manager was also the owner. She sat in a chair beside what had been the bar, at one side of the room. Her hands were folded in her lap, her head lolled on one shoulder, her mouth was open, and she was asleep.

This woman was a virago. In the old days, she once hit a brakeman with a rubber bung starter, and he died. She was acquitted because the brakeman was drunk and she pleaded self-defense. She was feared and respected by the men among whom she lived. In Paris, in '93, she would have been a commanding figure. In the Nail Mill Addition of Hardiston she was a plague. But as she sat here now, asleep, her old hands folded in her lap, she invited not fear nor disgust but just compassion.

She was merely a tired old woman, asleep.

She was still asleep when the street door opened and four men came in.

The floor of the office was a foot below the level of the street. The first of the four men tripped and stumbled over this descent; and this slight sound woke the woman. She got to her feet with scrambling quickness, and from behind the breastwork of the dusty bar, surveyed her visitors. Her eyes were failing, and she thrust her head forward and twisted it on one side that she might see the better.

When she saw who the leader of the four men was, she straightened up with relief and said, her voice openly contemptuous:

"Oh, it's you, Kite?"

It was. V. R. Kite, Jack Routt, and two of Kite's satellites. Kite glanced at the men over the checkerboard, and at the boy. The old men, at their entrance, had looked up in fretful hostility, surrendered to the inevitable, and returned to their game. The boy continued to read.

"Hello, Mrs. Moody!" said Kite to the woman; and he stepped toward her and lowered his voice. "Is there a man—Wint Chase—staying here?"

Mrs. Moody grinned. The grin revealed a startlingly perfect set of false teeth, as beautiful as those of a girl of twenty. Their very beauty made them hideous in Mrs. Moody's mouth. She nodded.

"I want to see him."

"He's upstairs. I'll show you."

She turned around and took a lamp from a shelf behind her and lighted it. Then, with this in her right hand, and her petticoats gathered up in her left, she emerged from behind the bar and led the way to the stairs.

The four men followed in silence. Kite led, and Routt was on his heels.

The stairs were uncertain; but they made the ascent without disaster. Mrs. Moody led the way along a narrow hall to an open door, and stood aside here so that the others might enter. She was enjoying herself.

The four men went into the dark room, and the woman followed and set the lamp on the mantel. This lamp illumined the place.

The room contained a bed, a chair, and a wardrobe. On the chair were set two shoes. On the floor lay a hat and a coat and one sock. In the bed, sprawling on his back upon the dirty coverlet, was Wint.

The woman crossed and shook him by the shoulder. She screamed at him:

"Wake up, deary! Here's gentlemen to see you!"

Routt crossed quickly to her side, his face working. "Here. Let me!"

She pushed him scornfully. "And don't I know the ways of a drunk, at my age? Get back with you. It's me that has a right to bring him out of it."

She shook Wint again; and this time he came slowly back to consciousness. He gasped, flung out his arms, stirred. His mouth twisted as though at a bad taste on his tongue. They waited for his eyes to open, but after a moment he settled back into sleep again.

The woman looked up over her shoulder. "He's had a full dose. Since noon he's been so." She shook Wint again, yelled into his ear, cuffed him.

Thus presently he woke.

His eyes opened, though he still lay on his back. His eyes opened, and they wandered idly about the room, fixing a dull gaze now on this face and now on that. Wint was usually amiable when he was drunk, and so when he discovered Routt, he grinned and tried to sit up.

"Good ol' Jack," he said thickly. "Tried be a guardian t' me. I fooled 'm. No hard feelin's, Jack. Shake, ol' man."

He leaned on one elbow and thrust out an unsteady hand. V. R. Kite grinned wickedly, and Routt stepped forward and sat down on the bed and put his arms about Wint's shoulders.

"Wint," he begged. "Stiffen up! We've got to get you out of here."

Wint shook his head. "I'm comf'ble here. My hostess—" He waved a hand toward Mrs. Moody. "She's a lady. I'll stay right here. I'm always go'n' stay here, Jack."

Routt shook him gently, cuffed his cheeks smartly. "Wint! Wint! Come out of it! Come on. Let's go to my house. Let's go home."

Wint recognized the others. "H'lo, V. R.," he said amiably. "V. R., why this sudd'n s'lic'tude?"

V. R. Kite was not a bashful man. He was enjoying himself. "I came to take you home—take you to some respectable house," he declared. "This is no place for you."

Mrs. Moody broke into objurgations. But one of Kite's companions deftly hustled her into the hall, and silenced her there. Wint persisted:

"Why don' this place suit me all right? I wanna know, V. R."

Routt looked at Kite, and Kite said oracularly: "Because, my friend, the voters of Hardiston have elected you their next Mayor."

Wint was swaying a little in Routt's arms; and for a time his face remained blank. Then it assumed a puzzled look. In the end he asked, his voice less unsteady: "What's—that?"

"You're elected Mayor, Wint," Routt told him. "Brace up."

Wint sat up slowly, pushing Routt's arms aside. "You mean—my father, don't you?"

Routt shook his head; and Kite said pompously: "No, not your father. Yourself. The voters wrote in your name on the ballots...."

They saw a slow sweep of red flood Wint's face; and for an instant his eyes closed as though he were fainting. The flush passed and left him pale. He got up, stood erect, unsteady, then firm. He shed drunkenness as though it were a cloak, throwing it off with a backward movement of his shoulders.

They watched him, waiting; and V. R. Kite suddenly moved a little toward the door, half afraid.

Then Wint burst out on them. He waved his hands furiously. "Routt!" he shouted. "This is a poor joke. It's a damn poor joke. You Kite, you old whited sepulchre. You panderer, you worse than a prostitute—get out of here! Jack—I counted you my friend. You're all dogs, cowards, rascals! Get out! If I choose to lie drunk in this shack—I'll lie here. None of you shall stop me. It's not your affair. It's mine. Mine! Get out! The last one of you! Get out!"

He was so furious that they obeyed him. Routt tried to protest, but Wint gripped him by the shoulders and whirled him and thrust him toward the door.

They tumbled over each other into the hall. Even V. R. Kite lost his dignity. Wint pursued them, cursing them. He drove them to the stairs, down, stood above them with brandished fists. And when they had gone he still stood there for a space, trembling and alone.

Then he turned and went haltingly back into the room. He was no longer drunk. He was as sober as hell. He went into the room, stood at the door, frozen, ghastly white.

The lamp still stood on the mantel, and he crossed to it without knowing what he did. He stood before it.

There was a cracked mirror behind the lamp, above the mantel. Wint saw himself in it.

He looked into his own eyes for a long instant; and then his face twitched into a terrible, shamed, disgusted grimace. He lifted the lamp in both hands and sent it crashing into the grate in the fireplace. It splintered and shivered into fragments. The flame of the wick still burned, however, and the oil that had spilled caught fire, so that for a time the hearth and the grate were wreathed in blue flame.

Then the oil burned itself out. The room was left in darkness.

Wint went slowly across to the miserable bed and sat down on it. He gripped his head in his hands. After a little he lay down on his back on the bed.

Presently his misery and shame became so poignant that tears filled his eyes and welled over and flowed down his cheeks to the pillow. He ignored them.

Eventually, the silence in the room was torn by a single, racking sob.

END OF BOOK ONE

BOOK II

CHAPTER I

MULDOON

THE sun woke Wint in the morning; and the awakening was cruel. Level, white-hot rays burned through his eyelids as though they would char to cinders his aching eyes. He threw his arm fretfully across his face to keep off the glare and lay quietly on the shabby bed, groping back into the night and into the hours of the preceding day in a terrible effort to remember.

There was no more drunkenness in him. The shock of what they had told him had banished that. He was sober. Too sober, in all conscience, for any peace of mind. It was his loneliness that was most torturing. If there had been some one near, some one else in the room, for whose benefit it was necessary to play a part, Wint would have stiffened his resolution and laughed at the situation. But he could not play a part that would deceive himself. Alone in the dingy bedroom in that disreputable place, he burned with shame and tortured pride.

He began to fit together the pieces of the puzzle. He never doubted that it was true the voters had elected him. There had been truth in Jack Routt's eyes the night before, truth and a sort of triumph. Routt was a good fellow and a true friend; and he rejoiced, no doubt, that Wint had been so honored. Wint, thinking this, grimaced. He knew, without explanations, that his election was a joke; a colossal joke in the first place upon his father, and a grim jest at his own expense. He could imagine the cackling mirth of those who had engineered the thing; and this laughter that he seemed to hear lashed his ears.

He flung himself over on his face and buried his head in his arms and tried to think. He was full of rebellion. He would go away, leave this place, never return....

After a time, he lifted his head and moved his body and sat up on the bed, his feet on the floor. He sat up and looked about him and shuddered in a sick way.

The light of day made this room more hideous than it had been by lamplight. The shattered lamp lay in the grate, and there was a charred place on the floor near the hearth, where the oil had burned itself out, when Wint threw down the lamp the night before. Above the mantel hung the cracked mirror. In it from where he sat, Wint could see a distorted reflection of the ceiling of the room, and an angle of the wall. There had once been paper on this wall, and it had been cracked by the shrinking of the plaster, and picked away by casual fingers, and here and there it hung in short, ragged strips. The bare floor was unclean; the chair near the bed where Wint's two shoes now reposed was decrepit and lacked paint. One door of the big wardrobe hung awkwardly from weakened hinges. It was a little ajar, and Wint could see a disorder of rubbish inside. On the floor near the chair lay his hat and coat and one sock, where he had dropped them when he had come here and stumbled drunkenly to bed.

He held his head in his hands, and his fingers clenched in his crisp hair.

For some time, his senses had been catching hints of life in the building below him. The smell of burning grease had come up the stairs from the kitchen; and the grumble of voices now and then upraised in protest or abuse had reached his ears. Once he heard, from a distance and muffled by intervening doors and walls, the clamor of quarreling dogs. But these things did not penetrate his consciousness until a new and louder disturbance broke out somewhere below.

A dog barked, snarling and angry; another yelped. The two joined their voices in an angry tumult of sound. Then a woman's voice, the voice of Mrs. Moody, shouted abuse, and a door opened and cries and barks and snarls redoubled.

Wint lifted his head, in sudden recognition. He heard the thud of some missile that had missed its mark and clattered against the floor; and then he heard the scramble of hard-toed feet racing up the stairs, and the snuffing of eager nostrils. His eyes lighted softly; and he called: "Muldoon!"

There was a yelp of delight and a new scuffle of feet, and Muldoon plunged in through the open door and was all over Wint in a delirious joy at this reunion. The dog leaped up on Wint's knees; it tried to climb on his shoulders; its tongue sought to caress his cheeks; it nipped his hands lovingly; and all the time it whined a low whine of happiness. Wint, cuffing the hard and eager head, smiled in spite of himself at the dog's caresses; he smiled, and caught Muldoon by the ears and held him away and shook him affectionately.

"You, dog!" he scolded. "How did you come here? Eh, you?"

Muldoon wriggled in a desperate effort to explain; and then he stiffened in Wint's arms, and turned toward the door with hackles rising. Wint looked that way and saw Mrs. Moody, panting with the zeal of her pursuit. The virago came in; she bore a stick of firewood in one harsh hand; she made for Muldoon, and her old lips dripped blistering abuse.

Wint drew Muldoon close in his arms and held up a protesting hand. "Wait a minute, wait a minute!" he warned her. "What's the matter?"

She smiled mirthlessly, brandishing her billet and reaching for Muldoon's scruff. "I'm a-goin' to whale that pup, deary," she told Wint. "He's been around here all morning."

Wint hugged Muldoon closer. "Of course," he said, "he knew I was here."

She looked puzzled. "He ain't your'n, is he?"

"Sure," Wint told her. "He's some dog, too."

The woman's anger vanished. "Well, say now, if I'd a knowed that...." She laughed, her desolately beautiful false teeth glistening between her wrinkled lips. "He's drove my dog crazy. He come around here before day, and Jim heard him and tried to get out. Woke me up. I drove this one away; but he came back. Jim got out once, and they had it till I broke 'em up. And then a minute ago, Jim got out again, and when I went after 'em with this stove wood, that'n of your'n slipped by me and in and up th' stairs."

Wint rubbed Muldoon's head proudly. "He must have tracked me, found me out somehow," he explained. "I left him locked up. Hope he didn't hurt your...."

"Oh, Jim c'n take care of hisself. If he can't, he'll have t' look out." She looked around the room curiously. "You had callers last night. D'ye remember?"

Wint nodded, bending over the dog. "Yes—I remember."

The woman studied him. "Thought mebbe you was too far gone to know anythin'...." She waited for Wint to speak; but Wint volunteered nothing, so she remarked: "I see th' lamp got broke."

"I'll pay for it," Wint told her. She nodded.

"That's all right. All in the bill. You must've been tickled to hear about bein' elected."

Wint said nothing. The woman laughed harshly. "Never had a Mayor of Hardiston in my hotel before. Had some sheriffs, and a marshal now 'nd then. But no Mayor!" She shook with mirth at the thought. "I d'clare, I'll have t' raise my rates."

Wint looked at her steadily, with expressionless eyes. He was fighting to hide the humiliation which was stinging him; and he succeeded. His silence at last frightened the woman; she backed toward the door, babbling broken sentences. Only when she was in the hall, with an avenue of flight open to her, did she recover herself. "But I s'pose you'll forgit old friends, now that you're Mayor, deary," she told him.

Wint smiled bleakly. "Don't count on it," he said.

She seemed uncertain whether to take this as a threat or reassurance. "I was always a good friend to you," she reminded him.

He nodded. "Yes—you've been consistent, at least."

She wagged her old head, comforted and grinning. "I guess you won't forget," she told herself. And after a moment: "Will you be wanting some breakfast?"

Wint stroked the ears of Muldoon. "No," he said. "No." And he added thoughtfully: "Thank you very much."

"That's all right, deary," she assured him, and so turned at last and went haltingly down the stairs.

When the woman was gone, Wint sat very still for a space, staring at the empty doorway, thinking. Muldoon was on his lap, and Wint forgot the dog, although his hand still played automatically with Muldoon's ears. The dog was for a time content with this, moving its head now and then under Wint's hand to get full value from his caresses; but by and by it became conscious of his abstraction, and looked up into his face, and wriggled, and at last muzzled a cold nose under his chin and nudged upward against Wint's jaw until Wint emerged from his absorption and laughed and caught Muldoon's head in his hands and shook it. "There, boy," he whispered. "D'you think I'd forgotten you? No fear, Muldoon."

Having aroused his master, Muldoon in his turn decided to feign abstraction. He lay down, ostentatiously, across Wint's knees, and he pillowed his muzzle on his forepaws and lay there with eyes rolling up in spite of himself to watch Wint's face. Wint cupped the dog's lower jaw in his right hand and shook it gently. "What are they saying about me uptown, Muldoon?" he asked.

The dog moved its head, then fell into a motionless pose again. Wint bent over it, whispering, half to Muldoon and half to himself. "Laughing, of course," he said softly. "Laughing! The joke of years!" He smiled grimly. "Tough on dad. He'd set his heart on this Mayor business."

He looked across to the window, and his eyes hardened. "They meant it as much as a joke on me as on father," he reminded himself, and his eyes burned. He wondered how the plan had been carried through. Caretall and Gergue must have had their hand in it; they had probably united with V. R. Kite. It would be reasonably easy, he knew. His father had had no real popularity. Winthrop Chase, Senior, was not a likable man. He was not a vote getter. There was a self-conscious condescension about his good-fellowship.

Wint had never paid any great attention to local politics. He wondered idly what a Mayor had to do. He tried to remember some of the things Mayors had done in the past; and he found his only knowledge of the subject concerned with a Hallowe'en prank as a result of which he and two others had been haled before the Mayor's court and badly frightened.

"He must do something besides that," he assured himself. "But Lord— I couldn't even do that."

What was he to do? That was the thing he had to decide, and he must decide at once. What could he do? Was there any way by which he could nullify the election; resign; abdicate; get himself impeached? He thought of these projects wistfully. They took no concrete form in his mind. He knew nothing of the machinery of local government, knew nothing of the avenues of escape which might be open to him.

He only knew that he would not be made thus the butt of the town's mirth. His face flushed at the thought; and he got up abruptly and walked to the window, Muldoon pacing at his side and looking up wistfully at his master. He would not do it. They should have their trouble for their pains. They were fools. Impudent fools....

One thing he could do; one thing at least. He could go away. Hide. If he were not here, they could not force him to serve. So much was sure. He would go away....

This decision, Wint told himself, had cleared the air. He tried to believe that it solved all his perplexities; and he bent over Muldoon and cuffed the dog and romped with it across the room, to Muldoon's delirious delight. Then he began to whistle to himself, and so looked about and sat down on the bed, and drew on the sock which still lay on the floor. He had difficulty in fastening the sock supporter about his leg. The leg of the trousers obstructed him. He fussed over the thing until he was fuming again, and his face flushed with stooping. But at last the trick was done, and he took his shoes from the chair and put them on. He found that one of the laces was broken, no doubt by his drunken fingers when he had unlaced the shoes before removing them. This discovery whetted his resentment and disgust. He knotted the lace and hid the knot under an eyelet of the shoe, where it pressed on his instep and irked him. He kicked the shoe on the floor until it gave him some measure of comfort.

His hat and coat were on the floor. He put them on, brushing the dust from the coat with his hands, and afterwards with a flicker of his handkerchief. Then he crossed reluctantly to the speckled mirror and looked into it.

He saw that his face was dirty, and his collar soiled and crushed. He took the collar off and turned it inside out and replaced it, and it gave him some faint satisfaction to see the improvement thus effected in his appearance. But he was still ghastly. There was no water in the room; and he knew that the bathroom at the end of this upper hall was not made for cleanliness, so he wet his handkerchief with his tongue and scrubbed his face clean with that. The result had a forced and unnatural look, but he was constrained to be content.

He started slowly for the door, but his feet lagged. It was hard for him to make up his mind to face the world again. He thought, uneasily, of remaining here through the day and catching a night freight out of town; and he turned irresolutely back toward the bed, but Muldoon, at his knee, barked softly in remonstrance, and Wint bent and patted the dog's head and said softly: "Right you are, pup. We're not afraid of them. But Heaven help the man that laughs, Muldoon!"

The dog wagged its whole body, and barked again, as though in approval; and Wint smiled faintly and went again toward the door. He looked down and saw that his trousers were wrinkled, and he smoothed and tugged at them in an effort to give them some appearance of respectability. When he had done his best for them, he went toward the door again, and this time he did not stop. He went out into the hall, and to the stair head, and so down into the office of the hotel.

Like the bedroom, the office of the Weaver House suffered by daylight. Even the dingy and unwashed window panes could not keep out the pitiless sun; and the room's ugliness was exposed in hideous nakedness.

The room, save for the fact that the sun instead of a lamp lighted it, was as it had been the night before. The smoky lamp, still standing on the table, gave forth a smell of dirty oil which filled the place and fought with the reek of bad tobacco and the pungent smell of alcohol. Doors and windows were tight shut. At their corner of the table, above their checkerboard, still leaned the two old men. It was as though they had not stirred, the long night through. As Wint came down the stairs, a game ended, and their cackling voices broke into the familiar argument, while their stained old fingers swiftly rearranged the pieces for a new beginning. Then one moved a piece, and both fell silent, and the new game began.

Mrs. Moody sat at her place behind what had been the bar. The only change in the room since the night before was that instead of the reading boy, a man sat by the table. This man was unshaven, trembling, shrunken within his rumpled and baggy garments. His eyes were open, and his head wagged from side to side as he sat, and his lips moved in an interminable, mumbling argument with some one invisible.

Jim, the dog that was just a dog, was not to be seen.

Wint, with Muldoon at his heels, came down the stairs and stopped in front of the bar and nodded to Mrs. Moody. He reached into his pocket, and the old woman got up briskly and grinned at him, the enamel of her teeth a blinding white flash in her wrinkled old face. Her eyes puckered when she grinned; and she laid her hands, palms down, upon the bar.

"Going away, deary?" she asked.

Wint nodded. "What do I owe you?"

"Sorry I ain't got a bite to offer ye," she apologized. Then, with a sly glance at the men across the room. "Less'n you wanted to come out by the kitchen in back. A little drop...."

Wint shook his head. "Not to-day. How much?"

She told him and he selected a bill and gave it to her. She took it, and tucked up her apron and delved into the pocket of her loose skirt and produced a dirty, cloth bag. This bag was tied with a string at the top; and she untied the string, and rummaged inside, and found his change, and gave it to him. He took it from her; and as he did so, he turned at a shuffling step and saw the drunken man at his elbow.

This man peered at him; and Wint moved a little away from him. The man followed a lurching step, and grinned placatingly, and mumbled: "Wint Chase, ain't it?"

Wint nodded. "Yes." He tried to pass the man and get to the door; but the man thrust out a shaking hand.

"Shake!" he invited thickly. "Wanna shake hands with new Mayor. Voted f'r you, voted f'r you three times."

Mrs. Moody was leaning across the bar and watching and grinning. Wint hesitated, and then he took the man's hand and shook it, and tried to release it; but the man clung to it, and lunged closer, and put his other hand on Wint's shoulder. His weight fell against Wint's chest.

"New Mayor," he repeated uncertainly. "Good, nice new Mayor." He chuckled loosely and wiped his wet mouth with the back of his hand and gripped Wint's shoulder again, and regarded Wint seriously, studying him. "Good little man," he applauded. "Make dam' good Mayor f'r this little town."

He rocked on his feet, and Wint tried to put the man away without offending him, but the man staggered and clasped his arms around Wint's neck and giggled weakly on Wint's breast.

"This'll be a nice, wet li'l town now, eh, boy!" he exulted. "Eh, boy? Nice, wet li'l town...."

Wint, with a sudden revulsion that sickened him and stiffened his angry pride, thrust the man away and stepped quickly out into the street. He felt Muldoon brush against his legs, and he looked down at the dog and set his jaw.

"You, dog," he whispered. "They've tried one joke too many. Eh, pup? We'll stay and turn the joke on them, Muldoon. What say?"

Muldoon whined approvingly, fidgeting on eager feet; and Wint bent and clapped him on the shoulder. "Come on, you," he said softly. "Come on. Let's go home."

CHAPTER II

JOAN

WINT left the Weaver House at a little before noon, Muldoon trotting sedately at his heels. The street outside the hotel was empty; and Wint was glad of this. He followed it to the railroad tracks, intending to cross the yards and take a back street toward his home. But at the end of the street, he encountered Peter Gergue.

Gergue saw him coming, and stopped, and fumbled in the tangle of hair at the back of his head until Wint came near. Wint would have avoided him, but there was no way to do this, and so he said coldly:

"Good morning, Pete."

Gergue grinned slowly. "Why—right fair," he agreed. "Yes'r, it's a right fair morning—if you look at it that way."

Wint nodded. He would have passed by, but Gergue stopped him. "I was coming down after you," he said.

"Why?" Wint asked.

"Oh—I thought you might want company. Heard you was here."

"Want anything special?"

"We-ell—I did think of congratulating you."

Wint smiled coldly. "Thanks. That all?"

Gergue rummaged through his hair. "Thought you might have things to inquire about."

Wint started to say "No" to this, then changed his mind and looked steadily. "You—you mix in politics, don't you, Pete?"

Gergue looked startled. "Why—some," he admitted. "Why, yes, I might say—some."

"Friend of Congressman Caretall's, aren't you?"

Gergue spat, and nodded slowly. "I like to help him out—when I c'n manage," he agreed.

Wint smiled again. "Then you know how this thing happened."

"Some," said Peter.

"Explain it to me," Wint invited. "How was it worked? And—why?"

Gergue grinned slyly. Then he laughed, a shrill burst of merriment of a sort unusual in this man. When this mirth passed, he touched Wint's lapel. "Cleanest piece of work I ever see," he declared.

"How was it done?"

"Word o' mouth! Word o' mouth! Cong'essman knew folks was expecting something f'om him. He kept 'em expecting. Told everybody he was going to vote for a man named Chase. Got 'em worked up, sittin' on needles and pins and cockle burrs to know where the trick come in. Everybody knowed they was some trick. Then—last minute—he passed the word to V. R. Kite, and him and Kite passed the word around. Everybody figured it would be a joke on your paw. Whole town took it laughing, and went and done what Cong'essman told 'em t' do. Writ in your name...."

Wint smiled frostily. "Great joke, wasn't it?"

Gergue chuckled. "Fine. Take V. R. Kite. Tickled him half t' death. Like t' killed Kite."

"Caretall and my father are against each other, of course."

"Sure. Your paw comes to the Cong'essman, high and mighty, offering him this 'nd that. That wa'n't no way to go at the Cong'essman. Amos ain't used to it."

Wint nodded. "But why me?" he asked. "Why pick on me?"

Gergue waved his hand. "That made it more like a joke on your paw. Everybuddy knowed what your paw thinks of you. Figured it'd pupplex him. It did, too, Wint. It certainly did pupplex your paw."

"It would," Wint agreed. "But—I should think Caretall would as soon see my father elected as me."

"Yo'r paw had a little too much wind in his sails. Needed a little coolin' off. Amos gave it to him."

"But how about Kite?" Wint asked. "Why was he so ready to fall in with it?"

Gergue looked at Wint sidewise. "Why, he don't like yo'r paw so very much," he explained, with an appearance of frankness, "and besides that, Kite's wet, and your paw's dry. That stands t' reason."

"He figured I would be wet, of course."

Gergue nodded emphatically. "Natural," he said. "Natural, he figured that way."

"Did Caretall have that idea, too?"

Gergue wagged his head. "We-ell, now," he parried, "Amos don't lay so much on that end of it. He's a wet man, in politics; but he don't touch it hisself. I guess he just wanted t' give you a leg up—see what you'd do. Amos keeps his eye on the young fellows, that way."

They had crossed the tracks while they were talking, and now they met two men. Wint knew these men casually; they knew him. They were workmen; and they saw Wint and Gergue together, and grinned, and one of them called: "Morning, Mr. Mayor."

Wint smiled at them amiably. "Good morning."

"Congratulations!"

"Thanks." Wint's cheeks were burning. The men passed by, and he and Gergue started up the hill by a back street that led toward his home. Neither of them spoke. Presently they began to meet other men. One or two men scowled at Gergue, stared angrily at Wint; but for the most part they smiled covertly, and voiced congratulations. Their words seemed to Wint to mark covert jibes.

After a time the two came to a cross street that led toward town; and here Gergue halted and looked at Wint curiously. "Was there anything else?" he asked.

Wint shook his head.

"You wasn't thinking, maybe, of walking uptown?"

"Not now."

"Going on home, I guess."

"Yes."

Gergue nodded. "All right. When you come uptown, you might stop in and see me."

"I'll see," Wint told him.

"Amos aims to do right by you," said Gergue.

"Much obliged."

"You don't want to hold this against him."

Wint smiled slowly. "Good-by," he said.

Gergue nodded. "By-by," he responded. "I'll see you again."

He turned toward town, and Wint watched him for a moment, and then went on toward his home. Muldoon trotted sedately before him, ranging now and then across the street or into a yard to investigate some affair of his own. Wint walked swiftly, for he had an uneasy feeling of nakedness in the light of open day, as though every one he encountered must see the shame that was torturing him. He came to his home through a short cut that brought him by way of an alley to the kitchen door; and when he opened the door and stepped into the kitchen, he saw Hetty Morfee there. Hetty was rolling biscuits on a board, her sleeves rolled to the elbows on her creamy arms; and she turned at the sound of his entrance and stood with the rolling pin in one hand, brushing back the hair from her eyes with the other, and laughing at him softly.

"Oh, you Wint!" she said.

Wint closed the kitchen door behind him and faced the girl. "Is mother here?" he asked.

"She's in next door." She nodded her head reproachfully. "You certainly have started something, Wint."

"Where's father?"

"Uptown. He telephoned just now to know if you had come home. He ain't coming home for dinner."

Wint dropped his eyes for a moment, then lifted his head. "All right," he said. "I—I suppose he's mad as a hatter."

Hetty chuckled softly. "Mad as two of 'em," she declared. "You certainly have started something this time, Wint."

He looked toward the biscuit board. "Are those for lunch?"

"Uh-huh."

"How soon will they be ready?"

"Half an hour. You hungry?" She studied him, solicitude lurking in her eyes.

"Yes. I didn't have any breakfast."

The girl moved toward him with the quick instinct of woman. "You poor kid! I'll get you something now."

He lifted his hand impatiently. "Never mind. Or—just a glass of milk."

She laughed, crossing the room toward the pantry. "You just sit down and see." And while he still stood irresolutely in the middle of the floor, she was back with bread and butter and a glass of jelly and a bowl of milk. She spread these things upon the table, and cut the bread for him, and made him sit down and eat while she hovered over him, her eyes never leaving the brown head as he bent above his plate. Now and then she laughed softly, and more than once she repeated: "You surely have started something this time."

He ate ravenously. He had not realized his own hunger. But after the second slice, she stopped him. "Now that's enough," she declared. "You'll spoil your dinner."

He laughed, the first time he had laughed that day. "I guess not," he declared. "I could eat a house."

She smiled, carrying the viands back to their places. "Where was you last night?" she asked curiously.

He looked up at her, half resentful, half glad of her friendship and understanding. "Weaver House," he said.

She made a little grimace. "Golly! You must've been pie-eyed for fair."

He flushed, but he nodded. "Yes."

"And look what they've done to you. It don't pay, does it, Wint?"

He laughed. "I suppose not."

"What are you going to do?"

"I don't know."

"Your paw's awful mad."

He got up stiffly. "I suppose so. Well—he's been mad before."

"And your maw's upset."

"I'll be up in my room," he said. "Call me when dinner's ready."

She was back at her biscuits, laying them delicately in the pan. "Sure. Go ahead." The door closed behind him. When she heard the click of a latch, the girl stopped her work for an instant, and looked over her shoulder at the closed door. She remained thus for a space; then brushed her arm across her forehead as though a lock of hair distressed her, and went on with her task.

Wint went to his room, and threw aside his soiled garments, and bathed and was half dressed when Hetty called up the stairs that dinner was ready. He came down into the hall as his mother entered the front door. When she saw him, she lifted her hands, and ran at him, and poured out upon him a torrent of querulous complaint. "Wint, where have you been all this time? Your father is so mad. He's terrible mad at you. I never saw your father so worked up, Wint. I don't see what you had to go and do a thing like that for anyhow, Wint. I told Mrs. Hullis this morning I just couldn't see how you could do it. Your father was so set on getting elected, and everything; and he'd made so many plans, and when he came home last night I said to him—"

Hetty called from the dining-room door: "Dinner's ready, ma'am."

"All right, Hetty, I'm a-coming," Mrs. Chase assured her. "Wint, you come along. I want to talk to you. I don't see what you're going to do about it. I don't see—I said to your father last night that I just couldn't see how you could—"

Wint broke in: "Mother—please! It wasn't my doing. I had nothing to do with it."

"I said to your father last night, when he came home," she insisted. "He came home so mad, and everything. He was in a terrible state, Wint. He ramped and tore around here like he was a crazy man; and I said to him that I didn't see how a son could do a thing like that to him. He was tramping up and down, and he kept talking about you, and I said to him that I—"

"I tell you I had nothing to do with it, mother."

"I think Congressman Caretall ought to have something better to do than to come home here and stir up a son against his father. I told your father so; and I said—"

"He didn't stir me up against father, mother. It was a trick, a political game. I didn't know anything about it till they told me I'd been elected."

"I said to him that I just couldn't believe it. And he said if it wasn't true why weren't you here at home where you belonged? He said you were probably down at Caretall's, laughing at your father. And I said I just couldn't see how a son could do a thing like that to a father like him. Because your father has been good to you, Wint. He's been mighty good to you; and he's stood a lot. I said to him that he'd stood a lot, and he said you were probably off drinking again somewhere, and that you'd—"

Hetty came in from the kitchen with the plate of biscuits, and set them before Mrs. Chase, and looked at Wint and laughed and pressed her hands to her ears and grimaced at Mrs. Chase's unconscious head. Wint protested:

"Mother, I—"

Mrs. Chase broke in. "Hetty, those biscuits are just fine. I declare, your things always seem to come out better than mine. I wish I could do it that way. I wish your father was at home, Wint. He likes hot biscuits so. But goodness knows, he wouldn't have any appetite to eat anything to-day. Hetty told me when she called me to come home that he'd telephoned he wasn't coming. She told me you had come, and I came right over to tell you that I just didn't see how you could—"

Wint was glad at last to finish and escape. He went up to his room, his mother's words pursuing him. The reaction had set in; and he was terribly tired, and sick and full of sleep. He flung himself on his face on the bed, and he tossed there for a space, thinking miserably, and so at last he fell asleep.

He was awakened by a thrumming knock on his door, and sat up and called huskily: "Who's that?" The door opened, and his father came in.

His father came in, and shut the door behind him. Outside, Wint saw his mother. She was saying something; and the closing door cut off her words. His father ignored her; he slowly turned and faced Wint.

It was late afternoon, almost dusk. Shadows had begun to fill the room. Wint saw that his father's face was black; and he got up from the bed and stood there for a moment, and he saw that his father was trembling. He took a step forward. "Father," he said unsteadily, "I want to tell you I had nothing to do with this. I'm sorry. And I'll do whatever you say to make things right."

The restraint which the elder Chase had imposed upon himself fled before the wind of passion. He lifted his clenched hands as though he would bring them down upon Wint's head. "You! You!" he cried. "You're my son— and you join with drunkards and vagabonds and thieves to make a laughingstock of me."

Wint protested. "I did not! I knew nothing."

"Don't lie to me, Wint," his father cried. The elder man's anger was terrible. It swept away the poise with which he faced the world, it left him nothing but his wrongs; and these wrongs and his own rage somehow transfigured and ennobled him. In spite of himself, Wint had never respected and loved his father so much as then. He cried again, almost pleadingly:

"Dad...."

"Be quiet!" his father cried. "Don't speak. It is my time to speak. I have kept silent too long. You have disgraced me with your drunkenness; and now you make a joke of me before the world. You...."

"I tell you, I knew nothing of this till it was done."

"You lie. You lie, Wint! And even if it were true, you have made it possible by—by your debaucheries. You have given them the chance—you have made me the laughingstock—" he flung his arms wide. "Why even the Cincinnati papers have the story, Wint. They—the whole damned country knows...." His voice broke suddenly; his hands dropped at his side. Resentment fought with affection in Wint; and pride stiffened his voice as he said again:

"I told you I'd do anything, dad."

"Anything? What good will that do? You and Caretall—laughing at me! I won't stand it! I'll break Caretall if it kills me. Caretall is a scoundrel, a crook. He's debauched the town...."

He stopped suddenly, he became cold and still. "Come down to supper, Wint," he said shortly. "After that, you can get out. I've warned you enough—the last time. I'm through."

Wint stiffened. "Dad...." he said softly.

His father made a fierce gesture. "Be quiet! I tell you I am through." He whirled to the door, and opened it, and was gone before Wint could speak again. But while Wint still stood quiet, he returned and called: "I know where you were last night. That was enough. That alone. I'm through. Through!"

This time he did not return. And Wint waited for a space, and then, mechanically and automatically, he picked up his hat, and put it on, and went down the stairs. His mother and father were in the dining-room. He heard his mother's voice. But he did not go in.

He went to the door and out, and down the walk to the street. As he reached the pavement, the door opened behind him, and he looked back and saw his father standing there. For a moment, the two looked at each other; then the elder man turned his head, and went back into the house and closed the door.

Wint walked steadily down the street. He did not know where he was to go; he did not think of this. And so it was without his own volition that he came to Joan's home, and saw the girl sitting in a chair upon the veranda, a book in her lap.

Her eyes met his. Her eyes were very serious and sad; but Wint turned in, and came to the steps, and stood there before her. She smiled a little wistfully; and he said, under his breath: "Joan."

She made no move to answer him. He said again: "Joan...." And then: "Joan...."

She bent her head a little, but her eyes held his. "Wint," she said, so softly he could scarce hear her words. "Wint—I'm sorry. But—I can't go on. I can't—trust you, Wint. This is good-by."

He felt himself shrink a little at the word; and he stood still for a moment till his senses steadied. Then he lifted his head a little.

"I don't blame you," he told her.

She said again: "Good-by!" And he nodded and echoed quietly:

"Good-by, Joan."

For another moment, their eyes held each other. Then his dropped, and he turned and went down to the street again.

Half an hour later, Mrs. Moody was lighting the smoky-lamp in the office of the Weaver House when Wint came in. She saw him and grinned, and her teeth reflected the lamp's light like pearls. "Why, hello, deary! Back again?" she called.

He nodded. "The same room, please," he told her.

She bustled across to the stairs, and paused there and looked at him wisely "A little drop first, in the kitchen?" she invited.

He shook his head. "No—nothing."

And so presently he found himself in the place where he had slept that sodden sleep the night before.

CHAPTER III

THE STRATEGY OF AMOS

WINT had returned to the Weaver House in a numb revulsion of feeling. He was hurt and angry at the whole world; and he was wholly at sea as to what he should do. His instinct was to fight, to fight the thing out, to fight his father and to prove to Joan that she was mistaken in her condemnation. It was this instinct, with an unspoken thought that he would face the thing honestly, that sent him back to the hovel where he had spent the night before. That was where he belonged, he told himself. It was to such places that his father and Joan had consigned him. So be it. He found a grim sort of satisfaction in flaunting the stigma of his shame.

The greatest single force in Wint's life had always been his resentment of dictation. A devil of contrariness possessed him; a devil of false pride that made him go counter to all warnings for the sheer joy of opposition. Thus his best friends became his enemies; for their good advice and counsel thrust him into evil paths; and by the same token, those who thought themselves his enemies were as often as not his best and truest friends. There was a stubborn streak in Wint that ruled him; it was rare that the gentler side of him had the ascendancy. One of those rare moments had come when he faced his father on this day. He had been humble, shamed, regretful, ready to make any amends. But the elder Chase, writhing under the ridicule to which the day had subjected him, had been in no mood for gentleness; and the result of the interview of father and son had been a parting which left them both sore and resentful.

The first faint anger in Wint's heart grew swiftly. When he had seen Joan, and she had sent him away, he coupled her with his father in his thoughts. They were both against him; both thought him nothing better than a drunkard; both thought him a treacherous and ribald fool. And the consciousness of this lifted his head in anger, and stiffened his heart, so that he swore he would fight out the battle and prove to them they were wrong, and then throw his newly won victory in their faces. They thought him a drunken sot; very well, he would fight the fight on that basis. They thought the Weaver House was the place where he belonged; very well, he would fight his fight from that brothel. And it was in such fashion as this, wearing his own disgrace like a plume, that he returned to Mrs. Moody's disreputable hostelry.

When he was alone in his room, he sat down on the edge of the bed and lighted a cigarette. He rested his elbows on his knees, the cigarette dangling from his clasped fingers, and considered. And as he thought, his face hardened, hardened with the effort to control his own pity for himself. He was immensely sorry for his own plight, immensely resentful of the misunderstandings of which he was a victim. And he was terribly lonely. He missed companionship—Jack Routt, Gergue, even Muldoon. Muldoon would have been the most welcome of them all, but he had left Muldoon at home. He regretted this; and his regret at last became so keen that he could not bear it. With a sudden resolution, he tossed the half-burned cigarette into the grate, and went down the stairs and crossed the railroad and bent his steps toward home. Muldoon, at least, would not condemn him. Muldoon was a faithful sort; a good pup....

He took alleyways and unfrequented streets, and avoided chance encounters. Thus he came near his home without meeting any one, and he went in through the alley and halted under a cherry tree that shaded Muldoon's kennel, beside the coal house, and whistled softly. The dog might be in his kennel; he might be in the house; he might be roaming abroad in search of his master.

He whistled three times, and got no response. Muldoon was somewhere beyond hearing. He might be in the house; and if he were and heard Wint's whistle, Wint knew he would bark a demand that he be allowed to come out.

So Wint whistled more shrilly; a long, familiar call.

For a time he got no answer to this. He tried again, and this time he heard the faint sound of a muffled bark from inside the house. This bark came nearer, became clamorous, located itself at the kitchen door, where Wint could hear Muldoon's claws rattling on the panels.

He started toward the kitchen, then halted. For the windows were lighted; and at one of them Hetty Morfee appeared. She was wiping dishes, and when she came to the window she held a plate, gripped in a dishcloth, in her left hand, and shaded her eyes with her right as she tried to peer out into the night.

Muldoon's close-cropped head appeared beside her at the window for an instant, and he barked again. Wint shrank back into the shadow. He did not wish to be discovered and he was unwilling to risk encountering his father or his mother by going to the house. He shrank back into the darkness; but he whistled again, and this time Hetty left the window and opened the door, and Muldoon came out like a projectile, and found Wint under the cherry tree, and slavered over him.

Wint was so absorbed in the dog that he did not see, until too late, that Hetty had followed Muldoon. She came on him, under the tree, laughing softly. "It's you, is it?" she called.

"Yes."

"What's the matter?"

"I came for Muldoon. He's mine."

She chuckled lightly. "You're the original Mister Trouble, Wint. Your paw says he never wants to see you again, and your maw's gone over to tell the neighbors all about it."

"Where's father?"

"He stomped off uptown after supper."

Wint fumbled with the dog's head. "Thanks for letting Muldoon out," he said.

"That's all right. Don't you want some supper? Come on in."

"No."

"Where are you going to spend the night?

"The Weaver House."

She gave an exclamation of disgust. "That dirty joint!"

"They say that's where I belong. I can stand it if they can."

"Oh, don't be a nut!"

He turned away into the alley, Muldoon at his heels. She called after him: "What's your hurry?"

"Good night."

"Your paw'll come around."

Wint said nothing. He was moving away. She ran after him and caught his arm. "Wint! Don't be a nut! Come on back! He'll come around."

He released his arm and shook his head. "That's up to him," he said. "I've eaten dirt. All I intend to."

She lifted her shoulders, laughed. "Oh—all right. If there's anything you want from here, let me know and I'll get it for you."

"Thanks. And—good night!"

"Good night," she said; and moved back into the shadow of the coal shed and watched him disappear. Leaning there, one hand fumbling at her throat, she was a wistful and unhappy figure. But when Wint was gone, she laughed harshly, and turned back to her work in the kitchen.

If Hetty had wished to confirm Wint in his resolution to go his stubborn way, she could have taken no better means than to repeat her warning: "Don't be a nut!" He took a certain delight in being thus unreasonable. What he did was his own affair; it concerned no one else. And he returned to the Weaver House in a surprisingly peaceful frame of mind and climbed to his room and went to bed with Muldoon curled on the floor beside him, and slept soundly and healthfully.

He woke in the morning to find Muldoon sitting by the bed, watching him and waiting for him to stir. When he opened his eyes, Muldoon wriggled and yawned and licked his hand, and Wint chuckled, and got up briskly, and dressed himself and went downstairs. The office was empty when he came down, for the hour was early; and he went out without seeing any one, and followed the railroad tracks to the station. There was a lunch cart near the station; and he crowded in among the toil-grimed crew of the night freight and ate a Hamburg steak sandwich garnished with a biting slice of onion, and drank a great mug of steaming coffee. Some of the men recognized him, and they talked to him with an unwilling respect in their manner. He liked this. They did not seem to be laughing at him, although they professed interest in the manner of his election, and asked him how he had worked it, and what he was going to do now. He told them, honestly enough, that he had known nothing about it beforehand; and he told them, with equal honesty, that he was asleep in the Weaver House when the word was brought to him. They seemed surprised that he should state these things without attempt at palliation; and they seemed to approve of him for doing so. Their attitude gave him renewed confidence, so that he went up toward town with his head high, ready to look men in the eye.

He began to meet people at once. They were for the most part men going to their work; and some of them eyed him angrily, and some seemed inclined to laugh at him; but most of them, like the railroad men, gave evidence of a certain new respect. They hailed him with effusive cordiality as "Mr. Mayor," but they seemed a little afraid of the sound of their own words, a little afraid of what his attitude might be.

Wint had made his plans. He must get some clothes from his home, must cut himself off completely from his father. To this end he sought Jack Routt. Routt, like every one in town, went to the Post Office each morning for his mail; and Wint found him there.

Routt shook his hand heartily. "Wint, congratulations!" he said, under his breath. "This'll be a great thing for you. It will steady you, Wint."

Wint shook his head, some of the sullen anger of the night before returning. He had no wish to be steadied, and he said so. "I can take care of myself," he told Routt.

Jack nodded. "So you can. But you need something to hold you down. And this'll do it." He nudged Wint in the ribs, smiling slyly. "Y' know, you've been hitting it too strong lately. You don't know when to stop, Wint. This will put the brakes on. Make you tend to business."

Wint brushed his hand across Routt's face abruptly. "Cut it," he said. "Say, Jack, I want you to do something for me."

"Anything in the world."

"My father is sore. He thinks I was in on this. So he kicked me out last night."

"Kicked you out?" Routt was startled and indignant. "Why, say, that's—Where did you go? Why didn't you come over to my place?"

Wint said consciously: "No—I went to the Weaver House. They know me there."

Routt looked quickly around to see if any one had heard. "Sh-h-h!" he warned. "Say, that was a fool thing to do. Don't let any one find it out. You want to walk straight now—"

Wint cut in. "I want you to go out home and get my steamer trunk and pack it with some things. There's a blue suit in my closet. And shirts, and so on. Get my overcoat, too. Mother will show you—or Hetty."

Routt looked at him quickly. "Hetty who?"

"Hetty Morfee."

Routt looked at Wint and laughed softly. "Oh—she's working for you?"

"Yes."

"Nice kid, isn't she?"

"Yes. And—as I said—she'll help you if mother won't."

Routt nodded. "All right," he agreed. "I'll go out this morning. Where'll I send the trunk? Weaver House?"

"I'll send for it. You just pack it."

Routt touched Wint's arm. "I'll do it," he said again. "But Wint,—for the love of Mike, don't make a fool of yourself! Thing for you to do is to take hold, run the town right, and make a name for yourself. It's a great chance,

Wint. Make everybody see what you've got in you. And it'll be the making of you, Wint."

The distribution of the morning's mail to the boxes was ended just then, and the windows opened. Routt broke off and went to get his mail, and Wint, still resentful at Routt's insistence on the moral advantages of his situation, went to the window. Dave Howells, one of the postal clerks, was there; and before Wint could speak, he had offered his congratulations. These continual good wishes were beginning to irk Wint. He nodded impatiently. "Dave," he said, "I want you to hold my mail hereafter. Don't send it to the house."

"Oh, we always put it in your father's box," Howells told him.

"Well, don't do that. Hold it. I'll call for it."

The clerk wanted to ask questions, but decided not to do so. He took out a card and wrote something on it. "I think there's a letter for you in the box now," he said. "I'll give it to you."

Wint nodded; and a moment later the man handed him an envelope, and Wint turned away from the window. He met his father, face to face, at the door of the Post Office. Neither of them spoke.

Wint had dropped the letter into his pocket without looking at it. When he reached the hotel on the corner, he turned in, and sat down on one of the deep, leather chairs in the lobby, and drew out the envelope. The address, he saw, was typewritten. The letter had been mailed in town. The envelope was plain; and when he opened it he saw that the paper it contained bore no distinguishing mark.

The letter, like the address, was typewritten, and Wint read it once, and read it again with slowly kindling resentment. It said:

"*Dear Wint.*—

"You have made ducks and drakes of your life. And you have made yourself the butt of the town's jokes. And you have made those who loved you the objects of derision.

"But your election as Mayor gives you the finest chance a man ever had to retrieve those old mistakes, to make a man of yourself, and to make a fine town of Hardiston.

"Take hold. Work hard. Live straight. And be sure that there are some true friends who will watch you lovingly and sympathetically, and hope and pray for your success."

This letter was unsigned. Wint read it a second time, and then with tense, stiff fingers he tore it into little bits and dropped these bits into a wide, brass cuspidor beside his chair. As the scraps of paper fluttered from his hand, he clenched his fists; and he looked about to see if any one had been watching.

He hated this preaching, this morality, this harping on the hope of his redemption. He was all right; no harm in him. But they would not leave him alone. They nagged at him; nagged.... He hated it.

He wondered, as an undercurrent to this rage, who had written the letter. It might have been his father, or his mother, or Routt. Routt was a sanctimonious ass about some things. Or it might have been.... He thought it was probably the minister of his father's church; and he grinned with dry relish at the thought. The old man must have been sadly shocked at Wint more than once; and this letter sounded just like him. Blithering, self-righteous....

He lunged up from his chair, boiling furiously. All his determination to stick it out was gone. He would not do it, would not make a righteous spectacle of himself for the edification of these old women. He went out and turned up the street past the Court House, walking blindly, storming inwardly. He would get out of town, shake the dust of the place off his feet. Let them find a new Mayor.

He was still fuming thus when, in front of the Court House, he met Peter Gergue. Peter rummaged through his back hair and grinned at Wint. "Saw you coming," he explained. "Thought you might be looking f'r me. So I came down."

"I'm not looking for you," said Wint.

Gergue nodded. "All right," he assented. "Mind if I walk along with you? Going on this way?"

Wint halted in his tracks. "What's up?" he asked sharply. "What do you want?"

"Me?" Peter ejaculated. "Why—me? I don't want nothing."

"What are you so anxious to keep an eye on me for, then? I don't want you."

Gergue hesitated, and he looked across the street toward his office; and at last he leaned toward Wint and said slyly: "Tell you th' truth, it ain't me. Amos is over at my place. He see you coming, and he was worried f'r fear you'd come up and find him there. He knows you're mad at him. Don't want to see you. Don't want to listen to you. Knows you got a fair kick, and he don't like to listen to kicks."

Wint looked across the way, and then at Peter; and then, without a word, he started across the street. Peter went hurriedly after him. "Say," he begged, "you ain't going—"

"I'm going to tell that old scamp what I think of him."

Peter pleaded. "Oh, now, Wint—he'll be mad at me." He laid a restraining hand on Wint's arm. Wint shook it off.

"What do I care what he thinks of you?" he demanded. "Let go."

"You don't want t' see him, Wint."

Wint went stubbornly ahead. He turned into the stairs that led up to Peter's office; and Gergue sighed.

"Glory! Well—all right, then. I'll trail along," he said; and then he smiled at Wint's ascending back with amiable satisfaction and followed Wint up the stairs.

Wint had never been in Peter's office before. He halted in the doorway, struck by the slack disorder of the place. There were spider webs in every corner; there was dust everywhere. The soft floor had been worn by many feet till every knot stood up like a rounded knob, and every nail upreared a shining head. The door of the wardrobe hung open, revealing some battered books inside. The old, oilcloth-covered table at the window was littered with papers and rusty pens, and sagged weakly under the weight of the books upon it. At this table, when Wint came in, sat Congressman Amos Caretall. The Congressman saw Wint, and got up hurriedly, eyes squinting, head on one side. He looked distinctly apologetic; and when he saw Peter behind Wint, he eyed his satellite reproachfully.

Wint stormed across the room to face the Congressman; but even while he approached the older man, some of his anger died in him. Amos was so frankly unhappy, he was so apologetic, the tilt of his head was so plaintive. Nevertheless Wint cried: "What right had you to use my name in this way, Congressman?"

Caretall shook his head humbly. "Not a right in the world, Wint."

"It was a dirty trick. Underhand."

The Congressman nodded. "I know it, Wint," he assented. "I c'n see that now. All the trouble it's made and everything. If I'd knowed.... But you see, a man gets to playing the game, and he don't stop to think like he oughter."

"You hadn't any right to do it," Wint insisted; but he was weakening. Nothing is so disarming as acquiescence; and when a man condemns himself, it is human nature to wish to defend him.

"I know it," Amos repeated. "I ain't got a word to say, Wint. Except that I'll help to straighten things out so you won't have to serve."

Wint looked puzzled for a moment. "I—what's that?"

"I say, I'll help you fix things so you won't have to take it."

"What makes you think I don't want to take it?"

Amos spread out his hands like a man who has nothing to conceal. "Why, that's common sense. I'd ought to have knowed. It's a hard job. Prob'ly you couldn't swing it. Anyway, it means work, and stickin' to the grindstone; and you're a young fellow. You like your good times. You wouldn't want to be tied down to anything this way."

Wint laughed derisively. "You think you know a whole lot about me, don't you?"

Amos smiled. "Well, Wint," he returned. "I've seen some of life. I know a lively young fellow like you don't want to take on a job that means work. And you're right, o' course. It ain't the job f'r you. You ain't fitted for it. You couldn't manage it. You're right. I hadn't ought to have got you into this. But I'll help get you out. That's th' least I can do."

Wint looked at the Congressman with level eyes for a moment; and then he turned and looked out of window, saying nothing. Amos caught Peter Gergue's eye, and Peter winked at him. Amos said humbly: "I sure am sorry about this, Wint. It's made it hard for you. You can't stay here now. You might go over to Washin'ton, Wint. I c'd get you somethin' easy, there."

Wint turned back to him abruptly; and there was a catch in his voice. "Congressman," he said, half laughing, "you owe me something."

Caretall nodded. "That's right, Wint. 'Nd I'm ready to pay."

"All right. Here's what I want you to do." He hesitated, extended his hand. "I know I'm not fit for this job, sir," he said reluctantly. "But—if you'll give me a hand and help along—I'd like to tackle it."

Amos looked doubtful. "Now, Wint—don't you get wrong notions. No sense you're sticking in this mess. I'll get you out without any—"

Wint interrupted him angrily: "You can't get me out. Nor any one else. I'm in and I'll stay in. But—I'd like to have your advice and help when I need it."

And the Congressman yielded. He took Wint's hand. "All right," he agreed. "I'll back you. I don't know as you're right, and I don't know as you're wrong. If you can get away with it."

"I intend to."

Amos nodded. "Sure you intend to. But can you? Well—we've got to see." He hesitated, seemed to be thinking. "I hear your father and you've broke," he said.

"Yes."

"That's too bad. Where are you living?"

"The Weaver House," said Wint defiantly. But his defiance was misplaced. Congressman Caretall nodded approvingly.

"That's fine," he said. "Old Mother Moody sets a right good table, when she's a mind to. I wish I c'd live down there myself. It's a good plan." He looked at Wint and winked slyly. "Always a good plan to play to the workingman," he explained. "Good idea of yours, Wint. Living down there. Get the workingmen and the railroad men and all to sympathizing with you. They'll play you for a martyr, and back you strong. You'll make a good politician, Wint. I c'n see that."

Wint shook his head. "It's not politics," he said. "I—don't intend to stay there. Just till I get settled uptown. Somewhere."

Amos studied him. "Pshaw, now! That's too bad. It'd been a good play, Wint."

Wint laughed. "I'll play the game some other way."

The Congressman nodded. He remained silent for a moment, then said thoughtfully, "I was thinking.... You and me has got to do a lot of talking, planning. I wish you could come and stay with me till your paw comes 'round."

Wint shook his head. "Thanks," he said, smiling. "That's good of you. But I'll—" He hesitated; for through the window he had seen, across the street, Jack Routt and Joan together. They were talking briskly; and Joan was laughing at something Routt had said. Wint stared at them, with slowly burning eyes; and before he could continue Gergue nudged him in the side and told the Congressman smilingly:

"That 'uz a bad break, Amos. He can't come live with you."

Wint looked at him. "Why not?" he asked; and Amos said to Gergue:

"That's right, Peter. I'd forgot."

"Why not?" Wint repeated impatiently; he glanced again toward the two across the street.

"Why, he means Miss Joan wouldn't like it," the Congressman explained.

"Why wouldn't she?"

Gergue pointed across the street. "She'd soon teach you manners," he chuckled. "The Congressman here's got a nice-looking daughter of his own, you know."

Wint's hand clenched at his side. "You're all wrong there," he said curtly; and then to Amos: "I think I'll accept your invitation, after all," he said.

CHAPTER IV

INTERLUDE

THE weeks between his election and his inauguration Wint spent as a guest at Amos Caretall's home. At which the townsfolk put their tongues in their cheeks and smiled behind the back of the elder Chase. This open alliance between Wint and the Congressman was taken as confession that Wint's election had been planned between them; and after a day or two Wint perceived the hopelessness of denial, and perceived, too, that those who believed him concerned in the trick respected him the more for it. Therefore, Wint ceased to deny; and it was one of Amos Caretall's rules never to discuss a thing accomplished.

Between Amos and the young man, a strong friendship began to develop in these weeks. Congressman Caretall was a good politician, largely through the advice and counsel of Peter Gergue; but he was also a man of level head and good common sense, and he found beneath Wint's pride and stubbornness a surprising store of good qualities. A week after Wint went to live at his house, he said as much to Gergue.

"He's a fine boy, Peter," he declared. "Looks to me like a colt that hadn't been gentled right."

Gergue nodded slowly and scratched the back of his head, tilting his hat forward with his knuckles. "He has his points," he agreed. "But—he ain't set in th' traces yet, Congressman."

Amos looked at the man. "What's wrong?"

"Noth'n'," said Peter. "Noth'n'. But—there will be."

Jack Routt brought Wint's trunk to the Caretall house and, before he left that day, he took occasion to drop a word of warning in Wint's ear. "Look out for Agnes," was his warning. "She's the darndest little flirt you ever saw."

Wint lifted his head angrily. "Cut it out, Jack!"

Routt laughed. "I'm only giving you some good advice," he insisted. "You know—a certain young lady will not be pleased if you pay Agnes too much attention. And Agnes loves to make trouble."

Wint repeated: "Shut up! Drop it!" And Routt lifted his shoulders and obeyed.

Two or three days after the election, Wint remembered that he was supposed to be working in his father's office at the furnace. With an unadmitted twist of conscience, he went down to the office, half hoping to see his father and find some common ground for a reconciliation. But the elder Chase was not there, and the office manager greeted Wint coldly and told him that his place had been filled. Wint had ten days' salary due him, and the manager paid it punctiliously. Wint took the money without thinking, thrust it in his pocket, and went back uptown.

While he was in college, he had been on an allowance; since then his father had paid him a salary out of proportion to his deserts. This was one of the vanities of the elder Chase. His own youth had been hard and straitened; and he took a keen delight in lavishing upon Wint the money he himself had lacked. He did this, not to please Wint, but to please himself; and whenever Wint crossed him, he was accustomed to bring up the matter, to remind Wint of his good fortune as though it were a reproach.

"Be sure I never had money to spend, when I was your age," he was fond of saying. "And you roll in it. You ought to be ashamed, Wint. You ought to be ashamed."

Then he would give Wint twenty dollars and tell him to mend his ways; and afterward he would complain to Mrs. Chase of Wint's ingratitude.

Wint had always taken this money without scruple. Whenever inner doubts perplexed him, he would say: "He's got more than he can use. I might as well have it as any one else." In all honesty, he knew the falsity of such an argument; but he used it successfully to stifle the reproaches of his own heart.

A day or two after his visit to the office, however, Amos Caretall asked him: "Wint, you need any money?"

Wint shook his head.

"Didn't know but you might," Amos insisted. "Carry you over till your salary starts."

"I've got enough," Wint said. "Dad was always pretty liberal. Gave me more than I could spend."

Amos did not seem surprised at this. He nodded his head. "That's good," he agreed. "If any one had told me, I wouldn't have believed it. Wouldn't have believed Senior had so much sense. Keeps you in his debt, like, don't he? Keeps you d'pendent on him?"

Wint had never thought of it in that way, and he did not like the thought. He looked uneasy. Amos went on, puffing at his old black pipe: "Guess he figures to get it all back some way. 'F he sh'd come and ask you for something, after you're in, you'd naturally have to give it to him. Yes, Senior's a smart man."

They were sitting in front of the coal fire in Amos' sitting room; and for a time after that, neither of them spoke. Wint was thinking hard, and in the end he asked quietly: "Know any way I can earn a living till I'm inaugurated?"

Amos swung his head around, tilting it on one side, and squinting thoughtfully at Wint; and presently he smiled approvingly. "Guess you might," he said. "Might do some o' my letter writing. You'd learn things, that way. I never had no secretary. I'm allowed one. You c'n have the job, long's I'm here."

Next morning Wint mailed a money order to his father without explanation, and thereafter he drew a salary from Amos until his salary as Mayor began.

From his work for Amos, Wint learned many things. He got for the first time an insight into the scope of the Congressman's work, into the extent of his interests and influence. One of the things he learned was a sincere respect for Caretall's ability, and he also came to admire the shrewdness of Gergue. Wint did a deal of thinking in those weeks.

Living, as he did, as one of Caretall's family, he was thrown constantly with Agnes; and the girl put herself out to please him. She and old Maria Hale worked together in this. The girl discovered Wint's favorite dishes, and Maria produced them and brought them to a perfection that Wint had never known. It was Agnes' task to take care of the dusting and housework; and she began, after a time, to put an occasional cluster of flowers from the greenhouses next door in his room. When they talked together, she deferred to him with a pretty fashion of tilting her head and widening her serious eyes that he found exceedingly attractive. It stimulated his self-respect; and at the same time it gave him a new respect for her. Since she so obviously approved of him, there must be more to her than he had supposed. She was, he decided, a person of judgment. He had always thought her a giddy little thing with a brisk, gay tongue and laughing eyes. He found in her an unexpected capacity for silence and for attention. She encouraged him to talk about himself, about his plans; she sympathized with him, and advised him when he asked her advice. They became surprisingly good friends.

She suggested, one evening, that they telephone Jack Routt to bring Joan for a game of cards. Wint shook his head; and the girl, without asking questions, made her curiosity so obvious that Wint told her that Joan had cast him off. He leaned forward, elbows on knees and fingers intertwined, staring idly into the fire, while he told her; and the girl leaned back in her chair and listened and studied him, and when she finished she laid her hand lightly on his arm.

"It's a shame, Wint," she said.

Wint shook his head. "Oh—she was right!"

"She wasn't right. She ought to have stuck by you, and helped you fight it out."

Wint thought so too, and his respect for Agnes rose. But he said insistently: "No, she was right."

Agnes patted his arm, and then leaned back in her chair again. "It's fine of you to think so," she said.

One night Wint asked her to go uptown with him to the moving-picture theater. She was delighted, and she was gay as a cricket on the way. At the entrance of the theater, they came face to face with Jack Routt and Joan.

Wint felt his cheeks burn. Agnes greeted the other two with a burst of rapid chatter that covered the awkward moment. Routt studied Wint, and Joan nodded to him without speaking. Then Routt and Joan went inside, and Wint and Agnes sat three rows behind them.

While the picture was flashing on the screen, Wint watched the heads of the two. He could not help it; and when their heads, silhouetted against the light, leaned toward one another for a whispered word, he felt something boil within him. His reaction was to bend more attentively toward Agnes; and the gay little girl beside him responded to this new mood so that when the film was done and they filed out, she and Wint were the most obviously happy young couple in the house. They had ice cream together at the bakery next door, and walked home in comfortable comradeship, the girl's hand on his arm.

That night, Wint's sleep was disturbed and wretched; and next day when he met Routt at the Post Office, he stiffened with resentment. But Routt caught his arm and drew him to one side. "See here, Wint," he said, "Joan tells me you and she have quarreled."

Wint nodded.

"You ought to go to her and make it up, Wint. I don't know what it's about, but you ought to make it up with her."

"I've nothing to make up."

"She's a dandy girl."

"I've nothing against her."

"It makes her sore to have you chase around with Agnes."

"There's no reason why it should," Wint said stiffly. "She has no hold on me."

Routt hesitated. "Well, Wint," he said uneasily, "if that's so, you've no claim on her."

"Of course not."

"Then you don't mind my—showing her some attention? I don't want anything to come between us, Wint."

Wint laughed. "Go as far as you like, Jack," he said cheerfully. "You can't hurt my feelings."

Routt gripped his hand. "That's great, Wint." He looked about them, and then added slowly: "I think she likes me, Wint. I'm—in to win."

"Go as far as you like," Wint repeated.

They separated, and Wint went back to the house and remained in his room half the morning. He was tormented by angry pride and irresolution; he could not decide what to do. A recklessness took possession of him; he repented of his determination to stick, and fight out this fight to the end. He sought for some way out....

Muldoon had become a part of the Caretall household with Wint; and he looked out of the window now and saw the dog starting toward town at Agnes' heels. He made a move to whistle Muldoon back, then thought better of it. Joan might see Muldoon with Agnes; he hoped she would, hoped it would make her miserable.... He wanted Joan to be unhappy.

As the time for his inauguration as Mayor approached, Wint became more and more uneasy. He felt as though he were about to submit to bonds that would pin him fast; he felt as though he were on the steps of a prison. A fierce revolt began to brood in him and grow and boil.

He broke out once, in a talk with Caretall. He would throw the whole thing over, leave town, go away, never to return.

Amos agreed with this project perfectly. He agreed that Wint was not the man for the job, that it would mean hard work, and difficulties; he thought Wint was wise not to attempt it. He offered to straighten out any tangle and free Wint from the obligations of the office; and he offered to lend Wint money that Wint might make a start elsewhere.

His great complaisance angered Wint, so that he stubbornly declared that he would stick if every man in town urged him to go.

On the morning of the day before he was to take office, he met Jack Routt uptown, and Jack took his arm. They walked together toward Jack's office, and went in and sat down.

It was evident that Routt had something on his mind. He talked of the weather, of Agnes, of Joan; and Wint, watching him, saw that Routt was holding something back, and at last asked impatiently: "Jack, what's on your mind?"

Routt looked surprised. "Why—nothing."

"Yes, there is." Wint laughed at him. "What's the matter? Open up."

Routt hesitated; but at last he said frankly: "Well, Wint, I was wondering...."

"About what?"

"Have you been hitting the booze lately?" Routt asked.

Wint shook his head; his eyes hardened a little.

Routt seemed pleased. He thrust out his hand. "I'm darned glad, Wint," he said. "Congratulations! You ought to leave it alone. You're right."

Wint flushed angrily. "I haven't sworn off," he said shortly. "It—just happens—" He stared at Routt. "You didn't bring me up here to ask that?"

"Yes, I did."

"Why?"

Routt shifted in his chair and lighted a cigarette. "Never mind," he said. "Forget it, Wint."

Wint laughed unpleasantly. "Come on. I'm a grown man. What's eating you?"

Routt lifted his shoulders. "Well—fact is, some of the boys wanted to get up a little supper to-night, at the lodge rooms, in honor of your— inaugural. I told them nothing doing. Said you were off the stuff. They didn't believe it; and I promised to ask you."

Wint looked at him angrily. "You're not my wet nurse, Jack. That supper idea tickles me. It's on."

Routt protested. "No, Wint. I won't stand for it. You've stayed off the stuff this long; and it's the best thing for you. You can't stop when you once start. So—leave it alone."

Wint got up hotly. "Go to the devil!" he snapped. "Don't be an old woman. Who's running the thing?"

"Dick Hoover. But you leave it alone...."

"Rats! Tell Dick I'll be there. Or I'll tell him myself."

Routt lifted his hands in surrender. "Oh—I'll tell him," he agreed. "But you're a darned fool, Wint."

"Rats!" Wint repeated; and he grinned. He was unaccountably elated, as though he had shaken off restraining bonds. "Rats!" And he went out to the street with his head high.

Routt picked up the telephone and called Hoover. He was smiling.

CHAPTER V

ALLIANCE

WINTHROP CHASE, SENIOR, was thrown by his son's election to the office he had counted as his own into a passion in which rage and humiliation were equally commingled.

He was a man fed fat with vanity. He took himself very seriously. He lived a decent and respectable life in the eyes of all men, and he felt himself justly entitled to the respect of all men. He had, before this, seen the smiles of those few who dared mock him; but he had believed them a small minority. When three quarters of the town united in the jest at his expense, he was outraged inexpressibly. And when the city papers took up the story and for a time the whole state tittered over it, Chase trembled and shuddered with his own agony.

His first reaction had been anger at his son; and when he heard Wint had been found, sodden and stupid, in that room at the Weaver House, he cast the boy out of his life, hiding his own honest grief and sorrow under a mantle of resentment and accusation. For he loved Wint, and had wished to be proud of him.

In the beginning, his chief resentment centered on Wint, and he had toward Amos Caretall only that anger which one feels toward a treacherously victorious opponent. But about the time Wint sent him that money order, and stood on his own feet before the world, Chase's heart softened in spite of himself. He sought to make excuses for his son, and in this effort he found Caretall a convenient scapegoat. By degrees he convinced himself that Caretall had led Wint astray, playing on the boy's vanity and pride; and after that came the half conviction that when Wint denied all knowledge of the coup, the boy had told the truth. Then all Chase's anger centered on Amos; and as the first sting of his disgrace passed by, he began to look about him and seek to rebuild the shattered structure of his plans.

He had encountered Amos more than once upon the street since the election, though neither had carried their greetings further than a nod or word. But there came a day when Chase met the Congressman face to face in the Post Office at a moment when there were no others there; and when Chase nodded, Caretall stopped and tilted his head on one side and squinted in a friendly way at Chase.

"No hard feelings, is there, Senior?" he asked.

Chase looked at him, started to speak, flushed, checked himself; and at last said huskily: "Congressman, I want to talk with you."

Caretall nodded. "That's fair."

"Where can we talk?"

Amos scratched his head. "Tell you," he suggested. "I'll go along up to Pete Gergue's office. You go down t' your place, 'nd then come in the back way. Guess we don't want it known we're gettin' t'gether."

"Very well," Chase said stiffly. "I'll be there in half an hour."

When he climbed the stairs, Amos had sent Gergue away and was sitting at the oilcloth-covered table, slowly whittling a charge for his pipe. He got up bulkily at Chase's entrance, and motioned the other man to a chair across the table from his own. Chase sat down and Amos, lighting his pipe between his sentences, said slowly: "Chase...." a scratch of the match. "You don't want to hold this against me." A succession of deep puffs. "It's politics. All in th' game." A puff. "You was getting too strong for me. I had t' lick you." Puff, puff, puff!

Chase struck his fist with quiet vehemence on the table. "It was a dirty trick, Amos."

Amos shook his head, vastly pained. "Now, Senior," he protested, "don't go talking that way. 'Twas all in th' game. All in the game."

"It was a dirty trick," Chase insisted. "You played on my good feelings; you pretended to agree to an alliance with me; you got me off my guard—"

Amos held up a heavy hand. "Wait a minute," he protested. "Wait a minute, Senior. Let me get this here straight. You come to me with a prop'sition. Wanted to get together. Said you had me licked. I told you if you was elected Mayor, we'd hitch up. Ain't that right now, Senior?"

Chase moved angrily. "Strictly true," he confessed. "Strictly true. That's why I call it tricky. You came to my own meeting and said you were going to vote for me."

"Guess I said I was going to vote for a Chase, didn't I? Guess I did. And that's the way I voted."

"The town thought you meant me."

"Not long, they didn't. Word went around what I meant, all in good time."

Chase got to his feet, his head back, his face flushed. He leaned down to face Amos, and he slapped his right fist into his left palm. "I tell you it was a trick," he insisted. "You know it. It was unworthy. And I give you due warning, Caretall—I'm out for your scalp now. I propose to get it. Take your measures accordingly."

Amos puffed hard at his pipe. He, too, rose; he tilted his head thoughtfully on one side and squinted at Chase. "I don't like t' hear you talk that way, Senior," he said slowly. "You come to me and talked to me till you rightly showed me we ought to get together. I'm ready—even if you did get—"

Chase flung up his hand. "Stop!" he cried. The self-control which he had imposed upon himself was gone. "Stop! Man, man! D'you think I'm one to lick the hand that stabs me? You lie to me, trick me, make a fool of me and a joke of me before the state; and to cap it all you steal my own son out of my house—"

"Heard you was the one to throw him out," Amos interjected, but Chase went hotly on:

"You steal my own son, take him into your own home, turn him against me, persuade him to help destroy me...." His voice broke with his own rage and grief. "I tell you, Amos," he said again, leaning steadily forward, "I'm going to get you. Fair warning. Take your measures accordingly."

Amos looked out of the window; he puffed at his pipe; and at last he faced the other man again, and smiled. "Well, Senior," he said slowly, "if the land lies so—thanks for the word. As for them measures—I'll take them like you say."

For a moment longer, the eyes of the two men held each other. Then Chase turned stiffly on his heel, and stalked to the door and went out.

As he disappeared, Amos called: "G'd day!" But Chase made no answer, and Amos, left alone, grinned slowly to himself and shook his head.

After that interview with Amos, Chase began to emerge from the turmoil of anger and shame in which he had been fighting since the election. His head cleared and his brain cooled, and he began to plan, with a certain newly acquired shrewdness, his next steps against Caretall. In many matters, heretofore, the elder Chase had been as simple as a boy. Now he was becoming crafty. In the past he had honestly believed that the life of self-conscious rectitude which he had led was of a sort to inspire respect and affection. Now he knew that he was wrong, knew that he must always have been disliked or despised by half the town. He had always been benignly courteous; and this courtesy, which was more than half condescension, had made more enemies than friends. He had played a straightforward game; and he had lost.

Like other men before him, in the determination to change his tactics, he went too far. He threw himself into the fight to injure Caretall with an utter disregard for the conventions he had once observed; he sought allies where he might find them; and for the first time in his life, he tried to put himself in another man's place and guess what the other man would do.

The man into whose place he sought to put himself was Amos Caretall; and the result of his considerations of Amos's possible future plans threw Chase into the arms of his ancient enemy, into the shrunken arms of V. R. Kite.

The feud between Kite and Chase had never been a concrete thing. It was based upon a thousand minor incidents, none of them important in itself. Kite, as the leader of the "wet" forces in the town, and as the proprietor of half the liquor-peddling establishments, was a man very quick to resent "dry" activities. Chase had always been actively "dry." And Kite, curiously enough for one of his vocation, was a very thin-skinned man. He found offenses in words that were meant for kindness; he found a sneer in an honest smile.

It was a part of the manner of the elder Chase to smile and nod benevolently upon those whom he encountered. This was automatic with him; and he smiled at Kite with the rest. Kite, a man of fierce and violent temperament, knew that Chase had no kindly feeling toward him; and so he saw in these smiles only sneers. He had complained to Amos Caretall: "He's always grinning at me," when Amos asked why he hated Chase; and this was an old grievance with the liquor man.

Kite had been one of those who rejoiced most highly in Chase's humiliation; and for a week or two after the election, he went out of his way to meet Chase upon the street. On such occasions, he paid back with interest those grins he had resented; he spoke to Chase with exaggerated courtesy and extreme solicitude. He inquired after the other's health end spirits; he sympathized with Chase in his defeat.

These sports palled upon him only when he perceived the growing change in Chase. For Wint's father was in many ways at this time like a child that has been punished for a fault it does not understand. The elder Chase was groping for friendliness; he sought it wherever it could be found; and he took some of Kite's satiric inquiries in good faith and responded to them with such honest confidence that Kite was touched and faintly uneasy.

A few days after Chase's talk with Amos, he sought out Kite in the little Bazaar which the latter conducted. It was an institution like a five and ten cent store, and did a flourishing business. Next door to it was a restaurant, also owned by Kite, and reached by a communicating passage. In a room behind this restaurant, knowing ones might be served with anything in reason. But Kite went there only for his meals, and most of the hours of business found him at his desk in the rear of the Bazaar.

Chase frankly sought him there. He drew a chair up to face the wrinkled little man; and Kite was surprised, and cocked his head on his thin neck and tugged at his drooping side whiskers until he looked more like a doubtful turkey than ever. "Howdo, Chase?" he said.

Chase nodded. "Kite," he began frankly, "I want to talk to you."

Kite tried to grin derisively; he tried to reawaken the old enmity in his breast. But there was something appealing about Chase, and so he said nothing, only waited.

"Kite," said Chase, "Amos Caretall played a good trick on me."

Kite looked startled; then he grinned. "Yes, Chase, he did that," he said.

"You helped him."

Kite frankly admitted it.

"You helped him," said Chase, "because you thought with Wint in as Mayor, the town would stay as wet as you want it."

Kite hesitated, then he nodded. "Yes," he agreed. "Yes, that's so, Chase. What about it?"

Chase leaned back. "Amos made a fool of you," he said. "He's going to turn this town dry, with the man you helped elect."

Kite flushed; he leaned toward Chase with narrowed eyes peering out from an ambush of wrinkles; and then suddenly he threw back his head with his long, turkey neck rising raw and red from his collar, and he laughed cacklingly, so that customers in the front of his store looked that way to share the joke. Chase frowned angrily. "Well?" he snapped, "what's funny about that?"

Kite dropped a dry old hand on Chase's arm. "Oh, Chase," he choked through his mirth, "the notion of Wint making this town dry...."

Chase flushed. He started to speak. Kite interrupted: "Now don't get mad. Course, he's your son, but he does like his drop now and then, Chase."

"I tell you, Amos is planning to do it."

There was something so deadly sure in Chase's tone that Kite sobered and looked toward him. "Say, what makes you say that?" he demanded. "How do you know?"

"Amos has sense. He sees this question is the big one in this state. He's out for Congress again. He's not going to have it thrown at him that his man let this town soak itself illegally."

For the first time, Kite began to look worried. "Amos wouldn't do that. He told me—"

"Told you? He told me many things, too. But none of them were true."

Kite, suddenly, burst into flame like an oily rag. He threw up a clenched fist. "By God, Chase, he don't dare try it!"

"Dare? He'll dare anything."

Kite stammered with the heat of his own anger. "He don't dare!" he insisted. "Why, Chase—if he tries that—I'll—I'll—" With no sense that his words had been said before, he exclaimed: "I won't live in the town, Chase. I'll get out! I'll shoot him! Or myself."

Chase leaned forward. "I tell you, he's aiming to do it," he said steadily. "So sit down."

Kite gripped his arm. "Chase, you got to drill some sense into that son of yours. You got to tell him—"

"He's not my son now; he's Amos's. Living with Amos, doing what Amos says. Don't forget that."

There was a bitterness in Chase's voice which silenced Kite for a moment. Then the little man touched Chase on the arm. "See here," he said softly, "you don't like Amos any better'n I do."

Chase smiled mirthlessly. "I'm out for his hide," he declared.

Kite nodded, chuckling grimly. "He thinks he's a big man," he said. "He thinks he can run over us, play with us, use us and then give us the brad. But I tell you right now, Chase...." He lifted his open hand as one who takes an oath. "I tell you right now, Chase, if he tries that little trick—you and me'll get together, and we'll hang his old hide in the sun to dry."

"He'll try it," said Chase steadily.

Kite stuck out his hand. "Then we'll skin him."

"That's a bargain," Chase declared, and gripped the other's dry and skinny fingers.

It was in this fashion that these two enemies joined hands against the common foe.

CHAPTER VI

THE WHISTLE BLOWS

THE festivities in Wint's honor on the night before his inaugural were a great success, from every point of view.

There was nothing formal about them. They occurred in an upper room in one of the newer business blocks on Main Street. Only half a dozen young fellows attended them; but these were all chosen spirits, and congenial.

At half past nine, they were all pleasantly illuminated by their libations and the general good cheer of the occasion. At eleven, two of them were asleep quite peacefully in each other's arms upon a couch at one side of the room. These two snored as they slept. The others were playing cards, and the refreshments which had been provided were in easy reach. Wint and Jack Routt were among those playing cards. Routt never passed a certain stage of intoxication, no matter how much he drank. He reached this stage with the first swallow.

With Wint, it was otherwise. In such matters, he progressed steadily toward a dismal end. As eleven o'clock struck, he had just passed the quarrelsome stage and was beginning to pity himself. He opened a hand with three queens, but when Routt raised his bet, Wint threw down his cards and put his head on his arms and wept because he could not win. Then he took another drink.

After a little, he cried himself to sleep.

Toward one o'clock, Routt and Hoover took Wint home to Amos Caretall's. The streets, at that hour of the night, were utterly deserted. There was a moon, and the street lamps were unlighted as an economical consequence of this heavenly illumination. Wint was between Routt and Hoover. At times he took a sodden step or two; at other times he dragged to his knees upon the ground, wagging his head from side to side and singing huskily.

Hoover was almost as badly off as Wint; and now and then he joined in this song. Jack Routt was cold sober, and coldly exultant. His eyes shone in the moonlight; and he handled Wint with rough tenderness.

When they were about half a block from the Caretall home, Wint became very sick; and Hoover sat down in the middle of the sidewalk and giggled at him while Routt, leaning against a tree above the sprawling body of his friend, waited until the paroxysms were past and then caught Wint's shoulders again and dragged him to his feet.

Wint had thrown off some of the poison; he was able now to help himself a little more than before; and they got him to their destination. There Routt propped him against a tree before the house and shook him and tried to impress upon him the necessity of silence.

"Don't you sing, now, Wint," he warned. "Brace up. Have some sense. Keep quiet."

Wint pettishly protested that he liked to sing, and that he was a good singer; and he tried to prove it on the spot, but Routt gagged him with the flat of his hand until Wint surrendered.

"Cut it out, Wint," he insisted. "You've got to be quiet while we get you to bed."

Then Routt felt a hand on his shoulder, and some one drawled: "You've done your share, Routt. Go along. I'll tuck him in."

He turned and saw Amos Caretall. Amos was in a bath robe of rough toweling over his nightshirt; and his feet were in carpet slippers. Routt was tongue-tied for a moment; then he found his voice. "I'm mighty sorry about this, sir," he said. "I tried to keep him from drinking too much. But you can't stop him. He's such a darned fool."

Amos grinned at him in a way that somehow frightened Routt. "He sure is the darndest fool I ever see," he agreed. "But don't you mind, Jack. Boys will be boys. You and—who is it?—oh, Hoover. You and Hoover run along home. I'll tend to him."

"Don't you want me to help get him in the house?"

"I'll get him in. I've handled 'em before."

Routt hesitated: but there was nothing to do but obey, and he obeyed. Congressman Amos Caretall, in carpet slippers, nightshirt, and faded bath robe, watched them go; and then he turned to where Wint had slouched down against the tree and said kindly:

"Well, Wint—come on in."

Wint wagged his head and began to sing. The Congressman bent over him and slapped him expertly upon the cheeks with his open hands, one hand and then the other. The sting and smart of the blows seemed to dispel some of the clouds that fuddled Wint, and he grinned sheepishly, and got to his feet. Amos put his arm around him. "Come on, Wint," he said again.

They went thus slowly up the walk and into the house. Amos shut the front door behind them, and led Wint to the stairs and up them.

In the upper hall, one electric bulb was burning; and as they came into its light, Agnes came out of her room. Her soft, fair hair was down her back; her eyes were dewy with sleep; and a flaming, silken garment was drawn close about her. "What is it, dad?" she asked: and then saw Wint lurching along on her father's arm with nodding head and dull and drunken eyes, and she laughed softly and stepped toward him and shook her finger in his face. "Oh, you Wint! Naughty boy!" she chided.

Her father said sharply: "Get into your room, Agnes!" The girl looked at him, and at the anger in his eyes she turned a little pale and slipped silently away.

Amos took Wint to his room, where Wint fell helplessly across his bed and began instantly to snore. The Congressman looked down at him for an instant with a grim sort of pity mingled with the anger in his eyes. Then he bent and loosened Wint's shoes and drew them off; and afterward he took off the boy's collar, and unbuttoned his garments at the throat, and unbuckled his belt so that his sodden body should nowhere be constricted.

"I guess that'll do, Wint," he said slowly then. "You're too heavy for me to handle. Besides, Wint—you ain't right clean." He stood for a moment longer, then turned toward the door. At the door he looked back once, snapped out the light, and so was gone.

Wint's snores were unbroken.

The Caretall home stood in that end of town where the largest of the furnaces is located. A railroad siding passes this furnace, and a switching engine is busy here twenty-four hours of the day. The engine occasionally finds occasion to whistle; and the furnace itself has a whistle of enormous proportions; a siren whose blast carries for miles across the hills. This siren blows at every change of shift, it blows at casting time, and it blows at the whim of the engineer who may wish to startle some casual visitor or friend.

Persons who have lived long in this part of Hardiston grow accustomed to this great whistle. They sleep undisturbed when it rouses the night echoes; and they talk undisturbed when it shatters the peace of the day. It is even told of some of them that when the furnace went out of blast and its whistle was stilled, they used to be awakened in the middle of the night by the failure of the siren to sound at the accustomed time.

Wint's own home was in the other end of town. He had not lived long enough near the furnace to accustom himself to its noises; and they disturbed him. They penetrated his stupefied sleep on the night of this debauch. The steady roar of the great fires, which could be heard three or four miles on a still night, played on his worn nerves and tortured them; the sharp toots of the switching engine made him jump and quiver in his sleep like a dreaming child; and when he woke in the morning to find Amos shaking him by the shoulder, he was miserable and sick and his head throbbed with the beat of a thousand drums, and seemed like to split with agony. He wished, weakly, that it would split and be done.

When he opened his bloodshot eyes, Amos laughed and jerked him upright and shook some of the slumber out of him. "Come, Wint," he commanded heartily. "I've got a cold tub all ready. Jump in it. Got to get in shape, y'know. Inaugurated t'day."

Wint groaned and held his head in both hands. "Hell with it," he scowled. "Inaugural. Whole damn business. I'm not goin' to do it. Goin' sleep. Hell with it, I say."

He tried to drop back on the bed, but Amos laughed and caught him and dragged him to his feet. "Come out of it," he enjoined. "You'll be all right."

Wint shook his head stubbornly; then cried out with pain at the shaking. The fumes of the liquor were gone out of him; he was only dreadfully sleepy and dreadfully sick. He felt as though he were pulled and tortured by pricking wires that tore his flesh, and his eyelids were as heavy as lead and as hot as coals upon his bloodshot eyes. But he opened them, and said heavily: "No, Congressman Caretall. It's off. I won't do it. I'm through."

It was as Amos groped for a next word that the siren began to blow. This was the signal for the morning's casting. The engineer must have been in good spirits that morning, for he gave more than full measure on the blast. The whistle shrieked and roared till the very windows rattled and shivered in their places; and Wint, at the first sound, whipped up his hands to shield his agonized ears, and dropped on the bed and held his head and groaned until his groan became almost a shriek with the pain. Then, when the siren died into silence, he got dully to his feet, and glared at Amos, who said huskily: "I'd like t' kill man that did that. Like to dynamite that whistle. Anything— make it keep quiet."

Amos suddenly smiled; then he chuckled. "Well, Wint," he said quickly, "there's ways to make it keep quiet."

Wint looked at him with torpid interest. "I'll bite," he said. "Tell me one."

Amos waved his hands. "Why, f'r instance, the Mayor has power to enforce the abatement of a nuisance. Make them shut off that whistle, if it's a nuisance. Anything like that."

Wint swayed on his feet, and steadied himself with a hand on the foot of the bed. "Can the Mayor do a thing like that—on the square?"

"Why, sure," said Amos.

Wint grinned; a cracked and painful grin, but mirthful too; and he took a step forward. "Then say," he exclaimed. "Then say! There's something in this Mayor job, after all...."

"Sure there is!"

Wint gripped Amos' arm. "Lead me to that cold, cold tub," he enjoined.

END OF BOOK II

BOOK III

INTO HARNESS

CHAPTER I

ON HIS OWN FEET

THE inauguration of a small-town Mayor is no great matter for excitement. But Hardiston was interested in Wint, and wanted to have a look at him, so everybody came to see him step into his new responsibilities.

The Hardiston council chamber was on the second floor of the fire house. This was a three-story building of red brick, and a place of awe and wonder for the small boys of the town. The fire engine and the hose cart were kept on the ground floor, in front. Behind them were the stalls for the four sleek horses; behind the stalls again, a number of iron-barred stalls for human beings. Here were housed the minor criminals, arrested by Marshal Jim Radabaugh for petty peculations or disorders, and waiting for their hearings before the Mayor. These little cells were not designed to house prisoners for any length of time, and for the most part they were furnished simply with heaps of straw pilfered from the supply that was kept for the fire horses. The town drunkard, when the marshal got him, was treated as well as the fire horses; and this is more than may be said in larger towns than Hardiston.

At the left-hand side of the building there was an entrance hall, through which one passed to reach the stairs that led up to the council chamber. In the middle of this square hallway hung a rope, with a knot on the end. This rope disappeared through a hole in the ceiling. If you pulled it in the proper fashion, the bell in the steeple began a chattering, staccato beat like the clanging of a gong. This was the fire bell; and when it rang the fire chief came from his feed store across the street, and the firemen came from the bakery, and the hardware store, and the blacksmith shop where they worked; and the fat fire horses—they doubled in the street-cleaning department—came on the gallop from their abandoned wagons in the streets. Then everybody got into harness of one kind or another and went to the fire.

Everybody in town wanted to ring that fire bell. Any one who discovered a fire and reached the fire house with the news was privileged to do it. There was a tradition that a boy once tried to ring the bell and was jerked clear off the floor by the rebound after his first tug at the rope. This added to the wonder and the mystery of it. The boys used to hang around the doorway, watching this rope, and occasionally fingering it in a gingerly way, and wishing a fire would start somewhere so that they might see the bell rung.

It was through this hall where the rope hung that the people of Hardiston crowded to see Wint inaugurated. They went up the worn, wooden stairs into the council chamber, and they packed themselves in on the benches in the rear of the room. This was not only the council chamber; it was the seat of the Mayor's court. There was an enclosure, surrounded by a railing. When some of the bigger, or perhaps it was only the braver, men of the town came in, they sat inside this railing, tilting their chairs back against it, with a spittoon drawn within easy range. The crowd came early; and they talked in cheerfully loud tones while they waited. One by one the aldermen drifted in, the new ones and the old. And Marshal Jim Radabaugh was there; and the clerk and the other officials arrived and took their places within the enclosure. They were carelessly matter of fact, as though the inauguration of a new Mayor was an everyday matter. The boys, perched on the window sills, whistled, and giggled, and then subsided into frightened silence to watch with staring eyes.

Amos Caretall had let Wint sleep as late as possible this morning. Wint needed the sleep, and Congressman Caretall made it his business to study the needs of his fellow men. His Congressional creed, which he summarized upon occasion, was as simple as that. "If a bill's aimed to make you folks at home here more comfo'table, I'm for it," he would say. "If it ain't, I'm against it; and that's all the way of it with me." So he let Wint sleep this morning until the last minute, then shook him into wakefulness.

Even then, Wint might have thrown the whole thing over but for that whistle. He was sick and sore, his head hurt, and his eyes could not bear even the dim light of his bedroom. He told Amos he would not go through with it, that he would not be inaugurated. Then the whistle blew, and when Amos said it would be a part of his powers as Mayor to stop that plagued whistle if he wanted to, the idea struck Wint's sense of humor. He grinned, and decided there was something in being Mayor, after all, and climbed unsteadily out of bed.

After the tub of cold water which Amos had waiting for him, he felt better. After old Maria Hale's breakfast—fried eggs, and country-cured ham, and three cups of strong coffee—he felt better still. But he was not yet himself. Physically, he was acutely comfortable, blissfully comfortable. His legs and his arms felt warm; they tingled. His head did not hurt; it was merely numb. It was true that his tongue was furry and thick, so that he had to talk very carefully when he talked at all; but save for this precision of speech, there was no mark on him of the night before. He was young enough to recover quickly, his cheeks were red, his eyes were lazily clear.

But it was not to be denied that his head was numb. He was in something like a daze when he went out with Amos and started toward the fire-engine house. The day was bright and warm for the season, and the sun was cheerful. Wint enjoyed the walk. But he had to keep his eyes shut much of the time. The light hurt them. When he heard Amos speak to some one they passed, he also spoke. When Amos talked to him, he answered. But his answers were idle and unconsidered; he was too comfortable to think.

They went up some stairs after a while, and Wint understood that they had arrived. He heard people talking all together, and then one at a time. Men said things, and Amos nudged him, and he made replies. He could hear what others said to him. They mumbled hurriedly, as though over some too-familiar formula. There was nothing particularly impressive, or dignified, in the proceedings. The light from the windows at the back of the room hurt Wint's eyes, so he still kept them half shut. The people before him were merely black shadows, silhouetted against this glare. He could not see who any of them were.

After a time, some one—it sounded like a small boy—yelled: "Speech!" And others took up the cry, and Amos nudged Wint. So Wint stood up again and said with that careful precision which the condition of his tongue demanded: "I've nothing to say. I'll let what I do, do the talking for me."

That seemed to be satisfactory. Every one cheered, so that the noise hurt his ears. Then he sat down. A moment later, every one got up, and he got up, and they all began to crowd around him, and to crowd toward the door. Somebody came up and shook hands with Wint, and he recognized the voice of V. R. Kite. He had never liked Kite; the man was like a foul bird. A buzzard. The idea pleased Wint. He said cheerfully:

"To hell with you, you old buzzard."

He heard Amos chuckle, somewhere near him. Every one else stood very still. So Wint strode past Kite to the stairs, and Amos followed him, and Peter Gergue followed Amos. They went back home to Amos's house. Once, on the way, Wint asked:

"That all there is to it?"

Amos said: "Land, no, that's just the beginning."

Wint chuckled. He was beginning to enjoy himself. But he was very sleepy. When they got home, he went to bed and slept till dinner was ready, and he slept all the afternoon, and he went to bed for the night as soon as supper was done.

Amos had been thinking he ought to get back to Washington. He was glad Wint went off to bed, because there were two or three matters he wanted to attend to. One of these matters had to do with Jack Routt. Amos was not sure of his ground in that direction, but he had his suspicions. He sent for Peter Gergue after supper, and Gergue came quickly at the summons. They sat down before the coal fire, and Peter filled his pipe in careful imitation of Amos, and the two men smoked together in silence for a space, while Amos considered what to say.

Peter was one of those unfortunate men who do not like silences. This put him at a disadvantage before Amos, who could be silent indefinitely. It was Amos's chief superiority over Peter, and it gave the Congressman his mastery over the man. This night as always, it was Peter who spoke first. He puffed at his pipe, and he said:

"Well, Amos, you'll be gittin' back to Washin'ton."

Amos turned his head, tilted it on one side, and squinted at Peter. "I guess so," he agreed.

"Thought you'd be going," said Peter. "Wint'll miss you."

"Do you think he'll know he misses me?" Amos asked.

"If he did," said Peter, "he wouldn't admit it."

The Congressman nodded. "Wint's a cur'ous cuss. Peter."

"Yeah."

"He's a nice boy—give him a chance."

"We-ell, he's got his chance."

"What's he going to do with it, Peter?"

Gergue rummaged through his black hair thoughtfully. "Guess that depends on what he's let do with it. Somebody come along and tell him he ought to make a good Mayor, and he'll make a bad one, just to show he can't be bossed."

"That's right." Amos agreed. He considered, grinned to himself. "You know, Pete, if we could get Kite to sign on as Wint's guide, philosopher, and friend. Wint'd do all right."

Gergue considered, and he chuckled. "Sure. If he went contrary to what Kite said. And he would. Wint's always on the contrary-minded side of a thing."

"Now why is that?" Caretall asked.

"That's because he's who he is, I sh'd say."

Amos puffed deep at his black pipe. "Trouble is," he commented, "Kite wouldn't take the job. Not after what Wint handed him to-day. You heard that?"

Gergue grinned widely. "Yeah. The old buzzard. Say, that surely does hit Kite. The way he holds his head. I'd always thought of a turkey, but I guess a buzzard does it too. Like he was always looking over a wall."

"What I'd like to see," said Amos, "is some one that would guarantee to give Wint bad advice."

"We-ell," Peter told him, "I can do some of that."

"Trouble is, there's others will tell him to do the right thing."

"You talk like James T. Hollow," said Gergue. "Always trying to do what's right."

"I wonder," said Amos casually, "whether them that tell him to keep straight figure he'll do what they say?"

Peter understood that there was something back of the question; he studied Amos's impassive face. Then he thought for a minute, and nodded his head.

"You mean Jack Routt," he said.

"Yes," the Congressman agreed.

Peter considered. "I don't quite know about Jack," he said. "He lets on to be Wint's friend. But he don't help Wint any. Jack's got a way of telling Wint to do a thing that works the opposite every darned time."

"I've a notion," said Caretall, "that if Routt was to tell Wint to take care of his health, say, Wint'd go shoot himself, just to be different."

"That's right," Gergue agreed; and the two men sat for a time without speaking, their pipes bubbling, the smoke drifting upward lazily.

"Question is," said Caretall at last, "what are we going to do about it?" Gergue made no comment, and Amos asked: "What do you think, Peter?"

"I don't see through Routt," said Gergue. "I don't see what he's got on his mind."

"Looks to me that he's plain ornery," Amos suggested.

"I guess that's right."

"But that don't get us anywheres. I'd like to have him let Wint alone."

"He'd ought to."

"How can we make him let Wint alone?" Amos asked.

Peter considered that, fingers rummaging about the back of his head. "Routt's looking for something," he said. "Maybe he wants to be prosecuting attorney. Or something. I don't know."

"He never will be," said Amos.

"I guess that's right."

"Not as long as I can swing any votes here."

"Question is," said Peter, "whether he knows you feel that way."

"No," Amos told him. "He don't know."

Peter looked sidewise at Amos. "He might be bought," he suggested. "Or he might be scared. I don't know. He may be yellow. If he is, you could scare him."

Amos's pipe went out, and he rapped it into his palm and treasured the charred crumbs to prime his next smoke. "Peter," he said thoughtfully, "I'd like to see Jack. To-night."

Gergue was a good servant. He got up at once. "All right, Amos," he said.

Caretall went with him to the door. "I'm taking the noon train, to-morrow," he told Gergue.

"I'll be there," said Peter.

Amos shut the door behind him and went back to the fire. He sat there for a while, considering. Then he went out into the hall and called Agnes. She was in her room; and she came running down, very gay and pretty in a blue-flowered kimono, her hair down her back in a golden braid. Amos looked at her thoughtfully. There was always a wistful question in his eyes when he looked at Agnes. He met her at the foot of the stairs, and he asked:

"Agnes, how'd you like to go to Washington?"

Now the girl had gone to Washington one winter with Amos. And she had not liked it. Amos was just a small-town Congressman, one of scores. And his daughter was just a pretty girl, and nothing more. Amos was a small toad in that big puddle; Agnes had found herself not even a tadpole. And— that did not please Agnes. Here in Hardiston, she was the daughter of the biggest man in town; and she was the prettiest girl in town, some said. At least, they told her so. Jack Routt, and some of the other boys.

"I wouldn't like it at all, dad," she told Amos laughingly. "Washington is a dead old place beside Hardiston."

"I'm thinking of taking you," Amos said, watching her with something like sorrow in his eyes.

"I haven't any clothes," she protested. "I'm not ready, at all. I'd rather not go, dad."

"I'd rather you would," he repeated gently.

She pouted. "Why? You're always away. I'd never see you. I'd have nothing to do at all. I——"

"I'd rather not leave you and Wint alone here. Wouldn't be just the thing," her father insisted gently.

She laughed. "You funny old daddy. We'd have Maria for chaperon."

"Wouldn't be just the thing," Amos said again.

"I'm not going to eat Wint," she protested, half angry. "We get along beautifully."

"Guess you'd better go along with me," Amos told her.

She stamped her foot. "Dad, I don't want to."

Amos jerked a forefinger up the stair, head on one side, eyes steady. "Run along and pack, Agnes," he said. "Won't be much time in the morning."

Agnes began to cry. Amos watched her for a moment, watched her bowed head, and a load seemed to settle on the man's big shoulders. He turned back to the sitting room without a word. After a while, he heard her run up the stairs, every pound of her little feet scolding him, as a bird scolds.

Amos filled his pipe and began to smoke again.

Jack Routt came late. While he waited, Amos had smoked two pipes to the last bubble. When Jack knocked, he got up lumberingly and went to the door to let the young man in. "Come in," he said curtly. "Hang up your things."

He went back and sat down before the fire, and Jack Routt joined him there. Amos looked up at him sidewise. "Sit down, Routt," he said. "Take a chair. Any chair."

Routt sat down. "Gergue said you wanted to see me," he reminded Amos.

"Yes," Amos agreed. "I told him to tell you."

"Came as soon as I could," said Routt.

"That's all right," said Amos. "I wasn't in a hurry. I'm hardly ever in any hurry. Things come, give them time." The colloquialisms had fallen from his speech. Amos talked as well as any one when he chose; when he was with Hardiston folks, he talked as they talked. Routt was a college man.

Routt fidgeted in his chair. He had always been somewhat afraid of Amos. He wondered what the Congressman wanted now, but Amos did not tell him. He just sat, staring at the fire, smoking. Like Gergue, Routt was driven to break the silence.

"What did you want with me, Amos?" he asked.

Amos spat into the fire. "Wanted to talk things over, Jack," he said. "I'm going to Washington to-morrow."

"I've been expecting you'd go back."

"Well, I'm going."

Another silence, while Routt moved uneasily. At last he said: "You put Wint over, all right."

"Yes," Amos agreed. "I put him over." He looked at Routt then, with eyes unexpectedly keen. "Think he'll make a good Mayor, do you?"

"Well," said Routt slowly, "he'll be all right if he lets the booze alone."

Amos caught Routt's eyes and held them commandingly. "Jack," he said, "I want you to let Wint alone."

Routt asked angrily: "Me? What do you mean?"

"I don't want you giving him any advice, and I don't want you getting him drunk. I want you to let him alone. Is that clear?"

Routt protested: "I'm the best friend Wint's got."

"You're the worst enemy he's got," said Amos. "And you know it."

"You can't say that," Routt pleaded.

Amos did not let go the other man's eyes. "You got Wint drunk, day before election," he said. "You got him drunk last night. Routt, don't you do that again."

"I got him drunk? Good Lord, Congressman, Wint's a grown man. I'm not his keeper."

"I made you his keeper, before election," said Amos. "I told you to keep him straight. You didn't do it. You got him drunk. Now I tell you, let him alone."

"I tried to keep him from drinking," Routt urged.

"You said to him, 'Don't you drink, Wint. It ain't good for you. You can't stand it.' So he drank, to show you he could stand it. Just as you knew he would." Amos got up with a swiftness surprising in that slow-moving man. He said harshly: "Routt, get your hat and get out. And mind what I say. You let Wint alone."

Some men would have sworn at Amos, some would have defied him. Routt was the sort to promise anything. He said, with an assumption of straightforward frankness:

"Why, of course, if you say so, I'll keep away from him."

"See that you do," said Amos. "Now—good night."

When the door closed behind Routt, Amos stood for a minute in the hall, thinking. "Now I wonder," he asked himself. "Will he do it? Was he scared enough to keep hands off? I wonder, now."

Routt, half a block away, was grinning without mirth. "Damn him," he said to himself. "Him and Wint too. I'll...."

He wondered just what he had best do; and before he reached home, he had decided to go and see V. R. Kite.

Congressman Caretall and Agnes took the noon train, next day. Wint went with them to the station, and Amos had a last word for him.

"Don't you get the idea I've left you on your own, Wint," he said. "You'll need help. Things'll come up. When they do, don't you try to stand on your own feet. Just write me—or telegraph. And I'll come, or tell you what to do.

"You'll run into trouble. Don't you try to fight it alone. Just you call on me."

Then the train pulled out. Wint watched it go; and when it rounded the curve and disappeared beyond the electric-light plant, he grinned.

"Run to you when I need help, will I, Amos?" he asked good-naturedly, under his breath. "I guess not. You've left me alone. And I'm going to stand on my own hind legs. On my own two feet, by God!"

He turned and went swiftly back uptown.

CHAPTER II

JOAN TO WINT

THE months of that winter passed quietly in Hardiston. The excitement of the election was not forgotten; the drama of Wint's choice as Mayor became one of the stories to be told about the stoves on cold home-keeping days. But Wint himself was no longer an object of curious interest; he was just the Mayor. An inconsiderable figure in the town. There had been Mayors in the past, and there would be again. Never amounted to much, one way or another. Hardiston went along just the same; the winters were just as cold, the summers just as hot, the rains just as wet, the sun just as warm.

Hardiston is infamous for its winters and for its summers. In the spring or in the fall there is no lovelier spot. In the spring, apple blossoms clothe the hills; in the fall the woods are great splashes of flame against the dull green of the fields. But in winter the mercury drops far below zero, and climbs forty degrees in half a day. The snow comes tempestuously, eight, ten, twelve inches of it; and it melts as quickly as it comes. The roads turn into mud at the first snow; they remain mud till the increasing heat of the northing sun bakes them to dust. On Monday, every water pipe in town freezes tight; on Tuesday, violets bloom in sheltered corners about the houses. On a cold morning, adventurous boys skate on the film of ice that forms on streams and ponds; but by noon the ice is unsafe, and some one has broken through, and by mid-afternoon, it is freezing hard again.

This winter in Hardiston was like all others. The new Mayor stuck strictly to business. Jack Routt let him alone. When boys were arrested for misdemeanor, or children of a larger growth for more pretentious wrongs, they were brought before Wint and he passed sentence upon them, marveling that he, Wint Chase, should be passing judgment on his fellow man. At first, this feature of his work shamed him; later it awed him, and made him look into his own heart and ask whether he were fit for such a rôle. He tried to make himself fit.

To act as judge of the Mayor's court and to preside at council meetings comprised the bulk of Wint's official duties. They took only a fraction of his time. When the electric-light plant went out of commission with a broken cylinder head, Wint had to do the explaining; when a sewer became stopped up, he had to see that it was opened; when the old project for a sewage-disposal plant came up on its annual burst of life, he had to consider it. When Ned Howell filed his regular yearly suit for damages done to his pasture by overflow from the sewage-filled creek, Wint had to attend court and testify.

But—there was time on his hands and to spare. He did not know what to do with himself.

He did not undertake any crusades. A certain diffidence, in these first months, restrained him. He was not sure of his ground; he was not sure of himself. V.R. Kite's underlings continued to peddle their wares, and the Mayor's court had to deal, now and then, with one of Kite's bibulous customers. Wint dealt with them, but he did not dig for the root of the evil, to tear it out. Matters in Hardiston went on much as they had in the past. Men rose, did their day's work, ate, and went to bed again. Women likewise. The annual Chautauqua lecture course began and was finished; Number Four theatrical companies came to town with Broadway attractions, played one-night stands, and departed as they had come. The moving-picture houses had new films every day, and the same audiences day after day. The dramatic teacher in the high school organized a pageant, and it was presented to the eyes of admiring parents in the Rink. The high school played basket ball, the women played bridge, the men played poker of a night. Now and then the Masons or the Knights of Pythias gave a dance. The preachers preached sermons in which they tried to prove there was nothing the matter with the churches. The schools developed their annual scandal over the discharge of a school-teacher. There were the regular rumors of a new factory that was to come to town; and the rumors fell through in the regular way. Now and then a baby was born, now and then there was a wedding, now and then there was a funeral.

Wint stuck to his guns, and the world rolled majestically and interminably on.

When Wint took hold of his job, he wondered what there was for him to do. Dick Hoover told him. Dick was a lawyer, in with his father, who had the biggest practice in town. He showed Wint where to look, in the statute books, for the duties of a Mayor. Wint was surprised to discover that laws were simple, everyday things, having to do with life as it was lived. One day when he went to Dick's office to look up a statute, the book he sought was in use. To kill time, he took down a volume of Blackstone and peered into it curiously. He discovered that Blackstone said water was a "movable, wandering thing," and the description fascinated him. He read on....

The more law he read, the more interested he became. In January, he asked Dick Hoover if it were possible to study law in leisure hours. Hoover told him it was not only possible, it was easy. The end of January saw Wint putting in his spare time on calfskin-bound volumes of which each page was one-third reading matter and two-thirds footnotes. The first day he picked up a book of cases was marked with a red letter on his mental calendar. He found these cases as interesting as fiction.

He began to read law systematically. Dick Hoover's father was interested, helped him. The elder Hoover told Wint's father one day:

"Chase, your boy is going to make a lawyer before he's through."

The senior Chase looked at Hoover, half minded to resent the fact that his son had been mentioned in his presence. But—the old wound was healing. Men no longer took occasion to remind him of last fall's election with a jeer in their eyes. His conditional alliance with Kite had languished, because Wint had made no move to make the town dry. Chase hated Amos Caretall as ardently as ever; but he could not hate his son. That is not the way with fathers. He loved Wint; he had been, for some time, secretly proud of him.

He said to Hoover: "He's smart enough, if he sticks to it."

"He's sticking," Hoover told Wint's father.

Winthrop Chase, Senior, nodded indifferently, hiding the light in his eyes. "He never stuck to anything before," he said, and turned away.

He thought of telling Wint's mother, that night, but did not do so. When he spoke of Wint to her, it precipitated one of her endless remarks. They wearied him. But he had to tell some one, so he told Hetty Morfee, when he went to the kitchen for a drink of water. Hetty was washing dishes at the time, and she stopped with a plate in one hand and a dish-rag in the other, and listened, and said with a cheerful wistfulness in her voice:

"Wint's smart, sir. You'll be proud of him."

Chase was proud of him, but he would not admit it to himself, much less to Hetty.

"He's smart enough," he told her. "But he's ... He's...."

He turned abruptly and went out of the kitchen without saying what Wint was, and Hetty looked after him with understanding in her smile. Then her face became still and somber again. There was growing in Hetty's eyes a certain unhappy light. A desperate fashion of unhappiness, which no one was sufficiently interested to notice. She was not so cheerful as she used to be. And there was a helplessness about her.

Word of Wint's new industry spread slowly through Hardiston. It was Dick Hoover himself who told Joan of it. Dick was a Mason, and he took Joan to a Masonic dance one night. She spoke of Wint. "I have heard that he is studying law," she said. "Is it true?"

So Dick told her. "True as Gospel," he said. "And he's darned quick to pick it up, too. The principles.... Of course, it will take time. But I'd just as soon have him try a case for me now, as some of these...."

He went on enthusiastically. Hoover was always enthusiastic about things. He was an extremist. His friends were the finest chaps in the world, his enemies were the least of created things. But he had few enemies. People liked him, and he liked people. Joan liked him; liked him particularly this evening because he talked to her of Wint.

Joan Arnold was, in a way of speaking, a girl to tie to. There was a peculiar steadfastness in her. She was a little taller than Wint, and she was habitually grave and quiet, especially when she was with him. In his presence she had always been faintly abashed and reticent as a girl is apt to be in the presence of a man she cares for. Joan had always cared for Wint. In spite of the fact that she was a year or two his junior, they had played together as children: and they had grown up together. When they were little children, they fought as only good friends can fight. When they were a little older, Wint scorned her because she was a girl. A year or so later, she scorned Wint because she was at the age when girls resolve to have a career and never marry at all. But in their late teens, they were devoted to each other, so that the mothers of the town smiled when they passed by, and nodded to each other, and whispered, with the delight women take in such matters, that they were a nice-looking couple together. Wint's short, sturdy strength matched well the girl's slightly larger stature and her quiet poise.

The first passage of affection between them had come when she was eighteen, when he went away to college. Before that they had been much together, but none save the most casual words had passed between them. The night before Wint went away, he went to see her. He was feeling adventurous and heroic and important as a boy does feel when he leaves home for the first time. He talked vastly, of big things he meant to do, of his dreams. She thrilled to his dreams with the half of her that was still child; she smiled at his enthusiasm with the half that was already woman. They were sitting on the porch of her home. There were locust trees about the veranda. They sat in a two-seated swing, facing each other, Wint leaning toward her earnestly.

He became melancholy, and she comforted him softly. He did not want to go away, he said. She told him he would be happy. The movement of the swing made him lean toward her. There was a moon, and the September evening was warm, and the very air seemed trembling in a rhythm that beat upon them both.

When he got up to go, she got up at the same time, and the swing lurched and threw them together. Ineptly, he kissed her, fumblingly, on the cheek. She did not move, she trembled where she stood. He took her awkwardly in his arms, as though afraid she would break, and kissed her cheek again. He rubbed his cheek against hers. She looked at him with wide eyes, lips a little parted, and he kissed her lips. They were cool, unused to kisses.

The months thereafter, till Wint was expelled from college, passed smoothly with them. Too smoothly, too placidly. They wrote short, broken letters; they saw each other when Wint came home. They thought they were very happy; yet each was conscious of a lack in their happiness. There was no fire in it, none of the exquisite anguish of love. They missed this, without knowing what they missed. All went too well with them.

Joan wept on her pillow when he was expelled, but she did not let him see her weep. She reassured him. There was an unsuspected strength in her. Women are full of these surprises. They are indescribably dainty creatures, habitually clad in fabrics like gossamer, seeming light as air and fit to vanish at a breath, who reveal—in a bathing suit, for instance—a surprising physical solidity. It was so, spiritually, with Joan. She was so quiet and so still that Wint, if he had thought at all, would have supposed she was a simple girl and nothing more; but in the revelations of his disaster, she showed a poise and a power which heartened him immensely, and made him a little afraid of her. She was a tower of strength for him to lean upon, a miracle of understanding and of sympathy.

He had expected her to be shocked and revolted at the shame of his expulsion; she was simply sorry for him, and loved him none the less. Wint knew, then, how much he loved her. There is nothing that so inspires love in a man as to find himself beloved. This is the conceit of the creature!

Joan had told Wint that she was done with him, when the story of his drunken sleep in the Weaver House went abroad through Hardiston. But— she had done it for his sake. She thought there was good in him. How could she love him else? She thought it might come out if he had to fight; she thought his very stubbornness might save him. Joan had no illusions about Wint. She knew he was prideful and stubborn. But—she loved him. And so had told him she would have no more of him. With a reservation in her heart....

Thus what Dick Hoover told her made Joan happy; happier than Hoover could possibly guess. Another girl would have cried herself to sleep with happiness that night, but Joan was not given to tears. She lay awake for a long time, thinking....

Three or four days later, she met Wint on the street. They had met thus, often, for Hardiston is a small place. But heretofore they passed with a word, unsmiling. This time, Wint would have passed her in that fashion; but Joan stopped and spoke to him.

"Wint," she said.

He had been sick with hunger for a word from her for weeks. He stopped as though she had struck him, and his cheeks burned red as fire. He could not have spoken, for his life. He stood, hat in hand, face crimson, staring at her.

Joan knew what she wished to say. "I want you to know that I am proud of you, Wint," she said.

His impulse was to laugh, to reject her friendliness. The old Wint, stiff with pride, would have done this. But the old Wint was gone; or at least, he was going. This Wint who stood before Joan tried to find something to say, but all he found to say to her was:

"Oh!"

Joan smiled at him. "There was a time when I wouldn't have dared say this, Wint," she said. "But I do dare now. Stick to the fight, Wint. This is what I want to say."

He said, sullen in his embarrassment: "I'm going to."

"There was a time when you were not going to—just because I—your friends—told you to stick."

Wint looked away from her. "Well, that's all right," he told her uncomfortably.

"There's never any harm in having friends, Wint, and taking their advice," she said.

The old impatience burst out for a moment. "Don't preach," he said harshly.

"I'm not going to preach." She was afraid she had spoiled it all. But he reassured her, hot with shame at his own decency.

"It's all right, Joan," he said. "I know you mean to help. I'll try."

"Do try," she echoed softly.

He nodded, and she watched him, and at last added:

"I'd like to have you come to see me some time."

He hesitated, then he said swiftly: "All right. Some time. Good-by!"

He jerked his head in farewell and hurried away as though he were afraid of her. Joan watched him go, and she pressed her hand to her lips as though to still them.

CHAPTER III

ROUTT TO KITE

WHEN Wint left Joan, after their encounter on the street, he was walking in a daze. He stumbled, his head was down, his eyes were blank. He was stunned and humbled; and after he had left her, he began to feel defiant. He thought of words with which he could have crushed her and silenced her. Presuming to forgive him, to praise him. What right had she to do that anyway? He ought to have laughed at her.

Not that Wint did not love Joan. He did; but he was still, at this time, a boy and nothing more. And he had rather more than a boy's usual measure of stubborn contrariness in him. When his father, and his mother, and Joan, and every one else he cared for had bade him mend his ways, he had refused to mend them, and the thing had been a scandal on every tongue in Hardiston. When, in like fashion, father and mother and Joan bade him go to the dogs, whither he seemed surely bound, he had braced himself, fought a good fight, begun to make good. Now Joan was telling him he had made good, that he was all right. He had a reckless desire to go to the devil, forthwith, to prove her wrong.

He had met Joan at the corner by the Star Company's furniture store, an institution that was always holding fire sales and closing-out sales without either fires before or actual closings after. Their talk there together had not gone unremarked. Every one in town would know of it within the day. When they separated, Joan went away from town toward her home, and Wint went up Broadway toward the Court House. Not that he knew where he was going. But he had to go somewhere.

There were only one or two places in Hardiston to go to when you did not know where to go. You might go to the Smoke House, and shake dice for a cigar, or drop a nickel in the slot machine and see how your luck was running. Or you might drop in at the Post Office in the idle hope that a special train had come along with a letter for you since the last regular mail was sorted into the boxes. Or you might stop at one of the newspaper offices. The editors were always willing to talk, and there were usually two or three others there before you.

Wint headed, somewhat aimlessly, for the Post Office. But when he passed down Main Street, B. B. Beecham, editor of the *Journal*, called Wint in to look at proofs of some city printing. Wint always got on well with B. B. The editor never preached, he never seemed to have any particular interest in the wrong-doings of other people, he attended to his own business and let you attend to yours. A square-built man, with a big barrel of a chest and stocky shoulders, and a strong, amiable countenance. Wint went in at his hail; and B. B. got the proofs for him, and Wint began to look them over. B. B. chunked up the fire in the little round iron stove that had seen so many years of service it was disintegrating. It was bound together with wire to hold it together; and there were holes in the front of it through which the fire could be seen. The stovepipe went up at an angle like that of the leaning tower of Pisa, then made a back-handed elbow turn and ran along in a hammock of wire braces to disappear into the wall. B. B. thrust a bit of wood in through the door, down into the fire, twisted it upward, breaking up the clotted coals and ashes. Then he put on more coal, and shut the door, and the fire roared up the chimney. Wint was going over the proofs, figure by figure. They had to do with bids on a sewer contract. B. B. sat down at his desk with his back to Wint and busied himself with something.

B. B.'s desk was a roll top, its pigeonholes frazzly with letters and papers jammed into them to the bursting point. The desk itself was littered with newspapers and notes and notebooks and scratch pads made out of old order blanks. There was an old iron inkwell, a tin box full of pins, a pencil or two. In a little hexagonal glass bottle at one side, a newly hatched humming bird which had fallen from the nest and been killed was preserved in alcohol. Not so large as a bumblebee, and not nearly so impressive. For paper weight, B. B. used a witch ball, taken from the stomach of a steer that Ned Howell had butchered. A round, smooth, yellowish thing, with a hole picked in to show the hair inside. It was as big as a small orange, and looked not unlike one, save that the yellow was dull and muddy. On top of the desk were books, a big hornet's nest, an ear of corn. There was a curiously marked squash on the open iron safe in the corner; and in the rear of the office a stand-up desk and a smaller one at which a person might sit were littered with the miscellany of B. B.'s business.

While Wint was looking over the proofs, an old darky came in from the street. A ragged old man.... Wint knew him. He lived down the creek in a log cabin, and caught catfish, and farmed a plot of ground. His hat was battered, his coat was too big for him, his trousers slumped about his slumping shoes. His name was John Marshum. He took off his hat and looked around the ceiling of the office uneasily, as though he expected it to fall, and Wint and B. B. said hello to him, and he said:

"Howdy."

B. B. asked: "Is there anything I can do for you?"

The old negro gulped, and said: "I'd like tuh borry a paper and a pencil, ef you please."

B. B. gave him what he asked for, and the old man sat down at the desk in the back of the room, and bit his tongue, and gnawed the pencil, and began to write with infinite pains, slowly, the sweat bursting out of him with the effort. Wint and B. B. went on with their affairs.

After a while, the old fellow got up and crossed to B. B. and held out the product of his effort. "Heah's a paper for you, suh," he said. When B. B. took it, the old man hurried awkwardly out of the door and disappeared.

B. B. read the paper and chuckled, and Wint asked: "What is it?" The editor handed it to him, and he read the scrawl aloud:

"'John Marshum was a very plesint vister at this office Thursdy.'"

Wint laughed good-naturedly. "The poor old clown. Wants his name in the paper. You ought to put it in, just to make him feel good."

"I'm going to," said B. B. "Old John's one of my best friends in the county. He's been a subscriber twelve years, and always paid up. You'd be surprised to know how many don't pay up. And you'd be surprised how many people come in, just as he did, to get their names in the paper. I don't suppose you ever thought of that."

Wint passed the corrected proofs over to B. B. "One or two mistakes," he said, and the editor sent the proofs up for correction. "What do you do with the darned fools?" Wint asked. "Tell them advertising space costs money?"

B. B. looked surprised. "No, I print their names. That's what the paper's for—to print people's names. It makes them feel proud of themselves, and that's good for them. It's one way of helping them along, doing them good."

Wint grinned. "Never did me any particular good to see my name in print," he said. "Usually made me mad."

"It wasn't the fact that they printed your name that made you mad. It was what they printed about you."

"Maybe so," Wint admitted. "I didn't see that it was any of their business."

"That's the way the city dailies are run," B. B. agreed. "But a country weekly is a different proposition. I never print anything that will make any one mad. Not if I can help it. Not even a joke. A joke on a man's no good unless he can appreciate it himself."

Wint eyed B. B. and remarked thoughtfully: "I remember, when they stuck me in as Mayor, you didn't print the fact that my father was a candidate."

"No," B. B. agreed.

"I supposed that was because you and my father are—allies in politics and such things."

"No," said B. B. "I try not to print things that will hurt people. Mr. Chase felt badly about that."

"I don't blame him," said Wint slowly. "You know I had nothing to do with it." He had never talked so freely to any one as he was accustomed to talk to B. B. There was some strain in the editor that invited confidences. He knew as many secrets as a doctor.

"Yes, I know," he said.

"You know," Wint went on, abruptly, "people are funny, B. B."

"Yes."

"I'm funny, myself."

B. B. laughed in a friendly way. "Like the old Quaker who said to his wife: 'All the world is a little queer save thee and me, my dear; and even thee are at times a little queer.'"

"No," said Wint, smiling. "I include myself. I'm queer."

B. B. said nothing. Wint started to go on, but the words were not in him. He had a curious, sudden impulse to ask B. B. about his father; this impulse was like homesickness. But he fought it back. His jaw set stubbornly. His father had thrown him out. That was enough; he didn't ask to be kicked twice.

When B. B. saw that Wint was not going on, he spoke of something else. Then Ed Howe, one of Caretall's men, dropped in and cut a slice from a plug and filled his pipe in the Caretall fashion: and Wint listened to Ed and B. B. talk for a while before he got up and took himself away. He had found some measure of reassurance in his talk with B. B., not because of anything that had been said, but simply because B. B. was a reassuring man. A strong man. A strong man, and a wise man, with open eyes—and an optimist. Not all men who seem to see clearly are optimists.

In front of the Post Office, Wint ran into Jack Routt. Routt had been out of town for a month or so on a business trip, and Wint had seen little of him since Amos went away. He was glad to see Jack, and said so. They shook hands, and Wint bought Routt a cigar. Routt studied Wint curiously. He wondered if it were true that Wint was keeping straight and doing well. And to find out, he asked laughingly:

"Been over to see Mrs. Moody lately, old man?"

Mrs. Moody was that virago who managed the Weaver House, that woman of the hideously beautiful false teeth. Wint flushed uncomfortably at mention of her. "No-o," he said hesitantly.

"That's the boy," said Routt. "You keep away from her. You let the stuff alone. You can't monkey with it, the way some fellows can, old man."

And he watched Wint. There had been a time when this word would have acted as a challenge, when Wint would have snapped at the bait. But—Wint hesitated, he considered, he shook himself a little and said quietly:

"I guess you're right, Jack."

"You bet I'm right," said Routt.

Wint nodded. "Yes," he agreed.

When they separated, Routt went to his office and sat down with his feet on his desk to consider. And—he scowled. Matters were not going well with him. It did not suit him for Wint to keep straight. It did not suit him to lie supine under Amos Caretall's injunction to let Wint alone. The Congressman's command had irked him more than once, and more than once he had thought of V. R. Kite in that connection, and thought of going to Kite. He had a fairly definite idea that Amos would never help him along politically, and Kite might be able to. And—he remembered the word Wint had fastened on Kite on the day of his inauguration. He had called Kite a buzzard, and others had taken it up. The name seemed to fit; it tickled the sense of humor of Hardiston folks. But it did not tickle V. R. Kite. Kite ought to be ready to take means to crush Wint. And—that would please Routt. He had held off thus long in the belief that Wint would be his own ruin. He began to doubt this, now. It might be necessary to do something.

Routt was of mean stuff, small and tawdry. He had been what Hardiston called a mean boy, a trouble-maker. He had an infinite capacity for hate, a curious shrewdness that enabled him to fasten on another's weakest point. As boys, he and Wint had fought once. They fought over Joan, because Routt teased her till she cried. Wint had whipped him, though Routt was the taller and the heavier of the two. Routt had never forgotten that; but Wint forgot it as soon as the incident was over. Wint forgot, and Routt remembered. Circumstances threw them much together; they grew up as friends; Routt behaved himself; people decided that he had outgrown his meanness. Wint liked him, did not distrust him, accepted him for what he seemed—a friend.

But Jack Routt was nobody's friend. Sometimes, when he was alone, you might have seen this in his face. It was so now, as he thought of Wint; his countenance was twisted and distorted and malignant. In later years, it was to bear the marks of these secret and rancorous moments for any eye to see. Indelible and unmistakable. But just now Routt knew how to smile, how to be a good fellow....

He brought his feet down from the desk with a bang. He got up and reached for his hat. He had made up his mind; he would go and see Kite.

Kite was in town. Routt knew he would find the man in the Bazaar, the town's five and ten cent store. He went that way, but as he reached the place, Peter Gergue came along the street and Routt went past without entering. Just as well Gergue should not know that he was seeing Kite. Gergue would tell Amos. When Gergue had disappeared, Routt went back and turned into the Bazaar. Kite's desk was in the back of the store, but Kite was not in sight. The little man might be hidden behind the desk. One of the girls who clerked in the store—her name was Mary Dale, and she was a pretty, simple little thing—asked Routt what he wanted, and he stopped to talk to her for a moment. Routt liked pretty girls. He asked her if Kite was in, and she said he was at his desk, so Routt went back that way. He drew up a chair to face the little man, and Kite cocked his head on his thin neck, and tugged at his side whiskers. "Howdo, Routt," he said.

"Morning," Routt rejoined. "How's tricks, Kite?"

"All right." Kite looked suspicious. Routt offered him a cigar, which Kite declined. Jack lighted it himself, then said idly:

"Well, I just got back."

"Been away?"

"Yes. Columbus."

"Oh!"

"I see Wint hasn't closed down on you yet," Routt drawled.

Kite flushed angrily. "Of course not. Why should he? He's no fool."

"I said he hadn't shut down on you—yet," Routt repeated, and he emphasized the last word.

"He likes his drop now and then, same as another man."

"Hasn't been taking many drops lately, has he?"

"I'm not his guardian. How do I know? Long as he lets me alone."

Routt grinned. "I heard he didn't let you alone, day he was inaugurated. Called you a buzzard, didn't he?"

"The man was drunk."

"Name's kind of stuck, though. A darned, rotten thing like that will stick."

Kite was trying to keep calm, but he was an irascible little man. He snapped at Routt: "What do I care for names? They break no bones."

"Well, that's so," Routt agreed good-naturedly.

"Long as he lets me alone, I'm satisfied," Kite said again.

Routt nodded. "How long do you figure he'll let you alone?" he asked.

Kite's temper got away from him. "By God, he'd better let me alone!" He banged a clenched fist on the table. Routt drawled:

"Don't get excited."

"I'm n-not excited," Kite stammered. "But he'll let me alone. He don't dare to bother me. Why, Routt, if he tries anything, I'll—I'll get out of town. I won't live in the place. I'll take my money out of the dirty little hole."

"We-ell," said Routt, "you could do that, of course. That would suit him. He'd get his own way, then. You could get out. Or you might fight him."

"Fight him?" Kite snapped. "I'll fight him to the last dollar." He controlled himself with an effort. "But he's not going to start anything. I know him. He's inoffensive. A boy."

"Amos Caretall is no boy," Routt reminded him. "And Amos is backing him."

Kite remembered that Winthrop Chase, Senior, had told him this same thing; had warned him that Amos meant to use Wint to clean up the town. He and Chase had made an alliance on that basis. If Wint tried a crusade, they would go after Amos together, and hang his hide on the fence. They had sworn that together.... Now Routt was saying the same thing. He had been feeling fairly secure; he and Chase had made no move. Chase had wanted him to start a back fire against Amos, but Kite had been ready to let well enough alone.... Now Routt ... Routt was one of Caretall's men. He would be likely to know what the Congressman planned. Kite demanded angrily:

"What makes you think Amos is planning anything? He and I understand each other."

Routt laughed. "Amos would double cross his best friend and call it a joke," he said amiably. "You know that. Didn't he double cross Chase?"

"Sure. I helped him," said Kite defiantly.

"Next thing," Routt told him, "he'll double cross you."

Kite leaned across and gripped Routt by the arm. "What makes you say that? You and Amos are together."

"We were," said Routt, "but I told him a few things he didn't like. I'm no particular friend of Amos."

Kite said: "I'm not either. But as long as he plays fair with me, I'll play fair with him."

"What if he don't?"

"I'll smash him."

"You can't smash Amos," said Routt, "but you can hurt him."

"How?"

"Smash young Wint."

Kite snorted. "Pshaw! Wint's a boy."

"He's growing up. One of these days, he's going to send for Jim Radabaugh and tell him to clean up the town...."

"By God, if he does," Kite swore, "I'll tear him all to pieces."

Routt got up. "When you start in to do that," he said, "send for me. I might be able to help."

"I won't need any help to rip Wint Chase wide open."

"You send for me," said Routt insistently.

"All right. I'll send for you."

"I'll be here," Routt promised. When he went out through the store, he stopped and told Mary Dale she was the prettiest girl in town. Mary was pleased. She knew he didn't mean it; she was simple enough, if you like; but she knew there were probably other girls just as pretty as she was. Nevertheless, she was glad Jack had told her she was pretty. She thought it meant he was pleased with her.

As a matter of fact, it only meant that he was pleased with himself. But that was a thing Mary Dale could not be expected to understand.

CHAPTER IV

WINT TO JOAN

WINT had lived very comfortably that winter, in Amos Caretall's home, with old Maria Hale to take care of him. In the beginning, when Amos went away, he had protested at this arrangement. He told Amos he would go to a hotel, to a boarding house, hire a room somewhere.... He said he would not impose on Amos by living on his bounty.

Amos laughed at him and said Wint would not be living on any one's bounty. "I aim to charge you board and keep," he said. "And that's velvet for me, because I'd keep the house going anyway. Got to, to keep old Maria. If I ever let go of her, somebody'd grab her in a minute."

Wint knew it was Amos's habit to keep the house open and Maria in it, even when he and Agnes were both away; so he accepted the proposition. The board which Amos required him to pay was nominal; and Wint wanted to pay more. Amos shook his head.

"First thing you want to learn, Wint, is never to pay a man more than he asks, for anything. He'll think you're a blamed fool."

So Wint had been comfortable. Maria knew how to cook, she kept the house neat, she picked up after Wint's disorderliness. And she mothered Wint as her kind know how to do.

He was comfortable, but he was lonely, desperately lonely. Wint was a convivial young man. He liked to be with people. He had never been much in his own exclusive company. Some one said that it is not good for man to be alone; but it is equally true that it is not good for a man never to be alone. Solitude is good for the soul. It gives an opportunity for a certain amount of thought, for taking stock of one's self. If every one could be persuaded to an hour's solitary self-consideration each day, the world would be bettered thereby. It is hard to deceive yourself. Wint found out the truth of this in his solitary evenings that winter. He found himself forced to face facts, and face them squarely; he found himself forced to recognize his own mistakes.

Thus his loneliness did him no harm; but it did make him uncomfortable. The fact that he was much alone resulted from two or three circumstances and causes. His father had cast him out; so he saw his father and mother not at all. And he had been accustomed to see them every day, all his life. It is true there had usually been little pleasure for him in these encounters. His father's harshness, his mother's garrulous tongue had irked and angered him. They had worked at cross-purposes, as families are apt to do. There had been little obvious sympathy and understanding between them. Nevertheless, Wint found that he missed them; that he missed his father's overbearing accusations, and he missed his mother's interminable talk. Once or twice, when he met her on the street, he stopped to talk with her; and he took a certain comfort from the flow of breathless reproaches which poured out upon him at these times. Mrs. Chase was as unhappy that winter as a mother must be when her son is set apart from her; but she was loyal to her husband, and reproached Wint for his disloyalty.

Wint missed Joan, too. He missed her enormously. There was never any doubt that Joan was half the world to him. He had longed for her desperately at times; he had wanted to go and abase himself before her. But he would not; he was strong enough to keep to his own path. And Joan kept to hers.

The fact that Wint and Joan were thus at odds made Wint an awkward figure in any group of young people, because Joan was almost sure to be there. He knew this as well as any one. So when Dick Hoover asked him to go to the dances, he refused because Joan would be there; and when Elsie Jenkins asked him to a card party, he refused again, and for the same reason. But he did not tell Dick and Elsie what this reason was. As a consequence, people stopped asking him to the festivities of Hardiston, and Wint was left solitary.

Solitary, and lonely. He was so lonely, that night of Elsie's party, that he walked past her house for the sheer, hungry joy of looking in through her windows at the throng inside. He often walked about the town in the evenings, thus. Sometimes it was to pass Joan's home.... And he did a deal of thinking, and of wondering; and he made a resolution or two....

When Joan spoke to him, asked him to come and see her, Wint experienced a strange revulsion of feeling. He was unhappy, and he told himself he would never go; and he went uptown and dropped in on B. B. Beecham and had that innocuous and idle talk with the editor, which never touched on his troubles at all. Nevertheless, Wint emerged from the *Journal* office in a more cheerful frame of mind. People were apt to be more cheerful, and more optimistic, and more resolved, after talking with B. B. This was one of the virtues of the man.

Wint decided, after leaving B. B., that he would go and see Joan. Some time.... He decided he would not be in any hurry about it. Next month, perhaps, or next week, or in a day or two....

As might have been expected, the end of it was that he went to see her that night. For Wint was still half boy, with a boy's impatience; and he had been lonely for Joan for so long. After supper, with the long evening before him, and nothing to do, he thought of going to Joan. He swore he wouldn't go; but he wanted to, so badly. Why shouldn't he? She had asked him. He wouldn't and he would, and he wouldn't and he would....

In the end, he decided to walk out to her home and see if he could see her, through the window. There was snow on the ground, it was fairly cold. He bundled up in overcoat and cap and filled a pipe and lighted it, and set out. He would just walk past the house, come back another way, go to bed.... That would do no harm.

But even while he tried to tell himself this was what he meant to do, he knew that he would not come back without seeing Joan—if the thing were possible. And when he got to the house, he saw that it was possible. The shades were up at the sitting-room window; he could see her, reading before the fire. She was alone.

So Wint went reluctantly up the walk from the street, and he hesitated at the steps, and then he went up the steps, stamping, and knocked at the door. He heard Joan stirring, inside. Then the door opened, and Joan was there before him. The light behind her shone through her hair; her eyes were dark and steady.

The light fell on his face, and she said quietly: "Hello, Wint. I'm—glad you came."

Wint took off his cap, and held it in his hand. She thought he looked very like a boy. He said nothing; and Joan moved a little to one side and bade him come in. He went in, like a man walking in his sleep, and she shut the door behind him. Wint stood in the hall as though he did not know what to do. He wanted to run; but the door was shut.

She said: "Take off your coat." So he did, and laid it on a chair in the hall, and put his cap on top of it. Joan told him to come into the sitting room; and he said huskily:

"All right."

So they went in and sat down together before the fire. And Wint wished he had not come. He crossed his legs one way, then he crossed them the other. He folded his arms, he folded his hands in his lap, he cleared his throat, he leaned forward with his elbows on his knees. He did not look at Joan; but Joan watched him, and by and by she smiled a little, and her smile seemed like a caress upon his bent head.

Wint said abruptly: "Your people all right?"

"Yes," Joan told him.

He muttered angrily that that was good; and silence fell upon them again. He twisted in this silence, like a caterpillar on a pin. He was immensely relieved when Joan spoke at last.

"What shall we talk about, Wint?" she asked steadily. "Do you want to talk about your—fight? What are you doing?"

"No," he said dourly, staring at the fire.

Joan watched him, not resenting his sullenness, because she had understanding. After a little, she said gently: "I saw your mother the other day."

Wint shot a quick glance at her. He could not help it. "That so?" he asked.

Joan nodded, and she smiled a little wistfully. "Yes. She misses you. She and your father...."

"They haven't told me so," said Wint morosely.

"Have you talked with them?" she asked.

"No. My father—" For the life of him, he could not stifle the choke in his voice. "No, I haven't," he said.

"You couldn't, of course," she agreed, and she looked at him sidewise. "Of course, if you went to them, your father would think you were trying to make up. You couldn't do that." There was an anxiety in her eyes; the anxiety of the experimenter. Wint went by contraries. Joan knew quite clearly what she wanted; she wanted him to go to his father. Was this the way to lead him to make the first move?

She was frightened at what she had done when he looked at her angrily. "See here," he said, "do you want me to go to him? Do you think I ought to?" She was so frightened that she could not speak; but she nodded. Wint barked at her:

"Then why don't you say so? I'm sick of having people make me do things by telling me not to."

"I wasn't trying to—make you do it, Wint," she said; and she was almost pleading.

"You were; and you know it," he told her flatly. "Weren't you, now? Secretly trying to make me...."

Joan could not lie to him. "Y-Yes," she said.

"Then come out with it," Wint demanded; and he got up and stamped about the room, and words burst from him. "Joan," he exclaimed, "I've been

- 145 -

a fool, and I know it. Am one still, I suppose. Hate to be preached to and told what I must do, and mustn't. You know that. Result is, I'm always in trouble. Jack Routt, best friend I've got, does me more harm than my worst enemy—just trying to keep me straight. I've always known it, in a way. Knew I was a fool. But I've been just contrary enough to refuse to be preached to. That's the way I'm made. Only, for God's sake, don't you start trying to manage me." He hesitated, groping for words, and his voice was suddenly weary and lonely as he said: "You ought to be able to talk straight to me, Joan."

She did not answer for a moment; then she said simply: "I'm sorry, Wint. I was wrong."

That took the wind out of him. He had hoped she would argue with him. He wanted an argument, wanted a hot combat of words; he was full of things that he wanted to say. To show her…. Justify himself to her. But you can't argue with a person who agrees with you. He sat down as abruptly as he had risen, and stared again at the fire.

Joan asked, after a time: "Are you sure Jack Routt is really your friend, Wint?"

"Of course," he said, looking at her. "Why not? What do you mean?"

"I don't like him."

He laughed. "A girl never likes a man's friends. Jack's all right. He's a prince."

"Is he?"

"Sure he is."

Joan said no more about Routt. She spoke of other things, trivial things; and for an hour she and Wint managed to talk easily enough without touching on forbidden ground. It was not till he got up to go that they spoke seriously again. She had helped him on with his coat. At the door, he faced her; and he asked:

"Joan, d'you really think I ought to—patch things up at home?"

She answered him straightforwardly: "Yes, Wint."

He looked past her, eyes thoughtful; and at last he held out his hand. "Well, good night," he said. "Maybe I will."

They shook hands, and he went out and tramped swiftly back to Amos's house. There was a bounding elation in him; his head was among the stars.

CHAPTER V

WINT GOES HOME

WINT had thought of going to his father before he talked with Joan. He had tried advances now and then. Once he met the elder Chase on the street and stopped to talk with him, but his father passed by with a curt word of greeting. Another time, he saw Chase in the *Journal* office and went in. Chase and B. B. Beecham were talking together; but when Wint came in, his father got up and departed. Wint had said:

"Don't let me drive you away. I just happened in."

But the senior Chase said: "I was going, anyway," and he went.

These incidents had roused the old resentment in Wint, but they had hurt him more than they had angered him. And the hurt persisted, while the resentment died. He found excuses for his father. He blamed himself; and he thought of ways of approaching the older man with some hope of success, and discarded them one by one.

Seeing Joan gave him new confidence in himself. She had let him come to see her; his father could do no less. Wint had no illusions as to Joan. He understood that she wanted to help him, wanted to be proud of him; but he understood also that he was on probation. He had not proved himself, in her eyes. That must come with time. They had talked frankly enough together; but—they had merely shaken hands at parting. That was all; that was all he had any right to expect. He could wait—and work—for the rest.

It was much that she had asked him to come to her. It meant that he was no longer outcast in her eyes; and the realization of this gave him new self-respect. It was this very self-respect that enabled him to humble himself to his father. A man can be servile without being self-respecting; but self-respect and true humility are synonyms. Each implies a true self-appraisal. Wint was a man, doing his work among men. He was also his father's son; and it was as a son that he went to his father at last.

He found the elder Chase at home one evening. He had made sure that his father would be at home; but he was glad, when he got there, to find that his mother had gone next door. His mother could not understand; and no one else could talk much when she was about. Wint smiled when he thought of her; then his lips steadied. There was need for talk between his father and himself.

His father came to the door; and when he saw Wint, he stared at him coldly, and did not invite him to come in. Wint, with a sudden twinge of sorrow, saw that his father had changed and grown older in these last months. It seemed to Wint that his hair was thinner; there were new lines in his face; and his old benevolent condescension toward the world at large was gone. Wint said quietly:

"I want to come in and talk with you if I may."

Chase hesitated, even then; but—he had been lonely as Wint had been lonely. He stepped to one side and said: "Very well." Wint went in, and his father shut the door, and bade Wint come into the room off the hall that served him as library, and office, and den. He did not tell Wint to take off his coat, so Wint kept it on. Chase sat down at his desk, Wint took a chair facing him. He did not know how to begin.

Chase said: "Well, what is it you want?"

Wint hesitated, then he smiled a little wistfully; and he said: "I want to be—friends with you again."

His father abruptly looked away from him. Without looking at Wint, he asked:

"Why?"

Wint's right hand moved in a curious, appealing way. "Isn't it natural for a son to—want to be friends with his father, sir?" he suggested.

Chase said harshly: "I told you, once, that I no longer counted you my son."

"Those things don't go by what we want, sir," Wint urged. "I—am your son. And you're my father."

"Have you acted as a son should?" Chase asked coldly.

"No," said Wint, without palliation of the finality of the word, and Chase looked—and was surprised.

"You've realized it, have you?"

"Yes, sir."

There was one thing Chase wanted to do; and it made him feel ridiculous and ashamed of himself to want to do it. What he wanted to do was to take Wint in his arms. And both of them grown men! He shook his head, as though to brush this sentimental desire away. Foolishness! The young rip had made a laughingstock out of him. Yet here he was, ready to give in at a word.

He said: "I suppose Amos sent you."

Wint bit his lips, and his face set faintly; but his voice was quiet enough when he answered. "No, sir," he said.

"You tell Amos," Chase exclaimed, "that you can't pull his chestnuts out of the fire for him. And he'll be more anxious to get around me later on than he is now. Tell him that for me."

Wint shook his head slowly. "Amos didn't send me," he said again.

"Thought Amos told you everything to do?" his father asked. "Haven't got a mind of your own, have you?"

"Yes," Wint told him. "Yes, I think I have."

Chase considered, not looking at his son. He could not look at Wint and still hold himself together. After a while he asked:

"Well, what do you want? You haven't told me what you want."

"I want to be friends."

Chase flung that aside with a swift gesture. "I mean, what do you want to get out of me?"

"Nothing."

His father got up, glared down at Wint angrily. "Don't think I'm a fool, Wint," he said, in a rush of words. "You made me look like one, but I'm not. You linked up with Caretall to make a jackass out of me; you went out of your way to shame me by your own shamelessness. I kicked you out with your tail between your legs, as I should have done long before. Now you come whining home again. Don't try to tell me you're not after something. I know you are. If you don't want to say what it is, don't. That's your business. But don't try to make me a fool."

Wint had sworn to keep his temper; and he did. But he got to his feet with a swift, silent movement that startled his father. And when Chase broke off, Wint said steadily:

"I've told you the truth. It's true I misbehaved—badly. You have a right to be angry with me. It's true I did not know Caretall planned to stick me in over your head. You know that's true. As far as the rest of it goes ... I came here to-night just to tell you that I'm sorry for—the things I did. And I want you to know I'm sorry. You're my father. I'd like to have the right to come to you for advice; and I'd like to come to you for friendship, if nothing more. That's all. I've come." He turned toward the door. "I've come, and I'll go."

When Wint turned toward the door, his father's heart leaped as though it would choke him. He wanted to cry out to Wint not to go; he did cry out:

"Wait!"

Wint stopped and looked at him.

"Haven't you given me a right to think—to mistrust you?" the older man challenged.

"Yes," said Wint.

"You've shamed me; and you've come near breaking your mother's heart."

Wint found it hard to speak; and when he did speak, he said more than he had meant to say. "I want to make amends, sir," he told his father.

"There are some hurts that can't be mended," said Chase inexorably.

Wint nodded; his shoulders slumped a little, and he would have turned again to the door. "I've said all I can say," he explained, "so I guess I'd better go."

Chase shook his head. "See here, Wint," he said. "Listen." There was not yet friendliness in his voice; but there was a neutral quality that held Wint. "Listen," said Chase. "I've learned some things, too, Wint. It's only fair to say that I can see, now, I was a—bumptious father. And I've not changed. I'm too old to change. Probably there were ways where I wronged you. I don't doubt it."

"No," said Wint. "You were always decent to me."

"A father can be—decent to his son, without playing fair with him," said his father. "A father can—give things to his son, and at the same time rob him of better things by the giving."

"You did your part, sir."

Chase hesitated, eyes on the floor. "I did my best for you, Wint," he said. "I think I always meant to do what was—best for you. Did you always try to do what was best for me?"

"No," said Wint.

"I don't like our being at outs any better than you do," Chase went on. "It looks bad; and it's hard on your mother—and on me. Perhaps on you, too."

Wint said nothing. He was thinking that his father's thinning hair and lined face proved that the older man had—found it hard to be at outs with his son. He was ready to go a long ways to make it up to Winthrop Chase, Senior.

His father said abruptly, as though summarizing what had gone before:

"If you want to come home, Wint, I've no objection."

Wint had not thought of this possibility, and he said so. "I did not come for that," he told the older man. "I—just came to tell you, what I have told you."

"I'm willing to accept what you say at face value," said his father. "I understand you've—kept sober. I understand you're studying. I'm ready to let you prove yourself."

Wint smiled with quick satisfaction. "That's a good deal for you to offer me, sir," he said frankly.

"If you want to come home, you can."

"I hadn't thought of that till you spoke. I don't know what to—"

"Your mother would like to have you here," said Chase huskily, "if you care to come." It was as near a plea as he could bring himself.

Wint nodded with quick decision. "All right, sir," he said. "I'd like to come. I'll bring my stuff to-morrow."

They shook hands abruptly, with a curt word that hid their feelings. "Good night," said Chase, and Wint said good night, and his father closed the door behind him.

Wint felt, while he walked back to Amos Caretall's house, as though he had been stripped of a load, had been cleansed, had been made whole. The world had never looked so clean and bright to him before.

A few minutes after he left his home, Mrs. Chase came back from the neighbor's. She saw at once that something had happened; there was a change in her husband. He was flushed, and his eyes were shining. She asked:

"Why, what's the matter with you? Has anything happened? Is there anything wrong? You know, I said to-night, I told Mrs. Hullis, that I just had a feeling something was going to happen. I told Mrs. Hullis I just knew things were going to go wrong. Oh, it does look like we have more trouble all the time."

"Wint is coming home, Margaret," said her husband.

Poor, garrulous mother! For once she was shocked dumb. Her eyes widened, and she dabbed at them with her hand, as though a cobweb had stuck across them. She turned white, and she seemed to shrink and grow old. And she sat down slowly in the straight, uncomfortable chair she always used, and put her worried old head down in her arms and cried.

Chase touched her shoulder, awkwardly comforting her.

"It's all right, mother," he said. "He's coming home."

But Mrs. Chase didn't say anything. She just sat there, quietly crying. The tears wet through her sleeve till she felt them damp upon her arm.

CHAPTER VI

A WORD AS TO HETTY

PETER GERGUE wrote to Amos that Wint had gone home; and Amos got a letter from Wint with the same news, the same day. Wint's letter was straightforward, a little embarrassed. "I want you to know," he wrote, "that my father and I have fixed things up. I am living at home again. That doesn't mean I don't appreciate your kindness. But I thought I ought to go home if they were willing to have me, and they were."

Peter wrote more at length. Gergue, uncouth to look upon and rude of speech, was nevertheless an educated man, and a well-read man. There was nothing bizarre about his letters. He wrote that Wint and his father had come together. "From what I hear, Wint went home and told Chase he was sorry, and so on," Gergue continued. "I guess Chase took on some, at that; but he came around. He's wrapped up in Wint, you know, and always was. This has been a good thing for him. He's human now. He's not such a darned fool. Chase, I mean. If you don't look out, Chase will give you a run for your money yet.

"Wint's all right, too. Hasn't touched a drop, far as I can find out, since you left. He's studying law with old Hoover, and working at the job of being Mayor. Not setting the world on fire, either. Just the routine. Town's as wet as ever, and looks like it will go on being. I guess Wint is worried for fear folks will laugh at him if he starts a clean-up. Or maybe he doesn't want to. Or maybe he hasn't thought about it.

"He and Routt don't run around together much. Jack's been away. I wrote you about that. He's back now. Acts same as ever. Mary Dale told me he was in to see old Kite one day, and Kite went up in the air. She couldn't hear what they were saying. She thinks Jack is made and handed down. Maybe he is. I wonder what he wanted to go and see old V. R. Kite for?

"Kite was sore at you, right after election. Some one told him you was going to have Wint clean up the town. He made talk that he'd hang your hide if you did. But he got over that. He's lying quiet. Doing a good business, too, I should say. There were seven drunks in Wint's court last week.

"I asked Chase if he figured to run against you next fall. He said he was out of active politics. Active, he said.

"Guess you've seen about the new city government law. Means we'll have to vote for Mayor again, this fall, instead of a year from now. You figure to run Wint? I guess he'd take it. I guess he's just getting rightly interested in the job.

"See the session's likely to end along in May. You figure to come home then?"

Amos read these letters, read Wint's twice, and smiled at it; then re-read Peter Gergue's. That night at their hotel he told Agnes that Wint had gone to his own home. "Guess you'd better go back and keep Maria company," he said.

He half expected her to protest. Agnes seemed to be having a good time in Washington; she was very gay and much abroad. Jack Routt had stopped off for three or four days, during his absence from Hardiston, and she and Jack had been constantly together while he was in town. Also, there had been other amiable young men, before and after Jack. So Amos thought Agnes was enjoying herself, and hesitated to suggest her going home. But he made up his mind, before he spoke, that she should go. Amos never got into an argument unless he intended to win. This habit had established for him a certain reputation for infallibility.

But—Agnes did not protest. "I'm glad," she said. "I'm sick of this stupid old place."

Amos, head on one side, squinted at her humorously. "Well, there are some stupid things done here, anyways," he agreed. "When'll you put out for Hardiston?"

She planned to get some clothes. "I'll be along in May," Amos told her. "Guess you and Maria can go it alone till then."

Agnes was sure they could.

In Hardiston, Wint's home-going was a nine days' wonder. People made comments according to their own hearts. Some were glad, some were amused, some were caustic. The only one to whom Wint offered any explanation was old Maria Hale. The old negress loved him like a son; she was sorry to see him go. There were tears in her eyes when she told him so; they ran down her black cheeks, like drops of ink upon that blackness. It is easy to speak openly of simple, human emotions to such folks as old Maria. Wint said to her: "I want to go home to my father and mother. And they want me. I'm going to make it up to them for some of the things I've done." He would not have said as much as that to any other person in the world. But there was no sense of strangeness in saying it to the old colored woman.

She bobbed her withered head, and smiled through her tears, and cried:

"Da's right, Miste' Wint. Yore mammy 'nd pappy shore got to be proud o' you, boy."

"I hope so, Maria," he told her, and she patted his shoulder.

"'Deed and dey will."

When he left the house, she came to the door and told him he must come, now and then, and let her cook him a good supper; and he must come and see her. She would be lonely, in that big house, without no white folks around, she said. Wint promised to come; and she waved her blue gingham apron after him as he went down the street.

Muldoon was with him, scampering around him and about; and old Maria, watching Wint and the dog, said to herself as they disappeared:

"Shore will miss dat boy; but ol' M'ria ain't going to pester herself about not seeing dat dog."

She objected to Muldoon because he shed hairs on the rugs. But she had tolerated him for Wint's sake. Muldoon thoroughly understood her feelings; he used to sit with his head on one side and bark at her while she brushed up those tawny hairs and scolded at him. She declared he was laughing at her. More than once, Wint had been forced to make peace between them.

Muldoon did not seem surprised that they were going home; he took it quite as a matter of course. In fact, it is doubtful whether he noticed the change at all. Home, to Muldoon, was where Wint was. For that is the way of the dog.

So Wint went home, and Hardiston talked it over. V. R. Kite was glad to hear it. It meant, he decided, that Wint had shifted allegiance from Amos to his father; and while Kite had always mistrusted the elder Chase, he felt they had a common bond in their mutual antagonism toward Amos. Kite, in the last few months, had conceived a new respect for Winthrop Chase, Senior. "Chase," he was accustomed to say, "is a man of sense. Yes, sir; a man of sense."

Joan was glad; she found occasion to tell Wint so, simply and without elaboration. Wint said awkwardly: "Yes, I'm glad too. I guess it's better." And they never mentioned the change again. James T. Hollow, the little man whom Caretall had put up for Mayor against Chase, resented Wint's move. "It's desertion," he told Peter Gergue. "He is deserting Congressman Caretall; and after all the Congressman has done for him. It's not the right thing to do, Peter."

Gergue spat, and rummaged through his hair. "Can't always do what's right," he said.

"I'm afraid Amos will resent this," Hollow went on. Peter said he shouldn't wonder.

"If he does object, guess he'll know how to show it," he remarked. And Hollow agreed, and added admiringly that Amos always seemed to know just the right thing to do.

The *Hardiston Sun* and the *Journal* were both friendly to Winthrop Chase, Senior; so Skinner and B. B. Beecham made no comment on Wint's change of residence. But the semi-weekly *Herald*, which was an outcast with its hand against every man, politically speaking, said, under a headline: "The Prodigal Returns," that Wint, "whose break with the elder Chase dates from the election, when Senior was made a laughingstock before the state, has returned to the parental rooftree. Please omit fatted calves."

Sam O'Brien, the fat restaurant man, told Ned Bentley it was a good thing. "Young Wint's a fine lad," he said. "And he's on the right track. Does no good, never, to break with your blood and kin."

Thus each took his own point of view. It was a poor citizen of Hardiston who had nothing to say about the matter, except that those most concerned had nothing to say at all.

The actual home-coming was simple and undramatic. Wint sent his trunk out during the day after his talk with his father. In the late afternoon of that day, he happened to drop in at the Post Office for the late mail, and met his father there. They greeted each other casually; and Wint asked:

"On your way home?"

"I have to stop at the bakery."

"I'll go along," said Wint. And he did, while people stared with all their eyes. Old Mrs. Mueller, the comfortable little woman who owned the bakery, and who was always associated in Wint's mind with the delicious fragrance of newly baked bread, lifted both hands at sight of them together, then dropped her hands abruptly and wiped them on her apron and served them without a word. Before the door closed behind them, they heard her, behind the screen in the rear of the shop, volubly telling some one the news.

Wint and his father walked home without speaking once upon the way. They were both acutely embarrassed and uncomfortable. It was a relief to them both when they got to the house and Mrs. Chase met them in the hall. Chase dropped his hand on his son's shoulder—the involuntary touch, like a caress, brought the tears to Wint's eyes—and he said:

"Here's Wint, mother."

So Wint took his mother in his arms, and she hugged him, hard. "I knew you'd c-c-c-come home, Wint," she told him, through her sobs. "I was telling Mrs. Hullis, only the other day, that I'd—that I was just sure you'd come home some—"

"I've come, mother," said Wint.

"I knew you'd come, too. I told father there wasn't anything in you that would—I told him you'd be sorry, that you'd come and tell him so. Your father's a good man, Wint. He's tried to—"

Chase broke in. People who wished to say anything to her always had to break in on Mrs. Chase. He said: "Is supper ready, mother? Wint's hungry, and so am I."

"Yes, yes," she said. "It's all ready. Hetty's made two big pies, Wint. Apples, with cinnamon in them. Thick, the way you like them. Some of our apples, from the big Sheep's Nose tree in the back yard. They've kept wonderful this winter. We haven't lost hardly any; and they're as juicy—"

"Lead me to 'em," said Wint cheerfully. "Is Hetty a good cook?"

"She's fine," his mother assured him. "Hetty's a fine girl. I never had a harder worker. She don't seem right happy, sometimes; but she does her work, and that's all a body has a right to ask. She—"

Hetty herself came to the dining-room door, then, and told them that supper was ready. Wint said: "Hello, Hetty," and shook hands with her. She said:

"Hello, Wint." The old note of reckless courage and good nature was gone from her voice; and when he saw her more clearly, in the lighted dining room, he saw his mother was right. Hetty did not look happy. Her eyes were tired; and there were shadows beneath them. Her face was thinner, too. He thought she did not look well. During supper, while she waited upon them, he told her so. "You've been working too hard, Hetty. You don't look like yourself."

She said, with a twisted smile, that she was all right. There was a harsh note in her voice. It disturbed Wint; but he said no more. During the succeeding days and weeks, he grew accustomed to her changed appearance. He no longer thought of it.

In mid-April, Jack Routt came out to the house one night to see Wint. The visit seemed casual enough. He said he had thought he would drop in for a smoke and a talk. He came early, only a few minutes after supper, and Hetty was clearing away the supper dishes. When she heard his voice in the hall, she stood very still for a moment, looking that way. Wint did not see her. Routt laid aside his hat, and then he saw Hetty, and he called to her:

"Hello, Hetty."

She said evenly: "Hello, Jack."

Then Routt and Wint went up to Wint's room, and Hetty stood very still where she was for a little time, before she went on with her work.

Upstairs, Routt was saying: "I'd forgotten Hetty was working for you."

"Yes," said Wint.

Routt lighted a cigarette. "She's a beauty, isn't she?"

Wint nodded. "Not as pretty as she was in school. Remember what a picture she used to be, hair in a braid, and those cream-red cheeks of hers?"

"Guess I do," Routt agreed warmly. He looked at Wint and grinned. "Don't know that I'd want her living in the same house with me," he said.

"Why not?" Wint asked.

"Damned bad for my peace of mind."

Wint flushed. He was a curiously clean, innocent chap in some ways. He felt a little ashamed by the mere existence of the thought which had prompted Routt's covert suggestion. "I'm glad you dropped in, Jack," he said. "Good to see you here again. Like old times."

If he had been less busy with the work of his office, and with his study, Wint might have thought more about Hetty during the next few weeks. But—he didn't. They saw each other daily, and once or twice he realized that she was not as good-natured as she had been. There were times when she was sullen.... For the most part, however, he did not think of her at all.

Now and then he had short letters from Amos. Dry, friendly letters, with some impersonal advice sprinkled through them. In the third week in May, Amos wrote that he would come home, arriving the Thursday following. Wint was glad he was going to see Amos again. He had gone to Amos's house once or twice for the suppers Maria loved to cook for him, but when Agnes came home, he gave that up. Agnes bored him. She was too vivacious. Joan was quieter, calmer, infinitely strengthening and strong.... Jack Routt was seeing a good deal of Agnes, he knew. Routt seemed no longer bent on the wooing of Joan, though he had told Wint, months ago, that he meant to go in and win. Wint joked him, one day, about this, and Routt said frankly:

"You and she have made up. I'm not the sort of a chap that trespasses. When I see I've no chance, I know how to make the best of things."

Wint thought that was straightforward and decent in Routt.

Amos was to come home on the afternoon train, Thursday. Wednesday evening, Wint spent at home. Chase and Wint's mother went upstairs early to bed, but Wint was busy with a case book from Hoover's office, and remained downstairs, the book open on the table, the lamp beside him.

He did not realize that time was passing. Wint had a certain faculty for concentration; and the dead quiet of the sleeping house allowed him to enclose himself in the world of his thoughts. He heard nothing, saw nothing, knew nothing but the matter he was reading. He did not hear the clock strike midnight, and one o'clock.

But in the end he did hear some one come up on the back porch. That would be Hetty, coming home. He knew she had gone out for the evening. Listening to her step, he wondered what time it was, and looked at the clock and saw that it was within twenty minutes of two in the morning.

"Great Scott!" he said, half aloud. "As late as that?" And then, curiously, "What's Hetty doing out this time of night?" He listened; and he could hear no more footsteps, but he did catch the murmur of a man's voice. Indistinguishable.... Then Hetty's in a harsh, mirthless laugh. He got up abruptly and went out toward the kitchen. He could not have told what impulse sent him.

When he opened the door, Hetty was standing on the porch, facing him. There was no one with her. Wint said: "Alone, Hetty? Time you were getting in." He was good-natured.

She looked at him, and he saw that she was flushed, and her eyes were reddened, and her mouth was open. Her hair was a little dishevelled. She looked at him, and laughed, and said loosely:

"Oh, you Wint. Wint's caught me. Joke on me."

He saw that she had been drinking, and he was inexpressibly sorry and disturbed. Not that he was a stranger to drink; not that he frowned upon it from high, moral grounds. But—Hetty had been so beautiful, and so youthful, and so gay. She was so hideously soiled now. He was not disgusted; he was infinitely sorry for her.

Hetty laughed cracklingly. "Poor ol' Wint. 'Member when you came home so? Hetty put Wint t' bed. Now Wint'll have to put Hetty to bed. Mus'n't let Chase know, Wint. He's a moral man."

Wint said gently: "Of course not, Hetty." He took her arm. "Come in."

She was unsteady on her feet; and it seemed hard for her to keep her eyes open. He was afraid she would drop in a sodden slumber before he could get her upstairs. This fear haunted him during the moments that followed; it marked them in his memory. He was never going to be able to forget this business of helping Hetty slowly up the back stairs, and up to her third-floor room. It was only a matter of minutes; but they were fearfully long. And he was afraid she would go to sleep; and he was afraid she would laugh. Once he heard the laughter coming, in her throat, in time to press his hand over her mouth; and he could never forget the feeling of her loose, working lips beneath his hand. He was sweating and sick.

He got her to her room without turning on the lights. He got her to the bed and she lay down and seemed instantly asleep. He started for the door; and she called him back.

"Shame, Wint," she said mournfully. "Ain't going to take off my shoes? I took off your shoes, Wint. I took off your shoes."

She wore low shoes, little more than pumps. He thanked his fates for that, while his fingers fumbled for the laces. A tug loosed the knots, the slippers came off easily. Hetty was snoring before he was done, and he left her so.

He could hear her snoring, after he got out into the hall. It seemed to him his father, asleep in the front of the house on the second floor, must hear. He went down from the third floor to the second on tiptoe with excruciating care. And on down the back stairs to put out the lights, and put away his book, and come back up to his own bed.

He could not sleep for a long time. He was obsessed by a strange and persistent feeling of responsibility for Hetty. It was as though he felt himself to blame for this thing that had come to her.

Jack Routt would have laughed at such a state of mind; but it was very real to Wint.

CHAPTER VII

ORDERS FOR RADABAUGH

WINT had a talk with his father next morning; that is to say, the morning of the day Amos was to come home. He told the elder Chase that Amos was coming.

Chase nodded. "I heard so," he agreed.

"I want you to understand my relations with him," said Wint.

There was a time when the older man would have said that a son of his could have no relations with Amos Caretall. But Winthrop Chase, Senior, had been learning wisdom, and a certain tolerance. Also, he had no wish to lose Wint again. He told himself this was because Wint's mother was growing old, would miss him.

"Well," he said, "what are they?"

Wint had been dreading what his father would say; he had been afraid of anger, of abuse. He was immensely relieved at the older man's tone.

"Simply this," he said. "He put me where I am. That was tough on you; but I think it has been good for me. It's a strange thing to have the feeling that you can give men orders which they must obey; and that you have a—a sort of control over them. Dad, do you realize that I have to send men to jail every little while? It's a pretty serious thing to send a man to jail, when you know you ought to be in jail yourself, in a way. I've done some thinking about it; so you see, it's been good for me. It never hurts a man to think.

"The whole thing is, Amos has done me a good turn, sir. I can't help feeling grateful to him. Can't help feeling he's been a good friend to me. And—I want to be friends with him. And I want you to know there's no disloyalty to you in this friendship."

Chase considered for a little; then he said quietly: "You know, Amos played false with me. Deceived me—deliberately. And tricked me."

"I know it," said Wint. "It was politics; and in a way, it was dirty politics. But—he's been square with me."

"I'm not sure," said Chase, "that the whole business has not turned out pretty well, for you. For your sake, I'm not sorry." His voice stirred and quickened. "But by Heaven, Wint, Amos is no friend of mine! And some day I mean to break him."

Wint said: "That's all right. It's a fair game between you. But I don't want you to think I'm taking sides with him."

"What are you going to do?" Chase asked.

"I thought of meeting his train," Wint told him. "And—he asked me to have supper with them to-night, to talk things over. I thought I would."

"Suppose I tell you not to?"

Wint said wistfully: "I hope you won't, sir, because—I'm going to."

Chase nodded. "I suppose so," he agreed. "Well, Wint—you're a grown man. I shall not try to treat you—like a boy. Not again. I'm leaving it to you, Wint."

Wint said quickly: "I'm glad." He got up and, without either's suggestion, they shook hands, and looked into each other's eyes for a moment.

"All right," said Chase. "I'll tell your mother not to expect you for supper."

"Try to make her understand, will you?"

His father smiled. "Your mother doesn't always understand," he said. "But—she loves you, Wint."

"I know...."

He hesitated, wondering whether he should tell his father about Hetty. She had been sullen, avoiding his eyes, when she served breakfast. His father, or his mother, had a right to know.

Yet Wint could not bring himself to tell them. There would be no charity in them for the girl. And Wint had an infinite deal of tolerance for her. Give her a chance. He would not tell them. Not yet, at least. It could wait for a while.

He was conscious of a need to tell some one. Not for the sake of betraying Hetty, but to find some balm for his own soul. That sense of responsibility persisted; he could not analyze it, but he could not shake it off. A strangely haunting feeling, this.... It troubled him acutely. His thoughts dwelt on it all that day.

There was a drunken man in the Mayor's court that morning. An old man. Wint knew him. He was that man who had embraced Wint in the office of the Weaver House, on the morning after the election. The incident seemed to have happened infinitely long ago; yet it was horribly vivid in Wint's memory still. The man had treated him like a boon companion, a good, understanding comrade. He had assumed a fellowship between them; the fellowship of drink. The shame of it was that his assumption had been justified....

The man reminded Wint of the incident, this day in court. He was miserably sober when they brought him in, miserably sober, and trembling to be drunk again. "Don't be hard on a fellow, your Honor," he pleaded with Wint. "You know how it is. You remember. That day; day after you was elected. You're a good pal, Mayor, your Honor. Don't go to be too hard on a man."

He had been in court before; Wint had fined him, had sent him to jail. The futility of these measures came home crushingly to Wint just now. The man was not helped by them; he was as bad as ever. Worse, perhaps. A revolt against this whole system of punishment boiled up in Wint. He said, without considering:

"All right. Try to let it alone. Get out."

Young Foster, the city solicitor, looked surprised and pained as though Wint had insulted him. Marshal Jim Radabaugh grinned good-naturedly. The man himself crowded up to Wint's desk with his thanks, and poured them out, and at last whispered humbly:

"You haven't got a dime to give a man, have you, Mayor, your Honor? I'm shaking for a drink. You know how that is. Just a dime, your Honor."

Wint gave him a quarter, and Foster said: "Well, I'll be damned!" The man went out, calling blessings on Wint's head. Foster demanded: "What's the idea, anyway, Wint? He's a common souse."

"I'm sick of sending him to jail," said Wint hotly. "I'm not going to do it any more. What good does it do?"

"Keeps him sober, anyway. You as good as told him to go and get drunk again."

"Well, let him," said Wint. "What else is there for him to do?"

"Go to work."

"He looks fit for work, doesn't he?"

"Whose fault is that?"

"Yes," said Wint, "whose fault is it? Whose fault that he is what he is? Whose fault that he can buy a drink in a dry town? Whose fault is it, Foster, anyway?"

Foster laughed. "Well, what's the answer?"

Wint leaned back in his chair, eyes down, considering. He was thinking of Hetty; he could not help it. And the end of his thinking was this. He looked at Marshal Jim Radabaugh, and said evenly:

"Mister marshal, don't arrest any more men in Hardiston for being drunk unless they—commit other crimes." There was a bite in the last word.

But Jim Radabaugh only grinned and said: "All right, you're boss."

Foster started to protest. Wint asked: "Any more cases?"

"No. But damn it all, Wint! Listen—"

"I don't want to listen," Wint told him. "I'm through. Court's adjourned. Don't—"

"You're turning the town over to the bums," Foster protested.

"They can't run it any worse," said Wint, and took his hat and departed. Foster swore. Marshal Jim Radabaugh strolled up to the Bazaar to tell V. R. Kite this interesting news.

Wint met Amos at the train, and Amos shook him by the hand and looked him in the eye and nodded with good-natured approval. "Coming home for supper?" he asked.

"Surely. I wouldn't miss Maria's supper."

"You might say you wouldn't miss us, too," Agnes reminded him, clinging to her father's arm. "Mightn't he, dad?"

"Say it, Wint," Amos suggested. "Only way to have peace in the family."

So they let Agnes have her way, and she made the most of it. Peter Gergue came for supper, too; and Agnes sat at one end of the table, presiding over the coffee urn with a pretty assumption of the rôle of matron. She did most of the talking. The men were too busy with Maria's fried chicken. But afterward, when they were done, Amos and Peter and Wint went into the sitting room, and Agnes said she wasn't going to sit and listen to them talk politics. She was going to the moving-picture show. Amos told her to run along. He and Peter shaved their plugs of tobacco, and crumbled the slices, and filled their pipes; and Wint grinned at the exactness with which Peter copied Amos's procedure. He had filled his own pipe in more conventional fashion, from his pouch, and was smoking while they were still rubbing the sliced tobacco between their palms.

When the pipes were all going, Amos, as was his custom, sat in silence, waiting for some one else to speak first. Wint imitated him. And Gergue, who did not like silences, said at last:

"Well, Amos, you're home."

"Looks that way," Amos agreed.

"Hardiston ain't changed."

"No, Hardiston don't change."

"Same old town."

"Yeah, same old town."

Silence settled down upon them again. Wint was thinking of Hetty. She had been in his mind all day; she and the miserable man who had faced him in the court that morning. They were somehow linked in his thoughts; linked in a fashion that accused him. Accused him, Wint Chase, of responsibility for them. He groped for understanding, trying to guess why this was so.

Amos, abruptly, looked at Peter Gergue. "Pete," he said, "I want to talk to Wint."

Peter got up instantly. "Why, sure, Amos," he agreed. "I got to see some men, anyways."

"Be in your office in the morning?" Amos asked.

"Guess likely."

"I'll drop in."

Peter nodded, and Amos went with him to the door. When he came back, Wint was still sitting, nursing his pipe. Amos looked at him, sat down, looked at Wint again; and at last asked:

"We-ell, Wint, how's tricks?"

Wint said, after a little consideration, that he guessed tricks were all right.

"Like being Mayor?"

"It's—sobering," Wint told him. "It's a good deal of a job. For me."

"Tell you," said Amos. "Any job's a good deal of a job; if a man takes it serious."

Wint laughed. "Shouldn't wonder if I took this too seriously," he said.

"Can't be done," Amos reassured him. "Any man that has to look out for other men has a serious job."

Wint said nothing to that. He was wondering if it were a part of his job to look out for Hetty, and that drunken man of the court.

"That's what being Mayor amounts to," Amos remarked. "Found it so, haven't you?"

Wint stirred in his chair. "Amos," he said, "a thing happened last night. I feel like telling you about it. Don't need to ask you not to pass it on."

Amos tilted his head on one side, squinting at Wint wisely. "That's all right," he said. "Tell on."

The permission relieved Wint immensely; he felt as though he had been loosed from bondage. He told, in a swift rush of words, the story of Hetty. How she had come home last night. He went on, told about the man in court that day. He told Amos what had happened, what he had done, the order he had given Radabaugh.

Amos looked at him curiously. "Told Jim that, did you?"

"Yes."

"What did Foster say?"

Wint grinned. "Said he'd be damned."

"I reckon not," Amos decided, after a moment's thought. "He won't be. He's all right."

"He thought I was foolish. I suppose I was."

Amos said slowly: "Depends on why you did it, Wint. Depends on what was in your mind."

That set Wint thinking again, trying to decide just what had been in his mind. Amos smoked steadily, not looking at Wint at all. At last he said again:

"Yes, sir, Wint. Depends what was in your mind."

Wint assented thoughtfully. "I suppose so," he said.

Amos tried waiting in silence for him to go on; but Wint was busy thinking; he beat Amos at his own game without knowing it. He drove Caretall to ask:

"What was in your mind, Wint?"

The boy groped for words; he flushed uneasily, as though afraid of being laughed at. "Well," he said, "I had a fool sort of a feeling that I was to blame."

Amos nodded slowly. "Well," he said, "that's what I meant—in a way—when I said you had a job that meant taking care of folks. Hetty, and that old rip—they're folks, like any one else, like as not."

"Yes, they are," Wint agreed.

"Taking care of them; that's your job, Wint. Maybe that just means fining them, and sending them to jail."

"I tell you I won't do that again," Wint exclaimed. "I told you the order I gave Jim Radabaugh."

"We-ell," said Amos slowly. "That's all right. Far as it goes. Might go farther."

"Farther? How?" Wint demanded. "What can I do?"

"I hadn't anything pa'ticular in mind," Amos said carelessly. "Hadn't a thing in mind." He looked at Wint sidewise. Wint's face was white with the intensity of his thought. Amos said slowly: "Looks like a shame to have drunk folks around in as pretty a town as Hardiston."

"A shame?" Wint cried. "It's damnable."

"Guess most folks don't like it," Amos reminded him. "Town voted dry. Guess that shows most folks wanted it to be dry, don't it?"

"I suppose it does," Wint agreed. Amos looked at him; and Wint moved abruptly in his chair, and his eyes began to flame. The puzzle cleared; he began to understand. He began to understand himself, his own thoughts, his feeling that he was to blame for—Hetty. He began to understand, and his lips set. He said, half aloud: "By God, it means a fight! A hell of a fight in Hardiston."

"Fight?" Amos asked casually, as though he were thinking of something else. "I like a fight, I'd like to see a good one." And he added, after a moment: "I might take a hand; if it weren't a private fight, or something."

Wint sat forward in his chair, looked around the room. "Where's the telephone?" he asked.

"Telephone?" said Amos. "Why, in the hall."

Wint got up and went swiftly out into the hall. Amos listened; and he smiled, with a twinkling anticipation in his eyes. He heard Wint ask the operator to locate Jim Radabaugh and get him on the 'phone. Then Wint came back and stood in the doorway, waiting while she signaled for the marshal with the red light that was set on a pole in the heart of the town. Amos did not turn around to look at Wint. Wint did not move.

After a while, the 'phone rang twice. "That's us," said Amos, still without turning. "Our ring is two."

Wint went to the 'phone. Radabaugh, at the other end, said: "This is the marshal. Who's talking?"

"Wint. Mayor Chase."

"Oh! All right, Mister Mayor. What's on your mind?"

Wint said evenly: "I've instructions for you. If you are willing to carry them out, all right. If not, resign, and I'll fill your place to-morrow."

"You're the boss," said Radabaugh amiably. "I do what you say."

"Either do what I say or resign," said Wint again. "I want you to get busy and break up the liquor business in Hardiston."

There was a long silence, and Wint heard the marshal whistle softly under his breath. Then Radabaugh asked:

"In earnest?"

"Absolutely. I want the town cleaned up. I want it bone dry. Will you take the job? Or quit?"

"Why," said Radabaugh, "I'll just naturally take the job. I've been a-wishing I had something to do."

Wint spoke a word or two more, hung up, and came back to Amos. He sat down without speaking. After a little, Amos asked, looking at Wint sidewise:

"Going through with it?"

"Yes," said Wint. There was more resolution in the simple word than there would have been in lengthier protestations.

"We-ell, all I can say," Amos drawled, "is that this here is going to make an awful difference to V. R. Kite."

It did: a difference to Kite, and to Wint's father, and to Jack Routt; and a difference to Wint himself. A difference to Hardiston, too.

When Wint went home, at ten o'clock, the word was already humming around the town.

END OF BOOK THREE

BOOK IV

LINE OF BATTLE

CHAPTER I

MARSHAL JIM RADABAUGH

JIM RADABAUGH, the city marshal, that is to say, the chief of police, was a man not without honor in Hardiston. A good fellow, and a cool, brave officer. That he was a good fellow, every one who knew him could attest. He had no enemies. It was a pleasure to be arrested by him. There was an equable good nature in the man, and a drawling humor in the very tones of his voice which inspired good nature and good humor in return. He was a lean man, lazily erect, as though it were too much trouble to be stoop-shouldered. Black hair, black eyes.... A chronic bulge in his cheek that housed the wad of tobacco which he kept there. An intimate acquaintance with the intricacies of big-league baseball as set forth in the public prints; a repository of racing lore; a good pool player and a redoubtable hand at poker. All in all, a good man to keep the peace according to his lights.

People said he was easy-going, but every one knew he was no slacker of duty or of obligation. Three years back—that was before they elected him marshal—he had been under fire for the first time. It was on the interurban street-car line that ran from Hardiston "up the crick." Radabaugh sat in the front of the car, facing the rear; and a man in the middle of the car ran amuck with a revolver, shooting wildly. He killed one man, wounded another, in the seconds it took Radabaugh to charge down the aisle and overwhelm him. The conductor of the car, at the moment, was hiding under a rear seat; and the motorman had jammed off his power and jumped overboard, into a ditch that had more water in it than he had counted on. Radabaugh knocked the man over with a cuff of his fist, and pinned him, and took his gun away.

His friends told him he ought to run for office after that. He said he didn't mind. His business was not an exacting one. He and his brother were tailors, and his brother could handle the bulk of their work anyway. So Jim ran for marshal, and was elected. Thereafter, when he was not occupied with his official duties, he used to drop in at the tailor shop to help things along there. It was no sight for timid customers, trying on their new suits while Jim's brother chalked them in mysterious places, to see Jim come in and go to work. He always came in casually, spat in the appointed direction, then produced from one pocket and another his gun, his handcuffs, and his club. He was accustomed to lay these on one of the bolts of cloth which stocked the shelves, then seat himself cross-legged on the table, with a little cloth apron on his knees, and pick up the first task that came to hand.

His duties as marshal were not pressing, for Hardiston folk commit few crimes, and usually commit those away from home. When he was wanted during the day, the telephone operator called the shop. If she wanted to locate him after dusk, she flashed a signal light which called him to the telephone. For the most part, his time was his own.

And this is not to say that Jim Radabaugh had nothing to do. There was the case, for example, of the darky who was wanted for burglary in one of the cities in the southern part of the state. Jim got word that he was drinking in a hovel down by the creek, with two other men. So he went down there and strolled in and told the man he was wanted. Jim's hands, at the moment, were in his coat pockets. The darky pulled a revolver, jammed it against Jim's breast, and pulled the trigger. Nothing happened; that is to say, nothing happened to Jim. The darky's gun did not explode, but Jim's did. It burned a hole in his pocket, and it bored a hole in the darky, neatly amidships, in such fashion that there was no further occasion to trouble with that man. His body, laid open with two slashes of the coroner's knife that intersected on the bullet hole, was on view for a day or two in the undertaker's back room; and small boys went in to see it. They thought Jim Radabaugh was rather more than mortal, after that.

As a matter of fact, it had been a narrow squeak for Jim, as an examination of the darky's weapon proved. That unfortunate man had apparently been unable to buy revolver ammunition, so he had bought rifle cartridges of the desired caliber and whittled off the bullets to make them fit into the cylinder of the revolver. Perhaps he had hurried with this bit of preparation; at any rate, he left one of the bullets too long, and when he pulled the trigger, the bullet caught and prevented the cylinder from turning. Which undoubtedly saved Jim Radabaugh's life.

People agreed that was a good thing; for Jim was a good fellow. Wint's orders to clean up the town interested him. They meant some measure of excitement, and he liked excitement. He told two or three people, that night, and they spread the news. But Jim took no official step till next day. Then he set out to serve notice on those most concerned.

One of these people most concerned was a man named Lutcher. His place of business was on the second floor of a building that fronted on one of the alleys in the heart of town. You climbed an outside stair from the alley to Lutcher's door. Wint and Jack Routt went there, that night of Amos Caretall's first home-coming, from their interrupted billiard game. Lutcher's place was perhaps the best in town; that is to say, the surroundings were least sordid, and the wares he sold most meritorious. He was financed, of course, by Kite.

Radabaugh went there first. He had been there before, in his personal capacity. He had no scruples about such visits. Lutcher was a lawbreaker, of course; but the lawbreaking was tacitly accepted. There had been no orders against it. And Jim Radabaugh had no objection to a drink now and then. So he climbed the stairs from the alley to Lutcher's door, and knocked, and Lutcher opened the door and admitted him. This Lutcher was not a bad fellow, say what you will of his business. A big, bald man with a husky, whispering voice, and a habit of appearing in his shirt sleeves. He wore rather attractive silk shirts, chosen with no mean taste; and his vests were often remarked. Also, he smoked good cigars, instead of the well-nigh universal stogie of Hardiston; and he gave these cigars freely to his regular customers.

Lutcher had not heard the news, the night before. So he greeted Marshal Radabaugh good-naturedly, and told him it was pretty early in the day for a drink, and that he would lose his reputation if he came here by daylight in this fashion. Jim laughed at that, and asked cheerfully whether Lutcher had a good stock on hand.

"Ice chest full, and a sawdust bin packed with bottles," Lutcher told him. "What's yours? The same."

"Any reserve supply?" Radabaugh asked. Lutcher said there was no reserve; that he was expecting a shipment in a day or two. Radabaugh nodded.

"Got bad news for you, Lutch," he said.

Lutcher beamed. He was always an amiable man. "Can't make me feel bad, Jim," he said. "Shoot the wad."

"Going to close you up," said Radabaugh.

Lutcher laughed. "Fat chance, I guess. What're you trying to do? Work me for a snifter. All right. Say the word."

"Straight goods," Radabaugh assured him. "Mayor's orders."

"Wint's orders? That's a hot one." Lutcher chuckled, his gay vest heaving with his mirth. "Why, Wint's one of my regular customers."

"Ain't been in lately, has he?" Radabaugh suggested.

"No, not just lately. It wouldn't look right."

Radabaugh nodded. "He's in earnest, I'd say," he told Lutcher. "Anyway, I do what he says. He didn't say anything about confiscating the stuff, or destroying it. Said to stop the sale. So I've got to seal you up, Lutch."

Lutcher had been losing some of his amiability. He told Radabaugh so. "I'm a good-natured man," he said. "But this is no joke."

"No," said Jim. "It's no joke. Where's your ice box?"

"What in time do you think you're going to do?"

"Put a seal on it, and on that bin of yours. And drop in and look at the seals every day or two. And I'll take charge of shipments that come in, unless you cancel them. If you bust the seals, I'll have to take you into court, and Wint will soak you."

"You've got a Chinaman's chance," Lutcher told him scornfully. "Why, I've given that pup his pap for two years. I'm not going to stand for this. Not for a minute. You tell him so."

"If you'd rather have it so," Jim said mildly, "I'll pour it all out of the window, right now." He said this mildly, but Lutcher knew Jim's mildness was apt to be deceptive. In the end, he surrendered to the inevitable, because it was the inevitable. Jim placed his seals, and strolled away. Lutcher boiled out after him and hurried off to see V. R. Kite.

The marshal bent his steps toward the Weaver House, that infamous hostelry where Wint had spent the night of his election, and where he had been found next day. Radabaugh knew Mrs. Moody, the presiding genius of that place, as well as he knew Lutcher. He had always made it his business to know such folk. But Mrs. Moody did not receive him with the good nature Lutcher had shown. She had heard some rumors of what was to come.

The sunken office of the old hotel was little changed, when the marshal strolled in, since that night of Wint's election. The light of day, fighting its way through the dingy windows, served only to make the interior more squalid. The same old men played their interminable game of checkers on the table in the corner. The miserable dog that bore Marshal Jim Radabaugh's name sprawled beneath the table, its bony legs clattering on the floor when the creature stirred in its sleep. The boy, that boy who had been so painfully reading the literature of brewing on the night of the election, was not to be seen. It is to be hoped that he was out about some wholesome play. Radabaugh had a suspicion, founded on experience, that the boy was not in school. He never was. Mrs. Moody sat behind the high, bar-like counter. When Radabaugh came in, she got up with a quick, deadly movement like the stir of a coiling snake; and she smiled at the marshal with those hideously beautiful false teeth gleaming in her aged and distorted countenance.

"Why, good morning, deary," she said, terribly amiable. "I don't often see you down here any more."

"Morning, Mrs. Moody," said Jim. And stalked past the counter toward the door that led to that back room which overhung the creek. Mrs. Moody bustled after him and caught his arm at the door.

"Where you a-going, Jim Radabaugh?" she demanded. "You say what you want, and say it here."

Radabaugh shook his head. He knew such measures as he had used with Lutcher would not serve with Mrs. Moody. The patrons of the Weaver House had little respect for such flimsy things as seals. He knew, also, that there was no possibility of relying upon the word of Mrs. Moody. Many women, especially such women as she, have the attitude toward promises that the Kaiser had toward treaties. They consider them interesting only when broken. Radabaugh meant to destroy her stock of liquor; and he told her so.

Then she began to scream at him. The old men at the checkerboard brushed at their ears as though her screaming were a swarm of flies, harassing them. Jim pushed her to one side and went through to the back room. When he set about his business there, she attacked him with a billet of wood; and Jim subdued the old warrior as gently as might be, and told her to mind what she did. So she began to weep and wail and scream hysterically; and Jim emptied bottles through the trap-door into the creek, knocking off the neck of each bottle so that there might be no survivors. All the while, Mrs. Moody wailed behind him.

When it was done, he turned to her, brushing his hands. "Orders are, no more selling, ma'am," he said gently. "If you start up again, I'll have to take you in."

She was trying to placate him now. "Whose orders, deary?" she wheedled. "Who's doing this to old Mother Moody, anyhow?"

"Mayor," Jim told her; and she wailed:

"Wint Chase. Little Wint that I've put to bed here amany a time. He'd never go and do this, now. Who was it? Honest."

"Mayor," Jim repeated. "Straight goods. Hardiston has gone dry. This is serious, too. Don't you go to start anything, ma'am. Because I always did hate to arrest a lady."

"You'll just have to—you might just as well take me right off to the poor farm, Jim Radabaugh. I'm not making ends meet, even right now." Her withered old hands covered her face, and she rocked and wailed: "Eh, poor old Mother Moody! Poor old Mother Moody! You wouldn't take me in if I sold just a little bit, would you, now?"

He said he would; and when she saw he meant it, she dropped her attempts to conciliate him; and she cursed him through the corridor and through the office; and she stood in the door of her hostelry and cursed him as long as he could hear, so that even Jim Radabaugh's hardened ears turned red and burned with shame. It takes a brave man to face without inward shrinking the revilements of a thoroughly angry woman. Jim was glad to be rid of her.

He stopped, on the way back uptown, to warn a fly-by-nighter who ran a lunch cart near the station and served stronger drinks than coffee. This man denied any interest in Jim's warning; and the marshal could find no liquor about the cart. Nevertheless he served notice, and made a mental memorandum to see to it that the notice was obeyed.

Remained only V. R. Kite. Radabaugh grinned as he thought of Kite. Kite would take this matter hard; and when V. R. Kite took a thing hard, the sight was worth seeing.

But Kite was not in the Bazaar when he got there, so Jim strolled back up street and dropped in on B. B. Beecham. The editor greeted him as courteously as he greeted every one. "Good morning," he said. "Have a chair. Anything I can do for you?"

Radabaugh spat into the stove. "No," he said, readjusting the bulge in his cheek. "Just dropped in. Waiting to see Kite."

B. B. nodded. "Anything new with you?" he asked, for everybody was a source of news to B. B. Beecham. That was why the *Journal* was popular.

"We-ell, I have got a sort of an item for you," Jim told him. "Might be worth printing, maybe."

B. B. asked what it was; and Jim told him. "Wint's give orders that the town's going dry."

B. B. said: "H'm! Is that so?" And Jim said it was so.

"Guess that'll be an item folks will read," he remarked.

The editor shook his head. "We don't feel we can print such things," he said. "You see, it's bad for Hardiston, outside. Legally, the town is already dry."

"I never did have much of any use for laws," Jim drawled.

"I suppose this means some work for you."

"Can't say. Don't think so. There won't be much of it done, except a little, on the sly. Not after the word I've passed around."

"Well, it won't do Hardiston any harm. Even as things are, they are better than they used to be. I can remember thirteen saloons here at one time. How many have there been, under cover?"

"Three-four, regular," Jim told him.

"Very few people will really miss them," B. B. said. "People do so many things, just because they're in the habit, and the things are waiting to be done. It's surprising how much a man can give up without realizing that he's giving up anything. I don't suppose you ever thought of that."

"Can't say I ever did," said Jim, and spat into the stove.

"Like the horse in the story. You've heard about the horse?"

"What horse?"

"Oh, you haven't heard it? The horse that was trained to live without eating."

Jim looked mildly interested. "I'll say that was some horse," he remarked. "What happened to him?"

"Why, just as the man got him trained, the horse died," said B. B.; and Jim chuckled, and B. B. laughed in the silently uproarious way habitual to him. Then Jim saw V. R. Kite pass by on the way to the Bazaar and got up quickly.

"There's Kite," he said. "See you later."

He overtook the little man just inside the Bazaar; and Kite heard his step and turned and looked at him, and Jim saw that Kite knew. But he only said:

"Hello, Kite. Want to talk to you a minute."

"Come back to my desk," said Kite, and led the way, walking stiffly, head high, ever so much like a turkey. Jim marked this peculiarity to himself.

"Exactly like a man looking over a high fence," he thought. "I'll declare, it is."

Kite sat down, tugged at his side whiskers, and bade Jim speak. The marshal looked for a place to spit, saw none, swallowed hard, and said:

"Guess you've heard the orders."

"What orders?" Kite asked harshly. But his face was livid, and the veins stood out on his forehead with his effort at self-control.

"Mayor calls me up last night and tells me to stop whisky selling. Hardiston's gone dry."

"What has that to do with me?" Kite demanded.

The marshal did not grin. If Kite wanted to act that way, all right. It was the little man's privilege. After all, he was outwardly respectable enough, a pillar of the church, and all that.

"Thought you might be interested," said Jim.

"I am," said Kite. "I believe in the free sale of liquor. Every man must have an opinion, one way or the other."

Jim considered that. Then he got up. "Well," he said, "I've passed the word around. Don't know any one that's planning to keep on selling, do you?"

"No, of course not."

"Because if you do," said Jim slowly, "tell 'em not to do it. Because if there's any turns up, any selling, I'm going to come and ask you about it, Kite."

Kite boiled up out of his chair and waved his fist. "Get out of here, you rat!" he raged, holding his voice to a monotonous whisper that was more deadly than an outcry would have been. "Get out of here, before I...."

"Before you what?" Jim asked; and Kite checked himself, and pulled at his side whiskers, and sat down abruptly, staring at the desk before him.

Jim left him there. As he emerged into the street, he began to whistle. The whistle was ragged, but the tune could be identified. Jim was whistling:

"'There'll be a Hot Time in the Old Town To-night.'"

CHAPTER II

THE BREWING STORM

WINT lay awake for a while, the night after he had given his orders to Radabaugh. He had many things to occupy his thoughts. There was in him none of the elation which might have been expected; he had no zest for the fight that was ahead of him. He was, rather, depressed and doubtful of the wisdom of what he had done, and doubtful of his own strength and determination to carry it through. He was acutely aware that a great many people would say: "Well, Wint's got a nerve. A fish like him, trying to make Hardiston dry. I'll bet he's got a cellar full." They would say this, and they would have a right to say it. Wint thought, miserably enough, that he had been foolish to start trouble. He might better have let well enough alone.

The boy's stubbornness had played him false more than once in the past; this time it was to do him a good turn. A less stubborn person would have backed down, under the weight of these misgivings; would have canceled the orders given Radabaugh, and let matters slide along as they had slid in the past. But Wint, though he dreaded the ridicule that would follow what he had done, felt himself committed. They would laugh! Well, let them laugh! His jaw set; he swore to go on at any cost. On this determination, he slept at last.

In spite of his wakefulness, Wint was first downstairs in the morning. Hetty, sweeping out the sitting room, encountered him. He had not seen her the day before, except when his father and mother were about. Then she had avoided his eye. Now she looked at him sullenly, and said:

"Much obliged for getting me to bed, Wint."

"That's all right, Hetty. I remember you did as much for me."

She laughed harshly and defiantly. "Sure I did." Her eyes were watchful and on guard. Wint guessed that she expected him to reproach her, to warn her, to bid her mend her ways. But he did nothing of the kind.

"Forget it," he said. "It wasn't anything."

Something wistful crept into her eyes, as though she would have said more. But Mrs. Chase came downstairs, and Hetty went on with her work, while Mrs. Chase volubly directed her.

After breakfast, Wint and his father walked downtown together. The elder Chase asked stiffly:

"Well, how did you find Amos?"

"Same as ever," Wint said.

"Suppose he's home for the summer."

"I guess so."

He wondered whether to tell his father what he had done; but something held his tongue. It may have been diffidence, a reluctant feeling that to tell his father this would be like an effort to justify himself in the elder Chase's eyes. It may have been uncertainty as to what attitude the older man would take. It may have been a shrewd guess at the truth; that Chase would attribute the move to Amos, and oppose it on that ground. Wint had no illusions about his father's attitude toward the Congressman. Chase held Amos as his enemy, without compromise.

As they reached the first stores on the outskirts of the business section of Hardiston, they met Ned Bentley and another man, and exchanged greetings. Bentley grinned at Wint in a friendly way, and Wint knew that Bentley had heard of his order to Radabaugh. The elder Chase saw something had passed between them, and asked Wint:

"What's Bentley so cheerful about?"

"Why, I don't know," said Wint. "He's usually pretty good-natured."

He flushed at his own evasion, but the older man did not press the question, and a little later they separated.

Foster, the city solicitor—Foster was an earnest young fellow, and took his office seriously—was waiting for Wint in what passed as Wint's office, off the main room above the fire-engine house. Foster looked flurried; and he asked quickly:

"Look here, Wint, Radabaugh says you told him to clean up the town."

Wint nodded idly, fumbling among the papers on his desk. "Yes, I did."

"Well, what's the idea?" Foster demanded excitedly. "What's the idea, anyway?"

"The idea is to—clean up the town," Wint told him.

"You're in earnest?"

"Yes."

"You mean to stop bootlegging?"

"Yes."

"Good Lord!" said Foster.

The solicitor's consternation gave Wint confidence. He asked: "Why, what's wrong with that?"

"Wrong? Nothing's wrong. But you'll surely start something."

"I mean to stop something."

"There'll be an awful row."

Wint said quietly: "If you don't want to come through.... If you don't want to make it stick, help me out, why, now's the time to say so, and get out."

"Good Lord!" Foster cried. "Of course I'll stick. Nothing suits me better. I'm.... I tell you, you don't know what you've started. But I'm with you, Wint. All along the line. Absolutely."

Wint said: "That's good."

"It's a great chance for me," Foster said.

Wint chuckled. "Ought to do you and Hardiston both some good."

"Prosecuting all those cases."

"Oh, there won't be many cases," Wint said cheerfully.

"A lot you know. Why won't there?"

"Because," said Wint, "I'm going to see that the first man in here gets soaked, good and proper. I'm going to put the fear of—the fear of me into them."

"You can't scare those fellows."

"Well," Wint admitted, "that may be so. But I'm surely going to try."

Foster had amused him, and encouraged him; but when Foster was gone, and he was left alone, his depression of the night before returned. He locked his door. He did not want to see people. And he sat down to think.

Radabaugh came in a little before noon to report what he had done. Wint listened, studying the marshal. "Think Lutcher will keep straight?" he asked.

"I should think so."

"How about Mrs. Moody?"

"She'll need watching."

"See that you watch her."

"I'm right on the job," Radabaugh assured him easily; and Jim knew the marshal meant what he said. "I've left 'em run before, because there wasn't any kick made. If you say shut 'em off, I'll do it. That's all."

"I do say it," Wint told him. He got up and gripped the other's shoulder, something of the excitement of the coming fight already stirring in him. "Jim, we'll make Hardiston dry as a bone."

Radabaugh spat. "We-ell," he drawled, "it don't take much booze to wet a bone. But we'll see to it the stuff don't go sloshing around the gutters, anyway."

For his lunch, Wint went to fat Sam O'Brien's restaurant. He liked the place. The long, high counter, scrubbed white as the deck of a ship; the revolving stools before the counter; the shelves on which bottles of mustards and catsups and spices were ranged; and big Sam O'Brien in his vast white apron presiding over it all. There was a mechanical piano which played a tune for a nickel in the back of the restaurant, and it was jangling and tinkling when Wint came in. Half a dozen men were there before him; and they grinned when they saw Wint, and spoke among themselves. Sam O'Brien welcomed him with a chuckle. O'Brien was a jocular man. He set plate and knife and fork and a thick glass of water before Wint, and spread his hands on the counter, and asked in a booming voice:

"Well, how's your appetite, you bold crusader?"

Wint flushed, and said uncomfortably: "Cut it out, Sam!"

The restaurant proprietor had his own ideas of a joke; and he made the most of them. At Wint's words, he threw back his head and laughter poured out of him. He rocked, he slapped his great fist on the counter.

"Cut it out?" he repeated. "Oh, Wint, you're the funny man. Cut it out, he says! The whole blamed town. 'The booze is getting you, Hardiston. Cut it out,' he says!" He bellowed the words. "Cut it out! Cut it out! Oh, Wint, you'll be the death o' me."

There was never any use resenting Sam O'Brien. Wint laughed and said: "I'll be the death of you if you don't get me something to eat, Sam. Get a move on your old carcass."

After lunch, he had a word or two with men upon the street; but he did not want to talk to them. He wanted to get out of their way, out of sight. His nerves were beginning to jangle; he wanted something to happen. There was hanging over him a storm; he wanted the storm to break. He had a thought of going to V. R. Kite and flinging a defiance in that old buzzard's gold-filled teeth. He liked to think of Kite as an old buzzard; the phrase pleased him. Men will always be pleased to find they have used words tellingly. The gift of speech is what distinguishes man from the animals; it is right that he should vaunt himself upon it.

But in the end, Wint did not go to Kite; he went to Hoover's office and hid himself in a back room with a law book. Neither Dick nor his father was there when he arrived; he counted on not being disturbed. He did not want to be disturbed. He wanted to be let alone. He was mistrustful of himself, of his motives and of his powers.

In mid-afternoon, the telephone rang; and he answered, expecting a call for one or the other of the Hoovers. But when he spoke into the instrument, some one said: "Is this you, Wint?"

He said it was; and the some one said: "This is Joan."

Wint said: "Oh!" He was uncomfortable, wondering what she wanted, why she had called.

"I've just heard what you've done," she said.

"What's that?" Wint asked. "Done what?"

"About how you're going to—to clean up Hardiston."

"Oh, that," said Wint. "Yes."

"Central told me I could probably get you at the Hoover office."

"Yes. Yes, I'm here."

"I thought you might like to know that I'm glad you're going to do this."

"That's all right," he said awkwardly. The old, stubborn resentment at any praise was awake in him; but there was a curious tincture of happiness, too.

"It's a good fight, Wint," she said. "And—you'll win."

Wint laughed uneasily. "Oh, sure," he said. He did not want to talk about it; and Joan understood and said good-by. Wint stared thoughtfully at the telephone for a while; then he went back to his probing into the musty recesses of the law which he found so live and vital.

But he was unable to keep his thoughts upon the book. They wandered. He kept thinking about V. R. Kite. He kept wondering what Kite would do.

And he wished insistently that whatever Kite meant to do, he would do quickly. Wint was tired of waiting for the storm to break.

CHAPTER III

A HARD DAY FOR KITE

IF V. R. Kite had been wise enough to let Wint severely alone, in the days that followed, it is not at all improbable that Wint's resolution would have weakened. But if knaves were wise, they would not be knaves. So, instead of being left alone with his depression, and his doubts of himself, Wint was attacked front and flank; and the stimulus of battle proved to be exactly what he needed to forge his determination and whip his courage to the sticking point.

Kite first heard the news of what Wint had done from Lutcher, the amiable man in the distinctive vest, whose stock in trade Jim Radabaugh put under seal. Lutcher went straightaway to Kite when Radabaugh left him; and he found Kite still ignorant of what had come to pass. Lutcher took a decided pleasure in breaking the news to Kite. He found the little turkey of a man at his desk in the Bazaar; and he stuck his thumbs into the armholes of his vest and said in his husky, whispering voice:

"Well, Kite, we're closed up."

Kite had greeted Lutcher as pleasantly as he greeted any one. He was a little afraid of the big, bald man, and Lutcher knew it. He was as much afraid of Lutcher as Lutcher was of Jim Radabaugh. But he forgot to be afraid of Lutcher in this moment. He came up out of his chair like a Jack-in-the-Box—and Kite looked not unlike the conventional Jack-in-the-Box with his lean neck and his poised head and his side whiskers flying—and he snapped at Lutcher:

"What's that you say?"

Lutcher grinned, and wheezed: "I say we're closed up."

"Closed up?" Kite repeated, in something like a shout. "Closed up? What do you mean? Talk English, man."

Lutcher ran his thick finger around the soft collar of his silken shirt. "I mean Radabaugh's given orders not to sell any more stuff," he said. "What did you think I meant?"

"You're crazy," said Kite flatly. "Radabaugh wouldn't dare do that."

"Well, he's done it!"

"Jim Radabaugh? The marshal?"

"Sure," said Lutcher impatiently. "Can't you hear what I say? Came and sealed me up this morning. Said it was orders."

"Orders? Whose orders?"

"Mayor's."

Kite's clenched fists went into the air. "He can't do that," he said fiercely. "I won't stand for it. By God, if he tries to do that, I'll leave town. Or I'll kill the pup. Or kill myself. I won't stand for it, I tell you, Lutcher."

"Don't tell me," said Lutcher, amiable again in the face of the other's excitement. "Don't tell me; tell the Mayor."

Kite stood for a minute with staring, thoughtful eyes, as though Lutcher were not there. Then he grabbed his hat and started for the street. Lutcher looked after him, grinning with amusement. "The old buzzard does take it hard," he told himself. "Well, I should worry. What's he up to now?"

Kite had disappeared. When Lutcher got to the street, the little man was no longer in sight. Lutcher wondered what Kite had set off to do; and he loitered for a while in the hope of seeing the little man again. Kite's fury amused him. But Kite had not returned when Jim Radabaugh drifted into sight; and Lutcher did not want to see Jim again, so he effaced himself. He saw Jim go into the Bazaar, and come out again, and stop at the *Journal* office; and after a little, Kite came down the street from the Court House, and Radabaugh emerged from the *Journal* office, and followed Kite into the Bazaar. Lutcher wished he could be near enough to hear what they said, but there was no chance of it, so he departed.

Kite held on to himself while he talked with Radabaugh; but when the marshal was gone, the little man, in the shelter of his desk, fretted and jerked in his chair in a tempest of furious anger. There was no doubt about it; he did take this news hard. But one watching with a seeing eye might have discovered in Kite's anger something else; a touch of panic.

Perhaps fear is always a part of anger; perhaps it is one of the springs from which anger flows. But in the case of Kite, his fear and panic tended to quiet him and steady him and bid him go slowly and watch his every move. There had been a day when he would have leaped into such a fight as this, a terrible and furious figure. But Kite was getting old. There was something senile and pitiful in his fury now.

There in the rear of his busy little shop, with customers going and coming and the clerks laughing together, Kite twisted his fingers together and beat at his head with his clenched hands and tried to think what to do. He had been so sure that Wint would never take this step; he had been so sure that with Wint as Mayor, Hardiston would be safely and securely wet.

He had been so sure of Amos Caretall's good will. Chase and Jack Routt had warned him; but he had not believed their warnings, because he did not wish to believe. Wint was a drinker; it was just common sense that Wint would let the town go on as it had gone in the past. Kite had counted on it.

And now Wint had betrayed him. That was the word that sprang into Kite's mind. Wint had betrayed him. He felt an honest indignation at the Mayor. He was more indignant than he had been when Wint called him a buzzard. He had accepted that good-naturedly enough. Hard names broke no bones; besides, Wint had been quite obviously suffering from an overnight bout, that morning. Kite knew the mood; he was not surprised; and he was not resentful. But this was different. Damnably different. This was out and out treachery, betrayal. He had helped elect Wint; now Wint turned against him.

Kit felt acutely sorry for himself; he felt acutely reproachful toward Wint. And when Jack Routt dropped in, half an hour after Radabaugh had gone, with a triumphant light in his eye, Kite told him so.

"I didn't think Wint would do it," he said dolefully. "Routt, I didn't suppose Wint would do this to me."

Routt chuckled. "It's not Wint's doing," he said. "I told you this was coming, you know. It's Amos."

But Kite was in no mood for rage at Amos. "I don't know," he said. "This looks like Wint's doing. It's a boy's trick. A man like Amos would have seen the harm for Hardiston in such a move. No, Jack, Wint did this, himself."

Routt shook his head. "I know better. You get after Amos, and Wint will come to heel. I know them both, I tell you."

"I can't believe it," Kite insisted. "What motive could he possibly have?"

"Trying to get on the band wagon," Routt told him. "That's Amos. Trying to get on the dry band wagon."

"No, no, it's Wint. He's the one we must go to. He's the one we must work on. He's got to be stopped, Routt." Something of the old fire was reviving in Kite. "He's got to be stopped. Scared off. Called off. Something. I won't stand for such a state of affairs. Such a thing.... In Hardiston."

Routt grinned. "Well, what are you going to do about it?"

"Get after him. There must be a way. Don't you know a way to get hold of him and bring him to time? Must be some way, Routt. Think, man; think. What can we do? Scare him off?"

Routt looked at Kite in a curious, intent way, as though he thought there might be a hidden meaning in what the other man had said. "What's your idea exactly?" he asked. "What's up your sleeve?"

"Idea?" Kite echoed. "Idea is to get something on that young skate and make him call Radabaugh off. That's the idea. Get after him, heavy. There must be a way. Some way."

Routt smiled faintly, tilting back in his chair, looking at the ceiling; and he blew a long stream of smoke straight upward. Kite snapped:

"Well?"

"Well," said Routt, "there's something in that. There might be a way...."

Kite leaned toward him intently. "What is it?"

Routt waved his hand. "Nothing definite. Might develop. Hold off a while."

"I can't hold off," said Kite. "I won't hold off. Something's got to be done."

"Then you do it," Routt told him carelessly; and Kite pleaded with him.

"No, no. You do your own way. I'll try mine. We'll both work at this, Routt. Something ... I.... See what you can do. That's all. I'll see what I can do."

Routt got up. "Don't forget," he said, "that Amos is back of this."

Kite shook his head. "I don't think so. We'll hit Wint first. I don't want to buck Amos."

"You'll find," said Routt, "that you'll have to buck Amos."

After Routt left him, Kite sat for a while, fingers tapping nervously on his desk, wondering what to do next. And he wondered if it could be that Routt was right, that Amos was back of this move on Wint's part. Routt had said Amos would do this; so, Kite remembered, had the elder Chase. Chase had come to him, shortly after the election, to warn Kite that this was sure to happen. Were Routt and Chase right; was it possible that Amos had betrayed him?

Kite would not believe it. Not because he had any doubt of Amos's willingness to betray him, but because he did not dare believe that this was Amos's doing. If Wint had made the move on his own account, there was some hope of swaying him, or frightening him. But if Amos had prompted it and were backing Wint now, the situation was almost hopeless.

Therefore Kite refused to believe that Amos was responsible; he clung to the idea that the whole thing was Wint's own idea. Wint, then, he must fight.

He thought of Wint; and he thought of Wint's father again. There might be a chance to move Wint through his father. "If the boy has any sense of duty," Kite thought, "he'll do what his father says." He forgot that the elder Chase had always been a "dry" man. Politics takes little account of convictions; and Kite clutched at the hope that the elder Chase could change Wint's mind. Chase had offered him alliance, once; had offered him an alliance against Amos. He should be willing to show his friendliness now. Kite's eyes lighted with a faintly optimistic glint at the thought; and he took his hat and started forthwith down the street toward the furnace where Chase was to be found during the day.

He met a number of men; and he thought they all grinned at him with derision in their eyes. They must know what had happened; must be amused at this plight in which he found himself. The thought roused the anger in Kite, and strengthened him. He went on his way more boldly. By and by, at the end of the street, the smoky black bulk of the furnace loomed before him.

Kite did not like the looks of the furnace; there was such an atmosphere of harnessed power about it, and Kite was always a little afraid the power would break its harness. To reach the office, he had to go through the very heart of the monstrous thing. At the beginning of the way, a ten-foot flame hissed out of the very earth itself, at his right hand, so that he shrank past it timidly. Then he must pick his way through a corridor between structures like squat, brick ovens, below which living flame roared in a stream like a racing torrent. He could see this stream of flame. There was nothing to hold it, between the ovens. He trembled with fear that this stream would leap out at him.

When he passed under the stacks, pulsing with the rhythmic beat of life which stirred them, he could hear the roar of the fires inside, and the hiss of the air from the tuyères, and the sounds were like the ravenings of beasts to him. Kite felt immensely small, immensely insignificant. Toward the end of his way he was almost running, and he came out with vast relief upon the other side, and approached the iron-sheeted building which housed the furnace office and the chemist's laboratory. He might have come here by circling around the furnace, but even Kite had pride enough to face dangers, rather than avoid them.

He found the elder Chase at his desk; and Chase dismissed the stenographer to whom he had been dictating, and offered Kite a cigar. Kite refused it. He was by personal habit an abstemious man. "I never smoke," he said.

Chase nodded, a little ill at ease. He had tried to make an alliance with Kite, but he did not like the little man, and never would. He did not like Kite, and he was self-conscious about it, and felt that he ought to make up for his dislike by treating Kite with extreme courtesy. So now he asked: "Well, Mr. Kite," and Kite responded with a sharp question:

"What's this Wint's doing?"

There had been a time when such an inquiry frightened Chase; because, when people asked him such a question, he knew they meant that Wint was in trouble again. But he was coming to have a certain faith in Wint; so he was puzzled by Kite's question, and said so.

"I don't know what you mean," he told the little man.

Kite was surprised. "Good God! You must know. Didn't he tell you?"

"He's told me nothing in particular. What do you mean?"

"The young fool has given Radabaugh orders against any more liquor selling."

Chase's first reaction to this information was a leap of delighted pride. It was what he would have wished Wint to do; it was what he himself would have done in Wint's place. It was a decent, strong thing to do, and Chase was glad. Kite saw this in the other man's eyes; and he exclaimed challengingly:

"You look as though you were tickled, man. Don't you know this thing will ruin Hardiston?"

Chase knew it would not ruin Hardiston; nevertheless he was willing to humor Kite. So he asked: "Do you know the details? Tell me about it."

Kite laughed harshly. "You hadn't heard of it, then. He didn't tell you. It was Amos put him up to it, I guess, after all. But it looks as though he'd have told you, anyway." Kite was shrewd enough in his way; he understood that Chase, as a father, must be jealous of Amos's influence with Wint. And Chase reacted as Kite expected. His eyes clouded with hurt. Wint might have told him; should have told him. Instead, his son had laid him open to this new humiliation, the humiliation of hearing important news from a third person. And—Wint had had supper with Amos last night.

Chase struck back, in the instinct to defend himself. "You remember, I warned you Congressman Caretall would do just this."

"Sure I remember," Kite agreed. "That's why I've come to you. Want to get together with you. That was our understanding. I'm going to skin

Amos Caretall. Are you with me? That's the question." He was shrewd enough to rouse Chase against Amos, not against Chase's own son. And Chase considered the matter, inwardly hurt and sorry because Wint had not confided in him, and boiling with jealous hostility toward Amos.

"All right," he said at last. "You see I was right. What are we going to do?"

"Do?" Kite snapped. "We're going to make Amos run to cover. That's what we're going to do."

"After all," Chase reminded him, "I'm a dry man. I can't fight Amos on that issue."

"Dry?" Kite demanded. "What of it? What's that got to do with it? This is politics. Amos is no more dry than I am; but he plays the dry game because that's politics, and there are votes in it. He's trying to steal your thunder, Chase. If Amos grabs the dry vote, where do you come in? I tell you, we've got to lick him, man."

"How?" Chase asked at last. "What are we going to do?"

"First thing," Kite said, "is to get after Wint." He had been ready with the answer to this question. "Caretall is using Wint. Making a tool of him. A scapegoat. Wint doesn't know his own mind. Caretall's using him. We've got to get him out of Caretall's hands. Get him to work with you. You're his father. He ought to want to work with you. Oughtn't he?"

"He and I—understand each other," Chase said. He was not at all sure this was true, but he could not confess to Kite that he and Wint were less than confidants.

"Sure," Kite agreed. "Naturally. So the first thing to do is for you to go to Wint and tell him what he's up against. How he's being manipulated. Get him to rescind the order. Then we'll go after Amos, with Wint helping us, and clean him up."

"I don't know," said Chase reluctantly.

"Good God, man," Kite snapped, "can't you handle your own son?"

Chase got up and walked to the window, his back to Kite. His lips set firmly. Kite was right; he ought to be able to handle his own son, unless the world were all awry. After all, the dry question was only a pretext. Wint ought to train with him rather than with Amos. He would tell the boy so.

When at last he turned toward Kite again, the other man saw that he had won. "I'll see," said Chase. "I'll talk to Wint and see."

CHAPTER IV

CHASE CHANGES SIDES

WINTHROP CHASE, SENIOR, was thoughtful all that day; he went home in the evening still undecided as to what he should do. He was unhappy, hurt at Wint's reticence, disturbed as to his own course of action, and fiercely resentful of Amos's influence over his son.

His conscience was troubling him; and he was trying to quiet it with Kite's more or less specious argument that this was politics, not morality. If Chase had been asked to come out, point-blank, and champion the nonenforcement of the liquor law, he would have refused; and he would have refused with indignation at the suggestion. But the issue was not so clear as that. It was clouded by his dislike for Amos. It was not merely a question of enforcing the law; it was a question of balking Amos Caretall. And Chase was prepared to go a long way to put a spoke in Amos's wheel.

Wint had not yet come, when he reached his home; and he was glad of that. It gave him some leeway, gave him some further time to think. But his thoughts ran in an endless circle; his convictions countered his enmity toward Amos. It was only by small degrees that his attitude toward Amos crowded other considerations out of his mind. He was gradually coming to the point of decision when he heard Wint at the door. Mrs. Chase met Wint in the front hall, and told him hurriedly:

"Now, Wint, you're late again. You run right upstairs and wash your face and hands. Supper's all ready, and Hetty wants to go out, and I don't want to keep her waiting any—"

Wint laughed, and kissed her, and told her he would hurry, and he was gone up the stairs, two steps at a time, while his mother still talked to him. When he came down, his father and mother had already gone into the dining room. He followed them, answered his father's "Good evening, Wint," in an abstracted way, and sat down hurriedly. He did not look toward his father; he was conscious he had not done the fair thing in failing to tell the older man of his orders to Radabaugh. He felt guilty.

Mrs. Chase never allowed any gaps in the conversation to go unplugged; and since Wint and his father were both normal men, with normal appetites, she did most of the talking during the early part of the meal, while they ate. It was only when Hetty brought on a thick rhubarb pie and Mrs. Chase began to cut it that Chase said casually to his son:

"Well, Wint, I hear you've set out to clean up Hardiston."

Wint gulped what was in his mouth, and uneasily admitted that this was true. Mrs. Chase was talking to Hetty about the pie and did not hear what they said. Chase asked:

"What does Amos think of that?"

Wint looked for an instant at his father. "Thinks it's all right," he said.

Mrs. Chase came back into the conversation then. She had the aggravating habit of catching the tail end of a story or a remark and demanding that the whole be repeated for her benefit. "What's all right?" she asked. "What's all right, Wint? Who thinks it's all right? It keeps me so busy looking after things here that it seems like I never hear what's going on. What is it that—"

Chase told her quietly: "Wint has given Marshal Radabaugh orders not to allow any more selling of liquor in Hardiston."

Mrs. Chase was astonished. She said so. "Well, I never," she exclaimed. "You know, Wint, I never thought you'd do that. I think it's time, though, something was done. I told Mrs. Hullis ... I was saying to Mrs. Hullis here only yesterday that it was a shame, the way men were getting drunk. That Ote Runns, that beats my carpets, came here yesterday to do some work for me, and I paid him; and Mrs. Hullis saw him coming home from town that afternoon, and he couldn't even stay on the sidewalk, he was staggering so. I declare, it makes you feel like not paying a man like that for working for you, when he can go right off and spend his money on whisky, and his wife and children at home—"

Wint said, with a glance at his father: "Ote's not married, mother. He hasn't any wife; and as far as I know, he hasn't any children."

"Well, suppose he had," she demanded, "wouldn't it be just the same? I declare, Wint, you're always contradicting me. But I said to Mrs. Hullis I thought it was a shame, and she said she thought so too, and it is. You've done just right, Wint. I didn't think anybody could ever do that, or I'd have told you to do it before. I didn't know the Mayor had the say of that, Wint. I thought the Mayor was the man you went to when your dogs got into the pound. I remember Mrs. Hullis's dog got taken to the pound, three years ago, and she went to Mayor Johnson, he was then, and he got him out for her. And I told her—"

Wint had been watching his father. He had expected the older man to be proud of him, and had rather dreaded this pride. He had prepared himself to disclaim any praise that might come. But—Chase was not offering to praise him. There was no pride in his father's face; there was rather an uneasy regret, and it fired the antagonism in Wint, and made him feel like defending himself. He asked, interrupting Mrs. Chase, whether the elder Chase thought the orders should be enforced.

"I suppose so," Chase said, and Mrs. Chase lapsed into a momentary silence, pouring fresh tea into her cup.

"Don't you think it's a good thing?" Wint demanded challengingly. "Don't you—aren't you glad?"

Mrs. Chase said: "Of course it's a good thing. It ought to have been done long ago. It's a shame, the way things have been going on in this—"

Chase said to her: "Ordinarily, mother, I would think it a good thing. But in this case, it's a part of Amos Caretall's political game. A part of his—"

Wint looked at his father sharply, a word leaping to his lips. Mrs. Chase asked: "Congressman Caretall? Is he back here again, after the way he treated you? Wint, I should think you'd be ashamed to do anything to help him, after what he did to your father. I should think—"

Wint said quickly: "He has nothing to do with this. I decided to do it, and I gave the order, and I'm going through with it. Congressman Caretall isn't in this at all."

The elder Chase smiled and said: "You don't understand, Wint. I've known him longer. He's absolutely without principle or scruple. You know, for instance, that he's a wet man; but he's doing this for his own ends, using you—"

Wint protested: "He's not doing this. I'm doing it."

Mrs. Chase cried: "I should think you'd be ashamed, Wint, to do anything against your own father. He's been a good father to you, Wint. You know he—"

Wint cut in, almost pleading: "But, mother, you said yourself this was a good thing. To clean up Hardiston. And father's always been in favor of it."

"That was before I understood that Congressman Caretall was doing it to hurt your father. I don't think anything is good that hurts your father, Wint. You ought not to say that. You know I—"

"But he's not doing it to hurt dad, mother. I told you that. I'm doing it myself; he's not doing it at all."

"Your father understands these things better than you, Wint. Didn't he tell you Congressman Caretall was just using you? I shouldn't think you'd be willing to—"

The elder Chase said uneasily: "I know him better than you, Wint."

Wint pushed back his chair and looked steadily at the older man. "You talk like V. R. Kite, dad," he said.

Chase confessed his guilt by the vehemence of his protestations. "That's not so, Wint. And in any case, Kite is an honest man compared to Caretall. He plays square with his friends, at least. That's more than Amos can say."

Wint asked: "What makes you think Amos is playing crooked now? Not that he has anything to do with this...."

"I know him. He's always crooked. A crooked, double-crossing politician."

"I'm not defending Amos," Wint said stubbornly. "He's treated you badly. But he's been decent to me. I'll not turn against him. And anyway, this is my doing, my business. He's not in it at all."

"You said he was backing you."

"I said he thought I was doing a good thing. I expected you to think that, too."

Chase flushed uncomfortably. "Ordinarily, I would say so. If you'd done this without prompting from him, I would say so. But it's significant that you didn't; that you waited till he came home, and talked to you, and then gave your orders."

"I'd been thinking about it for a long time."

"But you didn't act without word from him, Wint. That's why I—regret it."

Wint asked harshly: "Listen! Do I get this straight? You'd have me let them go on selling whisky in Hardiston just for fear I am helping Amos by stopping them?"

"I don't like to see you letting Amos use you."

"Aside from that, isn't it a good thing to clean up the town, no matter what the motive?"

"You'll find in your law books somewhere the statement that the motive determines the deed," Chase told him.

"Don't you think it important to clean up Hardiston?"

"I think it important not to cement Amos Caretall's hold on this county, and this town."

Wint said angrily: "Forget Amos. Forget he exists. I'm asking a flat question. Why don't you answer it?"

Mrs. Chase interposed: "Don't you talk to your father so, Wint. Don't you do it. He knows best what's good for you, and for Hardiston, and for everybody. You know he—"

"Is whisky good for Ote Runns?" Wint demanded.

"Well, I guess it doesn't do him any hurt. It's not as if he had a wife and children, Wint, you know. You ought to do what your father says. He—"

Wint faced the older man. "Well," he asked, "what is it you say I should do, dad? In plain language. Just what do you claim I ought to do?"

"Refuse to let Amos Caretall make you his tool," Chase said steadily.

"Let Hardiston wallow in booze?"

"That's beside the point. Amos is the point."

Wint got up swiftly. "Amos is not the point," he said. "Hardiston's the point. Hardiston's the point, and I'm the point, too. If whisky is good for Hardiston, the town ought to have it. If lawbreaking is good for Hardiston, the lawbreaking ought to be permitted to go on. But if it's right and decent to keep the law, then I'm right. And if it's right to leave booze alone, then I'm right. And if I think what I'm doing is right, I ought to go on with it; and if I think it's wrong, I ought to drop it. Amos has nothing to do with it. Anyway, a bad man doing good things is a good man. If Amos were doing this, the fact that he's a crook wouldn't make it crooked. The whole thing works the other way. If Amos is doing this, and it's a good thing to do, then so far as this is concerned, Amos is a good man."

He flung up his hand. "I don't mean to hurt you, dad. I think you're wrong on this. I can't believe you want me to back down."

Chase had his share of stubbornness, of the pride which had been a pitfall before Wint's feet. He was too stubborn to admit himself in the wrong. He said swiftly:

"I do want you to back down. Call off Radabaugh. Tell Amos he can't make a monkey out of you. Can't get you to pull his chestnuts out of the fire.... Stand on your own feet. That's what I advise you to do, Wint."

Wint looked his father in the eye for a moment; then he shook his head as though to brush away a veil. "I'm sorry," he said. "I mean to fight it out on this line. Stick to it."

Chase said nothing. Mrs. Chase, silenced by the tension in the atmosphere, looked from father to son with wide eyes, and she was trembling. After a little, Wint asked gently:

"Does this mean—a break, father? Does it mean for me to get out of here?"

Chase got to his feet in swift protest. "No, no, Wint, not that." For a moment, he had an overpowering impulse to open his heart, promise Wint his support, offer the boy his hand. But he could not bring himself to do it. The stubborn, prideful streak was strong in him. He fought down the impulse, said simply: "We can disagree without fighting, I guess. That's all."

"You mean we're on opposite sides of the fence in this, dad? You really mean that?"

"Yes."

Wint's voice was wistful. "I—counted on you."

Chase flung toward the door. "I can't help it, Wint," he said harshly. "I can't link up with Amos Caretall. Not for any man."

When the door shut behind him, Wint stood still for a little, thinking hard. Then his mother touched his arm, and he looked down and saw that she was crying with fright.

"Wint," she pleaded, "don't you go quarreling with your father again. Don't you, Wint. Please.... He couldn't stand it. Not again, Wint. I told Mrs. Hullis when you were gone before—"

He put his arm around her affectionately; and he smiled. "There, mother, it's all right," he said. "Dad and I are all right. Don't you worry. We understand each other."

"I told Mrs. Hullis he couldn't stand it to have you go away again—"

"I'm not going away," Wint promised.

"Don't you...." she begged. "Don't you go, any more."

CHAPTER V

THE TRIUMVIRATE

A CONSCIOUSNESS of having acted unworthily does not make for a man's peace of mind. The plain truth of the matter is that after his talk with Wint at supper that night, Winthrop Chase, Senior, was ashamed of himself. Not that he admitted it, even in his thoughts; but it was obvious enough in his uneasiness, his inability to sit still, his restless movements here and there about the sitting room. Wint was not blind. He guessed something of what was passing in his father's mind, and wished there were some way for them to come together. But there seemed no move he could make to that end.

The older man at last announced that he was going to walk downtown for the mail. Wint said: "Good idea. I'll go along." But Chase said:

"I've got to see a man," and Wint understood that his father did not want his company, so he stayed at home when the older man departed.

Chase wanted to see Kite. He had no definite idea why he wanted to see Kite, but he felt the need of reassurance from some one, and he knew Kite would reassure him as to what he had done. So he went downtown to find Kite and talk to him. The Bazaar was closed. He telephoned Kite's home, and the old woman who kept house for him said Mr. Kite had gone uptown to see Mr. Routt. So Chase went to the building on the second floor of which Routt had his office, and saw a light behind the drawn blind in Routt's window and went up. He heard their voices inside, Kite's and Routt's, before he tried the door. The door was locked; and when he touched the knob, silence fell inside. Routt called: "Hello, who's there?"

Chase told him, and Routt said: "In a minute," and unlocked the door and let him in. Chase saw Kite sitting by the desk, his side whiskers bristling angrily.

There are no modern office buildings in Hardiston. Routt's office was on the second floor of the three-story building at the corner of Main and Broad streets. There was a hardware store on the first floor, and a lodge room on the floor above Routt's office. Routt and three or four others had quarters on the second floor. Routt's office faced the street; a single room with a hot-air register in the wall near the door. There were shelves around the wall, with a meager library of brand-new and little-used law books. Routt's desk was shiny, yellow oak. A diploma, or perhaps a certificate of admission to the bar, framed in mission oak, hung on the wall above the desk. There was an electric light in the middle of the ceiling, and it shed a bald and naked light over the three men who faced each other in the room.

Kite said: "Hello, Chase," and Chase responded to the greeting. Routt asked:

"How'd you happen to drop in? Glad to see you."

"I was looking for Kite," Chase said. "Heard he was with you."

Kite asked eagerly: "Looking for me, Chase? Good news? What's happened?"

Chase looked at Routt, with a curious, dull inquiry. The man was moving in something like a daze; he had not yet found himself in this new alliance. He was hating himself for opposing Wint, and he was flogging his courage to the venture. He wondered what Kite and Jack Routt were doing together. Routt was a Caretall man in politics; also he was a friend of Wint. Chase tried to puzzle this out, and Kite asked again:

"What's happened?"

"I—spoke to Wint," Chase said slowly.

Routt asked: "About withdrawing his orders to Radabaugh? He'll never do it."

"No," said Chase. "He'll never do it."

Kite cried fiercely: "He's got to. He doesn't understand. Didn't you tell him, Chase? Didn't you make him see?"

"I couldn't make him see anything. He would not change."

"He'll never change unless he's forced to," Routt said; and Chase looked at the young man and asked slowly:

"I thought you and Wint were friends, Routt?"

"We are," Routt declared. "He's the best friend I've got. That's why I don't want to see him made a fool of. That's why I don't want to see Amos make a fool of him. You're his father, but you feel the same as I do, that he's wrong, that he's got to be made change his mind."

"I thought you were with Amos," Chase insisted mildly.

"Amos and I have broken," said Routt hotly. "He tried to trick me as he tricks every one, and I wouldn't stand for it. That's all. I'm out to even things with him."

Chase looked around for a chair and sat down. Routt sat on the desk. Kite had not risen when Chase came in. The little man asked Chase now: "What did you say to Wint anyway? I should think he'd take your advice before he'd take Caretall's."

"I told him Caretall was using him, that he was being used to play politics."

"Well, what did he say?"

"Said this wasn't Amos's doing at all. Said it was his own idea, that he had given the orders, that he meant to carry them through. Said, even if it were Caretall's move, it was a good thing, and he was for it."

Kite snarled: "He's damnably moral, all of a sudden." And Chase felt a surge of resentment at the other's tone, and countered:

"He's right, you know. Booze is dirty business."

"It's my business," Kite snapped, stamping to his feet; and if Routt had not intervened, the old feud between Kite and Chase might have been revived, then and there. But Routt had no notion of permitting a break between these strange allies. He said cheerfully:

"Sit down, Kite. We're not talking about booze. We're talking about Amos Caretall. We're not trying to settle the moral issue. We're trying to settle Amos Caretall's hash. Question is, how are we going to do it?"

"That's right," Chase agreed. Caretall's name was like an anchor, to which he could make fast his disturbed thoughts. So long as he was opposing Amos, he could not go wrong.

Kite sat down, thinking; and he asked: "You say Wint told you Amos had nothing to do with this, Chase?"

"Yes. He probably thinks that's true. Caretall got around him, somehow."

Routt said: "Caretall's a shrewd man, he can get around other men. He knows the trick of it." Kite said nothing. He was thinking over what Chase had said. Routt continued: "What we want to do is to go out and get him."

Chase suddenly found the atmosphere of this room unbearable; he wanted to get out in the air. So he got up, and said harshly: "I'm with you on that. I'll do anything I can against Amos. Let me know what you decide."

Routt said: "Don't run away. Let's talk things over." But Chase told him he had business elsewhere; and Kite made no objection to his going. When he was gone, Routt told Kite:

"He'll have to be handled carefully. He's naturally a dry man, you know."

Kite said thoughtfully, as though he were considering another matter: "Yes, that's so."

"I've been figuring on what you suggested—getting a handle to control Wint," Routt told him. "You know, I think there's a way."

"To get something on Wint?"

"Yes. He's not such a terribly upright young man. Any one's foot is apt to slip."

"You mean his has slipped?" Kite asked eagerly. Routt only grinned.

"I'll let you know what I mean, in good time," he said.

Kite grunted. It was evident that his mind was busy with another angle of the situation. A little later, still abstracted, he took himself away.

While he walked home, he turned over and over in his thoughts his new idea.

CHAPTER VI

EVERY MAN HAS HIS PRICE

KITE'S new idea was one that appealed to the mean heart of the man. There had been a time when Kite was bold as a lion in evil-doing; but as he grew old, he was becoming timorous. He had, now, no stomach for a fight, talk as ferociously as he pleased. He wanted life to move easily and smoothly; and fighting jarred on him. He thought, with a self-pitying regret, that things had been going so comfortably. It was a shame that Wint had come along and started all this trouble. He was an old man, not made for trouble.

There was very little pride in Kite, and a good deal of the shamelessness of the miser. If he was a miser, his illicit business was his hoarded gold. He was ready to go to any lengths of self-humiliation to protect this treasure. He would fight if he had to; but he had no stomach for it. There must be some other way.

The suggestion of that other way had come from Chase. When Chase first warned him that Amos would turn Hardiston dry, Kite had refused to believe; when Routt repeated the warning, he was still doubtful. When Wint actually gave the orders he had dreaded, Kite was half forced to agree that Amos had tricked him, but even in the face of the fact, he had still clung in his heart to the hope that this was none of Caretall's doing, and that the two who had warned him were wrong.

He had hoped desperately that they were wrong, because if they were mistaken there was a chance to save himself without a fight. What Chase had told him this night strengthened his hope. Wint, Chase said, declared Amos had nothing to do with the case, that Amos had neither advised nor prompted his orders to Radabaugh, and that the whole crusade was his own idea and his own battle.

If this were true, if Wint were actually standing on his own feet, then there was a chance of coming at him through Amos. That was the thought from which Kite took hope. He and Amos were, on the surface, allies still. Amos would not willingly antagonize him. And if this move of Wint's were not Amos's doing, then Amos might be willing to take a hand on Kite's behalf, call Wint off, return things to their original condition, smooth Kite's existence into tranquillity again.

When he first conceived the idea, Kite cast it aside as grotesque and impossible. But it returned to his thoughts, and his hopes fought for it, until he convinced himself there was something in it; better than an even chance in his favor; worth trying, certainly. When he made up his mind to this—it was after he had undressed and got into bed that night—he dropped off into a restless sleep; and when he woke, as his habit was, at daylight, he began at once to consider what he should say to Amos.

He telephoned Caretall before breakfast and asked him when he could see him to talk things over. Amos told him good-naturedly that he could come right after breakfast. "I'm taking my ease, these few days," he said. "Staying at home in my carpet slippers, and smoking my pipe. Drop in any time."

"I'll be there in an hour," Kite told him. And Amos said that was all right, and hung up the receiver. Immediately, he telephoned Peter Gergue to come right over, and Peter joined him at breakfast in ten minutes. It was not even necessary for old Maria to set an extra plate for Peter. Agnes had overslept—she nearly always did oversleep—and Amos was breakfasting alone, with Agnes's empty place across the table from him.

Peter sat down there, and Amos helped him to fried eggs and bacon, and Maria gave him a cup of coffee. Amos said at once: "Kite just called up, Peter. He's coming over."

Gergue swallowed a gulp of coffee. "Guessed he would," he assented. "Guessed he'd have things to say to you."

"What do you guess he's got to say to me, Peter?" Amos asked.

"He'll want you to call Wint off, I'd say."

Amos looked politely regretful, as though he were talking to Kite. "Why, now, you know, Wint's his own boss. He does what he wants to do. I never saw any one that could run Wint, did you?"

"Not if Wint knew it, I never did."

"What have you heard, Peter?" Amos asked. "What did Kite do yest'day, when he heard the sad news?"

"Lutcher told him," said Peter. "Lutcher says he was wild. But when Jim Radabaugh saw him, he kept his head, and said it didn't concern him. I hear he had some talk with Jack Routt; and then he posted off down to the furnace to see Chase."

"To see Chase, eh?"

"What I hear."

"What about, Peter?"

"I sh'd guess he wanted Chase to call Wint off. Kite don't like a fight, you know."

Amos nodded. "V. R. Kite," he said pleasantly, "is a lick-spittle, Peter. That's what V. R. Kite is. I don't like to see Chase mixing with him."

"You know," said Peter, "Chase has changed some, since you put the laugh on him."

"Chase is all right," said Amos surprisingly. "He's had the foolishness knocked out of him. Peter, he'll make a good man, before he's done."

Peter looked at Amos sidewise and said he wouldn't be a bit surprised.

"But he makes a mistake to tie up to Kite," said Amos.

"Him and Kite had a talk with Routt, in Jack's office, last night," said Peter.

Amos chuckled. "Pete, it beats me how you find out things."

"I don't find 'em out," said Peter. "People tell me." He rummaged through the tangle at the back of his neck. "Looks like people aim to make mischief, so they tell me things to tell you that'll start a fight, and the likes of that. That's the way of it."

"This won't start a fight," said Amos. "I'm home for a rest."

Peter looked at him intently. "You backing Wint?"

"No."

"What?"

"Pete," said Amos thoughtfully, "this was Wint's idea. He figured it out, the right thing to do. He's started it. It won't hurt him a bit to fight it out. I'm going to stand by and yell: 'Go it, wife; go it, b'ar.' That's me in this, Peter."

"What are you going to tell Kite?"

"Going to tell him just that," said Amos.

They had finished breakfast and moved into the sitting room and filled their pipes. Agnes came downstairs in her kimono, hair flying, and kissed Amos and pretended to be embarrassed at appearing before Peter in her attractive disarray. Then she went out to her breakfast. The two men smoked without speaking. Amos had looked after his daughter with a certain trouble in his eyes; and Peter saw it. Peter did not like Agnes.

Peter had gone before Kite arrived. Old Maria let Kite in, and Amos called from the sitting room:

"Right in here, Kite. I'm too darned lazy to come and meet you. Leave your hat in the hall."

Kite obeyed the summons, and Amos said lazily: "Take a chair, Kite. Any chair." And when the little man had sat down: "Fine day, Kite. I tell you, there isn't any place that can beat Hardiston in May that I know of."

Kite said: "That's right, Amos."

"Yes, sir," Amos repeated. "They can't beat old Hardiston." He lapsed into one of those characteristic silences, head on one side, squinting idly straight before him, his pipe hissing in his mouth. You might have thought there were no words in the man. Kite said impatiently:

"Amos, I want to talk to you."

Amos looked at him, and said amiably: "Well, Kite, you'll never have a likelier chance. I don't aim to move out of this chair."

"Well," said Kite uneasily, "I want to talk to you about young Chase."

"Mayor Chase?"

"Yes. Wint."

"Oh!" said Amos, without any curiosity.

"I mean to say," Kite explained, "I want to talk about this move of his. You've heard about it."

"I hadn't heard he'd moved," said Amos. "Thought he was living with his paw. Where's he gone to now?"

"Damn it, Amos!" Kite protested, "don't fool with me. You know what I mean."

"Kite," said Amos, "nobody ever knows what you mean, even when you say it. You're such an excitable man."

"Well, who wouldn't get excited? I tell you, this is a—"

"What is?" Amos asked, interrupting without seeming to do so.

"This damned idea of enforcing a fool liquor law."

"Oh, that," said Amos.

Kite leaned forward. "Is it your doing, Amos? Did you get him to do this? Because if you did—"

"Why, man," said Amos, "I'm not Wint's boss."

"You elected him."

"You elected him as much as me, Kite. And I heard how he called you a buzzard. If he calls you a buzzard, what do you think he'd call me?"

"I hold no grudge for that," Kite explained. "He was drunk. Fact remains, he's friendly with you. I ask you, I'm asking you flatly: Did you prompt him to do this, or tell him to, or advise him to in any way?"

"Well," said Amos, "if you ask me, I'll say: No."

Kite slapped his knee. "I knew it," he exclaimed.

"Who says I did?" Amos asked. "Wint say I did?"

"No. He says you didn't. Chase and Routt claim you did it."

"Chase? And Jack Routt? Why, now, I take that unkind," Amos protested, in a hurt voice, and Kite realized that he had blundered, and hurried past the danger point.

"Well, if you didn't advise Wint to do this, what are you going to do now? Back him in his fight?"

"You know," said Amos, "Pete Gergue asked me just that. Ever hear the story about the lady and the bear, Kite? Bear chased the lady around the tree, and the lady's husband was up the tree. Lady yells to him to come down and kill the bear; but husband just sets on his branch, out of reach, and yells: 'Go it, wife; go it, b'ar.' Ever hear that story, Kite?"

Kite chuckled without any mirth in his dry old eyes. "No," he said.

"That man didn't figure to play any favorites," Amos explained. "And neither do I. Ain't often I get a chance to set back and watch a fight. This time, I'm going to. On the sidelines. That's me, Kite."

Kite protested instantly. "That's not the fair thing, Amos. You and I worked together to put him in there, with the understanding he'd let the liquor business alone."

Amos lifted his hand. "Understanding was that Wint weren't likely to monkey with it. You thought so. That's why you was willing to help me. I didn't make any promises, nor any predictions, Kite."

"But, damn it," Kite insisted, "you ought to be willing to help me out. I helped you out."

"It would hurt me, Kite, to know I sanctioned nonenforcement."

"Nobody would know."

"They'd find out. Things like that do get out, you know, Kite."

The little man tugged at his side whiskers feverishly. "Amos," he pleaded, "isn't there anything you can do for me? This is bad business. I can't stand it. I won't stand it. Isn't there anything you can do?"

Amos considered, then he sighed, and said good-naturedly: "Kite, you're an awful pest, stirring me up when I'm comfortable."

"You've got to do something."

"We-ell, I'll tell you. I'll take you to see Wint. You can put it up to him. That's the best."

"You'll back me up?"

Amos shook his head. "You and him can have it out. I'll not yell for either of you."

Kite protested: "A lot of good that will do."

Amos shrugged his big shoulders. "Well...." Kite got up hurriedly.

"All right," he agreed, before Amos could withdraw his offer. "All right, come on."

Amos looked ruefully at his feet, and wiggled his toes in his comfortable slippers. "I declare, Kite, I hate to put on shoes."

"Damn it, man, it's your own offer," Kite protested; and Amos admitted it, and groaned:

"All right, I'll come."

Wint was in a cheerful humor, that morning. He had been depressed by his father's attitude, disappointed that the elder Chase chose to oppose him. But at the same time, the opposition exhilarated him. After his father left the house, he went to see Joan for an hour; and without over-applauding the step he had taken, she spoke of the trouble and the opposition he would face, and the prospect pleased Wint. He took a cheerful delight in opposing people. He was never so good-natured as when he was fighting.

So Amos and Kite found Wint amiably glad to see them both. Amos sat on the broad window ledge, his back to the light, his face somewhat shadowed. Wint made Kite sit down near his desk; he himself tilted his chair back against one of the leaves of the desk, and put his feet on an open drawer, and asked what their errand was.

"Kite wanted to see you," said Amos. "Asked me to come along."

"No need of that, Kite." Wint said good-naturedly. "I don't keep an office boy. Anybody can see me any time."

Kite shifted uneasily in his seat, not quite sure what he meant to say. Amos prompted him from the window. "Kite don't think you ought to shut down on him," he said.

Wint looked surprised. "Shut down on him? What's the idea, Kite?"

Kite said, in a flustered way: "It's not so personal as that. You know, I'm by conviction a believer in the sale of liquor. I believe the people of Hardiston agree with me. I'm sorry to hear you've taken steps to stop the sale."

"Why, no," said Wint cheerfully, "the town voted against it. I had nothing to do with that. I'm just enforcing the law."

Kite smiled weakly. "There are laws, and laws," he said. "Some laws are not meant to be enforced. The people of Hardiston objected to the open saloon; they did not object to the unobtrusive and inoffensive sale."

"Oh!" said Wint.

"You didn't object to it yourself," Kite reminded him. "Isn't that so?"

He expected Wint to be confused; but Wint only laughed. "I should say I didn't," he admitted. "I liked it as well as any one. Same time, this isn't a question of liking; it's a question of the law." He leaned forward with a certain jeering earnestness in his voice. "Why, Mr. Kite, if I didn't enforce the law, Hardiston people could remove me for misfeasance in office, or something like that."

Kite said: "Bosh!" impatiently. And Wint asked him suddenly:

"What's your interest in this?"

"That of a citizen."

"Oh, I know you don't sell it yourself," said Wint, meaning just the contrary. "But, Mr. Kite, if you have any friends in the business, tell them to get out of it. It's dead, in Hardiston. Dead and gone."

Kite said weakly: "Amos and I came here to try and make you change your mind about that."

Wint looked at Amos. "That so?" he asked. "You think I ought to back down?"

"'Go it, wife; go it, b'ar,'" said Amos cheerfully. "That's me."

"Not taking sides?"

"No."

Kite explained: "Amos and I worked together to elect you, you know."

Wint eyed him blandly. "Well, I'm much obliged. But I don't see what that has to do—"

"You owe us some gratitude."

"I'm grateful."

"There's a moral obligation."

Wint grinned. "Kite, I'm afraid you're an Indian giver. I'm afraid you elected me, thinking you could use me. But I didn't ask to be elected, so I don't see—"

Hopelessness was settling down on V. R. Kite; hopelessness, and the desperate energy of a cornered rat. There was no shame in him, and no scruple. Also, there was very little wisdom in the buzzard-like man. He was to prove this before their eyes.

"Wint," he said, "Amos and I are practical men. You're practical, too, aren't you? There's no place for dreams in this world, Wint. It's a hard world. You understand that."

"You find it a hard world? Why, Kite, I think the world is a pretty good sort of a place. That's the way it strikes me."

"I—"

"Maybe it's your own fault you find it hard."

Kite brushed the suggestion away. He was obsessed with a new idea, a last hope. He said: "Wint, if you drop this, Amos and I can do a lot for you."

"You and Amos?" Wint looked at Amos again. "How about it, Congressman?"

"'Go it, wife; go it, b'ar,'" Amos repeated imperturbably.

"What I mean," said Kite, "is that we can send you to the legislature, or anything."

"Why, I'm not looking for anything," said Wint mildly.

Kite snapped: "Every man has his price." And when he met Wint's level eyes, and knew he was committed, he went on hurriedly: "I know that. If politics isn't yours, something else is. Speak out, man. What do you—"

Wint asked curiously, and without anger: "What's the idea, Kite?"

"I could give you a start in business. Help you.... I'm a business man, you understand. Anything...."

Wint laughed. "You're too vague."

Kite looked at Amos. He looked at him so steadily that Amos got down from the window seat, and whistled softly under his breath, and walked out of the office into the council chamber above the fire-engine house. He shut the door behind him. Kite leaned toward Wint. "Five hundred?" he asked huskily.

Wint chuckled. "I say," he exclaimed, "I had no idea there was any money in this job."

"A thousand...."

"I've always wanted to know what it felt like to be bribed."

"A thousand, Wint? For God's sake...."

Wint shook his head, still perfectly good-humored. "There's no question about it, Kite," he said. "You surely are an old buzzard. Get out of my nest, you evil bird!"

Kite protested: "Wint, listen to—"

"Damn you!" said Wint, still without heat, "do you want me to throw you out the window?"

Kite got up. Wint had not even taken his feet down from their perch. Kite said: "You'll change your—"

Wint's feet banged the floor; and Kite stopped, and he went swiftly to the door. In the doorway, he turned and looked back, his dry old face working. He seemed to want to speak. But without a word, he turned and went away.

Amos strolled back in. Wint looked up at him and chuckled. But Amos looked serious.

"Went away all rumpled up, didn't he?" Wint commented. "But he didn't have a word to say."

Amos nodded. "Not a word to say," he agreed. "But, Wint," he added, "knowing Kite like I do, I wish he had."

"Wish he had had a word?"

"I never was much afraid of a barking dog," said the Congressman.

CHAPTER VII

ANOTHER WORD AS TO HETTY

IF Wint had expected immediate conflict, he was to be disappointed. For after Kite left his office that day, nothing happened; neither that day, nor the next, nor the next. Amos told Wint that Kite would strike, in his own time, and strike below the belt. Wint laughed and said he was ready to fight, foul or fair. But—neither foul blow nor fair was struck. Radabaugh reported that his orders had been obeyed. Lutcher had left town, temporarily, it was said. His rooms off the alley were locked, and he had gone so far as to give Radabaugh a key, so that the marshal might make sure, now and then, that Lutcher's store of drinkables was not disturbed. One shipment did come in for Mrs. Moody. It was labeled "Canned Goods"; but Jim Radabaugh made it his business to inspect all sorts of goods consigned to Mrs. Moody, and he found this particular box contained goods in bottles instead of cans. He emptied the bottles into the creek, across the railroad tracks from the station, and told Mrs. Moody about it. She threw a stick of firewood at him, then wept with rage because he dodged it successfully.

For the rest, Hardiston was quiet. The lunch-cart man whom Radabaugh had suspected took his cart and left town. Kite met Wint on the street and greeted him as pleasantly as usual. Jack Routt cultivated him, and joked him about his ideas of morality. One night, at Routt's home, he offered Wint a drink. Wint looked thoughtfully through the smoke of his pipe as though he had not heard. When Routt repeated the offer, Wint declined politely.

The business of being Mayor occupied very little of Wint's time. Early in June, Foster, the city solicitor, brought a stranger to see Wint about a street carnival which wanted to come to Hardiston the last week in June. Wint agreed to grant the permits necessary.

"You understand," he told the man, "that this is a dry town."

The stranger winked, and said he understood. Wint shook his head gravely. "I'm afraid you don't understand," he said. "This is a dry town. There's no booze sold here. Last summer, I remember, there was some selling in connection with your carnival, here. If you try that this time, I'll have to close you up."

The man looked surprised and disgusted. "What is this, a Sunday school?" he demanded.

"No," said Wint. "Just a dry town."

"How about the games?"

Wint smiled good-naturedly. "Oh, don't make them too raw. I've no objection to 'The cane you ring, that cane you get.'"

"Hell!" said the man. "We won't make chicken feed."

"You don't have to come."

But the stranger said they would come, all right. After he had gone, Wint told Foster the carnival would bear watching. Foster agreed, but said the merchants wanted it. "Brings the farmers to town every day, instead of just Saturday, you know."

"I know," said Wint. "Well, let them come."

After a week of quiet, Wint decided that Kite and his allies had put the lid on. "But they're just waiting," Amos warned him. "Waiting till they get a toe hold on you, somehow. Watch your step, Wint."

Wint said he was watching. "I wish they'd start something," he said. "Hot weather's dull, with no excitement."

"There'll be enough excitement," Amos assured him.

Routt walked home with Wint one afternoon, talking over a proposition that he had brought up a day or two before. Since Wint was going to be a lawyer, he said, they ought to go in together. Wint was already so well advanced in his reading that Routt thought in another year or eighteen months he could take the examinations. "There's a big practice waiting for the right people down here," he told Wint enthusiastically. "Dick Hoover and I are going to get together when his father dies. The old man is pretty feeble. You come in with us. We'll do things, Wint."

Wint was pleased and somewhat flattered by the suggestion, and thought well of Routt for it. But he only said, good-naturedly, that it was still a long way off, and that there would be times enough to talk about the matter when he was admitted to the bar. Nevertheless, Routt dwelt on it insistently, so insistently that instead of turning aside toward his own home at the usual place, he came on toward Wint's father's house, still talking. It did not occur to Wint that there was any purpose in Routt's thus accompanying him. He had heard that Routt and Kite had been seen together, and asked Jack about it. Routt explained that he had to keep in touch with all sorts. A mixture of business and politics, he said, and Wint was satisfied.

When they came in sight of the house, it was still an hour before supper time; and Hetty Morfee was sweeping down the front steps and the walk to the gate. They saw her while they were still half a block away, and Routt said casually:

"Hetty still working for your mother, I see."

Wint nodded. "Yes; I guess she's pretty good."

Routt agreed. "If she'd only keep straight. But...."

"I don't think she's that kind," said Wint.

"I hope not," Routt assented. "Hope she doesn't—get into trouble. If she ever did, in this town...."

Wint said nothing; and Routt added: "She'd need a friend, all right." And again: "She'd need some one to take her part. But he'd be in Dutch, whoever he was."

He looked at Wint sidewise. They were near the gate now, and Wint said: "Come in and have supper."

Routt shook his head. "Not to-night."

Hetty looked up, at their approach, and Wint called: "Hello, Hetty."

She said: "Hello, Wint." Routt repeated Wint's greeting, and the girl looked at him with curiously steady eyes, and said:

"Hello, Jack."

Wint thought, vaguely, that there was some repressed feeling in her tone; but he forgot the matter in bidding Routt good-by, and went inside, leaving Hetty at her task, while Routt went back by the way they had come. Hetty watched him go. He did not look toward her, did not turn his head. She watched him out of sight.

Jack Routt took Agnes Caretall to the moving pictures that night. Wint saw them there. He was with Joan. Afterward, Routt and Agnes walked home together.

Routt did most of the talking, on that homeward walk. Now and then Agnes seemed to protest, weakly, at something he was urging her to do. One near enough might have heard him speak of Wint. But there was no one near.

When they reached her home, there was a light in the sitting-room window. That meant Amos was there; and Routt said he would not go in. "But you'll remember, won't you, Agnes," he asked, "if you want to do something for me?"

She said softly: "I do want to do anything for you."

He laughed at her gently. "How about him?"

"I hate him," she said, with a sudden intensity that was not pretty to see. "I hate him. Hate him, I say."

"What's he ever done to you?" Routt teased; and she said:

"Nothing," as though that one word were an accusation.

Routt put his arm around her; and she clung to him with a swift, terrified sort of passion, as though afraid to let him go. It seemed to embarrass him; he freed himself a little roughly.

He left her standing there when he hurried away.

CHAPTER VIII

AGNES TAKES A HAND

IF Jack Routt had meant to force Hetty into Wint's thoughts, he had succeeded. Wint was not conscious of this when he left Jack at his gate; he was thinking of other things. But during supper, an hour later, when Hetty came into the dining room, Wint remembered what Jack had said; and he looked at the girl with a keen scrutiny. He studied her, without seeming to do so.

He was surprised to discover in how many ways Hetty had changed, since she came to work for his mother. The changes were slight, they had been gradual. But they were appallingly obvious, under Wint's cool appraisal now. He tallied them in his thoughts. Her laughter had been gayly and merrily defiant; it was sullen, now, and mirthless. Her eyes had twinkled with a pleasant impudence; they were overcast, these days, with a troubling shadow. There was a shadow, too, upon the clear, milky skin of her cheeks; it was a blemish that could neither be analyzed nor defined. Yet it was there.

Hetty had slackened, too. Her hair was no longer so smoothly brushed, so crisply drawn back above her ears. It was, at times, untidy. Her waists were no longer so immaculate; her aprons needed pressing, needed soap and water, too, at times. She had been fresh and clean and good to look upon; she was, in these days, indefinably soiled.

After supper that night, Wint went out into the kitchen where Hetty was washing dishes. He went on the pretext of getting a drink of water. There had been a time, a few months ago, when Hetty would have turned to greet him laughingly, and she would have drawn a glass of water and given it to him. But she did neither of those things now. Instead, she moved aside without looking at him, while he held the glass under the faucet; and when he stepped back to drink, she went on with her work, shoulders bent, eyes down.

Wint finished the glass of water, and put the glass back in its place. Then he hesitated, started to go, came back. At last he asked pleasantly: "Well, Hetty, how are things going?"

She looked at him sideways, with a swift, furtive glance. And she laughed in the mirthless way that was becoming habitual. "Oh, great," she said, and her tone was ironical.

"What's the matter?" Wint asked. "Anything wrong?"

"Of course not. Don't be a kid. Can't I have a grouch if I want to?"

"Sure," he agreed amiably. "I have 'em, myself. Anything I can do to bring you out of your grouch?"

"No."

"If there is," he said, so seriously she knew he meant his offer. "If there is, let me know. Maybe I can help."

"I'm not asking help," she told him sullenly.

"Is there anything definite? Anything wrong?"

She said, with a hot flash of her dark eyes in his direction: "I told you no, didn't I? What do you have to butt in for?"

Wint considered that, and he filled his pipe and lighted it; and at last he turned to the door. From the doorway he called to her: "If anything turns up, Hetty, count on me."

She nodded, without speaking; and he left her. He was more troubled than he would have cared to admit; and he was convinced, in spite of what Hetty had said, that there was something wrong.

The third or fourth day after, Hardiston meanwhile moving along the even tenor of its way, Wint decided, after supper at home, that he wanted to see Amos. He telephoned the Congressman's home, and Agnes answered. He asked if Amos was at home.

"He went uptown for the mail," Agnes told him. "But he said he'd be right back. He'll be here in a few minutes."

"Tell him I'm coming down, will you?" Wint suggested, and Agnes promised to do so. Wint took his hat and started for Amos's home. He thought of going through town on the chance of picking Amos up at the Post Office; but the mail had been in for an hour, and he decided Amos would have reached his home before he got there, so he went on. Wint and Amos lived on the same street, but at different ends of the town. The better part of a mile lay between the two houses. The stores and business houses were the third point of a triangle of which the Chase home and Amos's formed the other angles.

The night was warm and moonlit; a night in June. The street along which Wint's route lay was shaded on either side by spreading trees, and lined with the attractive, comfortable homes of Hardiston folks who knew what homes should be. Wint met a few people: A young fellow with a flower in his buttonhole, in a great deal of a hurry; a boy and a girl with linked arms; a man, a woman here and there. At one corner, in the circle of radiance from a sputtering electric light, a dozen boys were playing "Throw the Stick." Wint heard their cries while he was still a block or two away; he saw their shadowy figures scurrying in the dust, or crouching behind bushes and houses in the adjoining yards. As he passed the light, a woman came to the door of one of the houses and called shrilly:

"Oh-h-h, Willie-e-e-e!"

One of the boys answered, in reluctant and protesting tones; and the woman called:

"Bedti-i-ime." Wint heard the boy's querulous complaint; heard his fellows jeer at him under their breath, so that his mother might not hear. The youngsters trained laggingly homeward; and the woman at the door, as Wint passed, said implacably to her son:

"You go around to the pump and wash your feet before you come in the house, Willie."

The boy went, still complaining. And Wint grinned as he passed by. His own days of playing, barefoot, under the corner lights were still so short a time behind him that he could sympathize with Willie. Is there any sharper humiliation than to be forced to come home to bed while the other boys are still abroad? Is there any keener discomfort than to take your two dusty feet, with the bruises and the cuts and the scratches all crudely cauterized with grime, and stick them under a stream of cold water, and scrub them till they are raw, and wipe the damp dirt off on a towel?... Wint was half minded to turn back and join that game of "Throw the Stick." The bewildering moonlight, the warm air of the night had somewhat turned his head. It required an effort of will to keep on his way.

Agnes opened the door for him when he came to Caretall's home. "Dad'll be here in a minute or two," she said. "Come right in."

Wint hesitated. "Oh, isn't he home yet?"

"No, but he will be." She laughed at him, in a pretty, inviting way she had. "I won't bite, you know."

"I guess not," he agreed good-naturedly. "But it's a shame to go in the house, a night like this."

She said: "Wait till I get a scarf. Sit down. The hammock, or the chairs. I'll be right out."

So Wint sat down, where the moonlight struck through the vines about the porch and mottled the floor with silver. Agnes came out with something indescribably flimsy about her fair head; and Wint laughed and said: "I never could make out why girls think a thing like that keeps them warm."

"Oh, but it does," she insisted. "You've no idea how much warmth there is in it."

He shook his head, laughing at her. "That wouldn't keep a butterfly warm on the Sahara Desert."

She protested: "Now you just see...." And she moved lightly around behind him and wrapped the film of silken stuff about his head. "There," she said, and looked at him, and laughed gayly. "You're the funniest-looking thing."

Wint unwound the scarf gingerly. "It feels like cobwebs," he said. "I don't see how you can wear it. Sticky stuff."

"Men are always afraid of things like cobwebs. Always afraid of little things."

Wint chuckled. "What's this? New philosophy of life?"

"Can't I say anything serious?"

"Why, sure. I don't know but what you're right, too."

He had taken one of the chairs. She sat down in the hammock. "Come sit here with me," she invited. "That chair's not comfortable."

"Oh, it's all right."

She stamped her foot. "I should think you'd do what I say when you come to see me."

"Matter of fact, you know, I came to see your father."

"Well, you're staying to see me. If you don't sit in the hammock, I'm going in the house and leave you."

Wint held up his hands in mock consternation. "Heaven forbid." He sat down beside her, as uncomfortable as a man must always be in a hammock; and she leaned away from him, half reclining, enjoying his discomfort. He could see her laughing at him in the moonlight. She pointed one forefinger at him, stroked it with the other as one strops a razor.

"'Fraid to sit in the hammock with a girl," she taunted.

She was very pretty and provoking in the silver light; and Wint understood that he could kiss her if he chose. He had kissed Agnes before this. "Wink" and "Post Office" and kindred games were popular when he and Agnes were in high school together. But—he had no notion of kissing Agnes, moonlight or no moonlight. He had come to see Amos. Amos's daughter was another matter.

"When is Amos coming home?" he asked. "Has he called up? Maybe I'd better walk uptown."

"He called and said he was starting," she assured him. "You stay right here. He'll be here, unless he gets to talking some of your old politics. I suppose that's what you came to see him for."

"Oh, I just happened down this way...."

She sat up straight. "Good gracious. You act as though it were a secret. Tell me, this minute."

"Why, as a matter of fact," said Wint good-naturedly, "I want to talk to him about a sewer the city's going to put in through some land he owns. I guess you're not interested in sewers."

She grimaced, and said she should say not. "I thought maybe it was something about the bootleggers," she said. "Everybody's talking about them. What are you going to do to them?"

Wint laughed. "That's like the instructions for destroying potato bugs," he said. "First, catch your potato bug."

"You mean you haven't caught any?"

"Not yet."

"Are you trying to?"

"Why, we've got our eyes open."

"I love to hear about criminals and everything," she said. "What will you do to them when you get them? Send them to jail?"

"Well, I'll do that, if I can't do anything worse."

She asked: "You're really going to—you really mean to get after them?" He nodded, and she laughed. He asked:

"What's the joke?"

"Oh, it seems funny for you to be so moral about whisky and things."

He grinned. "It is funny, isn't it?"

"I should think they'd just laugh at you."

"Well, maybe they do."

"I suppose you're just going to give them a lesson, and then—sort of let things go, aren't you?"

Wint shook his head. "No, I sha'n't let things go. Not as long as I'm—in charge."

"But lots of people will be awfully mad at you. Why, even your father buys whisky and things, doesn't he?"

"Yes, I suppose so. But he doesn't sell them."

"Well, some one's got to sell them to him."

"They'll not sell in Hardiston," said Wint. He was a little tired of this. "Looks to me as though Amos has stopped to talk politics, after all. Did you tell him I was coming?"

"Oh, yes," she assured him. "He'll be right home." She got up abruptly. "There's some lemonade in the dining room," she said. "Would you like some?"

"Every time," he said. "It's warm enough to make it taste pretty fine, to-night."

She came out with a tall pitcher and two glasses, and filled his glass and her own. They lifted the glasses together, and Wint touched his to his lips. Then he took it down, and looked at it, and said:

"Hello!"

"What's the matter?" she asked.

"There's a stick in this, isn't there?"

"Yes. I always put a little in. Peach brandy. I love it."

"Peach brandy, eh?"

"Yes. Don't you like it?"

"Well, I've been letting it alone lately I guess I'll not."

"Oh, don't be silly, Wint," she protested, and stamped her foot at him. "I guess a little brandy won't hurt you!"

"No, probably not," Wint agreed. "But I'm on the wagon, you see."

"You make me feel as though I'd done something wrong to offer it to you."

"Why, no. Only, I...."

They were so interested that neither of them had heard Amos, and neither of them had seen him stop by the gate for a moment, listening to what they said. But when the gate opened, Agnes saw him, and the sight silenced her. Amos came heavily toward the house, and Agnes called to him:

"Wint's here, dad."

Amos said: "Oh! Hello, Wint!"

Wint said "Good evening." Amos was up on the porch by this time, and seemed to discover the lemonade.

"Hello, there," he exclaimed. "That looks pretty good. I'm hot. Pour me a glass, Agnes."

She hesitated; and Wint said: "Take mine."

"What's the matter with it?" Amos asked good-naturedly. "Poisoned?" He lifted the glass to his nose. "Oh, brandy, eh? Well, got anything against that?"

"Oh, I'm on the wagon, myself, that's all."

Amos nodded. "Well, I never touch it. Not lately. Take it away, Agnes."

His voice was gentle enough; but Wint thought the girl seemed very white and frightened as she faced her father. She took pitcher and glasses and went swiftly into the house. Amos turned to Wint, and sat down, and asked cheerfully:

"Well, young fellow, what's on your mind?"

When their business was done, and Wint had gone, Amos sat quietly upon the porch for a while. Then, without moving from his chair, he turned his head and called toward the open door:

"Agnes!"

She answered, from inside. He said: "Come here." And she appeared in the doorway. He bade her come out and sit down. She chose the hammock, lay back indolently.

Amos filled his pipe with slow care and lighted it. His head was on one side, his eyes squinted thoughtfully. If there had been more light, Agnes could have seen that he was sorely troubled. But she could not see. So she thought him merely angry; and grew angry herself at the thought.

He asked at last: "You offered Wint booze?"

"Just some lemonade," she said stiffly.

"Booze in it," he reminded her. "Don't you do that any more, Agnes."

"I guess a little brandy won't hurt Wint Chase," she told him.

"Don't you do it any more," he repeated, finality in his tones. She said nothing; and after a little he asked, looking toward her wistfully in the shadows of the porch: "What did you do it for, Agnes? What did you do it for, anyway?"

She shrugged impatiently. "Oh, I don't know."

"What did you do it for?" he insisted. There was an implacable strength in Amos; she knew she could not escape answering. Nevertheless, she evaded again.

"Oh, no reason."

"What did you do it for?" he asked, mildly, for the third time; and Agnes stamped to her feet. When she answered, her voice was harsh and hard and indescribably bitter.

"Because I wanted to get him drunk," she said. "He's so funny when he's that way. That's why."

She stared down at him defiantly; and Amos saw hard lines form about her mouth. Before he could speak, she was gone indoors.

Amos sat there for a long while, after that, thinking.... His thoughts ran back; he remembered Agnes as a baby, as a schoolgirl. She was a young woman, now.

He thought to himself, a curiously helpless feeling oppressing him: "I wish her mother hadn't've died."

CHAPTER IX

A WORD FROM JOAN

WINT found himself unable to put Hetty out of his mind, next day. He had overslept, was late for breakfast, and ate it alone with Hetty serving him. When she came into the dining room, he said:

"Good morning."

Hetty nodded, without answering. And he asked cheerfully: "Well, how's the world this morning?"

She said the world was all right; and she went out into the kitchen again before he could ask her anything more. Wint, over his toast and coffee, wondered. He was beginning to have some suspicion as to what was wrong with Hetty. But—he could not believe it. It wasn't possible. It couldn't be.

A certain burden of work shut down on him that day and the next, so that he forgot her in his affairs. He saw her every day, of course; but they were never alone together. His mother was always about. And there were other matters on Wint's mind. He was glad to be able to forget her. Wint, like most men, was willing to forget a perplexity if forgetting were possible. And Hetty kept out of his way, and seemed to resent his interest.

He met Agnes on the street one morning, and she stopped him and talked with him. She was very gay and vivacious about it, touching his arm in a friendly way now and then to emphasize some meaningless word. Her hand was on his arm thus when he saw Joan coming, a little way off. He did not know that Agnes had seen her some time before, without seeming to do so. Agnes discovered Joan now with a start of surprise, and she took her hand off Wint's arm in a quick, furtive way, as though she did not want Joan to see. Yet Joan must have seen. Wint was uncomfortably conscious that he had been put in an awkward light; but he supposed the whole thing was chance. Nothing more.

Agnes exclaimed: "Why, Joan, we didn't see you coming." Her words conveyed, subtly enough, the impression that if they had seen Joan coming, matters would have been different; and Wint scowled, and looked at Joan, and wondered if she was going to be so foolish as to mind. Then Agnes turned to him and said:

"Run along, Wint, I've something to say to Joan." And he looked at Joan, and thought there was pique in her eyes; and he went away in such a mood of sullen resentment as had not possessed him for months. It stayed with him all that day: he reverted into the prototype of the old, sulky, stubborn Wint who had made all the trouble.

Agnes and Joan walked uptown together, and Agnes chattered gayly enough. Agnes had always a ready tongue, while Joan was of a more silent habit. Agnes said Wint had come down to see her, a few days before.

"That is, of course," she explained, "he pretended he came to see dad. But he telephoned, and I told him dad wasn't at home, but he came anyway. We sat on the porch and drank lemonade. That night the moon was full. Wasn't it the most beautiful night, Joan? I think Wint's a peach. I always did. I never could see why you and he quarreled. Seems to me you were awfully foolish. I'll never have a fuss with him, I can tell you."

There was too much sincerity in Joan for this sort of thing; she was almost helpless in Agnes's hands. That is, she did not know how to counter the other girl's shafts. She did say: "Wint and I haven't really quarreled. We're very good friends."

Agnes nodded wisely, and said: "Oh, I know." She looked up at Joan. "Was it about that Hetty Morfee, Joan? I know it's none of my business, but I can't help wondering. I shouldn't think you'd mind that. Men are that way. I know it doesn't make a bit of difference to me. Not if—Well, I sha'n't quarrel with Wint over Hetty, I can tell you."

Joan had turned white. She could not help it; and Agnes saw, and added cheerfully:

"Of course, you can't believe half you hear, anyway. But they do say that she.... No, I'm not going to.... I never was one to tell nasty stories about people, Joan."

Joan could not say anything to save her life. She had to get away from Agnes, and she managed it as quickly as she could. She was profoundly troubled, profoundly unhappy. She had not realized how much Wint meant to her. The things which Agnes intimated made her physically sick with unhappiness at their very possibility. She finished her errands as quickly as she could, and hurried home. On the way, she passed Agnes and Jack Routt together, and they spoke to her, and she responded, holding her voice steady. She was miserably hurt and unhappy.

At home, she shut herself in her room to think. There was a picture of Wint on her bureau, a snapshot she had taken two or three years before. Wint had changed since then. The pictured face was boyish and round and good-natured; Wint's face now had a strength which this boy in the picture lacked. Wint was a man now, for good or ill.

She had, suddenly, a surge of loyal certainly that it was for good, and not for ill, that Wint was become a man. There was an infinite fund of natural loyalty in Joan; she had been prodded by Agnes into a panic of doubt, but when she was alone, this panic passed. A slow fire of anger at Agnes began to burn in her; anger because Agnes had meant to injure Wint, not because Agnes had hurt her. In Wint's behalf she took up arms; she considered Agnes; she questioned the girl's motives, she went over and over the incident, trying to read a meaning into it.

There is an instinctive wisdom in woman which passes anything in man. In that long day alone, thinking and wondering and questioning, Joan came very near hitting upon the whole truth of the matter. Nearer than she knew. She came so near that before Wint appeared that evening—he had arranged, a day or two before, to come and see her—she had begun to hate Jack Routt.

She did not know why this was so. She had never particularly liked Jack Routt; yet he had always been cheerful, an amiable companion, a good fellow. Also, he was Wint's friend, and Joan was loyal to Wint's friends as she was to Wint. But—All that day, she had thought, again and again, of Jack's eyes when she saw him with Agnes. She told herself there had been something hidden in them, something she could not define, something meanly triumphant. She mistrusted him; and before Wint came to her, she hated Routt. And feared him.

Nevertheless, she and Wint talked of matters perfectly commonplace for most of that evening together. They were apt to talk of commonplace things in these days; because safety lay in the commonplace. There was a strange balance of emotions between Wint and Joan. A little thing might have tipped it either way. At times, Wint wished to bring matters to an issue; he wished to cry out to Joan that he loved her. But he was restrained by a desperate fear that she was not ready to hear him say this. He was afraid she would cast him out once more. And—he could not bear the thought of that. It was something to be able to see her, talk with her, be near her. He dared not risk losing this much.

Thus they talked of ordinary matters, till Wint got up to go at last. Joan went out on the porch with him; he stopped, on one of the steps, a little below her. He had said good-by before Joan found courage. She asked, then:

"Wint! Will you let me?... There's something I want to ask you."

He was surprised; his heart began to pound in his throat. "To ask me?" he repeated. "Why—all right, Joan. What is it?"

"Are you and Routt pretty good friends, Wint?"

"Yes," he said, at once. "Jack's the best friend I've got."

"Are you sure?"

"Of course. What's the idea, Joan?"

She said reluctantly: "I don't know. Only—I don't seem to trust him. I don't like him. I'm afraid of him."

He laughed. "Good Lord! Jack's harmless; he's a prince."

"I don't think he's as loyal to you as you are to him," she said.

Wint exclaimed impatiently: "The way you girls get down on a fellow! Jack's all right."

Wint's impatience made Joan quieter and more sure of herself. "I'm not sure," she repeated, and smiled a little wistfully. "Just—don't trust him too far, Wint."

"I'd trust him with all I've got," Wint said flatly. "I think you're—I'm surprised at you, Joan." The stubborn anger roused in the morning when Joan came upon him with Agnes reawoke in Wint. His jaw set, and his eyes were hard.

Joan was troubled; she wanted to say more, but she did not know how. And—she could not forget Hetty. She had not meant to speak to Wint of Hetty; but Joan was woman enough to be unable to hold her tongue. Also, Wint's loyalty to Routt had angered her; she was willing to hurt him—as men and women are always willing to hurt the thing they love. She said slowly:

"Did you know people are beginning to talk about Hetty Morfee, Wint? You and Hetty!"

Wint's anger flamed; he flung up his hand disgustedly. "You women. You're always ready to jump on each other. Why can't this town let Hetty alone?"

"I only meant—" Joan began.

"I don't care what you meant," Wint told her. "You ought not to pass gossip on, Joan. I hate it."

"I don't see why you have to defend her," she protested; and he said hotly:

"I'm not defending her. She doesn't need defending. If she did, I would, though. Hetty's all right."

Joan drew back a little into the shadow of the porch. After a moment, she said:

"Good night, Wint."

He said harshly: "Good night. And for Heaven's sake, forget this foolishness. Routt and Hetty.... They're all right."

She did not answer. He said again: "Good night," and he turned and went down to the gate, and away.

Joan watched him go. She thought she ought to be angry with him, and hurt. She was surprised to discover that she was rather proud of Wint, instead; proud of him for being angry, even at her, for the sake of his friend, and for the sake of Hetty.

She was troubled, because she thought he was wrong; but she was infinitely proud, too, because he had stuck by his guns.

CHAPTER X

THE STREET CARNIVAL

JOAN'S warning as to Jack Routt, her word as to Hetty, and Wint's rejection of both warning and advice did not lead to a break between them. They met next day, and Wint had the grace to say to her:

"I'm sorry I talked as I did yesterday, last night. I was tired, and—all that. I'm sorry."

"It's all right," Joan told him. "It's natural for you to stick by your friends."

"I needn't have talked so to you, though."

She laughed, and said he had been all right. "I guess you've been imagining you were worse than you really were," she told him. "It's quite all right, really."

"But I'm sorry you—dislike Jack," he said. "He's an awfully decent sort."

"Is he?" she asked. "Then I'm glad you and he are friends."

"That's the stuff," Wint told her. "That's the way to talk."

Thereafter, for a week or so, life in Hardiston went quietly. V. R. Kite still bided his time; there was no liquor being sold; Ote Runns went home sober, day after day, with a look of desperate longing in his eyes. That sodden man who had embraced Wint in the Weaver House so long, whom Wint had jailed more than once for his drinking, suffered as much as Ote, or more. He came to Wint and unbraided him for what he had done. "It ain't the way to treat a fellow," he told Wint, pleading huskily. "You know how it is. I just gotta have a drink, Mister Mayor. I just gotta. I told Mrs. Moody she's gotta give me a drink, and she told me you wouldn't let her. You ain't got a thing against me, now, have you?" The miserable man's fingers were twitching, his lips twisted and writhed. "If I don't get a drink, I'm a-going to kill some-buddy, I am."

Wint did not know what to do. He could see at a glance that the man was suffering a very real torment. He had himself never become so soaked with alcohol that his system cried out for it when he abstained; but he knew what torture this might be. He had an idea that candy would alleviate the man's distress; but the idea seemed to him ridiculous, and he put it aside. Yet there was an obligation upon him to do something.

He did, in the end, a characteristic thing, an impulsive thing; and yet it was sensible, too. There was no saving this man. Highest mercy to him was to let him drink himself to death. Wint told him to come to the house that night; and he gave the poor fellow a quart bottle from his father's store. The derelict wandered away, calling Wint blessed. They found him under a tree in the yard next door, in the morning, blissfully sleeping.

The story got around, as it was sure to do. The man told it himself; he boasted that Wint was a good fellow. V. R. Kite heard of it, and waved his clenched fists and swore at Wint by every saint in the calendar. Also, he sent for Jack Routt. "We've got him," he cried. "He can't put over a thing like this on me, Routt. I'll not stand for it. I'll run him out of town. Or get out myself. Damn it, Routt, he's a hypocrite! He's a whited sepulcher. I'll—"

Routt laughed good-naturedly, and held up a quieting hand. "Hold on," he said. "We'll have better than this on Wint before long. Good enough so that I—I'll tell you a secret, Kite."

Kite looked suspicious, and asked what the secret was; but Routt decided not to tell. Not just yet. "Wait till the time comes," he told Kite. "A little later on."

So Kite waited.

Toward the end of June, the street carnival came to town for a week's stay. These carnivals are indigenous to such towns as Hardiston. They resemble nothing so much as an aggregation of the added attractions which usually go with a circus, broken loose from the circus and wandering about the country alone. A merry-go-round reared its tent and set up it clanking organ at Main and Pearl streets. Down the hill below the tent, the snake-eating wild man had his lair; and below him, again, there was an "Ocean Wave." Along Pearl Street in the other direction the Museum of Freaks and the Galaxy of Beauty were located. Main Street itself was given over to venders of popcorn, candy, hot dogs, ice-cream sandwiches, lemonade, ginger pop, and every other indigestible on the calendar. There also, you might, for the matter of a nickel, have three tries at ringing a cane worth six cents, or a knife worth three. Or you might take a chance in the great lottery, where every entrant drew some prize, even if it were only a packet of hairpins. The arts and crafts were represented by a man who would twist a bit of gilded wire into likeness of your signature for half a dollar.

The first tents of the carnival began to rise one Saturday morning; and all that day and the next, the boys of the town and the grown-ups, too, watched the show take shape. It was almost as good as a circus. At noon on Monday, the carnival opened for business, with the ballyhoo men in full voice before every tent. The moderate afternoon crowd grew into a throng in the evening, when the kerosene torches flared and smoked on every pole, and the normal things of daylight took on a dusky glamour in the jerky illumination of the flares.

Every one went uptown to the carnival that first evening. Wint was there, and Jack Routt, Agnes, Joan, V. R. Kite—every one. In mid-evening, the quieter folk drifted home, but Wint stayed to watch what passed. A little after eleven, he bumped into a drunken man.

In spite of his warning to the advance agent of this carnival, Wint had been expecting to see drunken men. It was the nature of the carnival breed. He wandered back and forth till he came upon Jim Radabaugh, and called the marshal aside.

"Jim," he said, "they're selling booze."

Radabaugh shifted that lump in his cheek, and spat. "So?" he asked mildly.

"I want it stopped," said Wint. "If you pin it on the carnival bunch, I'll shut them up."

"I'll see," Radabaugh promised.

"Come along, first, and let's talk to the boss," Wint suggested; and they sought out that man. He was running the merry-go-round; a hard little fellow with a cold blue eye. Wint introduced himself; and the man shook hands effusively.

"My name's Rand," he said. "Mike Rand. Glad t' meet you, Mister Mayor."

Wint said: "That's all right," and he asked: "Did your advance man give you my orders?"

"What orders?"

"I told him I didn't want any booze peddling."

"Sure, he told me."

Wint jerked his head backward toward Main Street. "I ran into a drunk up there," he said.

Rand grinned. "Can't help that. We're not selling any."

"I'm holding you responsible," said Wint. "If there's any sold, I'll cancel your permits."

The little man stared at him bleakly. "You've got a nerve. You can't pin anything on us."

"I can't help that," Wint told him. "In fact, I don't care. If there's booze sold, you get out. If I pin in on any man, he goes to jail. Is that clear?"

"What is this town, anyway—a damned Sunday school?"

"If you like," said Wint sweetly; and he and Radabaugh turned away. Rand's engine man left his throttle to approach his chief and ask:

"What's up? Who was that?"

"Mayor of this burg and the marshal. Say we've got to shut down on the booze."

"Like hell!"

Rand grinned. "Sure. He can't run a whoozer on me."

When he left Radabaugh, Wint ran into Jack Routt, and they strolled about together through the crowd. Once they saw Hetty, and Wint thought she was unnaturally cheerful and gay. He wondered if it were possible she had been drinking again; and he stared after her so long that Routt asked:

"Takes your eye, does she?"

"I was wondering," said Wint.

Routt touched his arm. "You take it from me, Wint, you want to keep clear of her. I'd get her out of the house, if I were you. They're beginning to talk."

Wint asked angrily: "Who's beginning to talk? What about?"

"Everybody. About Hetty—and you, naturally."

"I wish they—I wish people in this town would mind their own business."

Routt grinned and said: "You act as though there was something in it."

"Don't be a darned fool."

"Well, I'm telling you what people say. If I were you—you're a public official, you know, in the public eye—I'd be careful. Tell your mother to get rid of her. Safest thing to do."

"I'm not looking for safe things to do." Wint liked the defiant sound of that.

Routt nodded. "I'd be worried, if it was me. That's all."

"I'm not worried," said Wint. "Hetty's all right. And if she weren't—I don't propose to be scared."

"We-ell, it's your funeral," Routt told him.

Wint laughed. "I guess it's not as bad as that. It's almost twelve. I'm going home."

CHAPTER XI

FIRST BLOOD

IT was upon the carnival that Wint was to score first blood in his fight to clean up Hardiston. Mike Rand, carnival boss, was a hard man, willing to take a chance, afraid only of being bluffed. So he took Wint's warning as a challenge. Nevertheless, for the sake of making things as sure as might be, he went to see V. R. Kite. He and Kite had known and understood each other for a good many years.

He dropped in to see Kite Tuesday morning; and the little man remembered his church connections and his outward respectability, and worried for fear some one had seen Rand come in. His worry took the form of resentment at Rand's imprudence. "Ought to be more careful," he protested. "Have more sense, man. I have to watch myself in this town. Don't you know that? I have a position to keep up. You're all right, of course." This as Rand's eyes hardened in a stare that made Kite wince. "But I can't afford to be hitched up with you openly. It wouldn't do either of us any good."

Rand said dryly: "You don't need to worry about me. I can stand it."

"I can be useful to you now, whereas my usefulness would be gone if I were less respected."

"Respected, hell!" said Rand without emotion. "Don't they call you 'The Buzzard' around here? I've heard so. That don't sound respectful."

"That's a jest," said Kite. "Nothing more."

"Pinned on you by this shrimp Mayor, wasn't it?"

"Yes. Good-naturedly. He was drunk."

"Drunk? Him?" Rand lifted his hands in pious horror. "I thought he was one of these 'lips-that-touch-liquor-shall-never-touch-mine' guys, to hear him talk."

"He's not drinking now; not openly. He was a sot, a few months ago. Dead drunk in the Weaver House, the night he was elected Mayor. I saw him there."

Rand drawled: "I'll say this is some town." He leaned forward. "What I want to know is: how about this booze? He serves notice on me that I'm responsible if any's sold. How about it? Will he go through? Or is it a bluff?"

Kite considered. "I don't know," he said.

"Has he shut you down?"

"He gave us orders not to sell; and we're not selling. But we're not idle. We're preparing to spring a mine under that man."

"He's got you bluffed."

Kite's face twisted with a sudden rush of fury. "I tell you, we're going to destroy him—blast him!—in our own good time."

Rand studied the little man; then he nodded. "Well, that's all right. Just the same, he's got you shut down."

"Yes."

"Has he pulled any one yet for selling?"

"No."

"How about the marshal? Is he reasonable?"

"I believe he will obey the Mayor's orders."

"Only question is the Mayor's nerve, then?"

"Yes."

"And you haven't tried it out?"

"No; we're waiting to strike when we're sure of winning."

"Hell!" said Rand disgustedly. "He's got you bluffed. I don't believe he's got the nerve to go through with it; but one thing's sure. He's got your number, you old skate."

Kite answered hotly: "If you're so brave, why don't you go ahead and fight him?"

"Are you with me?"

"I'm not ready to fight."

Rand got up. "Well, I am. I never dodged a fight yet. You watch, old man; you'll see the fur fly yet."

He stalked out, head back and shoulders squared aggressively. Kite watched him go, and nodded to himself with a measure of satisfaction. He was perfectly willing to see Wint forced to fight—provided some one besides himself did the forcing. Rand looked like a fighter.

Wint and Jack Routt met, on the way uptown after supper that day. Routt asked if Wint were going to the carnival again, and Wint nodded. "Keeping an eye on it," he said.

They went to the Post Office first; and Routt stopped at his office. "Come up," he said. "I'll only be a minute."

Wint went up with him. Routt dropped a letter or two on his desk; then from a lower drawer produced a bottle. "Don't mind if I mix myself a highball, do you, Wint?" he asked cheerfully. "I don't suppose you'll feel called on to arrest me."

"Go ahead," Wint said. Routt poured some whisky into a glass, filled it from a siphon.

"You're wise to leave the stuff alone," he said, between the first and second sips from the glass. "It's bad stuff unless a fellow can handle it."

Wint nodded uneasily. There was no physical craving in him; nevertheless there was an acute desire to drink for the sake of drinking, for the sake of being like other men, for the sake of defying the danger. "That's right," he said. "I'm off it."

"At that," Routt remarked, the highball half gone, "I guess you've shown you can take it or let it alone. I lay off of it myself, once in a while, just to be sure I can."

"Oh, I don't miss it," Wint said brazenly.

"Sure you don't," Routt agreed. "You're no toper. Never were. Any one likes to drink for the sake of being a good fellow. That's all I drink for." He finished the glass, poured in a little more whisky. "Long as I'm sure I can stop when I want to, the way you have done, I go ahead and drink whenever I feel like it."

Wint nodded. Routt looked at him with a curious intentness. "Another glass here, if you'd like," he said.

"I guess not."

Routt laughed. "All right. You know best. If you can't let it alone when you get started—"

"Oh, I can take a drink and quit."

"Want one?"

"No, I don't think so."

Routt chuckled. "Funny to see you afraid of anything," he said. "I never expected to see it."

Wint got up abruptly. The old Wint would have reached for the bottle; this was the new Wint's impulse. But he fought it down, steadied his voice. "Jack," he said, a little huskily, "you're a friend of mine. I don't want to drink, never. Don't offer it to me. Some day I might accept. Don't ever offer me a drink, Jack. Please."

Routt was ashamed of himself, and angry at Wint for making him ashamed. "Hell, all right," he said, and dropped the bottle into its place. "Come on, let's take the air."

At a little after eleven that night, Mike Rand sought out Wint. Wint was standing before the cane booth, watching the ring-tossers. Rand pushed up beside him and touched his arm, and Wint looked around. The carnival boss said harshly:

"Hey, you!"

Wint looked around at him, and said quietly: "Evening. What's the matter?"

"Your damned hick marshal has pulled one of my men. I want to bail him out."

Wint took a minute to consider this, get his bearings. He had not seen Radabaugh all evening. He asked Rand: "You mean he's made an arrest? What's the charge?"

"Claims the man was selling booze to a bum."

"Was he?" Wint inquired gently.

"Was he" Rand growled. "No, of course not. You must think we're bad · men, coming here to dirty your pretty little town. He was selling liver pills, or pink tea. What the hell of it? I want to bail him out."

"No bail accepted," said Wint quietly. "He'll have to stay in the calaboose over night."

Rand exploded, as though he had been half expecting this. He said some harsh things about Hardiston, and some harsher things about Wint, none of which will bear repeating. In the midst of them, Wint stirred a little and struck the man heavily in the mouth with his right fist; at the same time, his left started and landed in the other's throat, and the right went home again on Rand's hard little jaw. Rand fell in a snoring heap.

Wint was curiously elated. He looked around. A crowd had gathered, and some of the carnival men were pushing through the crowd. There was a belligerent look about them. Then he saw Marshal Jim Radabaugh elbowing through the circle, and Wint was glad to see Jim. He called him:

"Marshal, here's a man I've arrested."

That halted Rand's underlings. Rand himself was groaning back to consciousness. Wint pointed down at him. "Take him to jail," he said.

One of the carnival men protested. Wint turned to him. "Close up your shows, all of you," he told the man. "Your permit's cancelled. Get out of town to-morrow."

Radabaugh had Rand on his feet; he gripped the man, his left hand twisted in the other's collar. Two or three of Rand's men surged toward them, and Radabaugh's gun flickered into sight. It had a steadying effect; no one pressed closer.

All the fighting blood had flowed out of Rand's smashed lips. He was whining now: "Come, old man, what's the idea?" Wint and Radabaugh marched him between them through the crowd. Two or three score curious, cheering or cursing spectators followed them to the cells behind the fire-engine house. Rand submitted to being locked up there with no more than querulous protests. He seemed thoroughly tamed. He asked for a lawyer, but Wint said there was no need of a lawyer that night. Two of the fire department, on duty, had come out to see the business of locking up this second prisoner. Radabaugh bade them keep an eye on the cells, and they agreed to do so. Then the marshal scattered the crowd. Wint washed his bruised hands in the engine house. After a little, Radabaugh came in; and Wint asked:

"Is it true you got a man selling?"

"Yes. The capper at the lottery."

"How'd you get him?"

Radabaugh chuckled, and shifted the lump in his cheek.

"Saw Ote Runns," he said. "Figured Ote would nose out any loose booze, so I kind of kept an eye on Ote. He talked to two or three men, and finally to this fellow. They went in behind the billboard by the hotel, and I saw him slip Ote the bottle and take Ote's money. So I nabbed him."

"Ote? Get him too?"

"Yes; him and his half pint. I let him keep it. He was pretty shaky. Needed it, I guess."

Wint nodded. "Be around in the morning?" he asked. "I'll be down early."

Radabaugh assented. Wint hesitated, then he said: "Good work, Jim."

The marshal grinned. "Well," he told Wint, "from the looks of Rand's face, you did some good work, too."

They shook hands. There was a distinctly mutual liking and admiration in their grip. Then Wint started for home, and Radabaugh went back to keep an eye on his prisoners.

One of Rand's men went to V. R. Kite with the news of the trouble; and Kite, uncertain what to do, sent for Jack Routt and told him what had happened. This was at midnight. "I've got to stand by Rand," Kite said. "The question is, are we ready to get after Wint?"

Routt shook his head. "Time for that. Hold off," he advised.

Kite asked impatiently: "How long? What makes you think you can get anything on him?"

"It's ripe," said Routt. "Apt to break any time. I've been working on it."

In the end, he persuaded Kite to wait. "Well, then," Kite asked, "what are we going to do about Rand?"

"He's got to take his medicine."

"He won't. He'll fight."

"I'll tell you," said Routt. "I'll go see him. Fix it up with him."

"Can you do it without Wint's finding out?"

Routt laughed. "I'm a lawyer. I've a right to have clients, even in the Mayor's court. I'll take their case."

Kite, in the end, agreed to that. When Routt left the little man, he intended to go direct to the jail; but on the way, he changed his mind. As well to let the men cool their heels. It would make Rand more ready to listen to reason.

He went up Main Street toward the carnival, and found that the tents were coming down, one of Radabaugh's officers keeping a watchful eye on the proceedings. Wint's orders that the shows be closed could not be evaded. This much, at least, he had scored. Routt went home and did some thinking.

He appeared at the jail half an hour before Wint came to hold court; and Radabaugh let him talk with Rand and with the other man. When Wint appeared, the two were brought into court, with Ote Runns as a witness, for good measure. Wint was surprised to see Routt. Jack nodded to him, and came up to Wint's desk, and said: "Rand sent for me. Wanted me to take his case. He knows he's licked, I think. He'll take his medicine, if you don't make it too stiff."

"I'm charging him with assault and with using profane language," said Wint.

"Assault?" Routt laughed. "Thought it was you that did the assaulting."

"He made threats. Threats constitute an assault. You know that as well as I do."

Routt nodded. "Oh, sure." He added: "You know, the carnival's shut up. It's costing Rand money. You might go as light as you can."

"I'm going to give the other man the limit," said Wint.

"That's all right," Routt agreed. "Rand's sore at him for getting caught. He'll let the poor gink take his medicine."

Wint nodded abstractedly. Foster, the city solicitor, had just come in, and Wint beckoned to him, and asked: "What's the worst I can do on a charge of illegal liquor selling?"

"Two hundred dollars' fine on the first offense," Foster told him.

Three minutes later, the offender was protesting that he could not pay such a fine; he was appealing desperately to Rand. Wint bade the carnival boss stand up. Rand got to his feet.

"I'm sorry for this business," he said humbly. "I thought you were just trying to save your face. Running a bluff."

"Are you paying his fine for your friend?" Wint asked coldly.

Rand said: "No, blast him! If he wants to get caught by a hick constable, let him take his medicine. Work it out."

"I wouldn't call Radabaugh a hick to his face," Wint suggested in a mild voice, and Rand apologized.

"I didn't mean a thing," he said.

Wint, in a swift hurry to be done, told him: "You're fined ten for assault, and five for profanity. And costs."

"That's all right," Rand cheerfully agreed. "I'll pay."

Wint nodded, disgusted at the man because he submitted so tamely. He sat back in his chair, listening idly to what Routt was saying, paying no apparent heed. Rand settled his fines and costs with the clerk, shook hands with Routt, and departed. When he was gone, Wint sat up with new energy.

"I hope we're rid of him for good," he said.

"You are, I'll say," Routt told him. "He's had all he wants."

The carnival got out of town that day; but before he departed, Rand had a word with Kite, and Kite comforted him. "Don't worry," Kite said. "This won't last. You'll make a harvest here, next summer."

Rand said ruefully: "I'm not making any harvest now. And they tell me you helped elect this guy."

"He was a common drunk, then. How could I know?"

Rand fingered his swollen face gingerly. "I'll say he's got a punch."

"He won't have any punch left when we're done with him," Kite promised. "Wait and see."

"I'm waiting," said Rand. And a little later, he and his cohorts went their way.

CHAPTER XII

POOR HETTY

IN mid-July, Wint at last found out the truth about Hetty. That is to say, he found out a part of the truth; enough to make him heartsick and sorry.

His eventual enlightenment was inevitable as to-morrow morning's sunrise. A more sophisticated young man—Jack Routt, for example—would not have remained in the dark so long. But Wint, aside from noticing that Hetty looked badly, and aside from some casual consideration of Routt's repeated warnings, gave very little thought to his mother's handmaiden. There were too many other and more important things to occupy him. His work as Mayor, his studies, his Joan. Joan was bulking very large in his life in those days. He found understanding, and sympathy, in her. They were better than sweethearts; they were friends. The other—this thought must have been lying, unspoken, in the mind of each—the other could wait and must wait till Wint had proved himself for good and all. Then.... Once in a while, Wint allowed himself to look forward, and to dream. But not often. The present was too engrossing to give much time for dreaming of the future.

So, though he saw Hetty daily, when she served the meals at home, or when he went into the kitchen, or when he encountered her at her cleaning in the front part of the house, Wint gave her very little consideration. His mother protested, once in a while, that Hetty was growing lazy. "She slacks things," the voluble little woman said. "She leaves dust about; and she's not so neat as she used to be. I declare, you just can't get a girl that will keep up her work. They all get so lazy after a while, but I did think that Hetty was going to be—"

Wint's father said, tolerantly, that Hetty was all right; that she was a good cook, and did her work well enough, so far as he could see. The elder Chase had always been a good-natured man; but a new generosity in his appraisal of others was developing in the man now. He had been in some trouble of mind since that day in May when Amos Caretall came home. Chase was oppressed by the conviction that he had acted unworthily in that matter; yet he could not admit as much. His hostility toward Amos would not let him. The result was that he felt at odds with his son; that they avoided discussions of the town's affairs; that they lived together in a polite neutrality. It was working changes in Chase. He was becoming, in some fashion, a sympathetic, rather likable figure. You felt he was unhappy, needed comforting.

So, on this day, he spoke well of Hetty; and because Mrs. Chase was always the loyal mirror of her husband's opinions, she also ceased to criticize the girl. Wint had heard the conversation, but it made little impression on him. He was thinking of other things; wondering, for example, when Kite would make the first move in the conflict that was sure to come. He had heard, that day—Gergue told him—that Routt was thinking of running for Mayor against him in the fall. Wint was having difficulty in understanding that. He knew Routt was his friend; and, of course, political opponents might still be personal friends. Nevertheless.... The thing puzzled him. It did not jibe with his opinion of Routt.

After supper that night, the elder Chase went downtown. Wint had some writing to do, and went upstairs to his room to do it. Mrs. Chase had a caller, Mrs. Hullis, from next door. They were sewing and talking together in the sitting room. Wint could hear the murmur of his mother's voice, steady and persistent. Mrs. Hullis was a good listener.

About an hour after supper, Wint realized that he wanted a drink of water. There was water in the bathroom; but there was a filter on the faucet in the kitchen, and Hardiston water needed filtering. It was pure enough, clean enough, but there was a proportion of iron in it that sometimes gave the water a slightly rusty color. So Wint went down by the back stairs, in order not to disturb his mother, into the kitchen.

He found Hetty sitting in a kitchen chair with her arms hanging limply and her feet outstretched before her. The girl's whole body was slumped down, as though she had fainted; and at first Wint thought this was what had happened, for Hetty's eyes were closed. He cried out:

"Why, Hetty? What's the matter? Are you sick?"

And he went quickly toward her across the kitchen.

But when he spoke, Hetty opened her eyes and looked at him, and shook her head. "No," she said, in the sullen tone that had become habitual to her. "No, I'm all right."

"You are not," Wint protested. "You're as white as a rag." He saw the dishes piled in the sink. "You've not cleaned up after supper. How long have you been this way?"

Hetty closed her eyes wearily, and opened them again, and managed a smile. "Oh, I'm all right, Wint," she said. "You're a nice boy. Run along. Don't bother about me."

Wint laughed. "I'm not bothering. I want to help. What happened?"

"I—just felt terribly tired—all of a sudden," she said. There was a suggestion of surrender in her voice; as though the barriers of reserve were breaking down. "That's all, Wint; I'm just tired."

"You need a rest," Wint agreed. "You've been plugging away, taking care of us, for a long time, now. Come in and lie down on the couch in the dining room."

Hetty shook her head in a frightened little way; the bravado was going out of her. She seemed very helpless and feminine. "No, no," she protested. "I'll be all right as soon as I rest a little. Do run along, Wint."

Wint put his hand on her forehead. "There's more than just being tired the matter with you. You're sick, Hetty. Your head's hot. I'll tell you, you go up and go to bed, and I'll clean up down here. I'm a champion dish washer."

Hetty laughed wearily. "You're a champion decent boy, Wint," she said. "But you'll just have to let me alone. There's nothing you can do for me."

"I can see that you go up to bed."

"No, no; I'm all right. Nearly."

Wint started for the door. "I'm going to telephone for a doctor," he declared. "You're sick, Hetty. That's the plain English of it. I'm going to telephone."

She had moved so swiftly that she startled him; moved after him, caught his arm, shook it fiercely. "You'll not telephone for any one, do you hear?" she told him hotly. "You let me alone, Wint. What do I want with a doctor!"

Wint was honestly uneasy about her. He said: "Then let me call mother. She's a good hand to make sick people well. She—"

"No, no, not your mother," Hetty protested. And half to herself she added: "Not your mother. She would know."

The little phrase was profoundly revealing. "She would know." It struck Wint like a splash of cold water in the face. "She would know." It told so old a story. Wint understood, at last; and Hetty saw understanding in his eyes, and braced herself to defy him. But Wint only said softly:

"Hetty? That.... You poor kid! I'm so sorry."

Hetty laughed harshly; and her face began to twist and work and assume strange contortions, and abruptly she began to cry. She turned and groped her way to the chair again, and sat down with her head pillowed on her arms on the table, and sobbed as though her heart was broken. Wint stood very still, stunned and miserable, watching her. There was no sound at all in the kitchen except the sound of Hetty's racking, choking sobs. In the stillness, Wint could hear the even murmur of his mother's voice, three rooms away, as she talked to Mrs. Hullis. He could almost hear the words she said. And Hetty sobbed, with her head on her arms.

Wint went across to her and touched her head with his hand; and she brushed it away with an angry gesture, as a hurt dog snarls at the hand that comes to heal its hurt. She was like a hurt animal, he thought; she was quite alone in the world. Worse than alone, for she was here in Hardiston, where every one would make her business their business. For that is the way of small towns. Wint was terribly sorry for her, terribly anxious to help her. He had no thought, in this moment, of Jack Routt's warnings; and if he had remembered them, they would only have hardened his determination to help her. Which may have been what Jack intended.

He said: "Cry it out, Hetty. Then I want to talk to you."

She said thickly: "Go away. Let me alone." But Wint did not move, while she cried and cried.

He stood just beside her. Hetty at last shifted her position, so that she could look down between her arms and see his feet where he waited. She said again:

"Go away."

Wint chuckled comfortingly. "I'm not going away," he said. "This is the time your friends will stick by you. I'm going to stick by you."

"I don't want you to," she said. "I don't want any one to. Go away. Let me alone. Let me do what I want to."

Wint said: "You mustn't think this is too desperately hopeless, Hetty. I'm going to do anything I can; and mother will take care of you."

She lifted her head at that and looked at him and laughed in a hard, disillusioned way. "A lot you know about women, Wint," she said.

"I know that you think things are darker than they are," he assured her. "You'll see. We'll manage. Mother and I."

"Your mother'll order me out of the house, minute she knows," said Hetty unemotionally.

Wint protested. "No; you don't know her. Mother couldn't hurt any one. You'll see. She'll do everything."

Hetty got up and went to work on the dishes like an automaton. She had to busy herself with something, or she would have screamed. She was trembling, hysterically astir. Wint watched her for a little; then he said:

"You're going to let us help you."

"All the help I'll get will be a kick," she said. "Your mother won't want the like of me in her house."

"You don't know her," he insisted. "Mother's fine, underneath. She's always doing things for people. You'll see."

Hetty looked at him sideways, smiling a little. "You never would believe anything was so till you'd tried it, Wint," she told him. "But you're pretty decent, just the same."

He said, studying her: "You're looking better already. Feeling better?"

She nodded. "It helps some—just to tell some one," she admitted. "And the spell is over, anyway."

"Having friends always helps," he told her. "You'll find it so." She smiled wistfully; and he went on: "I'm going to speak to mother to-night."

Hetty said: "Well, she's got a right to know. I'll pack up my things."

"After Mrs. Hullis goes."

"Why not tell her, too? Your mother will, first thing in the morning."

Wint laughed. "You like to look at the black side, don't you? I tell you, it's going to be all right."

She whirled to face him, and said, under her breath, with a terrible earnestness: "All right? All right? If you say that again, I'll yell at you. You poor, nice, straight fool of a kid. You talk like I was a baby that had stubbed its toe. And all the time, I'd better be dead, dead. This is no stubbed toe, Wint. Wake up. Don't be a—"

And abruptly she collapsed again, weeping, into the chair.

Wint said insistently: "Just the same, Hetty, you'll see I know what I'm talking about. Things will come out better than you think."

She cried: "Oh, get out of here. Get out of here. You poor little fool."

Wint went up to his room. Mrs. Hullis was still with his mother. He would wait till Mrs. Hullis was gone.

CHAPTER XIII

THE MERCY OF THE COURT

MRS. HULLIS stayed late, and Wint had time to do some thinking before she finally departed. But he did very little. He was in no mood for thinking. It was characteristic of Wint that when his sympathies were aroused, he was an unfaltering partisan; and there was no question that his sympathies had been aroused in behalf of Hetty.

It was equally characteristic of him that he wasted very little time wondering who was to blame for what had happened; and that he wasted no time at all in considering what Hardiston would say about it all. He was going to help the girl; he had made up his mind to that. The rest did not matter at all.

He counted on his mother's sympathy and understanding; and when, after a time, he heard her showing Mrs. Hullis to the door, and heard their two voices upraised in a last babel as they cleaned up the tag ends of conversation and said good-by, he went out into the upper hall, to be ready to descend. Hetty had gone upstairs a little earlier; he could hear her now, moving about in her room.

His mother went out on the front steps with Mrs. Hullis, to be sure no word had been forgotten; and when she came in after her visitor had gone, Wint was waiting for her. She said: "Why, Wint, I thought you'd gone to bed long ago. I told Mrs. Hullis you were studying the law books up in your room. Mr. Hullis is a lawyer, you know. She says he brings his books home and sits up half the night, but I told her you were always one to go early to bed, ever since you was a boy. And she said she—"

Wint took her arm good-naturedly. "There, mother," he interrupted. "I don't care what Mrs. Hullis said. I want to talk to you about something that has just come up. Come in and sit down."

Mrs. Chase, like most talkative women, was habitually so absorbed in her own conversation and her own thoughts that it was hard to surprise her. She took Wint's announcement as a matter of course; and they went into the sitting room arm in arm, and she picked up her sewing basket and sat down in the chair she had occupied all evening, and began to rock primly back and forth while she stretched a sock on her fingers to discover any holes it might have acquired. "...do get such a comfort out of talking to Mrs. Hullis," she was saying, as she sat down. "She's such a nice woman, Wint. I never could see why you didn't like her more. She and I—"

Wint said: "I don't want to talk to you about Mrs. Hullis, mother. I want to talk to you about Hetty."

Mrs. Chase did drop her work in her lap at that. "About Hetty?" she echoed. "Why should you want to talk about Hetty? Wint! You're never going to marry her, are you? I—"

Wint laughed. "No, no. Not that Hetty isn't a nice girl; and she'll make some fellow a mighty fine wife. But I want to—"

"There," said Mrs. Chase, immensely reassured. "I knew it couldn't be that. I always knew you and Joan.... I said to Mrs. Hullis to-night that you and Joan were friendly as ever. She's a nice girl, Wint. I don't see why you don't get married right away. Your father and I were married before—"

Wint said, persistently bringing her back to the point: "I don't want to talk about Joan, either, mother. It's Hetty."

"Well, I should think you would want to talk about Joan," Mrs. Chase declared. "She's worth talking about. I'm sure she wouldn't like it very much to know you didn't want to talk about her, Wint. She—"

"Mother," Wint insisted. "Hetty needs our help. I want you to—"

Mrs. Chase looked at him with a face that had suddenly turned white and cold. She put one trembling hand to her throat. "Wint?" she asked, in a husky whisper. "What's the matter with Hetty? What are you talking about? What is the—"

"Hetty's going to have a little baby," said Wint gently.

Mrs. Chase exclaimed: "Wint! You're not.... You haven't.... It isn't you?"

"No, no," Wint said impatiently. "Of course not. I—"

"The shameless girl!" his mother cried, all her alarm turning into anger. "The shameless hussy. In my house. I declare—"

"Please," her son protested. His mother got up.

"She sha'n't sleep another night under my roof," she declared. "I never thought to live to—"

"Mother," said Wint, so sternly that his mother stopped in the doorway. "Come back," he told her. And she obeyed him, protesting weakly. "Sit down," he said. "Hetty needs our help. Don't you understand?"

When a wolf is injured, his own pack pulls him down; when a crow is hurt, his fellows of the flock peck him to death relentlessly; but wolf and crow are merciful compared to womankind. There is no deeper instinct in woman than that which condemns the sister who has strayed. It is true that, in many women, the compassion overpowers the cruelty of wrath. But Mrs. Chase was a very simple person, elemental, a woman and nothing more. She sat down at Wint's command; but she said implacably:

"I won't have her in the house, Wint. A girl like that. I should think you'd be ashamed to stand up for her. A shameless, worthless thing.... You can talk all you're a mind to, but I'm going to send her packing. You and your father have your own way, most of the time, but this is once that I'm going to have mine. I always knew she was too pretty for any good. Pretty, and impudent, and all. I won't have her—"

Wint asked: "Hasn't she worked hard enough for you? Done her work well? Tried to do what you wanted?"

"Course she's done her work, or I wouldn't have kept her. That hasn't a thing to do with it, Wint. I'm surprised at you, standing up for her. I told Mrs. Hullis, only the other day, that she was too pretty for her own good. I might have known she would get into trouble. The nasty little—"

"Mother," Wint cried sharply, "I won't let you talk like that. I told Hetty we'd help her; and she said you'd be against her; and I wouldn't believe it. I can't believe it. A poor girl without a friend anywhere, in the worst kind of trouble, and you—"

"Wint, I don't see why you stand up for her if you aren't—"

"You know I'm not. Don't be ridiculous, mother. But I've known her all our lives. Grew up with her. And I'm going to—"

His mother shook her head positively: "I'm not going to have her in the house, Wint. You don't need to talk any more. That's all there is to it. I won't!"

"I counted on you."

"Well, you needn't to count on me any more. I know what's best; and I'm not going to have that shameless—"

She was interrupted, this time, by the arrival of Wint's father. They heard the front door open, and heard him come in. Wint got up and went to the door that led into the hall. The elder Chase was hanging up his hat. Mrs. Chase, behind Wint, was talking steadily. Wint said to his father:

"Come in, will you? Mother and I are talking something over."

Chase nodded; but he had news of his own. "Heard uptown to-night that Routt's going to run against you in the fall," he said. "Did you know that, Wint?"

Wint nodded. "I'd heard so."

"I thought you and he were good friends."

"We are," Wint said good-naturedly. "But that doesn't prevent our being political enemies. He's had some break with Amos. Come in, dad. I want you to hear—"

But the older man heard it first from Mrs. Chase. She came across the room to meet them, pouring it out indignantly. "And Wint wants me to keep her," she concluded. "Wants me to keep that girl in the house after this. I told him—"

Chase asked: "What's that? Wint, what is this? Hetty—in trouble?"

"Yes, sir," said Wint. "I found it out to-night; and I promised her we'd stand by her. Help her."

Chase demanded sharply: "What right had you to commit us? If she chooses to destroy herself, how does that concern us? I'm surprised at you, Wint. It's impossible."

Wint said, in a steady voice: "She needs friends badly. She hasn't any one to turn to. And Hetty's a good sort, underneath. I told her—"

"Why doesn't she turn to the man?" Chase interjected. "He's the one that ought to—"

"As a matter of fact, I haven't thought of him," said Wint. "But if he were likely to help her, it seems to me he would have taken a hand before this. Don't you think so?"

"Don't I think so?" Wint's father was outraged and angry. "I don't think anything about it. It's no concern of ours, so long as she packs herself out of here. Let her get out of her own mess."

"I'm going to make it a concern of mine," said Wint, his jaw stiffening. "I'm not going to see her turned adrift. I'm going to help her."

Chase looked at him keenly. "By God, Wint, is this your doing? Are you—"

Wint said, a little wearily: "That was the first thing mother asked. You people don't think very highly of me, do you?"

"Isn't it the natural question to ask?" his father demanded. "Isn't it the only possible explanation of this attitude on your part? Is it true, young man? That you—"

"Have it any way you want," Wint exclaimed, too angry to deny again. "I don't care. The point is this. Hetty is in trouble; she needs friends. I've promised that we would help her. I've promised you and mother would back me up. I counted on you."

Chase lifted his hand in a terrible, silent rage. "You want to shame us, your mother and me, in the face of all Hardiston. I tell you, Wint, whether it's your doing or not, you're crazy. If it's you—then we'll give her some money and get rid of her. If it's not, then she gets out of here to-night. Inside the hour."

Wint said, half to himself: "We'd have to send her away, in any case. Somewhere. For a while."

Chase laughed bitterly. "All right. If this is a new scrape you've got yourself into, I'll buy you out of it. How much does the girl want?"

Wint flamed at him: "It's not my concern, I tell you. You ought not to need to be told."

"Then get her out of the house," Chase exclaimed; "as quick as you can. Or I will. Where is she?" He turned toward the door.

But Wint was before him; blocked the doorway. "Father," he said. "You and mother.... I've promised her help. Promised you would be good to her."

"The more fool you. She goes out to-night."

"If she goes," Wint cried, "I go with her. You can do as you please."

For a little after that, there was silence in the room. Wint stood in the doorway, head high and eyes hot. His father faced him. His mother stood by her chair, across the room, her lips moving soundlessly. It was she who first found voice. She came toward Wint in a clumsy, stumbling little run; and she caught his arms, and she pleaded with him.

"Don't you do that, Wint. Don't you. Don't go away and leave us again. We're getting old, sonny. Your father and I. Your old mother. Don't you go away. We'd.... We couldn't ever stand it again. We—"

Wint said gently: "I don't want to go. I want to stay at home here with you both, and be proud of you, and love you."

"You shall stay," she told him. "You shall. Anything you want, Wint, sonny. I don't care whether you did it or not. I'll be good to her. I will, Wint. If you'll stay—"

The boy said, half abashed: "I don't want to seem to drive you to it. Only—I've promised her. I can't break my word to her. Please, can't you see?"

"It's all right," his mother protested. "I'll do anything." She clutched her husband's arm. "Tell him to stay, Winthrop," she begged. "Don't let him go away. We'll take care of Hetty."

Chase said: "You're making lots of trouble for us, Wint." He smiled a little unsteadily. "We're too old for so much excitement. You'll have to remember that. Remember to take care of us—as well as Hetty."

Wint could not hold out. He said: "All right. I won't go away. Do as you think best about Hetty. I hope you'll let her—"

"I'll keep her," his mother cried. "I'll be as good as I know to her."

And his father echoed: "We'll take care of her, Wint."

"You're doing it because you want to," Wint pleaded. "You don't have to. I'll stay anyway. But I—hope you'll want to help her, anyway."

"Yes," Chase said. "We'll keep her—because we want to. Do what we can."

But they were not to keep her very long, for Hetty's time was near. It was decided that she should go to Columbus for a little while, returning to them in the fall. Wint wrote a check to cover her expenses. Hetty's old sullenness had returned to her. She took the check without thanks, and tucked it away in her pocketbook. She was to go to the train alone, to avoid talk.

The night of her going, Jack Routt met V. R. Kite, and took Kite to his office. And he told him certain things, an evil elation in his eyes. Told him in detail that which he had planned.

Kite listened with eyes shining; and at the end he said: "He'll deny it. What can you prove?"

"This proves the whole thing," said Routt triumphantly, and slid a slip of paper across the desk to Kite. Kite looked at it. A check, drawn by Winthrop Chase, Junior, to the order of Henrietta Morfee.

The buzzard of a man banged his hard old fist upon the table. "By God, Routt!" he cried, "we win. We'll skin that cub. We'll hang his hide on the barn!"

Routt reached into the drawer of his desk. "And that means," he said, "that it's time to have a drink. Say when?"

END OF BOOK IV

BOOK V

DEFEAT

CHAPTER I

SUNNY SKIES

AT this time, and for a long while afterward, it seemed to Wint that all was well with the world. He had some reason to think so. He kept his promise to Hetty; and that matter, which had threatened to cause a difference between him and his father and mother, had resulted in the end in a closer understanding between them. They had let him see their dependence on him; they had let him see something of the depths of affection in their hearts for him. The Chases were not a demonstrative family; not given to much talk of these matters, and Wint found their attitude in some sort a happy revelation. His father began, in an uncertain way, to defer to Wint; the elder Chase began to ask his son's advice, now and then; he seemed to have recognized the fact of Wint's manhood; he seemed to have discovered that Wint was no longer a boy. There was a new respect in his bearing toward his son.

Wint's mother had changed, too; she was, perhaps, a little less loquacious. She and the elder Chase were beginning to be proud of Wint; and this pride forced them to see him in a new light. Not as their boy, their son, their child; but as a man whom other men respected.

For Wint was respected. That was one of the things that made the world look bright to him. He was surprised to find, as the days passed, and as it was seen that his orders to clean up the town were being enforced, that good citizens rallied to him. Hardiston was normally a law-abiding, decent place; its people were normally decent and law-abiding people. They would not have condemned Wint for failure to enforce the law. In fact, with his antecedents, they had expected him to fail. They were the more pleased when he did enforce it; and they took occasion to let him see it. Also, they took occasion to tell the elder Chase that his son was doing well; and Winthrop Chase, Senior, took a diffident pride in these assurances. Chase was never a hypocrite, even with himself; he could not forget that he had urged Wint to rescind those orders to Radabaugh.

Wint found a surprising number and variety of people rallying to his support, in those days after his clash with the carnival men and his victory in that matter. Dick Hoover's father, for example; a solid man, a lawyer of the old school, and one who spoke little and to the point. Hoover told Wint he had done well.

Wint said he had tried to do well.

"You understand, young man," Hoover drawled in the slow, whimsical fashion that was characteristic of him. "You understand, I'm no teetotaller, myself. I've been accustomed to a drink, when I chose, for a good many years. This—crusade—of yours has made it damned inconvenient for me, too. But it's a good cause. I've no complaint. More power to your elbow!"

Wint laughed, and said: "I guess there would be no kick at anything you might do, sir."

Hoover nodded. "Oh, of course, I could bring the stuff in if I chose. But a man can't afford to be on the wrong side in these matters, you know; not if he wants to keep his self-respect. And I can do without it. I can do without it. Stick to your guns, young man."

"I'm going to," Wint told him, flushed and proud at the older man's praise. "I'm going to, sir."

Peter Gergue came to Wint, scratching the back of his head and grinning a sly and knowing grin, and told Wint he was making votes by what he had done. "That's a funny thing, too," said Gergue. "Man'd think you'd make a pile of enemies. But I could name two or three of the worst soaks in town that say you're all right; got good stuff in you; all that." Gergue scratched his head again. "Yes, sir, men are funny things, Wint."

Wint had never particularly liked Gergue, because he had never seen under the surface of the man. He was coming to have a quite genuine respect and affection for Amos's lieutenant. "I'm not doing it to make votes," he said good-naturedly.

"That's the reason you're making votes by it," Gergue assured him. "And that's the way politics goes. Take James T. Hollow now; he's always trying to do what is right. He says so hisself. But it don't get him anywhere; and I reckon that's because he does what's right because he thinks there's votes in it. You go ahead and do it anyway. Maybe you do it because you think it'll start a fight. Make some folks mad. And instead of that, they eat out o' your hand."

Wint nodded. "Even Kite," he said. "He made some fuss at first. But it looks as though he had decided to take it lying down."

Gergue shook his head. "Don't you make any mistake about V. R. Kite," he warned Wint. "He don't like a fight, much. Getting too old. But he'll fight when he's got a gun in both hands. He'll play poker when he holds four aces and the joker. V. R. will start something when he's ready. I wasn't talking about him."

"I'm ready when he is," Wint declared.

"He won't be ready till he thinks you ain't," Gergue insisted.

But Wint was in no mood to be depressed by a possibility of future trouble. In fact, he rather looked forward to this potential clash with V. R. Kite. It added to the zest of life.

Old Mrs. Mueller, who ran the bakery, whispered to Wint when he stopped for a loaf of bread one night that he was a fine boy. "My Hans," she said gratefully. "He is working now; and that he would never do when he could get his beer regular, every second day a case of it. And there is more money in the drawer all the time, too."

And Davy Morgan, the foreman of his father's furnace, told Wint that save for one or two irreconcilables, the men at the furnace were with him. "And the men that kick the most, they are the ones who are the better off for it," he explained, in the careful English of an old Welshman to whom the language must always be an acquired and unfamiliar instrument. "William Ryan has never been fit for work on Mondays until now."

Murchie, Attorney General of the state, who lived up the creek, and who had been a speaker at the elder Chase's rallies in the last mayoral campaign, happened into town one day and told Wint he had heard of the matter at Columbus and that people were talking about him, Wint Chase, up there. "They knew old Kite, you see," he told Wint. "He comes up there to lobby on every liquor bill; and they like to see him get a kick in the slats, as you might say. But you'll have to look out for him."

"I'm going to," Wint assured Murchie.

"If you can down Kite, there'll be a place for you at Columbus, some day," Murchie predicted. "They don't like Kite, up there."

Sam O'Brien, the fat restaurant man, stopped laughing long enough to tell Wint he was all right, had good stuff in him, was a comer. "The Greek next door," he explained. "He thinks you're a tin god. He runs the candy store, you know. Says there never was so much candy sold. He'll vote for you, my boy. If he ever gets his papers. And learns to read. And if you live that long."

Wint got most pleasure, perhaps, out of the attitude of B. B. Beecham. He had an honest respect for the editor's opinion on most matters. Every one had. Beecham was habitually right. In his editorial capacity, he took no notice of what had come to pass in Hardiston. When the carnival men were arrested, he printed the fact without comment. "Michael Rand was fined for assault and improper language," the *Journal* said. The other man for "illegal sales of liquor." And the "permit of the carnival for the use of the streets was canceled." Thus the news was recorded, and every man might draw his own deductions. B. B. was never one to force his opinions on any man, which may have been the reason why people went out of their way to discover them.

Wint stopped in at the *Journal* office one hot day in July. B. B. was in his shirt sleeves, and collarless. He wore, habitually, stiff-bosomed shirts of the kind usually associated with evening dress. On this particular day, he had been working over the press—his foreman was ill—and there were inky smears on the white bosom. Nevertheless, B. B.'s pink countenance above the shirt was as clean as a baby's. There was always this refreshing atmosphere of cleanliness about the editor. Wint came into the office and sat down in one of the chairs and took off his hat and fanned himself. The afternoon sun was beginning to strike in through the open door and the big window; but there was a pleasantly cool breath from the dark regions behind the office where the press and the apparatus that goes to make a small-town printing shop were housed. Wint said:

"This is one hot day."

"Hottest day of the summer," B. B. agreed.

"How hot is it? Happen to know?"

"Ninety-four in the shade at one o'clock," said B. B. "Mr. Waters telephoned to me, half an hour ago."

"J. B. Waters? He keeps a weather record, doesn't he?"

"Yes. Has, for a good many years. We print his record every week. Perhaps you haven't noticed it."

Wint nodded. "Yes. I suppose every one likes to read about the weather. Even on a hot day."

B. B. smiled. "That's because every one likes to read about things they have experienced. You won't find a big daily in the country without its paragraph or its temperature tables devoted to the weather, every day in the year. And a day like this is worth a front-page story any time."

"You know what a day like this always makes me think of?" Wint asked; and B. B. looked interested. "A glass of beer," said Wint. "Cool and brown, with beads on the outside of the glass."

The editor smiled. "The beads on the outside of the glass won't cool you off half as much as the beads on the outside of your head," he said. "Did you ever stop to think of that?"

"Sweat, you mean?"

"Exactly. You know, when troops go into a hot country, they get flannel-covered canteens; and when they want to cool off the water in the canteens, they wet the flannel and let it dry. The evaporation of your own perspiration is the finest cooling agency in the world."

"May be," Wint agreed. "But it doesn't stop your thirst."

B. B. said good-naturedly: "A thirst is one of the handicaps of the smoker. I quit smoking a good many years ago. A non-smoker can satisfy his own thirst by swallowing his own spittle. I don't suppose you ever thought of that?"

"Is that straight?"

"Yes, indeed."

Wint asked amiably: "Mean to say you wouldn't have to take a barrel of water to cross the Sahara."

"Oh, when the bodily juices are exhausted, of course...."

Wint grinned. "I'll stick to my beer."

B. B. laughed and said: "I expect a good many Hardiston men are cussing you to-day because they can't get beer."

"I suppose so. I've a notion to cuss myself." He added, a moment later: "You know, B. B., it's surprising to me how little fuss has been made over that."

"You mean—the—enforcing the law?"

"Yes. I looked for a row."

"Oh, you'll find most people are on your side. You know, most people are for the decent thing, in the long run. That's what makes the world go around."

"Think so?"

"Yes, indeed. If that weren't so, where would be the virtue in democracy?"

"Well," Wint said good-naturedly, "I've always had an idea that a democracy was a poor way to run things, anyway. About all you can say for it is that a man has a right to make a fool of himself."

"Well, that's about all you can say against slavery, isn't it?"

Wint considered. "I don't get you."

"There were good men in the South before the war, owning slaves," said B. B. "And the slaves were better off than their descendants are now. Materially; perhaps morally, too. But that doesn't prove slavery was right." He added: "The darkies had a right to make fools of themselves if they chose, you see. Their masters—even the good masters—prevented them."

"I suppose that's what a benevolent despot does?"

"Exactly."

"If it wasn't so hot, I'd give three cheers for democracy." He considered thoughtfully, fanning himself with his hat. "But that's what I'm doing, B. B. I'm refusing to let some that would like to, make fools of themselves with booze."

B. B. shook his head. "Not at all. It's not your doing. The people are doing it themselves. They voted dry; they elected you to enforce their vote. See the distinction?"

"Think I've done right, then?" Wint asked.

And B. B. said: "Yes, indeed." Wint got a surprising amount of satisfaction out of that. Because, as has been said, he valued B. B.'s opinion.

So, on the whole, that month of July was a cheerful one for Wint. Things were going his way; the world was bright; the skies were sunny.

The first cloud upon them came on the second of August. It was a very little cloud; but it was a forerunner of bigger ones to come. Wint did not, in the beginning, appreciate its full significance. In fact, he was not sure it had any significance at all. It merely puzzled him.

His month's statement from the bank came in. When it first came, he tossed the long envelope aside without opening it; and it was not till that night that he compared the bank statement with the balance in his check book.

He discovered, then, that there was a mistake somewhere. The bank credited him with more money than he should have had. He said to himself, good-naturedly, that he ought not to kick about that. Nevertheless, he ran through his canceled checks, comparing them with his stubs, to see where the difference lay.

He located the discrepancy almost at once; and when he discovered it, he sat back and considered its significance with a puzzled look in his eyes.

The trouble was that his check to Hetty, for her expenses in Columbus, had never been cashed; and Wint could not understand that at all.

CHAPTER II

A FRIENDLY RIVALRY

THIS matter of the check that he had given Hetty stuck in Wint's mind, disquieting him. This in spite of the fact that he tried to forget it, told himself it had no significance, that it meant nothing at all.

He gathered up the other canceled checks and put them back in the bank's long, yellow envelope, and stuck the envelope in a drawer of his desk. Hetty had not yet cashed the check; that was all. She would cash it when she needed the money. He tried to believe this was the key to the puzzle.

But it was not a satisfactory key; and this was proved by the fact that his thoughts kept harking back to the matter during the next day or two. When he gave Hetty the check, he had expected her to cash it before she left town. In fact, his first thought had been to draw the money himself, and give it to her; but this had been slightly less convenient than to write the check. So he had written the check, and given it to her, and now Hetty had not cashed it.

It was characteristic of Wint that he saw no threat against himself in this circumstance. Wint was never of a suspicious turn of mind. He was loyal to his friends and to those who seemed to be his friends; he took them, and he took the world at large, at face value. So in this case, he was not uneasy on his own account, but on Hetty's. For Hetty had needed this money; yet she had not cashed the check.

He knew she needed the money. Her wage from his mother left no great margin for saving, if a girl liked to spend money as well at Hetty did. She could not have saved more than a few dollars; twenty, or perhaps thirty.... Besides, she had told him she needed money. When he told her she had better go away, she had said: "A fat chance of that. Where would I get the money, anyway?" It was this that had led him to write a check for her.

She had needed the money; she had accepted it. That is to say, she had accepted the check, but had not cashed it. Not yet, at least. Why not? What was the explanation?

His uneasiness, all on Hetty's account, began to take shape. He remembered the girl's sullen hopelessness, her friendlessness. She had been ready to give up, to submit to whatever misfortunes might come upon her. There had always been a defiant, reckless, fatalistic streak in Hetty. And Wint, remembering, was afraid it had taken the ascendant in the girl. He was afraid.

He did not put into words, even in his thoughts, the truth of this fear. But he did write to a college classmate, who was working at the time on one of the Columbus papers, and asked him to try to locate Hetty at one of the hospitals. He told the circumstances. And two or three days later, the man wrote to say that there was no such person as Hetty in any hospital in Columbus under her own name; and that as far as he could learn, there was no one approximating her description.

When this letter came, it tended to clinch Wint's fears. He was not yet convinced that Hetty had chosen to—do that which writes "Finis" as the bottom of life's last page. But he was almost convinced, almost ready to believe.

It made Wint distinctly unhappy. He had an honest liking and respect for Hetty, an old friendship for the girl.

He did not tell either his father or mother of the matter of the check; nor did he tell them what he feared had come to pass. There was no need, he thought, of worrying them. There was nothing that could be done.

The long, lazy summer dragged slowly past, and nothing happened. Which is the way of Hardiston. That is to say, nothing happened that was in any way extraordinary. The Baptist Sunday school held its annual picnic in the G. A. R. grove, south of town; and every one went, Baptist or not, Sunday school scholar or not. Everybody went, and took his dinner. Fried chicken, and sandwiches, and deviled eggs, and bananas; and there were vast freezers of ice cream. And some played baseball, and some idled in the swings, and there were the sports that go with such an occasion. Cracker-eating, shoe-lacing, egg-and-spoon race, greased pole, and so on and so on, to the tune of a great deal of laughter and general good nature. And the Hardiston baseball team played a game every week, sometimes away from home, sometimes on the baseball field down by the creek, where the muddy waters over-flowed every spring. And Lint Blood, the hard-throwing left fielder who was fully as good as any big leaguer in the country, if he could only get his chance, had his regular season as hero of the town. And there were a few dances, where the men appeared in white trousers and soft shirts and took off their coats to dance; and there were hay rides, on moonlight nights; and Ed Skinner's nine-year-old boy almost got drowned in the swimming hole at Smith's Bridge; and Jim Radabaugh and two or three others went fishing down on Big Raccoon, thirty miles away; and the tennis court in Walter Roberts's back yard was busy every fine afternoon; and Ringling Brothers and Buffalo Bill paid Hardiston their regular summer visits. It rained so hard, for three days before Ringling Brothers came, that the big show had to be canceled, which made it hard for every father in town. And Sam O'Brien's brother caught a thirty-five-pound catfish in the river, and sent it up to Sam, who kept it alive in a tub in his restaurant for two days, and killed and fried it for his customers only when it began to pine away in captivity. And Ed Howe's boy fell off a home-made acting bar and broke his arm; and the Welsh held their County Eisteddfod in a tent on the old fair grounds, and John Morgan won the first prize in the male solo competition. Hardiston boys thought that was rather a joke, because John was the only entry in this particular event; and they reminded him of this fact for a good many years to come, in their tormenting moments. And the hot days and the warm days and the wet days came and went, and the summer dragged away.

In September, Joan suggested a picnic at Gallop Caves, a dozen miles from Hardiston; and Wint liked the idea, so they discussed who should go, and how, and in due time the affair took place. Joan and Agnes and two or three other girls made the domestic arrangements, with Wint and Dick Hoover and Jack Routt and one or two besides to look after the financial end, and the transportation. In the old days, they would have hired one of the big barges from the livery stable, with a long seat running the length of each side; and they would have crowded into that and ridden the dozen jolting miles, with a good deal of singing and laughing and talking as they went; but there were automobiles in Hardiston now, and no one thought of the barge.

They started early; that is to say, at eight o'clock in the morning, or thereabouts. There were three automobiles full of them, with hampers and boxes and freezers full of things to eat in every car. And they made the trip at a breakneck and break-axle speed over the rough road, and came to the Caves by nine, and unloaded the edibles and got buckets of water from the well behind the house at the entrance to the Caves. The farmer who lived in this house had an eye to business; and a year or two before he had put up a pavilion in the grove by the Caves, and had begun to charge admission. Besides the pavilion, there were swings, and there was a seesaw; and there were always the Caves themselves, and the winding, clear-watered little stream that came down over the rocks in a feathery cascade and wound away among the trees.

This day, they danced a little, in the pavilion—Joan had brought a graphophone—and when it grew too warm to dance, some of them went to climb about on the cool, wet rocks of the Caves; and some took off shoes and stockings, or shoes and socks as the case might be, and waded in the brook; and some sprawled on the sand at the base of the rocky wall and called doodle bugs. A pleasant, idle sport. The doodle bug is more scientifically known as an ant lion. He digs himself a hole in the sand like an inverted cone, and hides himself in the loose sand at the bottom of the hole. The theory of the thing is that an ant tumbles in, slides down the sloping sides, and falls a prey to the ingenious monster at the bottom. To call a doodle bug, you simply chant over and over:

"Doodle up, doodle up, doodle up...."

And at the same time, you stir the sand on the sides of the trap with a twig. Either the song or the sliding sand causes the bug to emerge from his ambush at the bottom of the pit, when you may see him for an instant; a misshapen, powerful little thing. If you happen to be an ant, he looks to you as formidable as a behemoth, bursting out of the sand and tumbling it from his shoulders as a mammoth bursts out of the primeval forest. If you happen to be a human, you laugh at his awkward movements, and find another pit, and call another doodle bug.

Routt and Agnes, Wint and Joan, all four together, investigated doodle bugs this day. They had a good-natured time of it till Jack Routt caught an ant and dropped it into one of the pits to see the monster at the bottom in action. The sight of the ant's swift end was not pleasant to Joan; and she looked at Routt in a critical way. He and Agnes seemed to think it rather a joke on the ant. Wint and Joan moved away and left them there and went clambering up among the rocks, and picked wintergreen and chewed it, and came out at last on the upper level, on top of the Caves. They looked down from there and shouted to the others below. And when they tired of that, they sat down and talked to each other for a while. That was one pursuit they never tired of.

Wint had been meaning to ask Joan something. It concerned that letter which he had received the day after his election as Mayor. The letter had been anonymous; a friendly, loyal, sympathetic little note. He had torn it up angrily, as soon as he read it, because he was in no mood for good advice that day, and the letter had given good advice. He could remember, even now, snatches of it. He had wondered who wrote it; and this wonder had revived, during the last few days, and he had considered the matter, and asked a question or two.

Now he asked Joan whether she had written it; and Joan hesitated, and flushed a little, and then said, looking at him bravely: "Yes, I wrote it, Wint."

He said in an embarrassed way: "But that was when you had told me you would have no more to do with me."

She nodded.

"I tore it up," he said.

"I thought you would." She smiled a little. "But I hoped you—would remember it, too."

"I do," Wint told her. "You said I had 'the finest chance a man ever had to retrieve his mistakes,' and you told me to buckle down."

"Yes, I remember," she agreed.

Wint looked at her, and his heart was pounding softly. "You said there were some who would watch me—lovingly," he reminded her.

For a minute she did not speak; then she nodded her head slowly; and she said: "Yes." Her eyes met his honestly.

Wint had been very sure, before he asked her, that she had written the letter; he had meant to remind her of this word, and if she confessed it, to go on. But now that he had come thus far, he found that he could go no farther. It was not that she forbade him; not that there was any prohibition in her eyes. It was something within himself that restrained him. Something that held his tongue, bade him not risk his fortune—lest, perchance, he lose it.

Any one but a blind man would have seen there was no danger of his losing it; but Wint, in this matter, was blind—for the immemorial reason. So all the courage that had brought him thus far deserted him, and he only said:

"Oh!"

That did not seem to Joan to call for any answer, so she said nothing; and after a moment Wint got hurriedly to his feet and exclaimed:

"Well, I'm getting hungry. Better be getting back, hadn't we?"

Joan looked, perhaps, a little disappointed. But she said she guessed so; and they made their way down to join the others.

After every one had eaten till there was no more eat in them, there was a general tendency to take things easy. The dishes had to be washed in the brook; and the girls undertook to do that. Dick Hoover found some horseshoes, and started a game of quoits. Wint would have taken a hand; but Jack Routt drew him aside and said:

"I'd like a little talk with you, Wint. Mind?"

Wint was surprised; but he didn't say so. "All right," he agreed. "Shoot."

Routt offered him a cigar, and Wint took it, and they walked slowly away from the others, back toward the Caves. Routt came to the point without preliminaries. "It's like this, Wint," he said frankly. "A good many people have been telling me I ought to get into politics."

Wint had ears to hear; and he had heard something of this. But he pretended ignorance, and only said: "I thought you were in politics. Thought you were linked up with Amos."

"I have been, in the past," Routt agreed. "But the trouble with that is, if you tie up with a big man, you get only what he chooses to give you. I've been advised to strike out for myself."

Wint said: "I think that's good advice. It ought to help your law practice, too."

"Matter of fact," said Routt. "They're telling me I ought to run against you."

"Against me?" Wint seemed only mildly interested. "For Mayor?"

"Yes. On the wet issue. You know my ideas on that. I'm not on your side of the fence there at all."

"Well, I don't find fault with any man's ideas, Jack."

"The trouble is this," Routt explained. "You and I are pretty good friends. Always have been. I don't want to start anything that will spoil that friendship."

Wint laughed and said: "Good Lord, Jack; I guess there's no fear of that."

"By God, I knew you'd say so!" Routt exclaimed. "Just the same. I was leary. You know what kind of a fellow I am. When I go into a thing, I go in with both feet. If I run against you, Wint, I'll give you a fight."

"Go to it. We'll show Hardiston some action."

"I'll lam it into you, Wint."

"Well, I can give as good as you send," Wint promised cheerfully.

"The only thing is," Routt explained, "I just want an understanding with you first; that is, I want you to know there's nothing personal in anything I may say. It's politics, Wint; and if I go in, it will be hot politics. If you'll promise to take it as that and nothing else."

Wint said easily: "I don't suppose you can tell Hardiston anything about me that it doesn't already know."

Routt grasped his hand. "Attaboy, Wint," he exclaimed. "You're a good sport. By God, I believe I'll go into it!"

"Come ahead. It's no private fight," Wint assured him.

"The only thing is, I wanted to know first. I want you to know I'm on the level with you personally."

"Well, I should say I know that, Jack."

Routt thrust out his hand. "Shake on it, Wint."

Wint laughed. "You're dramatic enough." But he shook hands.

They rejoined the others after a while, and Wint was glad of it. He had hidden his feelings from Routt; but as a matter of fact he was a good deal surprised and chagrined at Jack's news. He had heard rumors; but he had not believed Routt would come out against him. It was a thing he, Wint, would not have done.... It smacked, he felt, of disloyalty to a friend. He had even, for a moment, a thought of withdrawing and leaving the field free to Routt. But he put it away. After all, he was first in the fight; it was Routt who had brought about this situation, not he. He could not well avoid the issue.

Nevertheless, he was troubled. The world that had seemed so bright and fair a month ago had a less cheerful aspect now. His fears for Hetty, his anxiety over her, were always with him, faintly oppressive. Now Routt's desertion, his projected opposition. Try as he would to shake it off, Wint could not rid himself of the feeling that there were rough places on the road that lay ahead.

His anxiety over Hetty was relieved—though only to take a new turn—in the last week of September. For Hetty came back to Hardiston.

Wint met her on the street one day. He was immensely surprised; and he was immensely pleased to see her, safe and sound. He cried: "Why, Hetty, where did you come from?"

She looked around furtively, as though she would have avoided him if it had been possible to do so. "Didn't you expect me to come back?" she asked sullenly.

"Of course. But.... How are you? All right? Where have you been?"

"Summering in New England," she said ironically. "Where'd you think?"

"Mother's been wondering when you'd come back. She needs you."

"She'll have to go on needing me."

"Aren't you—"

"I've got a job in the shoe factory."

Wint said: "Oh!" He was disturbed and uncertain, puzzled by Hetty's attitude. He asked: "Is the.... Did you...."

"The baby?" said Hetty listlessly. "Oh, he died." There was dead agony in her tone, so that Wint ached for her.

"I'm sorry," he told her.

"That's all right. I can stand it."

He asked: "Did you need any money? The check I gave you never came through the bank."

"I lost it," she said.

"Why, you must have had trouble. You didn't have enough."

"I went in as a charity-ward patient."

"Columbus?"

"No. Cincinnati. I didn't want any one knowing."

Wint smiled in a friendly way and said: "I was worried about you."

Hetty laughed. "You'd better worry about yourself. Do you know people are looking at you, while you're talking to me? It won't help you any to be seen with me."

Wint said "Pshaw! You're morbid, Hetty."

"Besides," she told him. "I've got to look out. Mind my p's and q's. If I want to hold my job."

Wint flushed uncomfortably. "Why.... All right," he said. "But if there's ever anything...."

"Oh, I'll let you know," Hetty said impatiently, and turned away.

He had been afraid that she had killed herself; that her body was dead. He was afraid now, as he watched her move down the street, that something more important was dead in the girl.

It was at this moment that he realized for the first time that a man had been responsible for what had come to Hetty. He wondered who the man was; and he thought it would be satisfying to say a word or two to the fellow.

CHAPTER III

POLITICS

JACK ROUTT was as good as his word to Wint. Early in October, he announced his candidacy for Mayor; and he proceeded to push it.

In their talk at the Caves, he had warned Wint what to expect. But in spite of that warning, Wint had looked for no more than a polite and friendly rivalry, a congenial conflict, a good-natured tussle between friends.

He was to find that Routt had meant exactly what he said; that Routt as a political opponent and Routt as a friend were two very different personalities. On the heels of his open announcement that he was a candidate, Jack began a canvass of the town, and a direct and virulent assault upon Wint.

Wint heard what Routt was doing first through his father. The elder Chase came home to supper one evening in a fuming rage; and he said while they were eating:

"Wint, this Routt is a fine friend of yours!"

Wint looked at his father in some surprise. "Why, Jack's all right," he declared.

"All right?" Chase demanded. "Do you know what he's doing?"

"I know he's out for Mayor. That's all right. I've no string on the job. I want to be re-elected, just as a sort of a—testimonial that I've made good. And I intend to be re-elected. But at the same time, any one has a right to run against me."

"Nobody denies that," his father exclaimed. "But no one has a right to hark back a year for mud to throw at you."

Wint said: "Pshaw, there's always mud-throwing in politics."

Chase challenged: "Do you mean to say you think Routt has a right to do as he is doing?"

"Well, just what is he doing?" Wint asked good-naturedly.

"What is he doing? He's saying you're a common drunkard; that you always have been; that you are still, in secret."

Wint flushed with slow anger. "Well," he said, "if any one believes that, they're welcome to."

"But damn it, son, you're not!" Chase exclaimed; and there was such a fierce rush of pride in his father's voice that Wint was startled, and he was suddenly very happy about nothing; and he said:

"I'm glad you know it, anyway, dad."

"Damn it!" Chase repeated. "Don't you suppose I can see? Don't you suppose I have a right to be proud of my own son, when he does something to be proud of? Your mother and I have.... Well, Wint, we're—we're a good deal happier than we were a year ago."

Wint said gently: "I'm only sorry I didn't make you happy a year ago."

"That's all right," his father declared. "You were a headstrong youngster; and I didn't know how to control you. An unruly colt takes careful handling. I'm not a—tactful man. But I'll be damned if I can see how you can take this from the man you call your friend."

Wint smiled slowly, and he said: "That's three times in two minutes you've said 'damn,' dad. Cut it out. Don't get profane in your excitement. Routt's all right, really. Don't swear at him."

"Do you realize that he's saying you're drinking as regularly as ever, while you pretend to keep this a dry town?"

"Well, no one will believe him."

"You can find men to believe anything; and there are plenty in Hardiston that want to believe anything against you."

"Let them," said Wint confidently. "There are plenty who will stand back of me."

"But what are you going to do about it?"

"I'm not going to call names," Wint told him cheerfully. "I'll fight it out quietly and decently; and I'll win. That's what I mean to do."

"You act as though you had expected this."

"Well, as a matter of fact, Jack came to me and told me, before he told any one else, that he was going to run. And he warned me he was going to make it a real fight."

"A real fight? This is assassination!"

Wint laughed. "You're taking it too hard. I know it's just because you're—proud of me. Are you going to back me in this?"

Chase frowned. "As a matter of fact, Wint, I'm in a hard position. I want to back you—of course. But I can't stomach Caretall. If you weren't tied up with him."

"He's been a pretty good friend to me. Can't you take him on that ground?"

"If I tied up with him, I'd be called a bootlicker, and justly. After what he did to me, I can't cater to him and keep my self-respect."

"Pshaw, dad! The world has a short memory. That's all forgotten."

"I've not forgotten."

"Every one else has."

"I'm not talking about every one else. I'm talking about my own self-respect."

They had finished supper; and they got up and went into the other room. Mrs. Chase—she was doing her own work since Hetty had left her—began to clear away the dishes. In the sitting room, Wint said: "I've been counting on you, dad."

Chase said: "I'll do what I can—quietly. But I can not come out in the open and side with Amos. If he'd turn against you...."

Wint laughed. "I might kick up a row with him."

"You'll never regret breaking with Caretall. He's a crooked politician of the worst type, without honor. A traitor to his own friends. He'll be a traitor to you when it pleases him."

His son said quickly: "Don't. Please don't talk against him to me. Let's just not talk about him. After all, he's been square to me."

Chase flung up his hand. "All right. But how about Routt? Are you going to sit still and take the mud he's throwing?"

"Jack will be too busy to throw mud, pretty soon," Wint promised cheerfully. "Mud is trimmings. I'll bring him down to brass tacks."

"You ought to shut his lying—"

"Come, dad, don't take it so seriously."

"Well, then, you take it more seriously."

Wint laughed. "All right. You wait and see."

Nevertheless, he could not deny to himself that Routt's move troubled him. Not for its effect on his candidacy, but for the light in which it showed Routt himself. For all his loyalty, Wint thought it was unworthy. Thought Routt was hurting himself and sullying himself. He met Jack uptown that night, and told him so in a friendly way. "Do as you like," he said. "But I think it hurts you more than it does me," he suggested.

Routt laughed, and asked: "It's not getting under your skin, is it? I told you I'd give you a run."

"Pshaw, no. Say anything you like about me. But it doesn't get you any votes."

"You'll know better than that on the eighth of November," Jack told him; and Wint smiled and let it go at that. After all, it was Routt's own concern.

But if Wint took Routt's tactics equably, Hardiston did not. Hardiston folk love politics. The great American game is the breath in their nostrils. They have an expert's appreciation of the tactical value of this move and that; and they are keen spectators at such a battle as Routt and Wint were staging.

Wint would have liked to consult with Amos at this time; but it happened that Amos was out of town. He had gone to Columbus for a day or two. In lieu of Amos, Wint went to Peter Gergue, and asked Gergue how things looked to him. Gergue fumbled in his back hair in the thoughtful way he had and said he guessed Routt was making a lively fight of it, anyway.

"Do you think he's making votes?" Wint asked.

"We-ell," said Peter, "you can't always tell what folks will do. I'd say he's persuading every enemy you've got to vote against you."

Wint said: "They would, anyway."

"Sure."

"The question is, is he persuading any of my friends?"

"I'd say not."

"Then I don't need to worry."

Gergue spat at the curb. "Can't say. You see, Wint, there's about sixty per cent. of this town—or any town—that's neither enemy nor friend. Just neutral. Them's the votes you got to get."

"I don't believe Routt will get many of those votes by lies."

"Not if they're knowed to be lies."

"Every one knows they are lies."

"It's a funny thing," Gergue ruminated. "But lots of folks take a kind of pleasure out of believing lies about other folks."

Wint shook his head. "I don't believe Routt is accomplishing a thing."

"We-ell," said Gergue, "matter of fact, I'm thinking you may be right. Thing is, he's laying a foundation, like."

"What do you mean?"

"I mean he's laying the tracks. He's doing a lot of talk that won't be believed much now; but he might bring on something later along that would make folks say: 'Well, maybe that other was true, too.'"

"What can he bring?" Wint challenged.

"Has he got anything on you?"

"Every one knows all there is to know about me, I suppose."

Gergue scratched his head. "We-ell, I dunno," he said. "Anyway, that's what I was kind of thinking."

Wint met V. R. Kite one day, and the little man spoke to him so affably that Wint asked: "Well, how are things, Mr. Kite?"

"Excellent. First class, young man."

"I suppose you'll vote for me for Mayor?" Wint asked, grinning good-naturedly; and Kite chuckled and said he guessed not.

"Routt's more my style," he said.

"Don't waste your vote on a loser," Wint told him; but Kite said Routt might be a loser and might not. He left Wint with an unpleasant feeling that there had been a secretly triumphant note in the little old buzzard's voice.

Jim Radabaugh met James T. Hollow at the Post Office one morning, and said cheerfully: "Well, James T., how's it happen you're not out for Mayor again?"

"I try to do what is right," Hollow said earnestly. "But I really don't know what to do, Mr. Marshal. I have thought of coming out, but Congressman Caretall gives me very little encouragement."

"Don't encourage you, eh?"

"No. In fact, I might say he discouraged—"

"Well, now," said Radabaugh, "maybe you'd best just lie low."

Hollow looked doubtful and said he didn't know.

Thus all Hardiston talked, each man after his fashion. Ed Skinner of the *Sun* maintained a strict neutrality. He was closely allied with Wint's father; and the elder Chase held his hand. B. B. Beecham seldom let the *Journal* take an active part in local politics, except on broad party lines. And Wint—since he had the patronage of Amos Caretall—was of the same party as Routt, who had been Amos's ally. He carried the announcement cards of both men and let it go at that. But he went so far as to say to Wint, and to those who dropped in at the *Journal* office, that Routt's methods were not likely to be profitable. "It never pays to open up old sores," he said. "And it's never a good plan to say anything that will unjustly hurt another man's feelings. He may be in a position to resent it, some day."

Sam O'Brien, the restaurant man, told Wint that Routt would never get his vote. "I like nerve," he said, "and you've got it. You've made me laugh sometimes, Wint. Lord, I've thought you'd be the death of me. But you've took your nerve in your hands. You've got me, boy. More power to your elbow."

The first two weeks of October slid swiftly by. Wint heard Routt was planning for a rally or two; and he began to make his own arrangements to a similar end. But in mid-October, word came to him which put the mayoralty race out of his mind.

The word came through Ote Runns, that hopeless drunkard whose cheerful services were in such demand by Hardiston housewives at rug-beating time. Wint met Ote one evening, on his way home, and Ote was bibulously cheerful. He greeted Wint hilariously; and told him in triumphant tones that Hardiston was itself again.

Wint, with a suspicion of what was coming, asked Ote what he meant; and Ote chortled:

"'S a good ol' town. Good ol' wet town! Plenny o' booze now."

Wint asked Ote where he got it, but the man put his finger to his nose and shook his head. Wint left him and went on his way.

When he got home, he telephoned Radabaugh. "They're selling again, Jim," he said.

The marshal asked: "Who?"

"Don't know," said Wint. "I met Ote Runns with a load aboard. I want you to get after them right away."

"I'm started, now," said Jim Radabaugh. "I'm on my way."

CHAPTER IV

A CLOUD ON THE MOON

WINT was rather pleased than otherwise to learn that Kite and others of his ilk had resumed their illicit traffic in Hardiston. It gave him something to do. He had none of the instincts of a political campaigner; he could not for the life of him have made a really rousing speech. And it was next to impossible for him to ask a man for his vote. The old pride, the stubborn pride that had done him so much harm, was still alive in Wint; and this pride made him uncomfortable when he found himself asking favors.

He hated campaigning. If there had been no opposition for him to fight, if the way had been made easy before him, it is not unlikely that he would have quit the race. But there was opposition, and strenuous opposition. Jack Routt had kept his word; he was making a real fight out of it. When he encountered Wint, he was friendly—profusely so—and affable enough; but when he was canvassing, he made no bones of attacking Wint unmercifully, striking below the belt or above it as the moment might inspire him. He had dragged up Wint's old drunken record and aired it until people were beginning to ask themselves if there wasn't something in what he said, after all.

Against this, up till the middle of October, Wint had made a very poor fight indeed. He would not denounce Routt as Routt denounced him. As a matter of fact, there was no particular charge he could bring against Routt. Jack was no hypocrite, at least; he took an honest and straightforward stand. The liquor issue, for example. He was a drinker, he believed in it. And he said so. At the same time, he added that Wint was a drinker, but pretended not to be. He said Wint was a hypocrite.

The viciousness of Routt's campaign stunned Wint at first; he was half incredulous. The thing didn't seem possible. When he was forced to understand that it was not only possible but true, he was left at a loss. It was in the midst of his floundering attempts to find some means to advocate his cause that he got through Ote Runns the first word that the lawbreakers were at work again.

He grasped at that as though it were an opportunity. He telephoned Jim Radabaugh that night; and he sent for Jim the first thing in the morning and asked the marshal what he had discovered. Radabaugh shifted the knob in his cheek, and spat, and said he had discovered nothing.

"Did you find Ote?" Wint asked.

"Sure. I just listened, and then went where he was. He was singing, some."

"Question him?"

"Oh, yes."

"What did he say? Where did he get it?"

"He wouldn't say," Radabaugh explained.

Wint nodded. "I suppose not. What then?"

"We-ell, I scouted around."

"Find out anything?"

"Skinny Marsh had a skinful, too. And there was a drunk in the Weaver House when I drifted over there."

"Is it Mrs. Moody that's selling?"

Radabaugh shook his head. "I guess not."

Wint banged his desk. "Damn it, Jim! Who is it, then?"

"I couldn't say."

"Well, I want you to find out."

Radabaugh spat and considered. "They's one thing," he suggested mildly. "You might not have thought of it."

Wint grinned. "You talk like B. B. Beecham. What is it, Jim?"

"I mean to say," said Radabaugh, "this didn't just happen. What I mean is, it didn't just happen to happen. It was meant."

Wint studied him. "What's in your mind?"

"They'd have held off till after election, maybe," Jim suggested. "Looks to me like they're starting this to hit the election somehow. I can't say just how. Don't know. But it looks to me it was meant."

"You mean they're trying to discredit me, say I don't enforce the laws."

"Maybe that. Maybe something else. Just struck me it was something."

Wint got up abruptly. "I don't give a hoot. This campaign business bores me, anyhow. But I'm not going to stand for this. You get busy, Jim. If you need help, say so. I'll bring a man in from outside, if necessary. But I want to grab the man that's selling. You understand?"

"It's your funeral," said Radabaugh cheerfully, shifting the bulge in his cheek. "I'll do my do."

"Go to it," Wint told him. "I'm leaving it to you."

But nothing happened. A week dragged past; a week in which it was reasonably clear that Wint was losing ground to Routt. Wint himself saw this as quickly as any man, and it troubled him. He asked Peter Gergue for advice—Amos was still out of town—and Peter told him to get up on his hind legs and rear and tear, but Wint shook his head. "I can't do that. It isn't in me. The whole thing makes me sick."

"You've naturally got to do it," Gergue assured him. "Routt's telling 'em to vote for him; and he's telling them the same thing, over and over, till they know their lesson like a parrot. That's advertising, Wint. Keep a-telling them the same thing till they know what they're to do. You got to. Might as well come to it first as last."

"I can't ask a man to vote for me."

"Why not?"

Wint grinned, and flushed, and gave it up. And Gergue told him again that he would have to make a noise if he wanted to be heard in Hardiston; and he left Wint to think it over.

B. B. Beecham, a day or two later, gave Wint the same advice, but to more purpose. Wint had dropped in at the *Journal* office casually enough, and talked with two or three others who were there before him, till they drifted away and left him with B. B. Wint asked:

"Well, how do things look to you, B. B.?"

B. B. looked doubtful. "You're not making a very strong campaign," he said.

Wint nodded. "I know it. It goes against the grain."

The editor was surprised. "Is that so? Just how do you mean?"

"Oh, I hate to ask a man to vote for me. I hate to ask favors."

B. B. smiled. "Who are you going to vote for, on the eighth?"

"Why, Routt, of course. I can't vote for myself."

The editor looked blandly interested, and commented: "Well, if that's the case, of course you can't ask any one else to vote for you?"

"Why not?" Wint was puzzled.

"You know yourself better than they do. If you can't vote for yourself—"

"Oh, it isn't.... Why, you naturally vote for the other fellow?"

"This isn't a class election at college, you know," B. B. reminded him. "It's more serious. Not play. You want to remember that. But if you don't think enough of yourself to vote for yourself...."

Wint laughed. "All right," he said. "I'll vote for myself. You've persuaded me."

B. B. nodded. "Who do you think will make the best mayor; you, or Routt?" he asked.

"I don't...." Wint flushed. "Why, I...."

"Routt?"

"No, by God!" Wint exclaimed angrily. "I've done a good job; and I'll do another. He'd open the town up. Let things go."

"Do you want to be Mayor? For your own sake?"

"Why, yes."

"Like the job so well?"

"No, not particularly. But I want—well, it would show that people think I've made good."

"If you're going to make a better Mayor than Routt, your election is best for the town, isn't it?"

"I suppose so."

"Then it's best for every man in Hardiston, isn't it?"

"In a way."

B. B. tilted back in his chair and lifted his hand in a gesture of confirmation. "That's what I was getting at. The fact of the matter is, when you ask a man to vote for you, you're not asking him to do you a favor. You're asking him to do himself a favor. I don't suppose you ever thought of that."

Wint grinned. "Well, no."

"It's true?"

"I guess it is."

B. B. leaned forward. "Then go out and say so. Start something. Keep telling them to elect you; tell them louder and longer and oftener than Routt does, and they will."

This was so like what Gergue had said that Wint told B. B. so; and the editor nodded and said Gergue was a wise man. "But I can't do it," Wint protested. "I don't know how. I'll never make a speaker."

B. B. considered that for a while: and then he said: "You know, printed advertising was invented by the first tongue-tied man."

"I don't get it," Wint confessed.

"He had something to sell, but he couldn't tell people about it, so he put an ad in the papers; and after that, every one got the habit."

"You mean I ought to advertise?"

B. B. said that was exactly what he meant. And Wint was interested; he asked some questions. He had heard of advertising rates as things of astounding proportions; and so he was surprised to find that a full-page advertisement in the *Journal* would only cost him ten dollars. He laughed and said he could stand half a dozen of those. B. B. told him to put an advertisement in each Hardiston paper, and let them appear in every issue till the election. "Say the same thing, over and over, in different ways," he advised. "Try it. You'll be surprised."

In the end, Wint decided to do just this. B. B. helped him write the advertisements. In them, Wint recited what he had done and what he meant to do, but briefly. In each full, black-lettered page, the burden of his song was just three words, repeated over and over:

"Vote for Chase; vote for Chase; vote for Chase."

Amos came home toward the end of October; and when Wint heard he was in town, he telephoned and made arrangements to see him at his home that night. When he got there, Amos was upstairs. He called to Wint to go into the sitting room and wait, and Wint went in there and sat down. After a moment, Agnes came in to restore a book to its place on the shelves, and Wint got up and stood, talking with her. He thought she seemed uneasy, on edge. Her eyes went now and then through the open door toward the stairs down which Amos would come. She fumbled with her hair, and a lock became disarranged and fell down beside her face.

She said, abruptly, that there was something in her shoe; and she held to his arm with one hand, and stood on one foot, and pulled off her slipper and shook it, upside down. Then she seemed to lose her balance and toppled toward Wint; and he caught her in his arms. She straightened up and pushed him away with what seemed to him unnecessary force; and then turned and went swiftly out into the hall without a word. He looked after her, and saw Amos, halfway down the stairs, watching them with a curiously grave countenance; and Wint, for no reason in the world, was confused, and felt his face burning. He looked down and saw Agnes's slipper on the floor, where she had dropped it; and he slid it out of sight under the bookcase before Amos came into the room. He was sorry as soon as he had done this; but Agnes had somehow contrived to make him feel guilty. He could hardly face Amos when the Congressman came into the room. He had a miserable feeling that everything was going wrong; all the trifles in the world seemed conspiring to harass him.

But Amos seemed to have seen nothing. He was perfectly amiable, bade Wint sit down, filled his black pipe, squinted at Wint with his head on one side and asked how things were going.

Wint said they were going badly; and Amos smiled.

"Why, now, that's too bad," he declared.

"I wasn't made for a campaigner," Wint said. "I'll never be able to make a speech."

"You write a good ad," Amos told him; and Wint asked:

"You've read them?"

"I guess everybody's read them."

"Are they all right?"

"First rate. They'll do."

Wint said impatiently: "I'm sick of the whole thing."

Amos studied him. "Routt getting under your skin?"

"No. He's playing it pretty strong, though."

"I'll say he is."

"Of course, it's just politics. He and I are as friendly as ever."

"Oh, sure," Amos agreed indolently. "He told you so, didn't he?"

"Yes. He came to me, in the beginning."

"I heard so."

"I don't know how to answer him—the line he's taking," Wint explained. "That's all."

"Don't have to answer him, do you? Don't have to answer a lie."

Wint laughed uneasily. "Just the same, he's stirring people up."

"I never heard of anybody being permanently hurt by a lie but the liar," said Amos.

Wint leaned forward. "I tell you, Amos, I want to be elected. I've gone into this; and I want to win. Routt and I are friendly enough; but he started this fight, and I want to beat him. I want to beat him to a whisper. I'd like to see him skunked. I don't care if he doesn't get two votes in Hardiston. That's the way I feel." His fierce enthusiasm dropped away from him; he said hopelessly: "But I'm darned if I know how to manage it."

Amos nodded slowly. "Sick of it, eh?"

"Yes."

The Congressman puffed for a while in silence, thinking; and Wint waited for the other man to speak. At last Amos looked at him and asked curiously: "Wint, you dead set on being Mayor?"

Something in his tone put Wint on guard. "Dead set? Why?" he asked.

Amos lifted a hand. "Why, just this," he explained. "I've been talking around, here and there. Far as I hear, they've heard about you in Columbus. The way it strikes me, right now, if you was to run for the House, say, you could get it; and you'd have a good start up there. That's all."

Wint laughed uneasily. "That can come later. Maybe."

"Thing is," said Amos, "if you was to get licked for Mayor, it'd hurt you."

"I'm not going to get licked," Wint exclaimed. "I'm going to win."

"Well—maybe," Amos agreed. "Only I just want you to know that if you'd rather try for something else, I'd back you to the limit."

"You mean after election? Next year?"

"I couldn't do much if you was licked."

Wint leaned toward him. "Just what do you mean?"

"Just what I say."

"Are you asking me to withdraw?" Wint asked. His heart was in his mouth. "I know you and Routt have always worked together. Do you want me to get out and let him have it?"

"I'm not asking you to do a thing. I'm offering you a good excuse to—maybe—dodge a licking."

"I'm not going to get licked," Wint insisted. "And if there's a licking waiting for me—by God, I won't dodge!"

Amos looked at him curiously. "Well, that's all right. I just put the thing up to you."

"But I owe you enough," said Wint, "so that if you asked me to quit—I'd do it."

"I'm not asking you."

"Then," Wint declared, "I stick; and I win."

Amos moved a little in his chair; and he sighed. "Well," he drawled, "I'm watching you."

Wint left Amos, a little later; and he walked home with a weight on his shoulders. He had counted on the Congressman; but—this was half-hearted support at best that Amos was offering. Wint was puzzled, he could not understand; and he was depressed, and worried, and unhappy. He had an impulse to get out, throw the whole matter to one side, forget it all; but on the heels of the thought, his jaw hardened and he shook his head.

"No," he said. "No; I'll stick it out to the end."

He would have been more concerned, and he would have been thoroughly angry, if he could have heard Agnes Caretall talk to Amos when he had left. She came in to retrieve her lost slipper; and she was fuming indignantly. Old Maria Hale, setting the table for breakfast as she always did, the last thing at night, overheard a word or two of their talk. She heard Agnes exclaim:

"I don't see how you can be so calm, just because you elected him. But that doesn't give him any right to think he can do a thing like that with me."

And she heard Amos's slow, even voice reply:

"No; it doesn't give him any right."

"I should think you could say something," Agnes cried. "Your own daughter!"

Maria heard Amos say something about "fooling." And Agnes retorted:

"It wasn't fooling! It was—plain insulting!"

"Well, we can't let him do that," Amos agreed drawlingly. Then Maria departed to the kitchen and heard no more. She had paid no particular attention. The old darky lived in a world of her own. A quiet world. A world that was not far from coming to its end. She was very old.

After Agnes left him and went upstairs Amos sat for a long time, very still, before the fire. His eyes were weary, and his calm face was troubled.

Once he lifted his glance from the fire and saw a picture of Agnes on the mantel; and he got up and took it in his big hands. It had been taken two or three years ago; and it was very beautiful. A gay, happy face; the face of a child without cares. A good face, Amos thought. An honest one.

He compared it in his thoughts with Agnes as she was now; and the trouble in his countenance deepened. After a little, he said to himself as he had said once before: "I wish her mother hadn't 've died."

He put the picture slowly back on the mantel, and sat down and once more became motionless, staring into the fire. To one watching him it would have seemed in that moment that Amos, too, was very old.

CHAPTER V

A LOST ALLY

CONGRESSMAN Amos Caretall staged, next morning in the Post Office, one of those dramatic incidents which had checkered his career and done a good deal to make him what he was. These scenes were meat and drink to Amos. He liked to hark back to them and chuckle at the memory. In Washington, last winter, for example, he had told over and over the story of his speech at the rally of Winthrop Chase, Senior; his pledge to vote for a Chase, and the sequel to that pledge. The thing appealed to his sense of humor.

This morning he met Wint in the Post Office and snubbed him. And within half an hour all Hardiston knew about it, and was talking about it. The way of the thing was this.

Wint had met Jack Routt on the way uptown; and they came up Broad Street together, and down Main to the Post Office. Wint was thoughtful and a little silent; Routt expansively amiable in the fashion that had become habitual with him since the campaign opened. He asked Wint, jocularly, whether he was downhearted, and Wint said he was not. Routt told him he would be. "You'll be ready to quit before I'm through with you, old man," he warned Wint. "You'll be ready to crawl into your hole. Oh, I'm laying for you."

"Go ahead," Wint told him quietly.

"All your ads in the papers won't do you a bit of good, either. That's good money wasted. You have to get out and talk to the voters, Wint. Take a tip from me. It's the word of mouth that does the trick."

Wint said if this were so Routt would surely come out on top. "You've used word of mouth pretty freely," he remarked.

"Getting into the quick, am I?" Routt chuckled.

"Why, no. I just commented on the fact that...."

Routt asked solicitously: "Look here. You're not sore, are you? You know, the understanding was that this was to be a real fight."

"Of course," Wint agreed. "And I'm not sore. Go as far as you like."

A moment later, Routt said: "I heard Amos was going to throw you down. Anything in that? If he does, you haven't got a chance."

"Nothing in it," Wint told him. "I had a talk with Amos last night."

Routt laughed and said Amos's promises didn't amount to anything. "Is he backing you; or is he holding off?" he asked. "I haven't heard that he's doing much."

"You'll hear in due time," Wint told him.

He thought, afterward, that it was a curious coincidence that Routt should have said this about Amos on this particular morning. It was almost as though Routt had really had some foreknowledge. But at the time, the question made no great impression on him.

When they turned into the Post Office, the mail had not yet been distributed, and the windows were closed. There were perhaps a dozen men there, waiting before their boxes, talking, smoking, spitting on the floor. Routt and Wint took their places among these men; and Routt stuck near Wint. There was some good-natured chaffing. And after a little, Amos and Peter Gergue came in together. Every one had a word for Amos. It was a minute or two after he came in the door before he worked back through the groups to where Routt and Wint stood. He looked at the two, head on one side, and Wint said:

"Good morning, Amos."

Amos squinted a little; then, without replying to Wint, he turned to Jack Routt, at Wint's side, and thrust out his hand. "Morning, Routt."

He and Routt shook hands, and Wint went a little white with surprise, still not fully understanding. Routt said cheerfully:

"Back in time to see the election, Amos."

Amos nodded cordially. "And back in time to shake hands with the next Mayor, Routt," he said. "You're making a first-rate campaign. If you need any help—"

Routt took it all as a matter of course. Wint had stepped back a little; he was leaning his shoulders against the wall, and it seemed to him the world was swimming. "I'll surely call on you," Routt said.

Amos turned toward his mail box and unlocked it. Gergue shook Routt by the hand. "Morning, Mister Mayor," he said; and then, casually, to the other: "H'lo, Wint."

Every one had seen; no one had a word to say. The windows opened as sign that the mail was all distributed. Every one bustled forward to open their boxes; and they went out, ripping open letters and papers, talking in low voices, glancing sidewise at Wint. Routt had gone out with Amos and Peter. Wint pulled himself together, got his mail, and went out into the street by himself. Hardiston seemed like a new town; it was changed, terribly changed, by a word or two from Amos.

Every one seemed to know what had happened, almost as soon as it had happened. The people who spoke to him on his way to Hoover's office—he was planning a day with the law books—seemed to Wint to be grinning maliciously. He was still dazed, unable to think clearly. When he was settled in the back room with the leather-bound books, Wint tried to put his mind on them; but he could not. He was groping for understanding. He felt as a child feels, when it has received a blow it cannot understand. He was incredulous. The thing could not have happened; but it had happened. The ground was cut from under his feet. Cut from under his feet. He was lost, helpless. He had been supported for so long by Amos; he had felt the Congressman's substantial strength upholding him for so many months that it had come to seem to him as an inevitable feature of his very life. He did not see how he could go on without it.

Yet in the end he had to believe, had to accept the new condition. He remembered Amos's attitude, the night before. Amos had suggested his withdrawing from the fight; the Congressman had almost asked him to withdraw. He had refused; now Amos would force him. Would beat him to his knees. At least, Amos would try to do that. A slow anger began to grow in Wint; a slow determination not to be beaten. Or if he was to be beaten, he would not be beaten without a fight. In simple words, Wint got mad; and he always fought best when he was mad. His resolution hardened; a certain fire of inspiration came to light within him. He began to make plans to meet this new contingency. He would go to the people of Hardiston with the facts. Appeal to them. Prove to them that he deserved their good will; and that he deserved their votes. An hour after the scene in the Post Office, Wint was more determined to win than he had ever been before. Even Amos was not invincible. The man could be beaten. Not only in this fight, but in others. Wint began to cast forward into the future, and plan what he would do.

Dick Hoover came in, after a while, and gripped him by the shoulder. "I say," he exclaimed excitedly, "they tell me Amos has thrown you down. Is it true?"

Wint nodded. "Yes," he said crisply.

Hoover swore. "The dirty, double-crossing hound. What are you going to do?"

"Lick him," Wint replied.

Hoover looked doubtful. "Lick him? You can't, Wint."

Wint said nothing.

"Can you?" Dick Hoover asked.

"I'm going to," said Wint.

Hoover banged his fist on the book that lay open before Wint. "By God, you'll find some that are willing to help!"

"I know it," Wint agreed.

"My father and I.... Whatever we can do."

"Thanks!"

"Get after him, Wint," Hoover urged. "Show him up. No one has ever gone after Caretall the right way. Start something. The people are always looking for fun, for a change. By God, I believe you can do it!"

"I told you I was going to," Wint repeated.

That night, his father spoke to him of the matter. The elder Chase had heard it during the day, had heard what Amos had done. And there was fire in his eye. He had no sooner come into the house, before supper, than he called:

"Oh, Wint!"

Wint was upstairs, getting ready for supper. He answered: "Hello, dad."

"Coming down?"

"Right away."

"Well, hurry."

Wint was surprisingly cheerful. The elation of battle was on him. He chuckled at the impatience in his father's tone; but he did make haste, and a moment later joined the other man in the sitting room. The elder Chase was standing, stirring about, his face hot and angry.

"Look here, Wint," he exclaimed, without parley. "I hear Amos Caretall turned you down, to-day."

"Yes."

"In the Post Office."

"Yes, this morning."

"Told Routt he was going to win."

"Just that, dad."

Chase threw up his hands furiously. "By God, Wint, I told you he'd cut your throat! The dirty...."

Wint put his hand up to his neck. "Cut my throat?" he repeated. "I seem to be all here."

"You wouldn't believe me, Wint. But I warned you."

"Yes, you did."

"What do you say now to this fine friend of yours? Damn the man!"

"I say he's started trouble for himself."

"What do you mean?"

"I mean I'm going to prove that when he said Routt would be elected, he was either a fool or a liar."

Chase banged his hand on the table beside him till the lamp jumped in its place, and the shade tilted to one side. Mrs. Chase came bustling in just then, and straightened it, and protested anxiously: "I declare, Winthrop, you're the hardest man around the house. You do disturb things so. I don't see—"

"Caretall has turned against Wint," Chase told her.

She nodded wisely. "Well, didn't you always say he would?"

"Of course I did. Wint wouldn't believe me. Now he's done it."

"He ought to be ashamed of himself," Mrs. Chase declared. "But I always did think you were wrong, Wint, to be so friendly with a man who had treated your father as he did. He—"

"I know you did, mother."

Chase cried: "You take it almighty calmly, Wint. Isn't there any blood in you, son? Don't you ever get mad? Damn it, the man ought to be kicked out of town."

Wint laughed good-naturedly. "Oh, I don't know. He has a right to support Jack if he wants to."

"A right? What have his rights to do with it? By God, I'd have more respect for you if you could get good and mad!"

Wint chuckled. "I'll try to work up a fever if you like. I always want your respect, dad."

Chase said in a softer tone: "You always have it, Wint. You've earned it. But it makes my blood boil to see Caretall do this to you. To my son."

"It's terrible," Wint agreed whimsically; and Chase protested:

"I believe you're laughing at me."

Wint shook his head anxiously. "No. But I don't see that it does any good to get excited. I'm aiming to keep my head—and my job."

"You're going to fight?"

"Fight?" Wint echoed. "Why, dad, you won't be able to see me for dust."

"You've waked up at last. You're not going to sit back and let Routt lie about you, and let Amos trick you."

"I'm going to fight," said Wint. "Also I'm going to win."

Chase exclaimed: "I believe you can. If you try."

"You know," said Wint, "in a way I'm glad this has happened."

"Glad?" Chase asked. "For God's sake, why?"

Wint touched his arm in a comradely way. "Because now you and I can line up together. Fight side by side. I'd rather have you with me than Amos."

Chase said, with a sudden humility: "Amos might be able to help you more than I can."

"I'd rather have your personal vote than all the votes Amos can swing."

"You'd have had that, anyway."

"Well, isn't that worth being crossed by Amos?"

Chase said: "But don't fool yourself, Wint. Don't imagine this is going to be easy. Caretall is powerful."

Wint said with a slow energy: "I've done some thinking, dad. Amos is powerful. But—I don't know just how to say it, but what I mean is this. I think I've been a good Mayor. I've tried to be a good one, anyway. And if a fellow tries to do the right thing, it seems to me the world has a habit of turning his way. I've done my share, straight out and out. And I'm going to the voters on that record. If there's anything in—democracy—then I can beat Amos. He's cleverer; he's better at tricks and contraptions. But he can't beat the right thing, dad. And—I've a hunch that the right is on my side, on our side, in this."

"Right or wrong," Chase declared, "we'll lick him if there's any way in the world it can be done." His eyes lighted. "I believe I can get Kite to line up with you."

Wint shook his head. "No."

"I think I can," Chase urged. "He hates Amos."

"I don't want him," said Wint. "This is a clean fight."

"You want all the help you can get."

"All the decent help. There are enough decent folk in town to put this thing through."

"You can't be too squeamish, Wint."

"I'm too squeamish to take help from Kite," said Wint. "That's flat, dad. Put it out of your head."

Mrs. Chase was still doing her own work. She called them to supper, just then; and while they ate, she told them how tired she was. "I declare," she said, "I wish Hetty would come back here. I saw her, uptown, yesterday; and I asked her to. But she wouldn't. Said she had a better job. I told Mrs. Hullis last night that the girl—"

"Hetty never cooked a better supper than this," her husband told her; and the little woman smiled happily, and bridled like a girl, and said:

"Now, Winthrop, you're always telling me things like that, when you know they're not true. I'm just a—"

Wint laughed: "Quit apologizing for yourself, mother. It's a darned bad habit. Tell people you're a wonder, and they'll believe you. I've found that out. That's the way I'm going to be re-elected."

"You can tell them that, but you have to back it up," his father reminded him. "Brag's not so bad, if there's something to base it on."

"Well, isn't there?" Wint asked quietly; and his father's eyes lighted, and he cried:

"Yes, son, by Heaven, there is!"

Wint made no move, during the next day or two; but he laid his plans. He intended to do a great many things in the last week before election. He would concentrate his effort in those last days, so that the effect should not have time to disappear. He talked with Dick Hoover, and Dick's father; he talked with others. And he was surprised to find that such loyal supporters of Amos as Sam O'Brien and Ed Howe and even James T. Hollow were inclined to support him. Support him in spite of Amos. Sam told him as much.

He met Sam at the moving-picture show that night; that is to say, he met Sam just outside. And Sam and Hetty Morfee were together. That surprised Wint; he had not even known that they were friends. But it was obvious that they were very good friends indeed. When he stopped to speak to them, Hetty looked at him with an appealing defiance. He wondered if Sam knew. He did not think it would matter. Sam was the sort who could, if he chose, forgive.

He spoke to Sam of the coming election; and Sam said: "Sure, I'm for you. Amos's all right in Congress. But he'd make a mighty poor Mayor. I'm for you, Wint, m'boy. You've got nerve; and you're funny, sometimes. Lord, but I've thought there was times when I'd die laughing at you. But you're there, Wint. You can have me."

He and Hetty went away together, and Wint watched them, forgetting what Sam had said in wondering about Sam and Hetty.

He got further comfort the next day from a man as close to Amos as Peter Gergue. Peter told him it looked as though Routt would win. "But there's a pile that'll vote for you," he added. "It ain't hurt you much, Amos quitting." He looked all around furtively, and fumbled in his back hair, and said: "Amos didn't do you such a bad turn, even if he meant to. I might give you a vote myself, Wint. I don't know but I might."

Wint laid plans for rallies on Friday and Saturday nights of the week before election. On Monday and Tuesday of that week, he worked all day, preparing the words he meant to say at those rallies. It was tough work; it was hard for him to put his own determination into words.

Tuesday night, the first of November, there came a diversion. Jim Radabaugh telephoned to him at midnight, summoning him out of bed. When Wint answered the 'phone, the marshal asked:

"That you, Wint?"

"Yes."

"You r'member you told me to get after the bootleggers?"

"Of course."

"Well, I've done that little thing."

Wint exclaimed: "First rate. You mean you've arrested some one?"

"I should say I had."

"Who?" Wint asked.

"You know Lutcher?"

"Of course."

"Him," said Radabaugh.

CHAPTER VI

KITE TAKES A HAND

THAT Radabaugh should have arrested Lutcher was almost as though he had arrested Kite himself; and Wint knew it. It brought matters to an issue, direct and unavoidable. Lutcher, for all practical purposes, was Kite. His arrest meant an open defiance to the head and front of the opposition. Wint, characteristically, leaped at the chance. He might have been more lenient with a lesser man.

He asked the marshal: "Where is he?"

"Locked up," said Radabaugh.

"In the calaboose?"

"Yeah. Him and the fire horses are all little pals together."

"You've got the evidence?"

"Sure."

"No doubt about it?"

"Not a bit. I'll tell you—"

"That can wait till morning. What does he say?"

"Acts like he wasn't surprised. Acts like he expected it. Matter of fact, he pretty near invited me to pinch him."

Wint nodded to himself. "That means they're looking for trouble."

"I'd say so."

"Haven't seen Kite, have you?"

"Hear he's out of town. Be back Thursday."

"All right. We'll hold Lutcher till then and have it out."

Wint heard a gulp that told him Radabaugh was shifting that bulge in his cheek. "He's wanted to furnish bail," the marshal said.

"Nothing doing," Wint told him.

"We-ell—he's got a right to want to."

"We're sound sleepers here. You couldn't raise me with the telephone," Wint suggested.

"Lutcher's all dressed up in a yellow vest and everything; and he didn't fetch his jail pajamas with him."

"He can sleep in the yellow vest."

"It's your funeral," Radabaugh decided philosophically. "Whatever you say."

"That's right." And Wint added: "I'm glad you got him, Jim. Good work."

"Oh, he weren't so much to get. I told you he put himself in the way of it."

"Just the same, you had good nerve."

"We-ell—maybe so."

Wint went back to bed; but he didn't go to sleep. He was tingling with the pleasurable excitement of combat; and he was immensely pleased at this chance to give evidence of the sincerity of his fight for a clean Hardiston. Those orders to Radabaugh which had become something like a proverb in Hardiston.... This was their test. He meant that they should meet the test.

He could not decide whether the incident would help him or hurt him at the polls; it was impossible to tell. But—he did not care. Hurt or help, his course would be the same. Unchangeable. Lutcher should get the limit. Whatever the evidence justified. The rest was on the lap of the gods. Let them take care of it.

It may have been an hour or two before he was asleep again; and he woke in the morning a little tired because of the sleep he had lost. But the cold tub revived him; he was cheerful enough when he came down to breakfast; and when his father appeared, Wint told him the news.

"Something doing, dad," he said.

Chase looked at him in quick and surprised interest; and he asked: "What? What do you mean, Wint?"

"Did you hear the telephone last night, about midnight?"

"No."

"I did," said Mrs. Chase. "I thought I heard the bell; but your father was asleep, and I wasn't sure. I came to the head of the stairs, but you were already down."

"I answered as quickly as I could. The bell only rang once or twice."

"Who was it?" Chase asked quickly.

"Radabaugh. Jim. The marshal. He's arrested Lutcher."

"Lutcher! What for?"

"Bootlegging!"

Chase uttered an involuntary exclamation. "Lutcher? He's Kite's right-hand man."

"Absolutely."

"Radabaugh arrested him?"

"Yes."

"Has he got a case?"

"Jim always has a case, when he makes an arrest."

"But Lutcher.... He's shrewd. Knows how to cover his tracks."

"He didn't cover well enough this time." Wint's elation was singing in his voice.

"But he—"

"As a matter of fact," said Wint, "Radabaugh thinks Lutcher allowed himself to be caught. Thinks he wanted to get arrested."

"By God, that doesn't sound reasonable!"

"He'll be sorry."

"They've got something up their sleeves, Wint."

"So have I!"

"You—What?"

"My arms," said Wint cheerfully. "With a fist on each one and a punch in each fist."

Chase looked uncertain. "They'll try some trick."

Wint touched the other's arm. "Don't worry. They've got to fight in the open, now. The time's short. And I'm not afraid of them in the open."

"They're treacherous. They'll strike behind your back."

"I'm not worried."

But the older man was worried. He said little more; nevertheless his concern was plain. Wint was sorry, a little disappointed. His father's uneasiness did not affect his own confidence. He was as sure of himself as before. But he had expected his father to be as confident as himself, as sure.

To him, the matter of Lutcher simply offered an opportunity for a telling blow; but it was evident that to his father the incident was rather a threat than an opportunity.

He and his father walked downtown together; they separated when Wint turned aside toward the fire-engine house where his office was. The older man gave him a word of warning there. "Go carefully, Wint," he urged. "Watch yourself."

"Don't worry."

"Be sure of the law, Wint. Don't make a mistake. They would jump on it."

"That's Foster's job. And I'm no ... I've studied up a bit."

"Take care."

"Right, dad."

They separated, and Wint went on to his office. Radabaugh was not there, but he appeared a little later. "I've just had Lutcher up to Sam O'Brien's for breakfast," he explained. "He wanted to go to the hotel; but I told him Sam had the contract to victual the city prisoners."

Wint chuckled. "Where is he now?"

"Down in the calaboose."

"Does he still want to furnish bail?"

"Says he does."

"Kite comes home to-morrow, doesn't he?"

"Yeah."

"Well, we'll let Lutcher out on bail till then. I'm curious to hear what Kite will have to say."

Radabaugh shifted the plug in his cheek. "Think he'll have anything to say?"

"Don't you?"

"We-ell, he might."

"Bring Lutcher up, and we'll turn him loose."

Lutcher came. Wint chuckled inwardly at sight of what Radabaugh had called a yellow vest. It was an ornate affair; no doubt of it. He was inclined to expect an outbreak from Lutcher, but the big, bald man was cheerfully amiable. Wint said: "Sorry we had to hold you in jail. The marshal tried to get me, but I'm a sound sleeper."

"Well, the bed wasn't soft," Lutcher admitted. "But I can stand it."

"I'm going to hold you till to-morrow," Wint said. "Unless you want to plead guilty and accept sentence now."

"Guilty? No, sir. You can't pin anything on me, Wint. You ought to know that."

"We'll see," Wint told him. "Want to stay in jail, or furnish bail?"

"Bail, of course. I can get any one."

"I'd rather have money."

"Check any good?"

"I'll cash it before you leave here."

Lutcher said amiably that that was all right, and asked the amount. Wint said "Four hundred." And Lutcher whistled, and protested: "That's pretty hard."

"Harder than the bed in the calaboose?"

Lutcher grinned, and wrote. Wint took the check and his hat and left Lutcher with the marshal. He went to the bank, drew the money, and deposited the cash to the city's account. "Just so there can be no question of stopping payment on that check," he explained.

Back at his office, he told Lutcher he was free to go. Lutcher, contriving to look dapper and well-dressed in spite of his night, took himself away. Then Wint turned to the marshal.

"Now, Jim, how about it?" he asked. "What's the case against him?"

Radabaugh shifted the knob in his cheek to clear the way for speech; and he sat down, and hitched his trousers up, and opened his coat and put his thumbs in his armholes. "We-ell," he said, "it was like this."

He had been scouting around for two weeks past, he said, according to Wint's orders, without discovering anything. But the afternoon before, an automobile had come into town with some boxes in the tonneau and a stranger driving. It made some stir on Main Street; and then it drove openly enough to Lutcher's place, on the alley. He had seen the boxes carried up Lutcher's stair.

"First off," he explained, "I figured it couldn't be what it looked like. Didn't seem as if they'd be so open about it. Lutcher had been lying low. I figured they might be aiming to get me excited, just to make a fool of me. So I held off a spell.

"But the thing stuck in my head. They might be trying a game, and they might not. I decided to keep an eye on Lutcher's place, and I did. All that afternoon."

Wint said: "They were brazen, eh?"

"I'd say so," Radabaugh agreed; and he shifted his plug and went on.

"Nothing happened, particular, all afternoon. I et my supper; and after it was dark, I took another walk down that way. Met Jack Routt coming out of the alley; and he stopped me and talked to me. It was on his breath. Plain enough. He must have knowed that; must have meant me to smell it. He was so darned open, I suspicioned there was a trick. So I still held off.

"But I took a walk through the alley about nine o'clock. All quiet. A light in Lutcher's place, that was all. Some men up there. I wondered.

"I walked through again, after a while. Sounded like they was having a game. Finally, about a quarter past eleven, I come along through, and some one yelled. Sounded boozy. So I says to myself: 'Jim, you're the goat. You got to bite, if it's only to see the joke.' So I went up the stairs. Quiet."

"No search warrant?" Wint asked.

"Why, no," said Radabaugh innocently. "I was just dropping in for a drink, like I'd done before. Some time back."

Wint grinned. "Of course. Go ahead."

"We-ell, the door wasn't locked," said Radabaugh. "So I knew I was meant to come in. And I went in. On in where they were. Four of them. Tuttle, and Harley, and Gates, and this Lutcher. I went in; and Tuttle throws a five-dollar bill to Lutcher and says: 'Here's for that last bottle, Lutch.'

"Lutcher took it. And he'd seen me before he took it. Then he got up and says: 'Hello, Jim. Have a drink?'

"So I told him to come along."

He stopped; it was evident that his story was done. Wint nodded. "Well, that's plain enough," he agreed.

"It's my evidence against theirs," Radabaugh reminded him. "But that's the way it's got to be."

"Your evidence is good enough for me."

"Sure. But he'll fight."

"We can't help that," Wint reminded him. "All we can do is—soak him." There was a sudden heat in his voice; and Radabaugh eyed him curiously and asked:

"In earnest, ain't you?"

"Absolutely," said Wint.

"Well, it never hurt any, to be in earnest. Go to it, boss."

Hardiston talked it over that day, and wondered what Wint would do. Most people thought he would sentence Lutcher; some declared he would wait till after election, for fear of influencing the vote. Sam O'Brien laughed at this view. "Wint wasn't ever afraid of anything," he declared. "Why man, you make me laugh. He'll soak Lutcher so hard Lutcher'll need to be wrung out like a sponge."

There were others who were loyal to Wint; and there were some few— not very vociferous except among those of like views—who were loyal to Lutcher. But for the most part, people waited. Waited for Kite to come home. This was his fight; that was understood. Lutcher was his man.

He came on the early morning train next day; and his coming was marked. Lutcher met him at the train. They came up the hill from the station together, and went to the Bazaar, and were alone there for a little while. Routt joined them presently. Routt would represent Lutcher in court, he said. But Kite laughed at that.

"It will never come to court, man," he told Routt. "You know that."

"I'm not so sure," Jack objected.

"Then we'll smash that young rip, flat as an egg," said Kite harshly, with a gesture of his clenched fist. "But he'll crawl, I say."

Lutcher got up. "I'm willing to see that," he declared amiably. "Come along and stage the show."

So they went down to the fire-engine house together, and they found the council room where Wint held court crowded with Hardiston folk who wanted to see what was going to happen. Radabaugh was there; and he told them Wint was in his office, in the rear. Kite bade Routt and Lutcher sit down. "I want to see the Mayor," he told Radabaugh, in a peremptory tone. "Take me in."

Radabaugh shifted the bulge in his cheek, and told Kite to stay where he was. "I'll see if he wants to see you," he said, and went into Wint's office. A moment later, he appeared at the door and beckoned to Kite, and there was an instant's hush in the big room as every one watched Kite go in. Then they began to whisper and talk together; and instantly were still again, trying to hear what Wint and Kite were saying. Radabaugh had shut the door behind Kite and stood, with his back against it, indolently studying the crowd.

They tried to hear; but they did not hear anything except a murmur of voices now and then. They could only guess at what had been said from what happened when Kite had been with Wint five minutes, or perhaps ten. At the end of that period, the door opened so suddenly that Radabaugh was thrown off balance. He stumbled to one side, and Wint came out and sat down at his desk. Kite was on Wint's heels; he whispered to Wint fiercely, but Wint, without heeding Kite, said to the clerk:

"Call Lutcher's case."

And at that Kite looked at Wint for a moment with a red and furious face, and then he turned and bolted for the stairs and was gone.

Wint's countenance was steady, his lips were white. He heard Radabaugh's story of the arrest of Lutcher; and when it was done, he asked Routt, who was appearing for Lutcher, whether the man denied anything. Routt hesitated, uncertain what Kite would wish him to do. He whispered with Lutcher. Then he stood up and said:

"He has decided to plead guilty, your Honor."

Wint nodded, consulted in a low voice with Foster, and said: "Two hundred and costs."

That was all. While Routt and Lutcher arranged the payment of the fine, the crowd began to disperse, a few lingering in the hope of some fresh sensation. And those who lingered and those who went their way were agreeing, one with another, that this matter was not ended.

"Kite's got something up his sleeve," Gates told Bob Dyer. "You wait and see."

And Dyer nodded, and grinned, and said: "Yes, wait till old V. R. takes a hand."

When every one was gone except Radabaugh, and Foster, and one or two others, Wint got up and went into his office and shut the door.

CHAPTER VII

A FEW WORDS TO THE WISE

THOSE minutes—five or ten—which Wint spent with V. R. Kite in his office behind the council chamber, before he sentenced Lutcher, left Wint depressed, shaken by foreboding. He was like one beset in the darkness by enemies he could not see. He felt the imminence of disaster without being able to avert it. The world was all wrong. Life had turned her thumbs down. There could be only destruction ahead.

He felt this, without being able to put a name to the peril. It was intangible; Kite had only hinted at it. But the little buzzard of a man had been in deadly earnest. Wint was sure of that. So.... There was nothing to do but wait for the blow to fall; and waiting is the hardest thing in the world to do.

Kite had come into Wint's office that morning with a smile in his dry eyes. It was a smile that had triumph in it; and it held also a certain mean magnanimity to a fallen foe. It was as though Kite knew Wint was beaten, and expected him to surrender, and was willing to accept the surrender while despising Wint for yielding. Wint had expected the little man to come in anger, with protestations, and open threats, and a desperate sort of defiance. He was prepared for these things; he was not prepared for the confidence in Kite's bearing. And his first glimpse of it disturbed him, made him uneasy.

Kite sat down without being invited; he put his hat on Wint's desk; and he said in an amiably triumphant way:

"Well, young man?"

He seemed to expect Wint to speak; but Wint had nothing to say to Kite. He replied: "You wanted to speak to me?"

"Not exactly," said Kite. "I wanted to hear what you have to say."

"I?" said Wint. "I have nothing to say, except what I shall say to Lutcher in court presently."

"Ah, yes, Lutcher," Kite murmured. "Lutcher, to be sure." And he nodded as though Lutcher were scarce worth considering, and kept silent, to force Wint into speech.

This trick of keeping silent, forcing the other man to make the advances, was a favorite with Amos Caretall. Amos had beaten V. R. Kite at the game more than once; but Wint had beaten Amos. He beat Kite, now. The older man was driven to speak first. He said, in a quick rush of words:

"You know you're done for. Done. Skinned. Licked. Down. What have you got to say?"

Before a direct attack, Wint recovered himself. He laughed. "I should say you were wide of the mark, Kite," he said cheerfully. "That is, if I know what you're talking about. The mayoralty?"

"Of course. Your hide is on the fence."

Wint shook his head. "I haven't felt it being removed; and they say the process is painful. So I would have felt it go."

"Don't joke, young man. You know what I mean."

"I know," said Wint, "that I'm going to be elected Mayor. I know Routt is licked. If that's what you mean."

Kite laughed, a harsh, short, mirthless laugh. "What's the use of bluffing? I tell you, I know."

Wint said a little impatiently: "You're talking in a mysterious way, Kite. I don't see your object. If you've no plain words in your system, we're wasting time."

"I've a plain word for you. Hardiston will have a plain word for you." There was a deadly menace in the little man's tone, and Wint felt it, and was a little impressed. But he managed a smile.

"I've a plain word for Lutcher, too," he said. "You're keeping Lutcher waiting."

"Oh, Lutcher," said Kite again. "You'll let him go."

"Hardly," said Wint; and Kite cried:

"I say you will. Don't be a fool. I tell you I know."

"You may know some things," said Wint slowly. "But you are wrong about Lutcher. He gets the limit."

Kite leaned forward; and his voice was almost kind. "Young man," he said, "you've good nerve. You're a good fighter. You're a vote getter, too, in an awkward way. If I didn't have the winning hand, I should be worried about what you can do. But I have; from the person who knows. You're beaten. You might as well accept it."

"If I'm beaten," said Wint, "I'll know it by midnight of the eighth. Not by your telling."

Kite lost his temper for an instant; and he cried: "You miserable little dog! With not even the grace to know you're whipped."

Wint said coldly: "Just what are you talking about, Kite? You wanted to see me. Well, here I am. What have you got to say? I'll give you about thirty seconds more."

"Thirty seconds?" Kite echoed. "You'll give me all the time I want. I tell you, you're done."

"What have you got to say?"

"Go out there, and.... No, first write out for me a notice of your withdrawal from the mayoralty fight. Then go out there and turn Lutcher loose. If you do these two things, they'll save you, for a while. And nothing else in the world can save you."

Wint—there could be no question of this—was frightened. He was afraid of the certainty in Kite's manner, afraid of the mystery behind the other's confidence. But it is braver to appear brave when you are frightened than when there is no fright in you; and Wint, frightened though he might be, was yet brave. He rose.

"Time's up, Kite," he said.

Kite exclaimed: "Don't be a fool. I don't want to ruin you. Save yourself, boy."

Wint opened the door and stepped out into the other room.

That was Thursday morning, five days before election. A fair, fine day of the sort you will see in Hardiston in the fall. The sun was warm, the air was crisp and dry. It was a day when simply living was pleasant; when to draw breath was a joy. Ordinarily, Wint would have drunk this day to the full. But there was abroad in Hardiston a whispered word; men looked at him curiously as he passed them. No one seemed to know exactly what was coming; yet they looked upon Wint as one looks upon a man about to die. Kite had said nothing. From the fire-engine house he had gone direct to his Bazaar and stayed there. One or two of his lieutenants visited him there during the morning.

Kite said nothing; no one had any definite word. Yet Hardiston was whispering its guesses. Somehow the rumor had gone abroad that Wint was done, that Kite was about to strike. There was a lively and an eager anticipation. It is always easy to anticipate the misfortunes of others; and there will always be those to rejoice in the imminent downfall of one who has held himself high. Wint had enemies enough; even some of those whom he had counted his friends looked askance at him this day.

When he went to the Post Office for the noon mail, he encountered Hetty on the street. Because he was thoughtful and abstracted, he spoke to her curtly. Hetty did not speak to him at all. She turned away her head. But Wint, already passing by, did not mark this.

He met B. B. Beecham in the Post Office, and stopped in with B. B. at the *Journal* office afterward. B. B. talked pleasantly of a number of things, till Wint could be still no longer. He asked abruptly:

"B. B., have you heard anything?"

The editor looked surprised. "How do you mean?" he asked.

"What's Kite up to?"

B. B. said: "I don't know. Is he up to something?"

"He came to me before court this morning and demanded that I withdraw from this fight and let Lutcher go."

"Demanded it?"

"Yes."

"On what ground?"

"He made some covert threat. He was not specific."

B. B. shook his head. "I hadn't heard."

"Oh, no one knows this," Wint told him. "I refused, of course, and fined Lutcher. Now every one in town seems to know that something is going to drop on me."

"What is there that he can bring against you?"

"Not a thing. Except the old stuff. What everybody knows."

B. B. nodded. "I should not worry, if I were you, if there's nothing."

"There isn't anything, I tell you," Wint exclaimed impatiently.

"Then what can he do?"

Wint got up, a little weary. "All right," he said. "I thought you might have heard."

B. B. shook his head. "Not a thing."

Wint went to Sam O'Brien's restaurant for dinner. It was a little after his usual hour, and there were only two or three others on the stools before the high, scrubbed counter. O'Brien waited on Wint himself, and Wint ate in silence, under the other's sympathetic eye.

When he paid for his dinner, O'Brien asked heartily:

"Well, Wint, m' boy, how's tricks?"

Wint looked up at the other and smiled wearily. "Rotten, Sam," he said.

O'Brien protested. "Lord, now, I'd not say that. As fine a day as it is."

"I wasn't talking about the weather," Wint told him. "It's just.... I guess I'm in the dumps, Sam. I've got a hunch. I've got a hunch something's going to drop on me like a ton of bricks."

"A hunch like that is bum company," O'Brien commented. "Where did you get it, Wint?"

Wint shook his head. "I don't know."

"Lord, boy! You act like you'd lost your nerve, Wint."

Wint said: "Maybe I have." He was terribly depressed, almost ready to drop out and surrender.

"You'd nerve enough when you soaked Lutcher, this morning," Sam reminded him. "I was proud of you, m' son. You've give me many a laugh, Wint, but I was proud o' your cool nerve this day."

"Oh, I'm not worried about Lutcher."

"I'd not be. Him nor his. The old buzzard of a Kite, neither."

Wint said: "I don't know. Kite's got something up his sleeve."

"That's as much as to say that he's tricky. It's these magicians that has things up their sleeves. Full of tricks. You stick to the middle of the road, Wint, and never mind their tricks. They'll trick their own selves."

Wint shook his head. "That's all right. But what can I do?"

"Do?" Sam echoed. "Why, fight 'em like that dog of yours fit Mrs. Moody's Jim." He nodded to Muldoon, curled as always near Wint's feet; and Wint dropped his hand to Muldoon's grizzled head. He was apt to turn to Muldoon in trouble. The dog was his shadow, always with him; but it was when he was troubled that Wint gave most heed to the terrier. At Wint's caress, Muldoon rolled his eyes up without moving his head; and Sam said:

"Look at him grin; the nervy pup. He's telling you to take a brace, m' son. You can't scare the dog."

"I'm not scared."

"You act damn like it," said Sam frankly; and Wint protested:

"It's only that I'm sick of it all. Sick of the fight, and the mud-throwing. And getting no thanks."

"Hell's bells," Sam exclaimed. "You talk like a woman!"

Wint looked at him curiously. "What's Kite up to, Sam? Have you heard?"

"Heard some rats say he would rip you up. And I told them you'd be doing some ripping, about that time. You're not going to make me out a liar, Wint. Are you now?"

"Oh, I suppose I'll fight."

He left the restaurant and walked down to Hoover's office and secluded himself in the back room; but his studies could not hold him. There was a curiously passive despair upon the boy. He could not shake it off. The whole thing seemed so little worth while. If there had been a chance to fight.... But the peril was intangible. He could not come to grips with it. He could not even be sure there was peril. He could not be sure of anything. Not even of himself. He asked himself despairingly: "Are you going to be a quitter, Wint?" And then thought hopelessly: "Oh, what's the use?"

In mid-afternoon, Dick Hoover looked in and said Gergue wanted to see Wint. Wint was surprised. "What does he want?" he asked. "Gergue?" He got up and went to the door and saw Peter waiting; and he called: "Come along in here."

Gergue came at the invitation. His hat was off; he was fumbling in the tangle of hair at the back of his neck. There was a curiously furtive uncertainty about the man. Wint thrust a chair toward Peter with his foot, and said: "Sit down." When Gergue was seated, and slicing a fill for his pipe, Wint asked:

"What's on your mind?"

Gergue looked at him sidewise, stuffing the crumbled tobacco into the black bowl. And he asked: "Wint, where do you figure I stand?"

Wint was surprised. "You mean—in this business between Routt and me?"

Gergue nodded. "Yeah."

"Why, with Routt, I suppose," Wint told him.

"Why d'you figure that?"

"You're tied up with Amos."

Gergue scratched a match. "Wint," he said, "Amos is a fine man. He does things his own way; but in the end, he pretty near always turns out pretty near right."

"Well, that's his record," Wint agreed. "He's usually on the winning side."

"Don't let that get away from you," said Gergue. "Don't you forget that, Wint!"

Wint laughed harshly; and he said: "I'm not likely to. I counted on him in this, you know."

Gergue leaned toward him. "Thing is, Wint, I'm wonderin' what you'd think if I told you something?"

"That would depend on what you told me."

"Something for your own good. Help you some."

Wint said, amiably enough: "I want to win this fight, Peter. But—after Amos's stand—I don't particularly want any help from him. I'd mistrust it."

"Say this come from me, personal."

"You're linked with Amos."

Gergue nodded resignedly. "Have it so," he agreed. "Anyway, I'm going to tell you."

Wint said: "All right. What do you want to tell?"

Gergue hesitated for a while, choosing his words. At last he asked: "You wondering what Kite aims to do to trim you?"

"Yes."

"Got any ideas?"

"No."

Gergue looked at him shrewdly. "Know any way he could hit at you?"

"No. Not with the truth."

Gergue hesitated; then he asked slowly: "Know any way he could hit at you with Hetty?"

"Hetty?" Wint echoed. "Hetty Morfee?"

"Yes. Her."

Wint was stupefied with surprise. "Good Lord, no!"

"She got any reason to be against you?"

"No. I—She's friendly, I think. Ought to be."

Gergue puffed at his pipe. Then he got up. "Wint," he said, "take it for what it's worth. I hear he's going to hit you with her."

Wint exclaimed angrily: "You're crazy, Peter. Or you're.... Look here, did Amos send you?"

"No."

"Is this some damned trick of his?"

"No."

"Well, what in God's name are you talking about?"

Gergue said thoughtfully: "I've said all I know. Think it over, Wint."

He went out, with a surprising quickness, and was gone before Wint could frame other questions. The young man was left to consider the thing.

When Wint went home for supper, he was still mystified; but he was beginning to grow angry. Angry at the mere suggestion that lay behind Peter's words. Angry at Gergue for saying them. And this anger was a more hopeful sign than his depression of the morning had been. He was fiercely resentful at Hardiston, at the whole world.

He met Joan, halfway home. That is to say, he overtook her on her way, and they walked home together. He was so absorbed in his own thoughts that he did not see there was something troubling the girl until she spoke of it. She said: "Wint, I met Agnes Caretall uptown."

He nodded, scarce hearing; and Joan said: "She's a good deal of a gossip, you know."

There was something in her tone which caught his attention; and he looked at her sharply and asked: "What do you mean? What did she say?"

"She said Mr. Kite was going to ruin you," Joan told him.

Wint laughed shortly. "Well, that's no secret. At least it's no secret that he wants to."

"She said he was going to," Joan insisted.

Wint asked: "How, since she knew so much, did she know how?"

Joan touched his arm. "Don't be angry, Wint."

But Wint was angry, even with Joan. He exclaimed harshly, after the fashion of angry men: "I'm not mad. What did she say?"

Joan told him. "She said they were going to link you up with Hetty."

Wint exclaimed: "Lord! You too? I'm sick of that tale. Hetty!"

Joan begged: "But there isn't anything, is there?"

Wint faced her hotly. "If you don't know without being told.... Can't I even count on you, Joan?"

"I only asked."

They were at her gate, and Wint lifted his hat abruptly. "Think what you like," he told her sharply. "Good afternoon!"

He left her there; left her, and Joan looked after him with troubled sympathy in her eyes, and something more. There was a mist of tears in them when she went on toward the house.

While they were at supper that night, the telephone rang, and Wint's father answered. After a moment he came back into the dining room. "Wint," he said, "it's Kite."

"Kite?" Wint demanded, pushing back his chair. "What does he want?"

"He wants to see you—and me. He says he'll be out here at eight. He wants us to be here."

Wint's face turned black with anger; then he threw up one hand. "All right," he cried, "tell Kite we'll be here."

CHAPTER VIII

POOR HETTY AGAIN

WHEN Chase came back from the table after telling Kite that they would expect him at the appointed time, Wint asked:

"Did he say what he wanted?"

Mrs. Chase exclaimed: "I don't think you ought to have let him come, Winthrop. I don't want that man in my house. He—"

Chase answered Wint. "No. Just said he wanted to see us." He was troubled; and he showed it. "What do you think he wants, Wint? Something about Lutcher?"

Wint shook his head. "I think he's going to hit at me. Somehow. There's been a rumor around town all day. They say he has something."

Chase asked quickly: "Has he? Has he got anything on you, Wint?"

"Not that I know of. There's nothing he could get. Nothing to get." He looked at his father in a quick, appealing way. "Dad, I wish you'd just remember that, whatever happens. You know the worst there is to know about me. Anything else is just flat lie."

His father nodded abstractedly. "Of course. But Kite is confoundedly clever. Now I wonder what he's—"

"I always told you, Wint, that you hadn't any business in politics," Mrs. Chase exclaimed. "I don't think it's decent, the way men talk about each other. Why, Mrs. Hullis told me that Jack Routt is going around saying the most terrible things about you. That you—"

"I know, mother. That's Jack's idea of a campaign. We'll show him his mistake next Tuesday."

"But he says that you—"

"Now, mother," her husband interrupted, "never mind. Wint, did you hear anything definite about Kite? What he's planning...."

Wint hesitated; he had heard something definite. Definite but incredible. That which he had heard could not possibly be true; he could not believe it. To tell his father would only disturb the older man; he could not be sure how Chase would react to the report. He held his tongue. "No, nothing definite," he said.

"Is he's coming to see you about it, he must have something."

Wint got up from the table. "Well," he said abruptly, "we'll soon know. It's after seven, now."

They went into the sitting room to wait; and the waiting was hard. Wint tried to read the daily; his father took a book from the shelves. But Wint's eyes strayed from the printed columns. He was in a curiously numb state of mind. This was part hopelessness, part the sheer suspense of waiting. Wint was one of those men who in their moments of greatest passion and excitement become outwardly serene and calm. Their own emotions put a physical inhibition on them so that they are still, and do not speak. Once or twice Chase glanced toward his son and saw Wint motionless, apparently absorbed, apparently quite at ease. But actually Wint was stirring to the throbbing of his heart, held still by the very fury of his own dread and anger and suspense.

At fifteen minutes before eight, some one knocked on the front door. Wint said: "There he is," and got up and went to the door; but when he opened it, Jack Routt stood there. Wint was surprised; he said slowly:

"Oh, you, Jack?"

Routt nodded, a little ill at ease. "Is Kite here?" he asked.

"No. He's coming."

Routt smiled ingratiatingly. "I don't know what he wants. He told me to meet him here about eight, to have a talk with you."

"Told you to?"

"Yes. I asked him what he meant; and he said to wait. I supposed he had made arrangements with you."

Wint said dully: "Yes, he has. He's coming." And after a moment, he added: "You might as well come in."

Routt grinned. "You're damned cordial," he remarked.

"Oh, that's all right," Wint assured him abstractedly. He was thinking so swiftly that he seemed stupefied. His father came into the hall, and Wint said: "Here's Jack Routt. Kite told him to come."

Chase looked at Routt uncertainly; and Routt said: "I'll get out if you say so."

Wint shook his head. "No. Sit down. Go on in."

They went into the sitting room; but before they could sit down, some one else knocked. This time it was B. B. Beecham. He stood in the door when Wint opened it, and smiled, and said:

"I'm not sure I understand, Wint. V. R. Kite telephoned me there was to be some sort of a conference here, about a matter for the good of Hardiston. I thought it curious that the word should come from him."

Wint laughed harshly. "All right, come in," he said. "I don't know any more about it than you do. I suppose Kite thought it would be cheaper to use our house than to hire a hall."

B. B. said simply: "I don't want to inconvenience you."

"Come in," Wint repeated. "I'm up in the air, that's all. Routt's here already. Kite will be along, I suppose."

"Routt?" B. B. echoed, in surprise.

"Yes; in there."

Wint and B. B. went into the sitting room where Chase and Routt were talking awkwardly. After the first greetings, no one could think of anything more to say. B. B. broke the silence. "I saw a robin to-day," he said. "They stay here, sometimes, right through the winter."

Birds and flowers were B. B.'s hobbies; he knew them all. And other people recognized this interest in him, and shared it. They liked his enthusiasm. Chase said: "Is that so? I had no idea they stayed. It doesn't seem to me I ever saw one in winter."

"They live in the sheltered places," said B. B. "You'll find them in the woods, and the brushy hollows, and around houses where there is a good deal of shrubbery. Especially if the people put out a lump of suet for them to feed on."

"Why, everybody ought to do that," Chase declared, with a quick interest. "You ought to tell them to, in the *Journal*, B. B."

B. B. smiled and said he was telling people just this, every week. He spoke of other birds. Chase seemed interested. Routt and Wint said nothing. Routt seemed uncomfortable; and that was a strange thing to see in this assured young man. Wint's eyes were lowered; he was thinking. Lost in a maze of conjectures. Kite would be coming, any minute now.

B. B. was still talking about birds when Kite came. Wint heard footsteps on the walk in front of the house, heard them come up the steps. There were several men. Not Kite alone. The sounds told him that. He waited, sitting still, till they knocked on the front door. Then he went out into the hall and opened the door and saw Kite standing there, his dry little face triumphant, malignantly rejoicing.

Wint looked at Kite steadily for a moment; and then he lifted his eyes and saw, behind Kite, Amos Caretall. And at one side, Ed Skinner of the *Sun*. He had thought there were others. But he saw no one else.

Kite stepped inside the door. Skinner and Amos stood still till Wint asked: "Well—what is it?"

Kite said then: "Come in, Amos. You too, Ed."

Amos, his big head on one side, his eyes squinting in a friendly way, drawled a question: "How about it, Wint? Kite says he's got something to talk over. Asked me to come along. But I don't allow he's got any right to ask me into your house."

"Come in, Amos. Both of you," Wint said; and Kite repeated:

"Yes, come in. I know what I'm talking about. This young man isn't likely to object."

"All right, Wint?" Amos asked again; and Wint nodded, and Amos lumbered into the hall. Then Chase came to the door that led from the sitting room into the hall; and at sight of Amos, he stopped very still, with a white face. Wint crossed to his father's side and told him quietly:

"It's all right. Kite brought him. It's all right, dad."

Chase exclaimed: "How do I know it's all right? I don't understand all this mystery. Kite, by what right do you use my house for a meeting place? What is all this, anyway? What is the idea, Kite?"

Kite smiled his dry and mirthless smile; and he said mockingly: "Do not fret yourself, Chase. Our concern is with this young man, with Wint. You shall hear." He was stripping off his overcoat in a business-like way. This was Kite's big hour, and he meant to make the most of it. He dropped the coat on the seat in the hall; and Amos and Ed Skinner imitated him; and Kite said briskly, rubbing his hands:

"Now, then, where can we have our little talk?"

Chase looked at Wint uncertainly; and Wint, still held by that curious inhibition which made his voice level and low, said quietly:

"The sitting room. Come in, gentlemen."

There were not chairs enough for them in the sitting room. Wint went into the dining room for another, and found his mother there, putting away the dishes. She asked in a whisper:

"Who is it, Wint? Mr. Kite?"

Wint nodded. "Yes, mother. Several men. You'd better go upstairs the back way."

He was so steady that she was reassured; he did not seem excited or disturbed. Yet was there something about him that made her think of a hurt and weary little boy; and she laughed softly, and put her arm around him and made him kiss her. He did so, patting her head; and then he said:

"There, mother. Run along."

She went out toward the kitchen, and Wint took the chair he had come for into the other room. He found the others all sitting down. Amos had slumped into the biggest and the easiest chair in the room. B. B. sat straight in the straightest chair, his round, firm hands clasped on his knees. B. B.'s legs were short and chubby; and his lap was barely big enough to hold his clasped hands. Ed Skinner and Chase were on the couch at one side of the room. Routt sat on the piano stool, twirling slowly back and forth through a six-inch arc. Kite, in the manner of a presiding officer, had pulled his chair to the table in the middle of the room and sat there very stiffly, his head held high in that ridiculous likeness to a turkey.

Wint placed his chair just inside the door, and sat down. He and Kite were the only composed persons in the room. B. B. looked acutely embarrassed and uncomfortable; Chase was angry; Skinner was nervous; Routt's ease was palpably assumed. And Amos was fumbling uncertainly with his black old pipe. He asked, when Wint came in:

"Your mother mind smoke in her sitting room?"

Wint said: "No; go ahead." He filled his own pipe, and Amos sliced a fill from his plug and deliberately prepared his smoke and lighted it. Kite seemed in no hurry to begin. He had taken a letter or two and a slip of paper from his pockets and was studying them in silence. Wint thought he recognized that slip of paper. A check.... It seemed to him that a cold hand clutched his throat. He felt a sick sense of the hopelessness of it all; a sick despair. Not so much on his own account.

Kite at last looked around the room, and said importantly:

"Well, gentlemen!"

Wint's father could be still no longer. He cried: "See here, Kite, what's all this tomfoolery? What's this nonsense? It's an outrage. Be quick, or be gone. I've no time to waste."

Kite looked at Chase; and then he looked at Wint and asked maliciously: "Do you bid me be gone, too, young man?"

Wint shook his head. "Say what you have to say," he suggested; and there was a great weariness in his voice.

Kite nodded. "I mean to." And to Chase: "You see, the young man understands it is in his interest to handle this thing among ourselves."

"To handle what thing?" Chase demanded. Kite cleared his throat.

"A matter," he said importantly, "that concerns first of all the good name of Hardiston. A matter that concerns, very intimately, the good name of your son. A matter that will be decisive in the mayoralty campaign now pending. A matter—" His poise suddenly gave way before the fierce rush of his exultation; and he cried: "A matter that will stop this damned Sunday-school nonsense of denying grown men the right to do as they please. That's what it is, by God! A matter that will show up this young hypocrite in his true light. If I were not merciful, I would have spread it before the town long ago."

He stopped abruptly, looking from one to the other as though challenging them to deny that he was merciful. No one denied it. B. B. cleared his throat; and the sound was startling in the silence that had followed Kite's words. Amos puffed slowly at his pipe and squinted across the room at Wint. Wint said nothing. He had scarce heard what Kite said; he was curiously abstracted, as though all this did not concern him. He was like a spectator, looking on.

Chase looked at his son; and there was fear in the man's eyes. For Kite was so terribly confident. Chase looked at his son, expecting Wint to make denial, to defend himself. But Wint said nothing; Wint did not lift his eyes from the floor. He only puffed slowly and indolently at his pipe, moving not at all.

Kite cleared his throat again; and his dry little eyes were gleaming.

"I have given this matter some thought," he said. "Some thought, since the facts came into my hands. And I must confess, at first they seemed incredible. I made investigations, I was forced to believe—the whole, black story." He paused again. He wanted some one to question him, but no one spoke. He went on:

"My first impulse was to cry the truth to the whole town. But I held my hand. I went to the city for the final proof. Got it. And when I came back, it was to find that this young man had caused the arrest of one of my friends, Lutcher, on a ridiculous liquor charge. Simply because Radabaugh discovered Lutcher and three others engaged in a game of cards, drinking as they had a right to do.

"I was indignant; but even then I was merciful. I wanted to give this young man a chance; and I went to him and offered him the chance to save himself."

He paused, moved one of his hands as though to brush the possibility aside. "But it is unnecessary for me to tell you that his chief trait is a blind and unreasoning stubbornness. It betrayed him, on this occasion. He rejected my offer; refused to take the easy way out.

"That was this morning. I considered. My chief concern was for the good name of Hardiston; that such a man should not be chosen Mayor. This seemed to me the simplest and least painful way to arrange his withdrawal. So I asked you to come here."

Amos drawled from the depths of his chair: "Did you fetch us here to talk us to death, Kite?"

Kite smiled bitterly. "No, Amos. Be patient."

Chase was watching Wint, still with that desperate hope in his eyes. They were all watching Wint; but Wint was looking at the floor, following with his eyes the pattern in the rug. This was the end. He had just about decided that. There was in him no more will to fight. He had been a good Mayor. If they didn't want to re-elect him—that was their affair. He would do no more. He had a sick sense of betrayal. His lips twisted in a bitter little smile.

Kite addressed him directly. "So, young man, we want your withdrawal from the mayoralty race. And this whole matter will end right here."

Wint still did not lift his head. His father thought the boy was shamed; and his heart was torn. Kite asked sharply: "Come! What do you say?"

Wint looked at Kite, then, for the first time; looked at him with a slow, steady, incurious gaze that made Kite twist in his chair. And he repeated, in a low voice:

"You want me to withdraw?"

"Exactly. Now."

Wint shook his head gently. "No," he said, "I won't withdraw."

Kite threw up one clenched fist in a furious gesture. "By God, if you don't you'll be run out of town!"

"I'm in the fight," said Wint steadily. He spoke so low they could scarce hear him. "I'm in the fight. I'll stay."

"Then I'll smash you, flat as a pancake. You young fool."

"Kite," Wint murmured gently. "I don't give a damn what you do. I'm in to stay."

Kite banged his fist on the table. "Then the whole story comes out."

"Let it come," said Wint.

"You mean you want me to tell these men here? The black shame?"

"Yes," Wint assented. "Tell them anything you please." He lowered his eyes again, resumed his study of the carpet, puffed at his pipe. Kite stared at the boy's bent head as though he could not believe his eyes, or his ears. He had counted so surely on Wint's surrender; he had been so sure that Wint would yield.

But Wint.... The fool sat there, passively defying him; daring him. Kite's face twisted with a sudden furious grimace. He jerked back his head. So be it. He flung defiant eyes around the room; he said abruptly, curtly:

"Very well. Here it is. This young rip is the father of Hetty Morfee's child."

There was a moment's terrible silence in the room. Then Jack Routt cried: "Good Lord, Kite, that can't be! Wint's a decent chap."

Kite snapped at him: "Can't be? It is. Here's the very check he gave her, to go away." He shook the slip of paper in the air. "What do you say to that?"

"I don't believe it," Routt insisted. "I've known Wint too long." He got up and strode across and gripped Wint's shoulder. "Tell him it's a damned lie, Wint," he begged.

Wint looked up at Routt with slow, steady eyes; and Routt, after a moment, could not meet them. He turned back to Kite, protesting Wint's innocence. Their wrangling voices jangled in the silence. B. B. pretended not to hear, stared straight ahead of him. Ed Skinner twisted uneasily where he sat. Amos, deep in his chair, was watching Wint; and Wint's father was watching Wint, too. Watching his son with a desperate, beseeching look in his eyes.

Wint did not see; he was looking at the floor; and he was thinking of Hetty, thinking what this would mean to her. That which had come to her was already guessed at, in Hardiston; now every one would know beyond need of guessing. She would be outcast; no saving her; but one black road ahead. For the thing would be believed. He knew that. People had been ready to believe before this; ready to accept the mere rumor. His own father, his own mother.... This had been their first thought when he wished to help

Hetty. Joan.... She had sought to question him. Yes, they would believe. Every one.

He was not angry at them for their credulity; he pitied them. That they should be so malignant, and so blind. He was quite calm, not at all sorry for himself. Sorry for them. And most of all, he was sorry for Hetty. He had always liked Hetty; a good girl, give her a chance. The stuff of good womanhood in her. Blasted now.... He wished he might find a way to help her. Some way....

A word from Kite to Routt cut through his thoughts. "If you won't believe me," Kite exclaimed, "will you believe her?"

"Hetty never said this," Routt protested; and Kite got up and went swiftly out into the hall, saying over his shoulder:

"Just a minute, then."

Every one looked toward the door, listening. They heard Kite open the front door and call:

"Lutcher."

A man answered, outside. Kite asked: "Is she there?" The man said:

"Yes."

"Send her in," Kite directed. And they heard the sound of moving feet.

So she had been waiting there, all this time, with Lutcher. Wint thought she must have been miserably unhappy as she waited. When he heard her step in the hall, he looked up and saw her. Her eyes met his for an instant; and Wint was curiously stirred by the pitiful appeal in them. As though she begged him to forgive.... Then her eyes left his. She came in and stood, just inside the door. Kite said:

"Sit down." He gave her his own chair, by the table. The girl moved apathetically across the room and took the chair. Kite looked down at her.

"Now, Hetty," he said, in the tone of one who questions a child. "I have been telling them what you told me. They think I am lying. Am I lying?"

She shook her head slowly; and Kite looked from man to man triumphantly. Routt cried:

"Hetty, you don't understand. He said Wint was your—your baby's father? That's not true. It can't be."

She looked at Routt; and there was a somber light in her eyes. She said, in a low, steady voice:

"Yes. Sure it's true."

Her eyes remained on Routt. He stepped back as though she had struck him. Wint raised his head and looked around the room; saw Amos squinting at his pipe; saw B. B. ill at ease, and Skinner squirming; saw his father white and shaken in his seat. Then Routt turned to him, exclaiming:

"Wint, for God's sake.... You heard what she said."

Wint hardly knew himself; he was, suddenly and surprisingly, very calm, and happy with an anguished happiness of renunciation. The old stubborn, prideful Wint would have denied, have fought, have sworn. But Wint looked at Hetty; he was terribly sorry for her. He surrendered himself to a great and splendid magnanimity.

"Yes," he told Routt. "I heard."

"But it's a lie!"

Wint got up slowly, looked around the room, studied them all; and he smiled. "Hetty would not lie about me," he said. "She and I have always been friends. We are going to be married, right away."

He held them a moment more with his steady gaze; they were frozen, every man. And then he looked at Hetty, and saw her eyes widen pitifully, and saw her face twist with anguish. And he smiled reassuringly, and he said: "It's all right, Hetty. Truly. Don't be afraid."

While they were still motionless, he turned and went quietly into the hall. Muldoon had been dozing under his chair; the dog scrambled up now and followed him. Wint got his hat and went out of the house, Muldoon upon his heels.

In the room he had left, every man was very still. Only poor Hetty crumpled slowly in her chair; and she dropped her head in her arms upon the table and began to cry, with great, gasping sobs. And she whispered to herself, so harshly that they all could hear:

"My God! My God! Oh, my God!"

END OF BOOK V

BOOK VI

VICTORY

CHAPTER I

THE WEAVER HOUSE AGAIN

THERE is a dramatist hidden in every one of us. We like to cast ourselves as heroes, as heroines, as villains of the piece. Make-believe is one of the fundamental instincts. It is human nature to construct a drama about our lives; it is also very human to seize dramatic situations.

There was a good deal of the dramatic in Wint. When he left his home that night, Muldoon at his heels, he was acutely conscious that his life was broken. He had lost everything. He had lost father, and mother; and he had lost Joan. They were irrevocably gone. Furthermore, he was beaten in his fight. There could be no question of this. Hardiston would overwhelm him. There was left for him in this world—nothing.

Wint was enough of a boy to take a keen delight in the tragedy of this; he was enough of a boy—or enough of a dramatist, for the two things are in many ways the same—to emphasize his situation, bring out the high lights, vest it in the trappings of drama. He did not think of himself as a hero, for having sacrificed everything for Hetty; he did not think of that phase of the situation at all. He had done that because it was the inevitable consequence of events. It was the only thing he could do. He took no credit to himself for the doing. But he did picture himself as broken or destroyed; and as he walked, more or less aimlessly, it was natural that his thoughts should cast back through the months to those other days when he had fallen low. Thus he remembered the Weaver House, and Mrs. Moody.

There seemed to him something appropriate and fitting in the idea of returning to the Weaver House this night. He had risen out of it; he would return to it. It was in such surroundings, now, that he belonged.

He turned that way.

It was no more than nine o'clock in the evening, or perhaps a little later, when Wint left his home. The day had been fine; the night was clear, and there was a moon. It was pleasant to be abroad on such a night. Wint took a leisurely course that brought him through the last fringes of houses above the railroad yards; and he followed the tag end of a street down the hill to the flats covered with slack and cinders. In the light of day, this was a hideous place, black and begrimed. But the moon could glorify even this. It painted blue shadows everywhere; it laid streaks of silver light along the rails; it touched a pool of water, a puddle here and there, and under the touch the water became quicksilver, alive and beautiful. A switching engine moved down the yard, and when the fire-man twitched open the door to replenish the fires, the glare shone in a pale glow upon his figure and back upon the tender. The long strings of cars, box cars with open doors, or coal cars loaded high, took on a beauty of their own in the night; and the winking switch lamps were like jewels, like rubies and emeralds shining in the moon.

He had to climb between two freight cars, on his way across the yard; and Muldoon scurried underneath them. Wint grimed his hands on the cars, and rubbed them together, cleansing them as well as he could, while he went on. He picked his way across the tracks, past the roundhouse where a locomotive slumbered hissingly, and on into the fringes of the locality where the Weaver House awaited him.

It is the custom in Hardiston that when the moon is full, be it cloudy or clear, the street lamps are not lighted. Thus the street along which Wint took his way was illuminated only by the moon. On either side, the dingy, squalid houses stood, with a flicker of light from one and another where those who dwelt within were still awake. A little later, he passed a store or two, and turned a corner, and so came to the hotel.

Something prompted him to stop outside and look in through the dirty window glass. It was so light outside, and the lamp inside furnished such a meager illumination, that Mrs. Moody saw him at the window; and she took him for some wandering ne'er-do-well, and came scolding to the door. "Be off," she cried, before she saw who it was. "Get away from there."

Muldoon snarled at her; and Wint said: "Quiet, boy," and to the woman: "It's me. Wint Chase."

She came out and peered up at him; and he saw her horribly even teeth shine like silver between her cracked old lips. "You, is it?" she exclaimed aggressively. "Well, and you don't need to come a-snooping around here. We're lawful folks, here. And you know it. So you can just go along."

He said: "I came for lodging;" and she backed away.

"Eh?" she asked.

"For lodging," he repeated. "Can you give me a room?"

"What's the matter with you, anyhow?" she demanded. "You had a fight with your paw again?" She was still aggressively and suspiciously on guard. He laughed, and said whimsically:

"Come; you wouldn't turn an old friend out. Let me have a room."

So she thawed, became her old, meanly ingratiating self.

"Why, deary," she protested, "you know old Mother Moody never turned a man away. You come right in now. Come right in where it's warm. Did you say you'd had a scrap with your paw?"

Wint went before her into the office of the squalid hotel. Muldoon kept close to his heels; and Jim, Mrs. Moody's dog, growled from beneath the table. Mrs. Moody squalled at him:

"You, Jim, be still."

Wint looked around him; it was curious to find the place so little changed. A train clanked past on the track that flanked the hotel. He could almost hear the gurgle of the muddy waters of the creek behind. The office itself was lighted, as it had always been, by a single oil lamp. It did not seem to Wint that this lamp had been cleaned since he was here before. It stood on the square old table in the corner, where the wall benches ran along two sides. The dog slept under this table; and the boy—the same boy—was leaning his elbows on the table by the lamp and poring with mumbling lips over a tattered, paper-backed tale. This boy's clothes were still too small; his wrists stuck out from his sleeves, his neck reared itself bare and gaunt above the collar of the coat. There was a strange and pitiful atmosphere of age and experience about him.

There was one change in the room, as Wint saw when he had persuaded Mrs. Moody to leave him to his own devices, and she had gone to her chair behind the high counter that had been a bar. This change lay in the fact that one of the two old checker players was no longer here. The other sat on the wall bench in the corner behind the table; the disused checkerboard lay before him. He was asleep, with sagging head, his occupation gone. His white beard was stained an ugly brown below his mouth. Wint wondered if the other old man were dead. Perhaps.

He did not wish to be alone, just then; he wanted companionship, friendly and impersonal. So he sat down beside the boy, and filled his pipe, and lighted it, and asked amiably:

"What are you reading, son?"

The boy was too absorbed to answer. He brushed at his ear with his hand as though a fly buzzed there, and turned a dogeared page. But the sound of Wint's voice so near him woke the old man; he stirred, opened his eyes, looked all about. And he reached across and laid a hand like a claw on Wint's arm.

"Play checkers?" he asked hoarsely. "Play checkers, do you?"

"A little," Wint said.

"I'll play you," the old man challenged. "I'm a good player. I always was. Played all my life. Played every night, right here at this table, with the best player in the county, for seven years." His skinny old hands were feverishly arranging the pieces, while Wint took his place by the board. "I beat him, too," the old man boasted. "Beat him lots of times. He'd say so himself. He would, but he had to go and die." There was resentment in his voice, as at a personal wrong. He said curtly: "Your move," and spoke no more.

Wint moved, the old man countered. On Wint's fifth move—he was an indifferent player—the old man cackled gleefully. "That beats you," he cried. "Heh, heh, heh! That beats you, now."

It did; and Wint lost the next game, and the next, as easily. His success put the old man in the best of humor. He laughed much between games, studying the board with fixed intensity while the play was in progress. Wint watched the old man as much as he watched the board; he studied the old fellow, with a curiously wistful eye. This old wreck of manhood had been a boy once; a baby once, in a mother's arms. No doubt she had dreamed dreams for him. Dreamed he might be President, some day. Might be anything.... This is one of the things that makes babies fascinating; their potentialities. There is no greater gamble than to bring a baby into the world. Wint, considering this, thought of Hetty's baby. The baby that had died. As well, perhaps. Otherwise, it might have come, some day, to playing checkers in the Weaver House. He put the thought aside abruptly. At least, it would have lived. Even this old man had lived. No doubt life had been reasonably sweet to him till his antagonist died. "Had to go and die...."

The old man accused him. "You ain't trying to play, young fellow. Now don't you go easy on me. I'll show you some things." And Wint gave more of his attention to the game.

He was playing when the door opened and Jack Routt came in; he did not look around till Jack exclaimed behind him: "Wint! By God, I thought you'd be here!"

He looked up then, and said: "Hello, Jack," in a calm voice, and went on with his play. Routt dropped on the seat beside him and caught his arm.

"Here, Wint," he protested, "I want to talk to you. Where'd you pick up that old duck? Listen. I want to.... Let's go outside."

Wint said: "Wait till we finish the game." The old man seemed unconscious of Routt's presence; and when Routt spoke again, Wint bade him be quiet, and wait. Only when the game was done did he rise. To the old man he said: "Thanks. We'll have another game. I'll beat you yet."

The other protested jealously at his going; but Wint said he must. Then, to Routt: "Come upstairs."

"Have you got a room?" Routt asked, amazed; and Wint said:

"Yes." And he went toward the stair. Routt followed him.

Mrs. Moody had given Wint that same dingy room in which he had spent the night of his election. They went there, and Wint bade Routt sit down. Routt sat on the bed; Wint stood indolently by the door. Routt exclaimed at once:

"Wint, I want you to know this wasn't my doing. You could have knocked me flat. I'm sorry as hell."

"Of course," Wint agreed.

"I want to know if there isn't some way we can fix it up," Routt urged. "There must be something we can do. Some damned thing."

"There's nothing to fix," Wint told him.

"Nothing to fix? Good God!" Routt shifted his position, reached into his pocket. "My Lord, but I'm knocked out. Shaky. I've got to have a drink. Mind?"

"Go ahead."

Routt produced a flask. He held it toward Wint. "Have a slug?" Wint shook his head. Routt drank, again asked: "Sure you won't?" Wint said:

"No."

"If I were in your shoes," said Routt, with the flask still open in his hand, "I'd want to soak myself in it. A good, stiff drunk. There are times when nothing else is any good."

"I used to think so," Wint agreed.

Routt took a second drink, wiped his mouth, screwed the cap on the flask and put it in his pocket. "If you want any, say the word," he suggested. "Now, Wint, what are we going to do?"

Wint, leaning quietly against the wall, stirred a little. "I'm going to tell you something, Routt," he said.

"Tell me? What?"

"This," Wint went on gently, eyes a little wistful. "This. That I—know you now. At last."

Routt sat for an instant very still; then he got to his feet. "Wint, what do you mean?"

"I thought you were my—friend," said Wint. "Stuck to that thought. People warned me. Amos, and father; and—Joan. Said you were not—my friend. But I believed you were."

"Damn it, I am your friend."

"I'm not sorry I held to you as long as I could," Wint went on impassively. "It's a good thing to have faith, even in—false friends. But—I know you now, Routt. You've made me drunk, played on the worst in me, slandered me, tricked me, played your part in this black thing to-night." He hesitated, and Routt started to speak, but Wint cut in.

"Are you—responsible for Hetty, Jack?" he asked.

"Am I?" Routt demanded. "Why, damn you, you said yourself...."

"If I thought you were," Wint told him evenly. "If I thought you had done that to her.... She was a nice girl. Clean. I think I'd take you by the throat, Routt, and kill you here."

Routt cried angrily: "You're crazy. What the hell! You said yourself that you...."

"In fact," Wint told him, "unless you go away, I am going to hurt you—even now. Without being sure. Hurt you as badly as I can."

Routt started to speak; then Wint's eyes caught his and silenced him. He stood for a moment, staring at the other.

And his eyes fell. He looked around gropingly for his hat, and he put it on. He went past Wint at the door; and he went past quickly, as though afraid of what Wint might do.

He went along the hall and down the stairs without speaking again.

Wint, left alone, stood still where he was for a time; then he stirred himself and began to prepare for bed. He moved slowly, indolently. Stripped off coat and collar, sat down to unlace his shoes. After a while, he crossed and opened the window. He felt, somehow, infinitely cleaner, healthier, since he had put Jack Routt out of his life. He felt as though he had washed smears of grime from his hands.

Yet there was a certain loneliness upon him, too; for he had lost one whom he had counted a friend.

After a while, he went to bed and slept peacefully enough till dawn.

CHAPTER II

A BRIGHTER CHAPTER

THE crowded events of the evening before had wearied Wint more than he knew; his sleep was dreamless and profound, and he might not have waked till midday if it had not been for Muldoon. The dog slept beside Wint's bed; but at the first glint of day, it became restless; and when the sun rose, Muldoon got up and walked stiffly across to the open window and propped his feet on the sill and looked out. The slight sound of his nails on the bare floor disturbed Wint, and he turned in his sleep; and Muldoon came back to the bed to see what was the matter. Wint's arm was hanging over the side of the bed, and Muldoon licked his master's hand. Which woke Wint effectually enough.

He opened his eyes, and at first he could not remember where he was. The dingy room.... He stared up at the cracked and broken ceiling. At one place, a patch of plaster had fallen, leaving the laths bare. It took Wint some little time to recognize his surroundings. But at last he remembered. He sat up on the edge of the bed, rumpling Muldoon's ears with his right hand, and looked around.

The room contained, besides the bed, a chair and a wardrobe. His clothes were on the chair. The sagging doors of the wardrobe hung open. There was nothing inside the decrepit thing. His eyes wandered toward the mantel. The cracked old mirror still hung there. His eyes fell to the floor, and he marked the charred place near the hearth, burned there that night of his election when at sight of his own image in the mirror he had smashed the lamp in a fury of shame. He remembered that night, now, and he smiled a little whimsically. It seemed his fortunes were always to be bound up with this dingy room.

Muldoon, disturbed by Wint's long silence, looked up at his master, and barked, under his breath, uneasily. Wint took the dog's head in both his hands and shook it gently back and forth. "What's the matter, pup?" he asked affectionately. "What's on your mind? What are you fussing about, anyhow? What have you got to fuss about, I'd like to know? Come."

Muldoon twisted himself free, and he snarled. It was a part of the game. Then he flung himself forward and pinned Wint's right hand and held it, growling. Wint took him by the scruff of the neck and lifted the dog into his lap; and Muldoon's solid body accommodated itself to Wint's knees and he lay there, perfectly contented.

"You stuck around, didn't you, boy?" Wint asked, his voice a little wistful. "The rest of them didn't give a hoot for Wint; but you stuck around. Eh? The rest of them didn't care. 'Get out. Good enough for him.' That's what they'd say. But not you, eh, Muldoon? You stuck. Even Jack Routt. Even Jack came only to offer me booze. And the rest of them didn't come at all. Only you, pup. You and I, now. But we'll show them some things. Eh?"

Muldoon rolled his eyes up at Wint and said nothing; and Wint lifted the dog from his knees to the bed. "There, take a nap while I'm dressing," he said. "Then we'll be moving on."

The dog stayed obediently on the bed; and Wint dressed, moving quietly to and fro. He did not hurry. He was possessed by an easy indolence. There seemed to be nothing in the world worth hurrying for. He was not unhappy; he whistled a little, as he dressed. But once or twice he remembered that his father had let him go without a word, and he winced at the thought. And once or twice he remembered that he had no friend now, anywhere, save Muldoon; and that was not pleasant remembering.

But for the most part, he put a good face on life. "After all, pup," he told Muldoon, "thing's can't be any worse. So they're bound to get better. And we'll just play that hunch for all it's worth. Why not? Eh?"

Muldoon had no objections; he wagged the stump of his tail and opened his jaws and laughed, dog-fashion, tongue hanging happily. Wint grinned at him, and sat down to tie his shoes.

Save for collar and coat, he was fully dressed when he heard through the open door the voice of some one who had come into the office of the Weaver House, downstairs. The voice was unmistakable. The newcomer was Amos; and when Wint realized this, he stood very still, and his face turned a little white. He waited without moving. There was nothing else to do.

He heard Amos and some one else coming up the stairs, guided by Mrs. Moody. "Right along here," the old dame was saying. "Always the same room. I always give him the best. That's the kind of a gentleman he is, when he comes to old Mother Moody. Right here, now."

In the doorway she said: "Here's the Congressman to see you, deary." And she stood aside to let Amos come in. Wint saw that B. B. Beecham was with Amos, on the other's heels. He watched them, steady enough by this time. He wondered what they had come for. To triumph? That would not be like B. B. Nor like Amos.

Amos turned and told Mrs. Moody to go. "And thank you, ma'am," he said. She went away, a little reluctantly. She was a curious old woman; she liked to know what went on in her hostelry. But—Amos had, when he chose, a commanding tone. When she was gone, he turned and looked at Wint, head on one side, squinting good-humoredly; and he said:

"Well, Wint, how's tricks?"

Wint hesitated; then he said: "Good morning, both of you."

Amos nodded. B. B. said: "Good morning."

Wint looked around at the sparse furnishings of the room. "You've caught me early," he said. "I'm not dressed yet." And he added: "I can't offer you both a chair, because there's only one chair."

"Me," said Amos, "I'll sit on the bed. B. B., sit down."

Wint remained on his feet. "Well," he asked, a challenge in his voice, "what's on your mind?"

Amos leaned back against the wall and began to fill his pipe. "Nothing much, Wint," he said slowly. "We come down here principally to shake you by the hand. Don't let me forget t' do it, before I go."

His tone was friendly and reassuring. Wint wondered just what he meant. He smiled a little, and said: "All right."

"Thought you might be glad to see your friends," Amos added; and Wint said, with lips a little white:

"I would be."

"Well," Amos told him. "Here's two of us."

Wint looked at the Congressman; and he looked at B. B. B. said quietly: "That was a fine thing you did last night, Wint."

Wint flushed, as though he were ashamed of what he had done. "I don't understand this," he said, a little impatiently. "What do you want? Out with it!"

Amos said: "Want to help you, any way we can."

Wint's eyes narrowed, and he flung out a hand. "You're too darned mysterious, Amos."

Amos lighted his pipe. "Well, Wint, I don't aim to be," he declared. "I'm talking straight as I know. B. B. and me are on your side; that's all. We're taking orders from you. We do anything you say."

Wint laughed, a sudden, harsh laugh. "I've heard they give a condemned man anything he wants—the last morning," he exclaimed.

Amos nodded. "Yes, I've heard tell o' that. But what's that got to do with this?"

"Plain enough, I should think."

"You don't count yourself a condemned man; now, do you?"

"I should think so."

Amos shook his head doubtfully. "And here I thought you said last night you didn't aim to quit."

"I don't. But I'll be snowed under—now. Of course."

"Well," said Amos, "that may be so. I ain't sure. Gergue will know, time he's talked around a spell. Prob'ly you are—are beat. But I've seen men beat before that turned out pretty strong in the end." He added slowly: "Anyway, licked or unlicked, I'm on your side, Wint. And always was."

Wint stared at him with a curious, threatening light in his eyes. "What's the idea? You turned me down cold, in public. Now you come whining around...."

"I'm not whining, Wint," said Amos cheerfully. "Do you think I'm whining, B. B.?"

B. B. smiled. "Congressman Caretall has his own methods, Wint. I know he seemed to be against you; but I also know that he's been secretly working for you, that every vote he can swing will go to you. He's been passing that word around for a week."

Wint hesitated, looking from one to the other. "I never caught you in a lie, B. B.," he said.

"It's true enough," the editor told him. "You see—" He looked at Amos, then went on: "You see, your father has no use for Amos. And Amos knew it. He also knew your father could do a good deal to help you win this election. But—Chase would not be on your side so long as Amos was with you. Do you see?"

"I see that much," said Wint. He was thinking hard.

"But your father has been working for you since Amos pretended to have turned against you. Hasn't he?"

"Yes."

"I don't suppose you ever thought of that," B. B. suggested; and Wint drew his hand across his eyes, and looked at Amos, and asked huskily:

"Is it true, Amos?"

Amos grinned; and he said: "I'm like you. I never knowed B. B. to tell a lie."

"But why didn't you tell me?"

"You can't keep a secret, Wint. You're too damned honest. Maybe you're too honest for politics. I don't know. Anyhow, I couldn't let on to you without your father seeing it in your eye."

Wint said, grinning a little shakily: "It hurt me a good deal, just the same."

"I guess you'll outgrow that."

"I suppose so."

He said nothing more for a minute; and Amos puffed at his pipe, and B. B. studied Wint, smiling a little at the young man's confusion. Wint was flushed; and he was happier than he had ever expected to be again. These two were true friends, at least. Not all the world had turned its back on him. He crossed abruptly and gripped their hands.

"Why, that's all right," said Amos, marking how Wint was moved. "If you hadn't run away last night, before we could move, I'd have told you then. I tried to find you, after. But no one seemed to know."

Wint nodded. "I just walked blindly, for a while. I could not go home. This was the first place I thought of."

Amos blew a cloud of smoke. "Well, that's all right."

"How did you find out I was here, now?" Wint asked. "Just guess? Or what?"

"Jack Routt is—spreading the word," Amos explained. There was a suggestion of something hidden behind his simple statement.

"Routt? Yes, he was here last night," Wint agreed.

"Yes, he said he was." Wint caught the implication in the Congressman's tone, and he asked:

"What's the matter? What does Routt say?"

"Well, as a matter of fact, he says you were down here last night, stewed to the eyes and getting steweder all the time."

Wint's eyes narrowed; then he laughed. "Oh, he says that?"

"Says it frequent and generous."

"He came down last night and suggested that I drown my sorrows," Wint explained. "I—" He hesitated. "You see, Jack and I—I've always counted him my best friend. But I seemed to see through him last night. I—don't count him my friend any more."

"We-ell," Amos drawled, "I can't say as I blame you for that. I'll say he don't talk friendly about you."

Wint, flushing, asked quickly: "You don't believe what he's saying?"

Amos shook his head. "I know a hangover when I see one; and I know when I don't."

Wint nodded. "I'm not starting in again on the booze at this stage of the game."

"No; I'd guess not."

Wint sat down beside Amos on the tumbled bed. "Now, Amos, let's get down to tacks. I said last night I was going to stick; and I meant it. I mean it all the more, now, with you to back me. The thing is—"

Amos turned his head toward the door. "Some one coming," he said; and Wint heard steps on the stair, and Mrs. Moody's cheerful harangue. He got up quickly. His father stood in the doorway.

In the long moment of silence that followed the appearance of the elder Chase, Wint put his whole heart into the effort to read his father's face. Was there anger there? Or shame? Or bitter reproach? Reason enough, in all conscience, for any one of these emotions. He stared deep into his father's eyes.

The elder Chase came into the room, one stiff step; and he looked at Wint, and at B. B., and at Amos. His lips twitched a little at sight of Amos, then set firmly together again. That was all.

Wint moved toward him a little. "Dad...." he said huskily.

His father's eyes searched Wint's. The older man's voice was shaking. He said slowly: "Routt is telling Hardiston you are drunk, down here."

Wint nodded. "Yes; I'd heard."

"I heard him telling men this thing."

Wint said nothing; the older man's face lighted fiercely. "I knew he lied, Wint. I knew he lied."

Wint flushed with the sudden rush of happiness within him. He looked from his father to Amos. "Dad," he said, "there's one thing. I know my friends now."

"Routt is no friend."

"I know."

"I always told you."

"Yes."

"He...."

Wint laughed softly. "Forget Jack Routt, dad. I've other friends. Amos, here."

Chase's face hardened; he said, without expression, "Amos?"

"He and B. B. came to me when I thought I hadn't a friend in the world. You and Amos have got to make it up, dad. You've got to. Please."

The older man hesitated; then he turned to Amos. "All right," he said. "I ... Wint's friends are mine."

Amos got up from the bed and took the offered hand; and he smiled shrewdly. "I did play you dirty, Chase," he confessed. "I admit it. But doing it—I played a good trick on your son. Didn't I now?"

Chase said slowly: "Yes."

"Wouldn't you rather have him as he stands?" Amos asked. "Wouldn't you rather have him as he stands—than the way he was a year ago?"

"Yes. God knows."

Amos said slowly: "When you're sorest at me—just give me credit for that."

Chase exclaimed swiftly: "It doesn't matter. It's past. Done. All I want is—my boy. You, Wint."

Wint was beginning to believe all was right with the world. He said slowly: "Even—after last night, dad? Hetty...."

"Yes," said his father.

"Mother?" Wint asked. "She'll.... Is she unhappy?"

"Why did you go away from us, Wint?" his father asked huskily. "Why did you run away?"

"I thought you wouldn't want me at home."

"We always want you."

B. B. caught Amos Caretall's eye; and he nodded slightly; and Amos understood. He said: "We'll be moving, Wint. See you uptown, by and by."

"Yes, I'll be up," Wint said.

"So long, Chase."

"Good-by," Chase told him quietly. Amos and B. B. went out, and along the hall, and down the stair. Wint and his father were left alone. For a little while they did not speak; then Chase said gently:

"Come home to your mother, Wint."

Wint asked: "Even—knowing this, what happened last night? You want me in spite of it?"

"Yes."

"In spite of—what I've done?"

Chase threw up his hand; he cried: "Damn it, yes. What do we care? Whatever you do...." His voice broke huskily. "You're always our son!"

Wint could not move for a moment; he was choking. At last he laughed, happily enough; and he touched his father's shoulder with one hand.

"Wait till I put on my collar," he said. "I'll come along."

Muldoon, as though in his dog mind he understood, began to prance and bark about his master as Wint prepared to leave the Moody hostelry behind him. Wint was as happy as the dog. He knew his friends, now. Knew the loyal ones. And his father, and his mother.... They loved him.

All was well with the world.

CHAPTER III

HETTY HAS HER DAY

WINT and his father walked home in a silence that was little broken. Across the railroad yards, up the hill. A new understanding of his father and mother was coming to Wint; some measure of comprehension of the completeness of their love for him. He marked that there had been no reproaches from his father, no questions, no scolding. That which had passed was to be forgotten, was to be ignored. He was their son; nothing else mattered in any degree. His father, on their homeward way, spoke of other matters, once or twice. He said the day was fine; he said Mrs. Chase would probably have breakfast waiting. Wint took the older man's lead, ignored what had passed the night before.

When they got to the house, his mother met him in the hall, and she put her arms around him and cried on his shoulder, and called him her boy. Wint cried, too, and was not ashamed of it. He kept patting her head, and saying: "There, mother," in an awkward way. She told him he must never go away from home again. Never; for anything....

He said: "I thought you would want me to go."

But she clasped him close, protesting.

She had breakfast hot upon the stove. The elder Chase had gone downtown as soon as it was day, to try to locate Wint. They ate together; and after that first moment in the hall, they did not speak of what had happened at all. When breakfast was done, Wint went into the kitchen with his mother to help with the dishes. She tied an apron around him, and laughed at him with a sob in her voice; and Wint laughed with her, and joked her, till the sob disappeared. His father looked in on them once or twice, then left them alone together.

Once, Wint broke a little silence by saying, his arm around her shoulders:

"Mother!"

She looked up at him with quick anxiety; and he said: "I'm sorry, for your sakes."

She said: "You didn't lie, Wint. Anyway, you didn't lie. There, dry that plate. So...."

He smiled a little whimsically. After all, he had lied. But they did not care whether it was true or false; these two. He was their son. The thought was glorious. He nursed it, treasured it.

When the work was done, and the dishes were being put away, they heard a step on the porch outside the kitchen. They both looked that way; and through the window saw Hetty. She passed the window, knocked on the door.

Wint looked toward his mother; and he saw that she was white as death. But even while he looked at her, she touched her mouth with her hand, and steadied herself, and went to the door and opened. "Hetty!" she said pleasantly, gently. "Hetty! Well, come in."

The girl came into the kitchen. She was pale, but she seemed very sure of herself. She looked from Mrs. Chase to Wint. "I want to talk to Wint," she said gently.

Mrs. Chase nodded. "You wait here." She went quickly out into the dining room. They heard her speak to her husband. She was back, almost at once. "Go into the sitting room," she said. "There's no one there."

Hetty went toward the door; but Wint at first did not stir. He was curiously ashamed to face Hetty. She stopped in the doorway, and looked back at him; and he pulled himself together, and untied his apron and followed her. In the sitting room, she sat down on the couch, and Wint sat by the table. She looked at him steadily, smiled a little.

He said: "Well, Hetty."

She laughed at him in a tender way. "Oh, you Wint!" she exclaimed, in a fashion that reminded him of the old, careless Hetty. He shifted uneasily. He felt as though he were guilty toward her. But there was no accusation in her voice. She shook a forefinger at him. "What got into you?" she asked. "Why didn't you tell them to go to the devil?"

There was no way to put it into words. He shook his head. "I don't know. It's all right."

"You knocked us flat; the lot of us," she said. "Wint, you pretty near killed me. You darned, decent kid."

Wint stirred uneasily.

"I thought I'd die," she said. Her voice shook, though she was smiling. "I...." She laughed. "You ought to have seen the others."

He asked awkwardly: "What happened? I haven't heard."

"Didn't your father—"

"No. I stayed at the Weaver House last night."

She laughed. "Oh, you. Leave it to you. To think of the fool thing to do."

He said soberly: "I was in earnest, Hetty. I meant what I said."

She nodded. "Sure you did. You're just a big enough fool to go through with it, too."

"Of course."

"You've got a f-fat chance, Wint," she said, and her voice broke, and she was very near crying through her smiles. "I've waked up, now. You've got a fine, fat chance of that."

"I don't hold it against you," he said. "I'd—be good to you."

"Don't be a nut, darn you! You'll make me cry. I came near crying myself to death, last night."

Wint's curiosity was awake; he asked again: "What happened?"

"Why, you knocked us all flat," she said. "I took it out in crying. Routt beat it after you. He was the first to move."

There was a curious, hard quality in her voice; and Wint asked: "Was it...." He bit off the question, furious with himself for asking. She said slowly:

"Never mind. That's past. I thought for a while I'd be better dead; but I know better, now. Nothing can kill you unless you want to be killed. Nobody ever fell so hard they couldn't get up. I'm going to get up, Wint, and go right on living."

He told her quickly: "Of course. I'll help. Honestly...."

She said fiercely: "You will not. If you think I'm going to let you go through with this—" She broke off, laughed. "Well, I was telling you what happened. Routt beat it after you. The rest of us sat still, me bawling. Then your father got up and ran out to the front door, and out to the street. While he was gone, Kite begun to stir. I looked at Kite. Believe me, Wint, he was squashed. He hadn't expected you to—do what you did. He looked like a dead man. He stuffed his things into his pocket and he pattered out into the hall. Then he came back; and he said to me:

"'Come, Hetty.'

"I said to him: 'You go where you're going, you old buzzard.' And I went on crying. It felt good.

"I heard Kite go out the front door; and then your father came back. He says: 'He's gone! Wint's gone!'

"Then he looked at me, and I couldn't look at him. And he went out and went upstairs.

"The rest of them went along, then. Ed Skinner went first. Then B. B. and Amos together. Amos says to me: 'Don't cry so, Hetty. Don't cry so.' I told him to shut up; and he went along. When they were all gone, I got myself together and went out. Lutcher and Kite were waiting at the corner. They stopped me; and Kite, he says: 'My God, what are we going to do?'

"I hit him in the face, hard as I could. Lutcher grabbed my arm; and I told him to let go, and he let go. I went on and left them. Went home and cried some more."

She laughed a little. "I'll say I felt like crying, Wint. That was your doing. Darn you!"

He said: "You mustn't feel badly."

"Badly!" she echoed, and her eyes were suddenly hard. "Wint, I could cut out my tongue." She moved abruptly, hid her face. After an instant, she turned to him again.

"There's no use in saying I'm sorry. They fed me up to it. Threats, and promises. If I'd do it, they'd give me—a rat of a man to marry. He said he'd marry me himself. But he'd said that before. He told me himself that he'd marry me if I'd do this. Marry me and take me away. I knew he was a liar, but I thought maybe he'd keep the promise, this time. I thought I had to have him, to be able to look people in the eye. Oh, I'm not making excuses, Wint. There isn't any excuse for me."

He said: "It's all right. Please don't feel badly."

"The thing is," she said steadily, "how am I going to make it up to you? What do you want me to do?" He did not answer at once; and she told him humbly: "I'll do anything you say."

He shook his head. "Nothing. I'm willing to go through with it."

She rose to her feet with a swift, furious movement. "Damn you, Wint!" she cried chokingly. "Don't you say that again. Ain't I sorry enough to suit you? Haven't you poured coals of fire on my head till—till my hair's all singed? Don't rub it in, Wint," she pleaded. "You've made me feel bad enough. I'll say I was ready to quit, last night. It wasn't worth a penny, to live. Then I thought I might make it up to you. So I—stayed alive. Don't you rub it in to me, now. Don't you say that again. I tell you, Wint, I went through something, last night." Her voice shook, she stretched out her hands to him. "For God's sake, Wint, don't rub it in any more!"

There were tears in her eyes, on her cheeks; her face was the face of one in torment. He took her hands; and he said gently: "Please—I didn't mean to make you unhappy. You've—really, you've made me happy. I thought every one would be against me. But Amos and B. B. came to me, offered me their friendship, and their help. And father came to me. I never knew before what friends I had. You've done that for me, already."

"I'll bet Routt came to you, too," she said, a terrible scorn in her voice. "He's a friend of yours, isn't he?"

"Yes," said Wint, "he came."

She was frankly crying, now; her shoulders shaking, tears streaming down her face. Her lips twisted; she held out her clenched hands. "I'd like to kill him."

"Don't cry," Wint begged. "Please."

She brushed her arms across her eyes and smiled at him. "All right. Now.... What do you want me to do? It's up to you."

"I don't want you to do anything," Wint protested. "It will all come out right in the end."

"I'm not going to stand and wait."

"Please. You'll see."

She stamped her foot fiercely. "I tell you, no. I was the goat, yesterday. They made a fool of me. But I'm grown up over night, Wint. This is my day. I'm going to tear things open—wide."

For all the harshness of her speech, there was a strange new gentleness about Hetty; and there was a new strength in her. Wint had never liked her more, respected her more. He said steadily: "You're wrong, I think. You're excited, to-day. I tell you, things will turn out better than you think."

The telephone tinkled in the hall; and Wint said: "Wait a minute, will you?" And he went to answer it.

Sam O'Brien, the fat restaurant man, was on the other end of the wire. He asked: "This Chase's house?"

Wint said: "Yes, this is Wint Chase. That you, Sam?"

O'Brien exclaimed: "Yes, it's me! Say, Wint—you're there, boy. You're a man."

"Pshaw!"

"Say, Wint," O'Brien cut in. "Is Hetty up there? They say at her room she started for there."

Wint glanced toward the door of the sitting room. "Yes," he said.

"Do me a favor?" Sam asked.

"Of course."

"Keep her there till I come."

"All right," Wint agreed. "What—"

But Sam had hung up. Wint went back to Hetty. He decided, for no reason in the world, not to tell her what Sam had asked him to do. She asked, as soon as he came into the sitting room:

"Who was that? Sam O'Brien?"

"Yes."

"What did he want?"

Wint laughed uneasily, and said: "He just wanted to tell me he was on my side."

Hetty nodded. "There's one decent man, Wint." There was a curious warmth in her tone.

"Yes, he is," Wint agreed.

"He's been fine to me," she said, a little wistfully. Then she put Sam aside with a movement of her hand. "Well, Wint, you want me to go ahead my own way?"

He hesitated; then he said: "Hetty, you're all right. I don't blame you for—anything. But I do want you to forget the whole thing. You'll see it will straighten out. Don't mix things up."

They heard his mother come into the dining room, across the hall, and busy herself there; and they kept silent till she went out into the kitchen again. A matter of minutes. Hetty moved once, crossing from her chair to stand beside Wint and touch his shoulder lightly with her hand. When Mrs. Chase had gone out of hearing, she said softly:

"I guess there's one person you'd like to have know the straight of this."

Wint's jaw set slowly with something of the old stubbornness; and he said: "No. She doesn't believe in me. She's made no move. I'll not."

She twisted her fingers into his hair and shook him good-naturedly. "You, Wint; you're as stubborn as a mule," she told him. "What would you think of her if she'd come running? After you'd said you were going to— marry me? What could she do? But she knows you're a liar, just the same. I'll bet she's just waiting."

Some one came up on the porch outside, and she looked sharply that way, and asked: "Who's that?"

"I'll go," Wint told her; and he went to the front door. Sam O'Brien was there. He had expected Sam. But Jack Routt was with him, and Wint had not expected to see Routt.

He looked from Sam to the other. Routt's collar, he saw, was rumpled; and there were little beads of perspiration on Sam's forehead. Wint hesitated. Sam said huskily:

"I know you don't want this skunk in your house, Wint. But is—she here?"

"Yes," Wint told him.

"Well, this thing wants to see her," Sam explained. "Speak up, you." He looked at Routt.

Routt said: "Yes." He ran a finger around inside his collar.

Wint moved aside. "Come in," he agreed; and they stepped into the hall. Then Hetty came out of the sitting room. She had heard their voices, heard what they said. She stood very still, looking at Jack Routt with inscrutable eyes.

Routt looked from Sam to Wint furtively. Then he looked at Hetty; and he moved toward her as though he expected violence. Two paces from where she stood, he stopped; he fidgeted. At last he said:

"Will you marry me?"

There was a parrot-like quality in his voice that made Wint, even in that moment, want to smile. Hetty did smile; she said quietly:

"I suppose Sam brought you here."

Routt looked at Sam; then he protested: "No. I wanted to come. Honestly."

"You never wanted anything honestly in your life, Jack," she told him; and there was as much pity as anger in her voice. "I wouldn't marry you. I wouldn't look at you. Not if you were the last man in the world."

No one said anything. They stood very still. Then Routt moved a little; and he turned, and he looked questioningly at Sam O'Brien. Sam had his hat in his hand. He dropped it, to leave his hands free. He opened the front door and stepped outside; and Routt followed him as though at a word of command.

Sam took him by the arm; then he closed the door. Wint looked at Hetty.

They heard a muffled, thudding sound. A hoarse cry. A scuffle of feet. The front gate banged.

When Wint opened the door, Sam was standing on one foot, precariously poised; and with his handkerchief he was carefully wiping the toe of his right shoe. Routt was not in sight.

Hetty came to the door beside Wint; and Sam looked at her humbly, and he asked:

"Will you walk along with me?"

Hetty, smiling a little tenderly, said: "You oughtn't to have done that."

"I can clean my shoe," Sam explained, as though that were the only consideration. "Will you walk along with me?"

She hesitated a moment; then she said swiftly: "Yes, Sam," and looked at Wint with a quick, laughing glance. "Yes, Sam, I'll walk along with you."

Sam looked at Wint. "We're much obliged to you," he said.

Wint nodded. Then Sam and Hetty went down to the gate; and Wint watched them go away together.

CHAPTER IV

WINT'S RALLY

IT was well toward dinner time when Hetty and Sam O'Brien went away together and left Wint. He watched them to the corner, and thought Sam was a good fellow. And a lucky one, too. There was a fine strength and pride in Hetty. No doubt about it, Sam was lucky.

When they were out of sight, Wint went into the house. His father had not yet come downstairs; Mrs. Chase was still in the kitchen. Wint settled himself in the sitting room, and filled his pipe, and went over in his thoughts the scenes this room had witnessed in twenty-four hours past. He looked back at them as though he had been an observer. He could not believe he had been chief actor in them all. It is, perhaps, this trait of the human mind which permits mankind to rise to emergencies. The emergency does not seem like an emergency at the time. It seems rather like the ordinary run of life; it is only in retrospect that the actors realize, and wonder at themselves. There is, during these great moments, a vast simplicity about life. It had been so with Wint; it was only now, as he thought back over what had taken place, that the drama of it caught him. And he wondered at it all; and most of all he wondered at himself.

His father came downstairs, after a little while, and joined him. The older man made no reference to Hetty's having been there; and Wint, at first minded to tell the whole story, to tell his father that Hetty was going to right the wrong she had done, decided on second thought to wait. It would be sweeter to anticipate their joy when they should hear the truth. So he held his tongue.

After a while, Mrs. Chase called them to dinner; and they went into the dining room together. Some impulse made Wint drop his hand lightly on his father's shoulder; and the older man reached up and took Wint's hand and held it, so that they crossed the hall with hands clasped, as though Wint were still a little boy. He was suddenly very proud of his father. And ever so fond of him....

At the dinner table, it was as though nothing had happened. Mrs. Chase was cheerful; she talked amiably of everything in the world except Hetty. Wint and Mr. Chase answered her—that is to say, they interrupted her with a remark now and then—while they ate. It was only when they both had finished that Chase looked at his son and said, a little awkwardly:

"You don't want to forget you have a rally arranged for to-night, Wint."

Wint exclaimed: "Good Lord; I had forgotten!"

"You're not going to give it up?"

"Give it up? No. But I'd forgotten all about it. I'll have to go uptown."

"You had made some arrangements, hadn't you?"

"Yes. Hired the Rink. B. B. is going to preside. That is, he said he would. And I asked Sam O'Brien to speak, and you promised that you would."

"I think I'd rather not," Chase said, flushing uncomfortably. Wint asked, smiling to take the sting out of his words:

"Not deserting me, are you?"

"No. I'll be with you. Sitting on the stage. But—I wouldn't know what to say, Wint."

"And Davy Morgan is going to speak." He pushed back his chair. "I'll go right uptown and make sure things are all right."

Chase said: "I'm glad you're not giving it up. I'll walk up with you, Wint."

His mother kissed him good-by at the door; and that was unusual. It was the only sign she gave of what she must have been feeling. Wint had sometimes thought, impatiently, that she was a babbling old woman, never able to keep a thought to herself. He was learning a new respect for her. And something more. He had felt that he was justified in counting on his father and mother to stand by him; but he had expected and been prepared for questions and perhaps reproaches. There were no questions; there was never a reproach. It is often tactful to keep silent; and tact is sometimes a shade nobler than loyalty, than many another virtue.

He hugged her close and hard, kissed her again; then he and his father walked away toward town. Shoulder to shoulder, swinging like brothers. They met people. Wint could see a furtive curiosity in the eyes of those they met. But he could bear that. He had anticipated coven jeers, perhaps an open jibe; and his muscles had hardened at the thought.

They went into the Post Office together, and separated there. Wint met Dick Hoover; and Hoover gripped his hand and clapped his shoulder and told him he was all right. That heartened Wint. On his way from the Post Office, he encountered V. R. Kite, face to face, in front of the Bazaar. Kite dropped his eyes and scuttled to cover like a crab in seaweed. Wint chuckled with amusement. Hoover said:

"He can't face you."

Wint laughed good-naturedly. "Oh, Kite's all right. He fights in the only way he knows...."

He left Hoover in front of the *Journal* office and went in. B. B. was there, stoking the decrepit stove, breaking up the clotted coals with a bit of wood, and pouring on fresh fuel. He greeted Wint smilingly; said:

"Good afternoon!"

"Hello, B. B.!" Wint rejoined, and sat down. "Still fussing with that stove?"

B. B., amiably enough, said: "Yes. It's a good stove. Perhaps it doesn't look as well as it might; but it heats this office. That's the way with a good many things that don't look very well; they manage to do their work better than the fine-looking things. Did you ever stop to think of that?"

"In other words," Wint agreed, "beauty is only skin deep, even in stoves."

"Well, I'd rather have an ugly stove that would draw and give heat than a fine one that wouldn't," B. B. declared; and Wint said he did not blame him. B. B. sat down at his desk, working and talking at the same time. This was a way he had; a way he had to have, for there was nearly always some one in the office to talk to him. Wint said:

"I almost forgot about my meeting to-night. Are you still willing to preside?"

B. B. said: "Certainly."

"I thought you might have changed your mind."

"No indeed. At the Rink, is it?"

"Yes."

"Who are your speakers?"

"I'm not having any fine talent," Wint said, smiling. "Just a couple of good friends of mine, Sam O'Brien and Davy Morgan. And if you'd be willing to say something—"

"Oh, I always talk when I get a chance like that."

"Sure."

"Is your father going to speak?"

Wint shook his head. "No," he said frankly. "Dad's all right. He's been absolutely fine. But—he says he wouldn't know what to say. He's no speaker, you know."

"I've heard him do very well."

Wint laughed. "You probably wrote those speeches for him yourself." And B. B. good-naturedly acknowledged the corn.

"About half past seven?" Wint asked, as he got up to go; and B. B. agreed to the hour, and said he would be there.

When he had left B. B., Wint telephoned the furnace to make sure of Davy Morgan; and Morgan said energetically that he surely would be on hand. "I've some few things to say, also," he declared. "I can talk when they get me mad, Wint. And I'm mad enough, to-day."

Wint said: "All right; go as far as you like. This is a fight. It's no pink tea." And he dropped in on Sam O'Brien. But Sam was not in the restaurant. His underling told Wint the fat man had been out all day.

"He went looking for Jack Routt," the man explained.

"He found him," said Wint. "Well, tell Sam I'm counting on him to be at the Rink to-night."

From the restaurant, he crossed the street to Dick Hoover's office. Dick and his father were busy, so that Wint was alone for a time. Then he decided people might think he was hiding; so he came downstairs and out to the street again, and went to the barber shop for a haircut. Jim Radabaugh was there; and Jim shifted the bulge in his cheek and shook hands with Wint and said:

"You're there, boss. I'd say you're there."

Marshall, the barber, violated all the traditions of his craft by being a silent man. He said nothing whatever while he trimmed Wint's crisp hair; and Wint was glad of that. He would not hide. But he did not want to talk overmuch. When he came out of the barber shop, he saw Amos and Sam O'Brien and Peter Gergue on the other side of the street. They were walking purposefully, coming uptown from the direction of Amos's home. They saw him, and Amos waved his hand in greeting; then Peter spoke to Amos, and left the others, and came across to Wint, scratching the back of his head. Wint said:

"Hello, Peter."

Gergue grinned. "Well, Wint, you've started something."

Wint nodded. "I suppose so."

"You've made 'em talk, Wint. That never hurt a bit."

"I think you told me that once before," Wint agreed, laughing.

"Well, and it's so," Gergue insisted. He looked all around, took Wint's arm. "Let's walk along," he suggested.

Amos and Sam had disappeared. Wint said: "I've been looking for Sam. I want to see him."

"What about?"

"He's going to speak at my meeting to-night. At least I want him to."

Gergue chuckled; and he gripped Wint's arm as though he knew a thing or two, which he might tell if he chose. "Oh, he'll speak," he said. "Sam'll speak."

"I've counted on him."

"You going to speak, ain't you?" Gergue asked.

"Why, yes. Naturally."

"Fixed you up a speech, have you?"

"Not yet. I'll—just say whatever comes up at the time. Anything."

Gergue shook his head. "I tell you, Wint," he said. "You better go on home and write you a speech. A good one, with flowers on it, and all."

"Oh, I don't need to."

"I've seen more'n one man get up on his hind legs and go dumb. Good idea to have something on your mind before you get up."

"We-ell, maybe."

"I tell you," Gergue said again. "You go on home and fix up something. Best thing to do."

"I want to see Sam."

"I'll see him."

Wint was more than half persuaded, before Peter spoke to him. He had thought of going home; he was tired. He wanted to sleep. He said: "We-ell, all right."

"That's the talk," said Peter. "You go along."

"So long, then."

"Fix you up a good one," Gergue advised him again. "Fix it up, and learn it, and all. You'll maybe be interrupted, you know."

"If there's any one there to interrupt," Wint said, in a tone of doubt; and Gergue cackled.

"Lord, there'll be some folks there. Don't you worry about that. You go home and fix you up a speech. You'll have a crowd."

So Wint went home, in mid-afternoon. He found the house empty. His mother, he thought, was probably next door, with Mrs. Hullis. He felt sleepy; and he went to his room and lay down. His father woke him, at last. Told him it was supper time.

At supper, Chase asked Wint's mother if she were going to Wint's rally. She said: "I don't know. I said to Mrs. Hullis this afternoon that I wanted to go, but I didn't know whether women went. And she said she didn't know either. But I told her I—"

"You'll have plenty of company," her husband told her. "From what I hear, the whole town is going to be there. Every one was talking about it this afternoon."

"Then I'm going," she said. "Mrs. Hullis wanted me to go with her; and I—"

"You go with her," Chase advised. "I'll be on the stage, with Wint."

She said: "I'll have to leave the dishes. There won't be—"

"I'll do them, mother, while you're dressing," Wint told her cheerfully. "Don't worry about that."

"Well, I don't know!"

In the end, Wint and his father did them together. Wint broke a plate, and Mrs. Chase called down the stairs to know what had happened, and protested that she ought to come down and do them. But they would not let her. Afterwards, they all started downtown together, Wint and his father, Mrs. Chase and Mrs. Hullis. Two by two.

It was dark; the early dark of a winter evening. They met people, or overtook them, or were overtaken by them; and Wint thought there were more people than usual abroad. The moon was bright again this night, bright as it had been the night before when Wint took his way to the Weaver House. That seemed more like weeks than hours ago. As they came nearer the Rink, they saw more people; and Chase said:

"You're certainly going to have a crowd."

Wint nodded. He was beginning to be nervous. He realized that this was going to be hard.

But it was only when they turned the last corner and started down the hill toward the Rink that he realized just how hard it was going to be. It seemed to him all Hardiston was there ahead of him. The crowd clustered in front of the Rink and extended out into the street; and more were coming from each direction. Mrs. Hullis and Mrs. Chase, ahead, were lost in the throng. Wint stopped; he turned to his father.

"We'll cut through the back way," he said.

Chase agreed; and they turned down an alley, and came circuitously to the stage door and went in. The minute he came inside the door, he heard the hum and buzz of voices. He could see out on the stage, with its stock set of a farmyard scene. There were chairs, and a table.

Amos, and Sam O'Brien, and B. B. and two or three others were waiting just inside the stage door; and Sam gripped Wint's shoulders and exclaimed: "Lord, but you give us a scare, Wint. Thought you wasn't coming. I was all set to go fetch you."

"Oh, I was coming, all right," Wint said nervously, one ear attuned to the murmur of the crowd. "Sounds as though there were a lot of people here."

"Every seat, and standing room in the aisles, and half of 'em can't get in."

Wint grinned weakly. "And I suppose they've got every rotten egg in town."

Sam stared; then he howled. "Rotten egg! Oh, Lord, Wint, you'll be the death of me. I'll die a-laughing. Rotten egg!" He turned to Amos. "Wint says rotten egg!" he cried.

Amos looked at Wint in a curious fashion; and he smiled. "It's half past seven," he said. "No need to make them wait."

Wint gulped. "All right. I'm ready as I will be."

Amos nodded. "Then it's your move, B. B."

B. B. cleared his throat. "Very well." He turned and started toward the stage. Sam shepherded Wint that way. Amos and Wint's father came side by side, the others following. Wint found himself out on the stage.

The glare of the footlights blinded him for a moment; but he heard the sudden, brief clatter of handclapping that greeted them. The stir was quickly hushed. His eyes, accustomed to the footlights, discovered that the house was banked full of people. Floor and gallery were jammed. Small boys clung to the great beams and steel rods that crisscrossed to support the roof. Some of them seemed right overhead. And everywhere Wint looked, people were staring at him. He felt the actual, physical weight of all those eyes, overwhelming him. He felt crushed, helpless; he had a curious obsession that he could not move hands or feet. He worked the fingers of his right hand cautiously, and was relieved to find that they answered to his will. He was dazed.

He became conscious that B. B. was on his feet, his hands clasped in front of him in a characteristic way; there was a little smile upon his face, and he was speaking in a low, pleasant voice. Wint could not catch the words; his ears were not functioning. His senses were numbed by that overpowering sea of faces in front of him.

He caught, presently, a word or two that appalled him. "...violate the usual order," B. B. was saying. "The principal speaker usually last.... Keep you waiting.... Lengthy introduction.... I believe you know him, now...."

He turned to look at Wint; and Wint, appalled and panic-stricken, saw the invitation in B. B.'s eyes. B. B. wanted him to speak first; but he was still tongue-tied and muscle-fast in the face of all those eyes. He shook his head weakly. Some one tugged at his elbow. Sam O'Brien. Sam whispered hoarsely:

"Get up on your feet, boy!"

Wint shook his head again, trying to find words to explain. Then a man yelled, out beyond those footlights. Other men yelled. Wint flushed angrily, his courage came back. They thought him afraid. Baying him like dogs.... He'd show them all....

He stood up and strode forward to the very lip of the stage. There was a moment's hush. He flung out one hand. "People...." he began.

But it was as well that Wint had not wasted time in following Gergue's advice to fix up a good speech; because on that one word of his, an overwhelming blast of sound struck him full in the face. A roar, a bellowing, a whistling, a shrilling.... Shouts and screams and cries.... He stiffened, furious. They were trying to yell him down. He flung up both hands, shouted at them....

Every one in the house was up on his or her feet. Some one threw his hat in the air. Order came out of chaos. A terrible, rhythmic order. The blare of sound dissolved into beats; they pounded on Wint's ears; he shuddered under the blow of them. His anger gave way to bewilderment. He could not understand. He bent lower to see more clearly the faces of those in the front row, just beyond the footlights. Dick Hoover was there. And Dick was yelling in a fashion fit to split his throat, flinging his fists up toward Wint, shrieking. Beside Dick, Joan. Her face stood out suddenly before Wint's eyes. She was crying; that is to say, tears were streaming down her cheeks. Yet was she happy, too. Smiling, laughing, calling to him.... She was clapping her hands, he saw. Then he discovered that others were clapping their hands, while they yelled at him. Everybody was clapping their hands....

Utterly bewildered, Wint whirled around to look at the men behind him. And there was Amos, both hands upraised, beating time to that appalling roar that swept up from the house before them. Beating time, leading them....

Sam O'Brien and Davy Morgan—they were both yelling like fools—came swiftly across the stage to where Wint stood. They caught his arms. He struggled with them, not understanding. They swept him off his feet, up in the air, to their shoulders.... Swung him to face the house.

The noise doubled; then it seemed as though an army of men swarmed upon the stage. So, at last, Wint understood. They were not trying to yell him down.

It is one of the most hopeful facts of life that all mankind is so ready to recognize, and to applaud, an action which is fine. Wint was in the hands of his friends. He thought, for a little while, that they would kill him.

When it was all over—and this took time, and left Wint sore and stiff from hand-shaking and back-slapping—the people began to drift away. And Wint escaped, off the stage, into one of the compartments that served as greenroom for theatrical folk. His father was there, and his mother. And Peter, and Amos, and Sam.

Every one seemed to be wild with exultation; they continued the celebration, there among themselves. And Wint heard how it had been done. Hetty had gone to Amos with the story. To Joan first, Sam told Wint. "I was with her," the fat man said. "You understand. I was with her."

Wint nodded, gripping Sam's shoulder. "She's fine," he said. "You're lucky. I understand."

Joan, Sam said, sent them to Amos, and Amos had arranged the rest; sent Wint home—Gergue was his agent in this—and spread the word through Hardiston. To-night had attested the thoroughness of his work.

Wint found a chance at last to thank Amos. They were a little apart from the others; and they talked it over briefly. Amos, Wint thought, was curiously subdued, curiously sad. He wondered at this. But he understood, at the end.

He had said: "Wonder what Routt will say to this, anyway? And Kite?"

"You don't have to—worry about Routt," said Amos.

Wint asked quickly: "Why not? Is he ... Is there something?"

"He took the noon train," said Amos. "And—Agnes went with him. She telephoned to-night. She says they're married."

Wint was so stunned that for a moment he could not speak; he could not move. He managed to grip Amos's hand; tried to say something.

"I've said to myself, more than once," Amos told him huskily, "that I wished her mother hadn't 've died." He began, slowly, to fill his pipe. Wint thought there was something heroic, splendid about the man. Facing life, driving ahead. And this to think upon.... He was sick with sorrow.

Amos was facing the stage; he said slowly, smiling a little, "but forget that. Here's some one coming for you to see her home."

When Wint turned, he saw Joan.

CHAPTER V

SEEING JOAN HOME

THEY walked home slowly, Wint and Joan. The moon was bright upon them; the streets were still filled with the dispersing throng. People spoke to them, then went discreetly on their way, and smiled back at the two. Wint and Joan said little; and what they said was of no importance. He told her he had seen her crying.

"I had to," she said. "I was so happy."

"I wasn't happy," Wint declared. "I was scared."

She said she didn't blame him. "It must have been hard to face them all."

He nodded. "I'll tell you; all that noise.... It—made me seasick. Something like that."

"I know," she said.

When they were halfway home, she told him that Hetty had come to her, that morning. Wint looked at her quickly.

"Hetty's all right," he said. "She'll be all right. She's found herself."

Joan nodded. "It's going to be a fight, for her."

"She'll win. Sam will help."

"I know. I saw that, this morning."

A little later, she said: "You—did the right thing. Foolish, maybe. But—it was fine, too. Foolish things often are."

Wint shook his head. "But I'd like to pound Routt."

"Don't," she said. "Agnes loves him."

Wint told her then what Amos had told him; and she uttered a low, pitiful exclamation. "I didn't know that," she said. "But—they may be happy. Agnes is good.... Loyal.... In her way."

"You knew she loved him?"

"Yes. I've always known. Agnes had talked to me."

"I hope Routt does—settle down."

Joan said thoughtfully: "There is something strong in him. Misdirected."

"I liked him," Wint said. "I can't help it, even now. He was my friend."

"I believe they will come out all right. I feel it."

Wint laughed at her gently. "Intuition?"

"Yes. You men call it a hunch."

Silence again, for a while. They came to her house. Wint thought the simple place was beautiful in the moonlight; he wanted, desperately, to go in. But there was a curious diffidence upon him, and he stopped at the gate till she said:

"Come. It's not cold, to-night. We can sit on the porch."

"You want me?"

"Yes, Wint." Her eyes said more than her words. He opened the gate, and they went up the walk to the house sedately enough, side by side. Any one might have seen.

The moonlight did not fall upon the porch. There was a shadowed place there. When they came into this shadow, Joan stopped, and looked at Wint. Her eyes were very dark. Something was pounding in his throat, so that he could not speak. He put out one hand, in an uncertain, fumbling way. Joan looked down at his hand, and smiled a little, and put her hand in his.

They stood thus for a little, hand in hand, facing each other. Wint said huskily, at last:

"I've—tried, Joan."

Her voice was clear and sweet as a bell when she answered. "You've done more than try, Wint," she told him. "You've—won."

So, without either of them knowing, or caring, how it happened, she was in his arms. And he kissed her; and her lips answered his. No cool kiss of a child, this. Months of longing and of yearning spoke through his lips, and through hers. Infinite promise of the years to come....

While they sat together on her shadowed porch thereafter, they could hear for a long time the murmuring voices of people passing on their homeward way. Some looked toward Joan's house; but they could not see Wint and Joan.

It was as well; for it is the way of Hardiston to talk. The way of a little town....

THE END

CPSIA information can be obtained
at www.ICGtesting.com
Printed in the USA
LVHW020905160622
721368LV00016B/130